STARTER

by

James E. Loyd and David B. Matheson

STARTER

Cover art and map by KibPrestridge.com
kib647@yahoo.com

ISBN 978-0-9905-763-9-6

Dreadnought Press
San Antonio, Texas

Foreword

This novel began as a memoir of growing up in the '50's and '60's in Alamo Heights, a small city surrounded by the much larger City of San Antonio. That notion slowly percolated in my mind until it grew into something a bit more ambitious, a drugs/crime mystery set in my old neighborhoods. Mulling over the concept, I realized I knew nothing about the necessary 'cop stuff', but did know someone who would, a high school classmate, David Matheson, a former San Antonio police officer. I hadn't seen him in years, but at a reunion I let him in on my little idea, and eventually we got around to writing this.

My idea was strongly influenced by a true story. During the summer of 1970 at the University of Texas, one of my friends was introduced to his first joint by a beautiful girl. I was there. That began his downward spiral into drug use, then dealing, then point-blank murder one night in Austin. Since that time, I've half jokingly said that I would strangle that girl for getting him started on drugs. That friend appears as Ricky Young in a series of flashbacks and dreams, each and every one true.

Another element of the narrative, mostly true, sometimes embellished and with names changed to protect both innocent and guilty, is the "cop stuff": the stories David tells from the perspective of the cop on the beat, the patrolman in his squad car, the homicide detective investigating murders and suicides. He has dozens of them, some introduced here as part of his history or in flashbacks triggered by events. Some are funny, some are gory, all are entertaining and fascinating. Some of the book falls into the Noir genre, but it's actually Noirer than Noir, heavily pigmented by the true cop stories, but also by one character's psychological descent into a rational madness and another's rising PTSD.

Finally, the story structure is simple, a three act play: first the characters' histories, then an unfolding tragedy, and finally a resolution, of sorts. The chapters alternate, beginning with David's alter ego Sam Thompson, an Alamo Heights Police Detective, then "my" character, Ian "Yonny" Jonas, the father of a son tragically dead of an apparent overdose. Sam's history is true to life, Yonny's only loosely similar to mine; Sam is photorealism to Yonny's impressionism. Their histories since high school could not be more divergent, but thirty years on, the two have a rendezvous with death.

James E. (Jimmy) Loyd
September, 2017
San Antonio

Prologue

September, 1997
Alamo Heights, Texas

The wooden tread squeaked softly, like an old mouse might, then let out a sharper crack as she lifted her foot. *This old house*, she thought, *showing its age. Not all that much older than me, though, maybe it's me.* She descended the flights carefully, cowboy-style at first, one foot against one wall, then the other, then gave up the bowlegged stretch and tightroped her way down along the right side.

On the last step she craned her neck around the corner, squinting into a coruscating silvery blue atmosphere. She couldn't see him at first in the flickering shadows, then spied a toe peeking from a blanket. Her husband had slouched into invisibility, sunken so low into their old couch. On the TV screen in the corner a dapper, bearded gentleman apparently dressed for a regatta or a polo match was speaking earnestly to a very tall man, not entirely amused by his look, a sort of Frankenstein meets Matt Dillon mix, *wearing one of those horrid jumpsuits Grandfather wore...* She smiled. *Yonny Jonas! A creature feature, at your age?*

She had made it halfway across the den to the bedroom, quietly, when the doorbell rang. She froze a moment, then relaxed—*it's a little early, he has his keys, doesn't he*?—then turned and bounded through the living room to the door. She looked through the peephole.

"What is it, Rachel?"

ONE

1

Senior Day, 1968
Hemisfair, Downtown San Antonio

Their extended clique had huddled on the mezzanine level of the Lone Star Beer pavilion until 3:30, when the reach of the administration finally ceased and they were on their own. Fake ID's came out, pitchers of beer were passed around and the cool cats were having their day.

On the way back uptown in Ricky Young's olive drab VW, Sam Thompson, sitting shotgun, made a crack, harmless and funny, but Yonny Jonas decided to take it as a declaration of war. He dumped his fresh cup of beer over the other's head, prompting instant, but errant retaliation, Mike next to him getting dowsed. Cans were shaken and spewed, beer flew, the windshield was coated from the inside just as they pulled up to his house. They left the car at the curb, then sprinted up the driveway as fast as their state allowed, passing his mother, surprised but delighted to see them, then jumping fully clothed into the pool.

He came up for air, expecting to see a ring of amber foam all around him.

His mother asked, "Did everyone have a nice time?"

That night, Sir John Falstaff's at Hemisfair: a long table of young men and women, obviously underage, chatting and laughing amidst pitchers and mugs of beer, Lofton Kline doing his best Roy Orbison off in a corner. One of the taller boys stands and extends his hand, taking a beautiful petite girl with long dark hair away from the noisy scene and onto the promenade. They find a suitably dark corner to kiss. But only for a few minutes until several friends come hooting loudly, gathering them for the next party.

2

1967
Alamo Heights

Sam Thompson grew up an Army brat, traveling all over the world. His father's current duty station was Fort Sam Houston in the heart of San Antonio. The family had transferred there from Schofield Barracks in the middle of the island of Oahu. It was Dad's second time at Schofield, the first being the late 1930's and early 1940's. He had described to Sam several times the little yellow skinned, slant-eyed bastards flying through Kolekole pass, firing shots indiscriminately at the barracks while the hung-over troops were still asleep that fateful morning in December, 1941.

Coming to Fort Sam meant Sam attended ninth grade at Cole High School on post. It was a rather small school and Sam played starting guard and defensive end on the freshman team. Next year he was due to start on the Varsity, but fate being the bitch she is, she had other ideas. That summer his parents decided they didn't want to live on post anymore and bought a house over in Alamo Heights, much to Sam's chagrin. Heights was a much bigger school and he didn't know if he could cut it. But when practice started, there he was, along with what seemed like several giant upperclassmen.

"24 Trap on 2," barked the quarterback to the anxious team. It was the first practice of 'two-a-days,' 95 in the shade with a humidity to match, the parched yellow grass on the practice field crying out for rain with each crunch of a cleat. About right for a South Texas August.

Sweat beaded from Sam's brow into his eyes as he pulled to his left from his right guard position. The left guard, Benny Something, they were new to each other, pulled to his right. The two collided.

Sam's helmet slid slightly, cutting the side of his lip as it did. *First day of practice and Benny can't pull in the right direction?* Sam flew into an immediate fit of rage and jumped on his teammate, hitting him furiously on the torso as hard as he could, causing Benny to throw up his breakfast and cry about the pain being inflicted by the new guy.

Three coaches and a booster, Benny's dad, came to the still prostrate player's rescue. One of the coaches said nothing, one sang the praises of Sam's aggressiveness and the other pulled at the scruff of Sam's jersey. Benny's dad wanted Sam thrown off the team and expelled from Alamo Heights, while at the same time cursing his son for allowing the new guy to best him. Sam just stood over him, grinning. Then he took off his helmet, wiped the blood from his mouth across the front of his white jersey and went back to work.

Three plays later, Sam's assignment had him pulling left again into the defensive guard, hitting him hard. He went down with his opponent on top of him—just like he planned it. Sam thought he had hit him pretty good, but the other just bounced back up and extended his hand, saying, "Good hit."

Sam looked up at him. "Couldn't have been too good a hit. I'm the one on the ground." He clasped the outstretched hand and levered himself up. "Sam Thompson."

"Ricky Young."

Their introductions were interrupted by a coach, full Cherokee by the looks of him, shoving their shoulders, yelling, "This ain't no date! Get back to your positions!" From that point on, Sam began getting a little more comfortable at the big school and slipped into his new role as a captain on the JV. After the older guys graduated, he started every varsity game his last two years.

He and Ricky became fast friends and since neither had a car that year, they walked home together after practices, a long walk, plenty of time to talk, to bond. After high school, they went their separate ways, Sam up to Tech, Ricky to Austin. After a year or so, they sort of lost track of each other. Sam had no problems getting into the swing of things up in Lubbock. He had heard it was a party school and vowed not to let its reputation down.

After his first year he wasn't invited back.

3

1968
Dallas

Yonny Jonas had it all figured out. He was tired, really tired, of school, of expectations, of grades, honors, all that. His strategy was simple, go to a decent college, preferably a party school, certainly not a grind, make stellar grades and four years later, decide what he wanted to do, take the entrance exams and go to graduate school.

His sisters had gone to SMU, majored in husbandry and stayed in Dallas. He had visited with his parents several times, had seen the college life and the frat scene from afar. So, fall of 1968 found him on the Hilltop, fitting right in, pledging a top fraternity, quickly learning to talk the frat talk, walk the campus walk. He was invited to join the Squires, an honorary men's spirit group. Midway through the football season he got tabbed to fill in for an injured upperclassman running Peruna, the Mustangs' black Shetland pony mascot, across the field after every score. Academically, he was on a different track from his pledge brothers who soon dubbed him Four Point, but he didn't let that interfere with his partying obligations. Even Hell Week was a breeze, once his Italian teacher offered him her office to hide and catch much-needed naps.

Midway through his sophomore year, his crowd sensed he had changed, abruptly so, quieter, more than a little withdrawn, no longer leading posses from the library to The Stables, their bar away from home. Puddy Purnell, his roommate, confided to a crowded lunch table, "Letters stopped coming. Phone bill's way down."

"Sounds like a girlfriend thing," said Thad Bumbry. "I'll talk to him."

He had stopped getting haircuts not long after he first arrived on campus and by Spring of sophomore year, had a mane falling to his shoulders; he definitely stood out in a generally clean-cut crowd. His brothers started calling him Junkie Jonas, amusing since he was one of a handful of his original pledge brothers never touching drugs, not even weed.

One noontime, Puddy was standing on the front steps between Leo and Cleo the lions, laying on some BS in his Lyoozianny drawl about some chick he had laid when he saw a figure ambling up to the house deliberately scattering the faded fall foliage at his feet. The frame and the lope were familiar, somehow, but not the face, at a distance looking reddened and battered, the head practically bald. "Good Gawd Almighty! It's Yonny! What happened? Some rednecks beat you up and shave you?"

Yonny laughed out loud for the first time in an age, his buddies thought. "Get out of my way, Pudster, you're keeping me from my lunch. I'll tell you, okay?"

At the head of the table, Thad ruffled what hair was left on his best friend's head, then exclaimed, "Kisses? What the fuck?"

"Easy, easy, easy." Yonny's face was covered with lipstick kisses, pink ones, some hot, some dark, mostly light pink, half a dozen clustered around his lips. "Simple, you idiots. The Thetas have this breast cancer thing going on, Miss Magnolia Devereaux,"—he strung out the names to *ooohs* and *ahhhs*—"asked me last fall if I'd donate my hair…"

A rich boy, arrogant and conceited, hissed, "Got a tax deduction?"

Yonny shot him a glance, shutting him up. "No, peckerwood. Try thinking of someone else for a change, huh? Wigs for women who have lost their hair. So I sat on the steps at the Student Center and Martha Burton and Cissy Reynolds tied my hair back and sheared me like the precious little lamb I am." As the laughter ebbed, "Then Stanley the mad barber finished the job, said he'd been waiting a long time to do it." Pointing to his face, "My admirers thronged me and adored me. I was really popular, guys, for about five minutes. And I did score a date with Naomi Harris tonight." He looked around. "Let's eat. Tennie, what are we having today?"

By this time, though, Yonny had already been accepted to transfer to UT, needing a change of scenery, needing it badly. He plunged right into the hedonistic Austin scene with his high school friends, but kept hitting the books hard unlike his party partners. When Senior year came, he already had his ΦΒΚ key and was headed for a double summa, everything seemingly under control. Except after four years he was still trying to figure out what he wanted to be when, if, he grew up. So, he let his inner instincts decide for him. He aced the GMAT then overslept for the LSAT. And thus was made the decision.

4

1969
San Antonio

At loose ends after his one year at Tech, Sam's dad got him a job at the Western Union office in the Activities Center at Fort Sam Houston. He wasn't the most organized person on the planet, but his boss at the Army and Air Force Exchange Service was, and a smartass second lieutenant from somewhere up North, to boot.

One day Sam had a money order to deliver to a soldier at Chambers Pavilion, the portion of Brooke Army Medical Center housing soldiers suffering the worst mental ravages of the Vietnam War. He checked in with the noncom at the front desk. "I'm here to deliver a Western Union money order to…" He checked the name again, "to a Private Robert Patterson."

The sergeant told Sam that this Patterson was being heavily medicated after a night full of flashbacks, dreams of battles he had experienced in the jungles thousands of miles away from home. He was escorted to a large room in one corner of which was a 12 x 12 heavy chain link padlocked enclosure—*your basic cage,* thought Sam. The sergeant unlocked the gate; inside was a flowered couch and non-matching loveseat, both at least twenty years old, by the looks of them, with a four foot long coffee table between. A similar cage next door had a 19" black-and-white RCA TV playing a commercial hawking a breakfast cereal—"Mikey likes it!"

Sam took a seat on the couch. The sergeant said he would be a few minutes getting Private Patterson; in the meantime he left the door open for another patient, a private who looked like he should have still been in junior high English trying to sneak a look down Molly's blouse. He nodded at Sam and took a seat in the love seat opposite, nodding his acknowledgement to the sergeant who had told him to behave and locked the gate behind him.

Another commercial came on. "Too bad you had to get a bald-headed one," said a little boy on the tube.

The newcomer looked at Sam and smiled, "I'm Brian McCoy," thrusting out his hand as a means of introduction. "Been to Nam yet?"

Sam flinched at the sudden movement, then leaned over to shake the soldier's hand. "No, no, I haven't been there… yet," he replied, nervously.

A movie came back on, an old World War II flick. The dialogue and background noise seemed a tad loud, but there was no way to turn down the volume. All of a sudden the scene changed to artillery and mortar rounds hitting a position. Without hesitating, the young man became Pvt. McCoy again. "Incoming!" he yelled as he dove headfirst under the safety of the coffee table.

Sam was frozen on his couch. The other screamed, "Get your fucking ass down here, Thompson! Now!"

Looking around for some help, Sam saw the sergeant running back into the cage as McCoy grabbed his ankles, still screaming. "Where's your rifle, Thompson? Where's your goddamned rifle? We gotta kill the little slant-eyed bastards!" In his mind, McCoy was still in Vietnam under heavy artillery fire from 'Charlie'.

Sergeant Jones finally keyed the lock.

The military draft was closing in on Sam, rapidly, too rapidly, he thought. No longer II-S, he was prime draft fodder. But there was talk of a new conscription system, a lottery based on dates of birth. Of course, there were the same lame deferments—being in college, studying or not, flat feet, asthma, and the not so appropriately named "Uncle Charlie," a name not revealed to Sam until much later. Seems "Uncle Charlie" was a United States Senator who pulled strings at Selective Service.

On December first, he watched the draft lottery on his little black and white TV, watched young lives, his friends' lives, plucked from a big glass jar by some old guy. Number One was September 14. Sam's birthday was November 13. Not too unlucky, he hoped, but it came up a lot sooner than he expected—126. Rumor going around was anyone under 200 would at least be called for a physical and maybe jerked into the service right away. He could still hope Tricky Dick and Henry the K would end the "Conflict", the "Peacekeeping Mission", the "Stopping of Communism"… *Oh, Hell, It was WAR! Young men, sons of mothers, boyfriends, fiancés, by the hundreds were dying each week. Even more were losing arms, legs, sight, minds…*

Next day he dropped by the 50-50 to see if any of his buddies were commiserating. A whole bunch was there, about half celebrating, the others were drowning sorrows and fears. He compared notes with the longer faces, felt a bit better that he wasn't having to cut off a fingertip or check out flights to Montreal. He couldn't help feeling something like envy, even bitterness, if he was honest with himself, at those guys whooping it up at the end of the bar, 300's, all of them, like Yonny Jonas who was crowing, "356! A day earlier or later and I'm down in the 100's!" He raised his longneck, "Thanks, Mom, Dad, well, Mom, mostly!"

After talking to one of his old teammates who had signed up for the reserves, he made a decision. At the Marine recruiting office downtown on Main, the recruiter tried to get him to sign up for four years, but Sam had been well-briefed and went straight for the Reserves. The frustrated recruiter smiled slickly, saying, "Well, this is your lucky day! I have one slot left and I can get you a delayed entry." Sam looked over the form and signed on the dotted line. He was going to be a Marine, well, maybe the JV, but still…

While he mulling his options, another friend had persuaded him to apply at the San Antonio Police Department. The department was delighted to see a big guy like him, and made the necessary arrangements to enroll him when he returned from active duty. So, he killed two birds with the same stone—the draft and gainful employment.

1970
San Diego

He enjoyed his remaining freedom, made the rounds with his buddies and even got himself engaged. Then it was time for boot camp. He flew to San Diego and at the airport he and a group were culled from the arrivals and herded into an olive drab school bus for the ride to the nearby Marine Corps Recruit Depot. There were seventy-one souls on board for the unknown. On the left side, some racial sorting had filled the seats with a lively and loud black cohort. Sam's side was mixed and quieter. The driver, a corporal, tried to get the left side to quiet down, was mostly ignored. *They have no idea...* One stood up in the aisle, swaying and singing, "I be so good-lookin' in my dress blues, yeah, gonna get me some pussy wearin' my dress blues!"

The corporal guided the big bus through the gate up to a low slung building. He killed the motor, rose and stepped down the stairs with a big smile and in a slow southern slur, "Ya'll better hang on t'your asses!"

Then the biggest black man Sam had ever seen walked coolly up the steps—blue slacks with a red stripe, long sleeved khaki shirt, Smokey hat. He planted himself at the head of the aisle, hands on hips, and started in the deepest voice, "Quiet!" That's all it took to turn that bus into a monastery. "My name is Gunnery Sergeant Willie Jackson. Welcome to the MCRD. Just because you're here don't make you Marines and I'm gonna make sure every day and night you understand what I mean! And you might just better go on and give your souls to Jesus, because your asses are mine!" He shot laser glares around the bus. "You fucking maggots got thirty seconds to get off my god-damned bus!" He made a show of glancing at his watch. "Twenty-nine already gone!"

In a flash, the windows on the port side had opened and the black recruits were crawling out and dropping to the ground. The rest, Sam included, got in line in the aisle and trooped out under the stare and shouts of the drill sergeant, too scared to do much else, sure as hell not going to say anything. Their new master explained how each of them would choose a pair of yellow footprints painted on the port side in the next five seconds. A few collisions and stumbles and eight seconds later, they were in place, staring straight ahead. They stood there for an hour in the sun, a quartet of burly drill sergeants striding to and fro amidst their ranks, getting in each recruit's face. He couldn't look around but he knew some of these guys were reservists, like him, the rest were regular and on their way to Viet Nam. He wondered, not that he expected to stay in touch, but how many of them would make it back?

Sam wasn't really sure what to expect and his father hadn't given him much advice, hardly acknowledging his soon-to-be Marine, being career Army, a Sergeant Major, the boss. From friends and acquaintances, he had heard stories of how hard it was, but once he got past the initial shock, learned the drill, he sort of enjoyed it. Belatedly thankful for the high school coaches who put him through the wringer in two-a-days, he was still in pretty good shape and handled the physical part pretty well.

Eighteen weeks of boot camp went by pretty quickly. After that, Sam and his platoon were to be shipped out to Camp Pendleton for Infantry Training Regiment. While waiting for their buses, one of the drill sergeants announced the smoking lamp was lit. A buddy reached for his pack of Marlboros in a sock only to find the pack was empty. Another sergeant passed by and noticed a Marine was out of smokes. He pulled out his pack and offered his last cigarette to the private, who responded, "I don't want to take your last one, Sir."

Sergeant Jones replied in his best command voice, "As long as I have one, maggot, you have one." That was one of the best lessons Sam learned in the Corps.

And there were moments of something else than physical exhaustion and mental abuse. One Saturday afternoon his platoon was marching on the parade deck. Four pretty girls in miniskirts were walking along the edge, probably to their boyfriends' Basic graduations. Sergeant Kelly turned them about, then doubletimed sixty horny young men right past the chicks. "Eyes right!" Everyone grinned. When the platoon had made a little distance, Kelly barked, "Platoon, halt! Right face!" He strode to front center and faced his men. "And now, Gentlemen, pray to the wind gods!"

Sam came home after Basic, lighter, leaner, and he hoped, tougher. He'd need it as a cop, he thought. He strode down the gangway into the satellite terminal wearing his service uniform, all olive, long belted jacket, tie, cover, the whole thing. His parents were waiting for him, he was glad to see, but even more to see Cheryl, his fiancée. Mama beat them all to give him a hug, then Cheryl. His father hung back, then came forward, stopped and saluted. "Looking sharp, Marine."

1971
San Antonio

Class 71-A at the San Antonio Police Department's Academy started at exactly 8:00 am on a March Monday. Sixteen young men set to change the world in some way. Some would live too long, some would die too soon, one from a heart attack, one during an angioplasty and one a suicide by girlfriend. After a prolonged and very heated argument he handed her his service revolver and said, "Just shoot me, bitch!" She did. He died. No more heartache because of a wandering woman… or so he thought. There was never one more faithful. Such is the suspicious mind of a cop.

In every cadet class there is a class clown and Sam's class was no exception. His clown was a guy named Ed, not Big Ed, not Little Ed, just Ed. Ed was always the first with a smartass remark, especially during the daily two hour Physical Training sessions. Every day, about halfway through, Ed would be flat on his back, hands behind his head, not doing situps with the rest of his class. The instructors would notice and yell at him, "What are you doing, cadet?" Ed always answered, "Cheating, Sir!"

Sam did not laugh along with the rest of his class. Sam hated it when Ed did that. Sam hated Ed. Sam was the class P.T. leader and when someone in the class wasn't doing the assigned exercise or fell out during a run, Sam would have to do twenty extra pushups. Sam very quickly grew tired of doing pushups and eagerly looked forward to the end of eighteen weeks of Academy.

5

1975
New York

After B-school, Yonny had gone to work for a Texas real estate developer making its first foray into New York, was doing well, especially for an outsider in what at that time was still a pretty closed circle of local landlords. In his very first solo presentation to a prospective corporate tenant he faced off at the Links Club on 62nd against John McDougall, the dean of the New York brokerage community, known for his abrasive, scorched-earth, hardball negotiating style. Having his company's CEO up from Houston didn't help much, even with the schmoozing over scotches.

But he had done his homework, had taken the client's requirements to a local interiors firm and browbeaten them into producing floorplans, not only for his building, but for the most likely competition, a local's building finishing up about the same time and about equidistant from the tenant's CEO's Park Avenue apartment. He ended his presentation with a chart showing a nine percent advantage in space, and therefore rent dollars, over the competition.

The normally gruff and voluble McDougall was quiet a few minutes, looking over the numbers, then the plans. He rose from his seat and steered his client to the far wall, saying something quietly yet intensely for several minutes. Returning to the conference table, he said, "Young man, very impressive, very impressive. We'll review, of course, but… you know the rest of your competitors aren't going to like you very much, don't you?"

As the laughter died down, Yonny responded coolly, "*Oderum dum metuant*, then."

All but McDougall missed that and were startled when he bolted from his chair, reaching over to shake Yonny's hand. "Excellent! A real estate guy who knows his Latin and can use it! Much better than the nitwits we normally deal with! Okay, then, thanks for coming. We'll get back to you."

As his group stood curbside waiting for their driver, his CEO asked, "What was that back there? Latin? What did it mean?"

"*If they won't love us, let them fear us*."

That prospect signed a huge lease a few months later, filling much of the new building. Yonny's limited Latin paid off; over the next few years, McDougall steered several large tenants his way. His reputation was being burnished in certain circles and tarnished in others, with more than a few New Yorkers taking note of who he was and what he was.

6

1976
San Antonio

That summer was very hot and sultry with the humidity easily as high as the temperature. Sam got a call to the 1100 block of Semlinger Road for an apparent DOA. In a weedy field strewn with trash stood a middle-aged black man waving the patrol car down as he approached. Visibly upset, he told Sam that his friend Freddy Johnson was dead over by their campsite.

Sam invited the man into the patrol car and drove him in the direction of their camp. The two men had apparently been living in a lean-to shelter fashioned of a tarp and a couple of pieces of plywood.

"How do you know your friend is dead?" Sam took out his notepad. "And your name is?"

"Hank Washington, Sir. Well, Sir, just wait 'til you sees him." Washington was trying to hold back his tears. "Freddy gots shot about two weeks ago over to Casper Walk, in those projects off I-35. He gots hisself shot breakin' in a man's car over there. The man caught him and popped a cap in his back," he said sadly. "Then I gots caught stealin' meat from the HEB on W. W. White."

As the patrol car bumped over the rutted lot, Hank said, "Looks like Freddy was getting' him some water outa the spring."

Sam looked sideways at the vagrant to see whether he was coherent or just babbling. "What are you talking about? I don't see anything, just that green mound over there."

He stopped the car and the other man got out. Sam asked him where he was going; the other merely pointed at the blob, choking up, unable to speak anymore. Sam got out of the car and when he looked closer at the green thing, he saw what he thought was a head butting out of a greenish mold. He had been fooled by what he thought were body parts a few months earlier, but this time, as he drew closer, he noticed maggots crawling over the outline of Freddy's bloated body. It was a horrific sight. Closer, the odor was overwhelming.

By this time a sergeant and two other patrolmen had arrived on the scene, followed by a Don's ambulance whose driver quickly surveyed the situation and advised the others he would be right back. When he returned, he had a six-pack of Cokes and half a dozen cigars, one each for the policemen and his attendant. The Sergeant asked, "What's all that for?" The driver held up the cigars, replying, "These will hide the stench of the body and the cokes will settle your stomachs, keep you from throwing up when the body pops."

"Say what?" exclaimed one of the patrolmen.

The driver just laughed and explained that the body was bloated with gases and other nasty stuff and would explode when it was picked up to load in the ambulance. "Better get a long stick or branch, or hell, just shoot him with a shotgun—he's already dead!"

Now the question among the officers was who would pick up Old Dead Fred and risk the smell and gases and "nasty stuff" that would surely permeate the immediate area. The sergeant decided as the ranking officer, he would not be picking up the body, that was for sure. He decided the three other officers would draw straws and proceeded to gather some dried grass strands, trimming several carefully. Sam was fortunate to draw the short straw meaning the other two patrolmen would be the lucky bastards to help ol' Freddy into the ambulance for his final ride.

The two unlucky souls weren't the least bit happy, but took off their uniform shirts and Sam Browne belts and went over to retrieve the body. On the way, Joe McAndrews spotted a dead tree branch to 'pop' the body. The sergeant laughed at him, telling him to quit wasting his time and just pick up the damned thing. Joe was closest to the legs so he bent over and grabbed what was left of them. That left George the head. He gently put his hands and arms under Freddy's chest. He tried not to put too much pressure on the rotting corpse, but the skin was wilting off and George was losing him. The body was slipping from his tentative grasp and he just had to let go. Ole Fred hit the ground fairly hard and exploded.

Green slime and maggots went flying in the immediate area. George and Joe attempted to flee with as little of the vile mess as possible on them, cussing and bitching as they ran. Sam and the sergeant likewise were on the run but when they stopped, they couldn't stop laughing, infuriating the other two officers who were covered in green slimy stuff, trying to slip out of their tee shirts and trousers.

Through all the chaos and confusion, no one had given any thought about how they were going to get what remained of Freddy into the ambulance. When they had all calmed down, Sam recalled seeing a city maintenance crew over on W. W. White earlier in the day. The sergeant went back to his car and called the dispatcher to ask the city to have the crew bring over their loader to pick up the remains. He turned back to his men, smoking their cigars and drinking their cokes, two of them down to their skivvies.

"Well, I'll be damned."

7

1977
New York

Yonny's date, his first Manhattan girlfriend for over a year now, was McDougall's wife's cousin's niece. When he made the introduction, he whispered, "*She's a handful. You have been warned.*" Tonight she was a bridesmaid in a wedding—*a merger*, they called it—of two socialites in an extravaganza that would have consumed the gross national product of several Third World nations. Even so, Gloria was of a family that could have bought and sold bride, groom and extended clans several times over, and maybe had, in days past.

They had hit it off instantly, and why not? She was, up to that very moment, the most beautiful girl he had ever met, slender, blonde, a nice but not extravagant figure, well-educated, now jaded, bored with the beautiful people set. And the eyes, gorgeous, wide like a baby's, deep emerald such as a poet might find himself lost in, but now, here at the reception, they were on the red side, rheumy. He knew that look, knew she had been in the ladies' snorting two, maybe three lines of coke, each side. Over the last six months she had starting using heavily, despite his objections, losing weight, now more of a scarecrow, a collection of protuberances under the sheets. *Concentration camp pin-up girl? Not to her face, of course.*

She weaved her way back to him, blowing kisses along the way, then clamped onto him, steadying herself. "Glory, damn it, you just have to lighten up on that crap. Look at you!" Just then, over her bony left shoulder, he caught his first glimpse of another standing at a perpendicular to him, observing askance the budding confrontation then turning her head away, the slightest moue flitting across her face. Now in profile, she was unmistakably prominent in a long black dress, her hair straight back over her head, threaded tightly through some sort of comb thing, cascading down to her waist.

Gloria was berating him loudly enough for anyone and everyone to hear, telling him to mind his own fucking business, *if she fucking wanted to get fucking high, she fucking would and he could just fucking kiss her fucking rich-as-Midas ass*. Then she turned to see what was distracting him. "Oh, so now you like the Jewgirls from Queens? Well, maybe you ought go over there and show her your circumcised pecker, she'd like that, I'm fucking sure."

Yonny drew his handkerchief out of his tux pocket. "Glory, here, let me wipe that stuff off your nose." He attempted to dab at her until she slapped his hand away, then slapped him hard across the face, pivoted and stumbled her way across the ballroom.

Sighing, he watched her walk away and out of his life then heard the distinctive sounds of retching. Turning back, he saw the dark-haired girl shaking her head at a clutch of well-dressed youths circling around some over-served unfortunate, hooting and chanting. Disgust clear on her face, she wheeled about and beelined his way. Not stopping, not even slowing, she took him by the arm and steered him toward the exits. "See me home tonight? Please?"

"Uh, sure." That was about all he managed to eke out.

"Or maybe another drink? Unless you've had too many, too?"

By the time they reached the elevators, he had introduced himself. "Ian Jonas. I go by Yonny most of the time."

"Yonny? What a stupid name! Where did that come from?"

"When I was little, I couldn't say Ian. It came out Yon. Which became Yonny."

"Cute."

"My friends call me Yawny."

She smirked at him as she stepped through an opening elevator door.

"Gets worse, or better, you might think. Yawny Joan-ass. Or Jackass, one or the other."

She laughed out loud. "I might like these friends of yours."

They went to Arcadia. The new girl, Rachel Polsky her name, stood discreetly aside as Yonny attempted to negotiate for a table. Fruitless, he turned and was about to suggest another spot when Rachel pinched his cheek lightly. "You boys from Texas! Let me give it a try." She strode aggressively toward the maître d's little pulpit, making sure he could see her approach with a rhythm that had her hips and her long tresses swinging along at odds with each another. She stopped short and summoned the gatekeeper with a long finger, speaking animatedly with hands as well as voice, then turned back to Yonny, beckoning.

As they were squeezed into their seats, she on the banquette, he in the little chair opposite, he ventured, "And how does that work?"

"Simple. This place, and all like it, has more than enough handsome young men on the hunt like you to fill every seat and spill over into the middle of Madison Avenue. Young women, on the other hand, preferably escorted by elderly lechers looking to impress, well, a somewhat scarcer commodity. Plus he thought I was a single, could probably pocket a hundred for making an introduction to one such."

"I see." He raised his water goblet. "The ways of the big city."

A waiter showed up after a decent interval. They had a light supper and a bottle of wine. She had closed up over their meal but then let the wine loosen her somewhat, still guardedly. "Yes, I knew who you were. My brother is in the family business." She noted his questioning eyebrow. "The Polsky Organization. Apparently you are a competitor of ours. And my… socialite… sister-in-law, the same who arranged my blind date, filled me in on your girlfriend there. So, yes, I know all about you."

"Yep, that's me. Former girlfriend, that is. Time for a change, or so it seems."

She discerned the mixture of relief and regret floating across his features and gently tapped his hand with a long lacquered fingernail, then laid her whole hand atop his. "Your Bible, your New Testament? We call it the sequel, you know. Doesn't it say somewhere in all that Messiah business that God doesn't close a door except as He opens a window?"

Yonny had never been able, never tried, really, to figure out the mother-daughter thing. His sisters were seven and nine years older, so he was just a kid when the teen scene screeched and screamed from room to room to slammed doors, and was outside playing most of the time anyway, or shut up in his room reading or building models or fiddling with the Wonders of the Universe with his Gilbert chemistry set, peppering the ceiling with by-products of his creations, and sort of shut it all out.

Not so with Rachel and her mother, no, the first salvos were loosed nearly the moment the taxi door opened at the house in Forest Hills. Funny, though, he and Miriam hit it off right away, or so he thought at the time. Didn't take long to figure out why, she let him in on it the first chance she had, at lunch at their club with Rachel's father off to the restroom, saying on the sly, "You showed Donny how to do it, cutie. Kicked his stuckup butt with whatever it was you did with Johnny McDougall. You know he and I went to high school together, well, next door, he's a Catholic, you know, I was at school next door, we saw each other all the time. He married my good friend Martha, have you met her?" Yonny absorbed her machine gun delivery with smiles and nods, then realized she had been staring at her retrognathic daughter-in-law the whole time. *So that's it?* He shook his head slightly, discreetly, he hoped. *Sheesh! What am I getting myself into?*

Almost from their first encounter, Rachel had tried to vaccinate him. "I had a very unhappy childhood."

"I find that hard to believe, looking at you now." He turned her face one way, then the other. "No scars, none that I can see."

"They're there. Trust me. No, it just happened, Yonnydoo. I'm not sure either of us knows how it started. I was always the leftover, that's one thing. My brothers got the attention, I was, well, I was your proverbial accident." Her older brother Emmanuel had fulfilled his mother's and her parents' dreams, becoming a highly regarded surgeon. The younger, not so gifted, had gone to work for his father, married a Jersey JAP, let her cajole and badger him into moving into Manhattan, stepping up to a higher profile, making the society pages. Esther and Donny, the nickname he preferred to Ezekiel, started running with a faster crowd, spending lots of money to enter the game. He put the family firm into some dodgier deals, one of them a casino in Atlantic City his wife pushed him into, now in danger of losing to foreclosure, something the patriarch had never, ever let happen, even if arms and kneecaps had to be offended.

None of which explained it all beyond the obvious leftover third child. "No, from the beginning," she said, "Mother was jealous of me. When I got older, eleven, twelve, it was clear I wouldn't need a nose job like Margie Kalmanowicz and Mother was envious." Miriam was a classic Semitic beauty, and Rachel owed her mother her own beauty, but daughter's nose was a bit more like her Nana's, smaller, finer, and that was a problem, she said. "And my hair? She never would allow me to cut it, even though she knew I caught hell at school for it. When the boys started appreciating it, though, then she wanted to cut it, but I wouldn't let her do anything more than trim it to my waist.

"And so it went, everything a power struggle. You see, she was unhappy, inside. Her parents were second generation here, her grandfather a doctor from Leipzig, married an Englishwoman, said they compromised over where to live and settled on America. He, Great-grandfather, had been friendly with Friedrich Engels, helped support Marx a little before emigrating. Grandfather was a communist, out-and-out Communist with a capital C. Didn't hurt his medical practice, not Lower East Side, not Upper West Side where they live now. He had been hauled before this commission and that committee and robustly defended his views, neither Stalinist nor Trotskyite, he was always clear to say. '*Pure Communism, not those parvenus,*' he would say.

"And when Mother met my father, a roughhewn type but a handsome devil back then, right before he shipped out in '44, she was eighteen and more than happy to try out her folks' enlightened morals. She got pregnant with Manny right away. Grandfather, well, Nana, really, was indignant at the notion of a Pole, Jew or not, impregnating her precious daughter."

He interrupted, "This is a brave new world for me, Rachel. I may not understand."

"Don't even try. Anyway, there was friction there, Mother began doubting their views and mores and all, and when Father returned home he married her right away and along came Donny." She showed him an absolutely vulpine grin. "Do you know the distance from an apartment at 85th and Amsterdam to Forest Hills, any address?"

"No clue, R. A few miles?"

"Wrong. Once again, Yonny, wrong-O. The right answer? Six hundred kilometers. I measured it. Leipzig to Łódź. Across a border, a gulf, really. And I chose the wrong side."

"Huh?"

8

1978
Westside San Antonio

The night had been extremely slow until the radio called. Sam answered, "Go ahead 9-1."

"9-1 at 1411 Washington Way for a theft," she directed.

"10-4," replied Sam.

Sam parked the patrol car and started up the walk to the apartments in the Lincoln Courts, a housing project for low income people, predominantly black, full of welfare and food stamps recipients, ex-cons, future cons. He was about to meet some of the project's finer citizens.

It was awfully dark. Sam made a mental note to write another report to the management to replace the street lights. He never saw it coming.

Slammed in the back of his head, he was knocked to the ground, dazed but not out. There were five of them. One for each leg and arm. One swinging a claw hammer.

He couldn't move to draw his .41 magnum. Try as he might, Sam couldn't fight free. He squirmed and rolled to no avail.

The one holding his right leg said, "Let's just kill the pig motherfucker!"

"No," said the one inflicting the hammer blows. "I be having too much fun."

Just about that time Sam heard the sirens, the most beautiful sound he had ever heard, better than any symphony, better, even, than Elvis. He imagined it was akin to angels singing. But before the bastards fled, he took a few more hits to the head and groin.

An ambulance was called and Sam was taken to the county hospital. There wasn't a part of his body that didn't bear the bruise of the hammer. Those on his head and face concerned the doctors most, twelve serious ones, fifty-four in all. Amazingly, the scans and x-rays revealed no major damage whatsoever, not one broken bone, not even a drop of blood spilled. Not even a concussion although the doctors kept him in the hospital another four days for observation.

On his return to duty, he discovered no official police report had been filed of the incident, most unusual involving bodily harm to a fellow officer. Sam wasn't happy about that. When he met one of the officers who rescued him in the parking lot, he asked why there was no report. The officer stood mute, merely handing him an envelope with a woman's handwriting on the outside. Inside he read:

One of your 'buddies' was found last night.
We'll take care of you.

Every few months after that, he found a similar envelope and message on the back table at roll call, the note written in the same beautiful cursive, something he would not easily forget. Four more. Then the notes stopped.

9

1979
New York

Damned telephone! He levered himself away from Rachel as quietly as he could, then scrambled across the cold concrete floor to the kitchen. They loved the space in the old leather works they called home now, but it was a hike from one end to the other. He grabbed the phone and breathed, "Yes? Hello?"

He listened a few minutes, then gulped and said, "How?

"Shit.

"Yeah, I'll come. When again?

"Okay. Yeah, see you there. No, not a problem, I needed to know, so thanks. See you. Yeah, bye."

He sat upright in bed, watching the lights of the city dim slowly as the eastern sun coated the façades uptown in pinks and yellows from crowns to shadows, the crenellations and voids and ornamentation becoming more and more distinct by the minute. Finally he got out of bed and went to shower.

When he came back, Rachel was awake, sitting up with the sheet wrapped around her. "Yonny, what's going on? Why are you up so early? Did I hear the telephone?"

"Yeah, yeah, you did. Joe called from Dallas, said he had just heard an old friend of ours had died."

"Oh, I'm sorry. Who? Have I met him?"

"No, he's been in Austin pretty much, not back home too much, I don't think. I don't know, actually. Not good."

"Not good?"

"Murdered. Opened his front door, someone blew him away."

"Murdered? I thought Texas was safer than this place," cocking her ears toward competing sirens racing then dopplering away. "What happened again?"

"Rachel, he was a druggie. A dealer. I guess pretty big time by now, probably a deal gone wrong, maybe a competitor. I'm just guessing." He watered up a bit, then, "Not about the drugs part."

"Are you going?"

"Hmmm?" He had lost himself somewhere in memory.

"To the funeral. Are you going?"

"Yes. I have to. Have to."

He stood at the back of the small crowd graveside at Sunset Park with Joe and Jack, two of his closest childhood friends. None of them were completely, totally surprised, just taken aback at the actuality, the reality of the crime. They had always just thought of him as Tricky Ricky, off on some tangent or another, his usual reckless mischief; even his friends who had stayed in San Antonio all along never really thought of him in terms of danger or even doing something illegal or deeply immoral, he was just Ricky.

As the line of well-wishers filed by his parents and sister, he lingered to join at the whip end. He knelt to the ground in front of Ricky's mother and took her hand, saying quietly, "Mrs. Young, Ivy, Ma'am, I'm Yonny Jonas." She finally lost the composure she had struggled to maintain all this time through the entire service, crying as she took both his hands in hers, massaging them, kneading them, saying over and over, "Yonny, Yonny, Yonny…"

He looked over at his father, a small man, he recalled, now a shrunken figure slumped in his seat, his face frozen in grief, an expression Yonny would never shed from memory, unable to speak, to move, to cry. He stood and leaned over to Ivy, giving her a light kiss on a wet cheek, then shook the father's hand and embraced Judy, the sister who had risen to meet him.

As he retreated to the safety of the rear rank, one girl said to another, just loud enough for him to hear, "That's Yonny Jonas? Boy, did I ever miss out!" He turned his head and smiled.

His flight had been delayed, he had missed the church service and just made it to graveside, so hadn't scanned the guests yet. He stepped to one side of the crowd as it broke up and checked out the faces. *No. Not here. No, not her, not here. Who was she?*

10

1980
San Antonio

Sam was a large man, 6'-2", 220 pounds, mostly muscle with an appropriate reserve of protective padding. He enjoyed his eating, especially his Mexican food. Whenever his beat allowed, he ate lunch at his favorite place, Lupita's, downtown. Wherever he ate, he always sat with his back to the wall, his eyes on the cash register, the comfort of a .41 Magnum at his side.

Lupita's was always crowded at lunchtime, close to the Bexar County Court House and the thousands of people working in the sky-scrapers within walking distance, even in the heat of summer. But this was March, a beautiful day for a short walk to lunch. It was especially crowded, the cool weather bringing more folks out. Waitresses were literally running from table to kitchen to tea and coffee station and back to table to keep up. Although Sam was in uniform, he picked up a pitcher of tea and a pot of coffee and began filling empty glasses and cups. After he served a table of sweaty construction workers, one of them started clapping. Others caught on and started clapping, too. Before long, the whole restaurant, Anglo and Hispanic alike, was standing and applauding Sam for his service. He bowed, filled a few more vessels and found himself a table.

Settling in, he placed his usual order. As he waited, he looked around and noted a chubby Hispanic boy holding his stare on him. Sam nodded and waved. The youngster returned the wave and nod, adding a smile and a blush.

Sam's food came and he thanked his waitress with a smile and a wink. Three beef enchiladas covered with enchilada sauce and melted cheese. Mexican rice and refried beans. A hard taco with picadillo—spiced hamburger meat, lettuce and tomato. Three masa harina tortil-las. All of that deliciousness spiced up with salsa verde and jalapeños. Sweet iced tea to wash it down. Heaven. He poured salsa verde on his enchiladas, rice and beans. He also liked to fill a flour tortilla with rice and beans and enchilada sauce and, of course, verde sauce. All done, he proceeded to dig into his culinary masterpiece.

He was halfway through his third enchilada when he looked up and saw the same young boy watching and giggling. His family was standing to leave when the boy walked over to Sam's table and pulled a shiny new nickel from his pocket. He laid it on Sam's table and said, "This will help pay for your lunch."

Sam almost choked on a mouthful of rice but managed to mumble *'thank you'* and shake the young man's hand.

After lunch he headed uptown to his Northside beat. He hadn't made it but a few blocks north of downtown when the call came in for a gunshot at an expensive apartment building on McCullough. Sam hit the lights and accelerated, reaching the site in a little less than three minutes. He parked in the circular drive and went inside. In the foyer, he met the building manager who led him up the curving staircase to the second floor. Number 210 was right in front of the stair, its door slightly ajar.

Sam asked, "What happened here?"

The manager replied, "We don't know. I called as soon as we heard what we thought was a shot. You came so quickly, we haven't tried to go in. We think there's a gun in there."

"So I heard. Please stand back." He drew his weapon, not knowing what to expect. Pushing the door open with his left hand, his pistol upright in his right, he entered cautiously, one slow step at a time, lowering his gun to ready position. He made his way through an expensively furnished living room, immaculately kept, looking around, listening for a sound. A on his left door was ajar– the bedroom, he thought—and he carefully pushed it open to survey the scene.

He immediately wished he hadn't. What he saw on the bed nearly cost him his fresh lunch, salsa verde and all. Lying on the bed was an older woman, late 70's, 80's, maybe. Blood was running out of her mouth, her right arm was dangling off the bed. As he closed, he could see her sky blue eyes darting about as she struggled to speak. His eyes drifted to a snub-nosed thirty-two beside her, then jerked up to the upholstered headboard splattered with blood and gray matter. He reached down and gently turned her head to see that side of her skull was no longer there.

All he could do was hold her hand in his as he called for an ambulance. When the attendants arrived, he retreated to the living room to distance himself from her moans. Outside was a small crowd of mostly older residents. Sam had always wondered why people wanted so badly to see what they didn't really want to see. He heard the gurney being wheeled out behind him and parted the crowd with a wave. As the gurney came alongside, he felt something. The woman pawed at his forearm, then grasped it firmly, surprisingly so. He laid his free hand atop hers, seeing in her eyes something he hoped he would never see again, terror, pain, regret, mostly regret? *For her life? Her sins? Her death?*

As they moved into the elevator, he felt her grip strengthen then evaporate, almost. He knew she was dead.

11

1980
New York

The tension between mother and daughter escalated to altogether new heights when Rachel announced she was pregnant. Married almost two years now, Rachel had adamantly refused to even consider motherhood, not so much because of her career at the DA's office, but because of, or to spite, her mother, her sniping, her pervasive interference. No longer could she keep Miriam at arms' length, nor avoid her pestering friends, nor stay away from Temple as much as she would like. The High Holy Days with the tickets, the jockeying for pews, all marinating in mother-daughter tension, all of that kept pushing her away.

"Rachel, dear, you must acknowledge your obligations, passing our faith down to your child, your children, yes? Bad enough you went and married a goy, but from Texas, yet! He will tear you from the Temple, will raise the child as some sort of cowboy or cowgirl! Disgusting! Please tell me you understand me, Rachel, and do not listen to my mother and father, not to those atheists!"

Rachel sighed, "Mother, I hear you. Listen, I have to go, I think I'm going to be sick…" She just managed to keep from slamming down the phone. *The Temple? Where was she when I wanted to do my bat mitzvah? Manny and Donny, yes, but me? A girl? Oh, right, she couldn't manage my tennis and her clubs and the Hebrew lessons, so one had to go. Guess which one. Now I do think I'm going to be sick…*

Things didn't improve that night when Yonny came home. He sat beside her on the sofa, turned to see what she was looking at, *the neighbors, maybe the construction guys across the street*? He placed his hand gently on her belly, felt her flinch. "Let me guess. Miriam called."

"Yep."

"Did not go well?"

"Nope."

He decided not to go any further down that dark dead end alley. "Something funny, odd, I mean, happened today. You want me to tell you?"

Taking the slightest of nods, maybe a twitch of a still smoldering temper, as a yes, he plunged in. "So I'm over on Third, talking to Brian Foster, the GC's site guy. You remember him, you like his wife, the Irishwoman?"

Again, a wisp of a nod.

"So we're in the trailer at the corner—the foundations are just coming up—and I look out the window and there are these four guys sitting in the way of everyone, it's a tight site, right? I mean just sitting, on lounge chairs—you know, those cheap woven web plastic things? All of a sudden, one of them jumps up and grabs a passing worker, shakes him, points at his coffee cup, yelling at him—I could just make it out—'*Chock Full o' Nuts! On the corner, four, with cream! Go get 'em!*'

"I looked at Brian and said, '*What's that all about? Who are those guys?*' Just then a loader came along with a bunch of rebar, had to stop for these guys, they wouldn't budge. I had seen enough and started to bolt out of the trailer when Brian caught my arm. '*Yonny, don't. I'll take care of it, nothing you need to get involved in.*'

"So he stepped down and went over. Brian's a big guy, played football at Penn State, I think, coal black, remember?"

"Handsome."

"Yeah, he is that. So he's talking to these guys, I hear them start on him, cussing him up and down, calling him a nigger and worse, one of 'em starts chest-bumping him. And you know what?" Not waiting for the not forthcoming reply, "He backed down. I mean, Brian could bench press me with you and baby Jonas on top, and he just backed off."

He saw Rachel was beginning to pay attention, so he went on, "That did it. I jumped in, feet first, started yelling at this big fat slob. Brian was tugging at me, but I kept at it until he finally put me in a bear hug and turned me around. '*Leave it, Yonny, we'll manage this. That's what we do, have to do.*' He squinted back at the slobs, '*We'll fix them, somehow.*'

"So now I'm turned around facing the trailer, away from these wiseguys, and here comes this other guy, tall, kinda lean, in a black suit and one of those old hats, a fedora, gray straw or something. I see him nod and wave to the guard and just waltz across the lot like he belonged. He went right past Brian and me, straight to the worst of that mob. By now Brian and I are turned back around and this character pokes Fatso in the chest with four fingers like this," he held his hand out flat, "and damned if the big guy doesn't just shrink away, turns to his boys and they pack up and leave." He snapped his fingers. "Just like that, they were gone, tails between their legs."

Rachel perked up. "Then what?"

"Then he just saunters off, back through the gate, hands the guard something and disappears behind the fence. Just like that."

"Who was he?"

"Brian said he didn't know, but I think he does. Anyway, that was the morning's excitement. Ready for the afternoon's?"

She looked questioningly at him.

"Well, I get back to the office, Steve is waiting for me. I had gone on to the Harvard Club for a lunch meeting, so I was a bit later than usual. Anyway, he's waiting for me, Donna says, with that look that says, *Get ready*. I step through his doorway, knocking on the jamb, he says, '*What the hell do you think you're doing? Don't you know anything about New York? The way things work here?*' His relationship with his boss had begun a long slide when he started bringing in the business, attracting attention, stealing the limelight. '*You know who those guys were?*'

"A bunch of slobs."

'*Right. A bunch of slobs. A bunch of slobs who just happen to be in the d'Urbino family. Does that mean anything to you? They control the masons' union, and with it, the concrete workers. You could have shut down the entire project for good!*'

"I sorta stammered a bit, then said I didn't know, but they were screwing up the job, screwing with Brian…"

'*I don't give a flying fuck! Jack Massengale called me right before lunch, had just got off the phone with Billy Gilmartin, who was threatening to, well, all sorts of things if we interfered with his means and methods. Said it would be my job.*' He kept his glare focused on me and went on, '*So, I said to Jack, maybe it's time.*'

"Time?"

'*Yeah. Time for a change. Find you something else to do so you don't screw up here anymore. Run that new project we're competing for.*'

Rachel sat up straight. "Yonny, doesn't that sound like a promotion? What project?"

"Cleveland."

It took the two of them all of ninety seconds to make the decision. Her father had been pestering her to pester her husband to join his business. Yonny had managed to deflect his attentions, pleading loyalty, that sort of thing. But he had hatched a notion, one he thought would float, namely, move back home to Texas to set up an operation taking advantage of the depression beginning to ravage the state's real estate markets. He held it close until a few months ago when he broached it to his wife, who, to his everlasting surprise, didn't even kick him in the teeth.

She had come to a somewhat similar conclusion herself, needing to put some space, a good distance between herself and her mother, especially as they were just then contemplating imminent parenthood. Today, she bought into it with as much enthusiasm as she would ever muster, which is to say, not a whole lot, but enough. "Let's go talk to Daddy."

12

1980
San Antonio

***H**e had been waiting and waiting for her near her car in the VA hospital lot. It was almost midnight. Her shift is over, where is she?*

In his rearview mirror he saw her, casually dressed, not in her nurse's outfit. She looked good. He got excited just looking at her. 'Yeah. Yeah.'

She walked right past him, didn't even say hello. Bitch. He jumped out of the car and waved his big butcher knife at her. 'Get in the car', he growled.

She saw the knife before the face, then recognized him. 'DeWayne, what are you doing? Leave me alone!' She turned and began running back to the hospital, frantically looking for the security guards. Where are they? Shouting for help as she fled, she stumbled and fell. Before she could rise, he was on her. He covered her mouth and told her to shut up. She tried to bite him, only to have him slam the hilt of the knife on her nose, immediately gushing with blood.

Then the pain in her side. She reached her hand toward the pain, only to have her hand slapped away. Then she felt herself being lifted off the ground. Weak, now, verging on shock, she tried feebly to fight back, but he was too strong. Now she slid across a knobbly surface, coming to rest against a wall. She looked around, saw she was in a car. The car was moving now. She lifted herself up only to be slammed down by the back of his hand. The pain was too great. She drifted in and out of consciousness only to be jerked against the seatback in front of her. The car had stopped. Through the red mist blanketing her eyes, she saw the door open, felt herself pulled out by her ankles, landing hard, knocking the breath out of her. She passed out again.

'Damn bitch! Wake up! I'm gonna fuck you.'

Barely conscious now, she lay limply against the rocky soil. Infuriated, he drove the knife into her kidney side and again below the shoulder. "Damn!' He zipped up his funky jeans, the ones he had hoped she would like. Looking around the lot, bare except for patches of agarita and brushy mesquite, he found a little hollow guarded by some bushes and began dragging her toward it. Dumping her, he tossed a few desiccated branches and prickly pear pads on top of her and headed back to his car. 'Damn! Bitch got her blood all over my new threads! Damn bitch! Nothing to do but go home'.

She was silent except for the few soft moans giving away her struggle for life.

"Here's what we've got. Someone grabbed a nurse in the VA parking lot about half an hour ago. Another nurse heard some screams as she was leaving her shift, saw a man she described as a medium-sized black beating on a woman then pushing her into a car. Security guard says he saw a brown sedan squeal out of that lot, an Electra deuce-and-a-quarter, got three numbers on it. So pretty quick we'll know where the perp lives, hopefully. Camacho has his guys on that angle. Meantime we need to check out the area on the west and north side of the Medical Center. We don't know where this guy went, but if it's a rape, he probably didn't go too far. There's lots of open land out there where he could take her. That's what we gotta assume. Scour the place. Here are your zones." Assistant Chief Nelson pointed at the wall map, calling out names as he did. Finished, he turned to his men. "Get out of here. Find her. Whatever you do, find her. If she's out there, well…"

Sam criss-crossed the area north of the intersection of Huebner and Babcock roads for several hours until he got the call to stand down. The suspect had been found at his apartment cleaning blood off his knife, his bloody clothes dumped in the kitchen sink. After he read the guy his rights, the detective in charge figured he could get him to talk pretty quick, but no such luck. Even after being booked on kidnapping charges, he refused to talk. After the first few hours, the patrolmen were sent out again.

Sam and some of his buddies went back to looking even before the order came down. But there was a lot of ground to cover, some of it still raw, undeveloped hill country scrub and scree, hard to get into the interior, a lot of it four wheel drive territory. But he kept looking, hoping against hope, day after day. On the fourth day, heading back to town on Babcock, his bladder started complaining. *Damn! Why now? Shouldn't had that last gas station coffee!* He pulled through a rough curb cut onto a caliche drive leading a dozen or so yards into a large vacant lot. He bolted out of the squad car and stiff-legged it toward a clump of brush, barely tall enough to hide his bulk. Just beginning his relief, he heard something. Turning sideways, he saw a patch of color. It was a blue halter top, torn and bloody. His eyes worked their way deeper into a gloom mottled with shifting patches of light, following soft sounds of breathing or pain, he couldn't tell. Then he saw her, first a foot and ankle, then a leg, then the other, then the rest of the body.

Sam tossed off the covering brush. She was naked from the waist up, covered in blood, sunburned where she wasn't. Her bony ribcage was heaving slightly, so slightly he hadn't noticed at first. Fighting his way under the thorns, he found a faint pulse in her neck. He jerked his walkie-talkie out of its holster and shouted repeatedly, "I found her! I found her! I found her!" He caught his breath. "She's alive!"

Sam leaned against the hood of his cruiser watching the stretcher load into the back of the ambulance, trying to remember his paths of the past few days, trying to figure out how he could have missed her, wondering if he could have saved her, saved her from her suffering. But she was alive, somehow, and now she had a chance at a life. *A chance she owes me. I'll get some leave. I want to be there for her, sit there waiting to hear if she can make it. Maybe she'll pull through, maybe someone will tell her I saved her, found her, at least. Maybe she's pretty, maybe...*

"Good work, Sam! Good work!" The Chief's voice jolted him out of his little reverie. "Sam, you'll be recognized for this. Let's just hope you've saved an innocent life." He looked at Sam's sallow face, his sunken eyes. "But I want you to take some time off. And I'd like you to see a specialist I think highly of, someone you can talk to, if you want." He pumped Sam's hand again and as he turned to walk off, he stopped. "Sam, how did you know to look there?"

Patty Montez clung to life for another twenty-four hours before dying. DeWayne Gustus Foster had refused to talk for four long days until Detective Camacho waved the blue halter top stained in maroon in front of him and let him know her blood matched that found on his knife and clothes. After nine months of incarceration and trial, he was convicted of capital murder and executed two years later.

13

1980
San Antonio

Rachel bravely endured a full hour of her mother's kvetching, then stood up, kissed her and walked out. At the door, patting her bulge, she turned to say, "November sixth, Mother. Be there, okay?"

The transition from SoHo to SoTex went about as smoothly as it probably could, if it were ever to have gone at all. Yonny's parents needed just a little prodding to make the move to join some of their friends in highrise living at 200 Patterson, leaving the house available to their son. He made a deal with his folks, then called his high school friend Skip to do a master bedroom addition on the first floor. Despite the usual delays and disasters, Rachel managed to endure both gestation and construction, going into labor the very day Yonny and some of his friends began moving furniture into the new addition. Jeffrey came into the world a few days early, and blissfully, her parents arrived only after she had come home and settled in.

It wasn't just her incandescent intelligence, the heritage of a succession of intellectual ancestors, that made Rachel so exceptional, but her street smarts, born, probably, of her difficulties with her mother, not to mention her father's history, and honed to an edge in her years with Rudy Giuliani at the Southern District. Keen to others' every nuance and foible, she innately seized upon those one or two things that made another tick, whether a witness or opposing counsel in the courtroom or her prospective, then actual mother-in-law. The first time she was brought home to meet his parents, she fell in love with Yonny's father, the sweetest, kindest man she had ever met, so unlike her own father yet a match for her sometimes acerbic banter, even as their politics were at the extremes. It was his mother she had to work on, both unsure of themselves, treading on a delicate tundra of religion and wealth and accents and upbringings. Inadvertently, unconsciously, she solved the conundrum with a passing comment on the plane back to

New York. "Yonny," she said, "you never told me your mother was so Southern!" She was right: his mother was his father's war bride from Georgia, brought back after the war to many raised eyebrows, he was sure. Yonny took care to relay her observation to the proper authorities and a bond was formed, although he persisted in claiming Mom didn't talk funny.

There was still the drama attendant to introducing her into an environment so very different from a lifetime in New York. He was surprised, pleasantly, when his mother said her bridge groups at the Club praised her down to the last matron. It didn't hurt that he had been invariably, if sometimes involuntarily, courteous and friendly to a fault to those fine ladies as he grew up. The meet-and-greet had gone exceptionally well, she said, and even those Mom had sworn never to speak to, ever again, for criticizing his long hair in college and then for marrying a Jewish girl, each and every one had fallen under her spell, partly genuine, partly contrived, a Potemkin Rachel for the Gentiles, down to the immaculate nails and discreet cleavage and especially the radiant smile, part Mona Lisa, part Joan Rivers.

1981

Rachel had played quite a bit of tennis growing up, won a few junior tournaments, then quit competing, spiting her mother. "Never was Bat Mitzvahed, Yonny. I told you that, yes? Hebrew classes would have interfered with travel tournaments, so my mother made the choice for me. I quit those tournaments not long after, but kept playing on my own. In college, too. Not for her, for me."

She began discreetly at the club, easing into it, doubles with some of the older women, then with some of the girls her age, making friends, or trying to. As she was walking off the court one early Spring afternoon, one of the men from the next court came over and started, well, hitting on her. "So you're the new girl? Aren't you from Queens? I'm from Stamford. Did we ever meet in New York…?" and on and on. She smiled, made an '*isn't that nice*' comment and went on her way. This one persisted over the next few weeks, but when he patted her butt under her pleated skirt, that was it. She turned to him and said loudly, "I'll make you a deal. We'll play. If I win, you leave me alone. If you win, you can keep on being a real creep." Her voice carried as well on the tennis court as in the courtroom, ringing across all the courts, probably all the way across the golf course to Fort Sam. As her playmates watched with mouths agape, she strutted to the opposite service line. "Best of three. Tiebreakers. My serve. Okay?"

Her tormentor took his position and proceeded to get his clock cleaned. Two sets, 6–3, 6–4, closed with an ace. She gathered her things and walked right past him, not bothering to shake hands or even look. As she left the courts, she turned and snapped, "Leave me alone!"

"And you were going to tell about this guy, when?"

She gave him the *maybe not now in front of the baby* look, then relaxed a bit. "Just happened today, Yonny. Just a little matter I had to take into my own hands. So I did. And it's done. By the way, I think I made a few new friends today, even if I did have to reveal my game."

"I'm sure you did both. And who was it? What's his name, in case I need to avoid him for the next few years?"

"Louis something. Julie or Sally told me, I wasn't really listening."

He laid down his fork. "Louis? Louis Goodman? Louie?"

"Well, crap!" She rolled her eyes and looked at infant Jeffy. "Sorry, kiddo. So, your high school friend Sarah's husband? Great, just great. And we're going to their big party next week?"

He grinned broadly. "And it's going to be big fun, dearie."

At Sarah's, she hung back at first, almost hiding behind Yonny, uncomfortable, even unsure of herself in front of her tennis antagonist and his wife. Yonny forced the issue, hailing Louis Goodman from across the living room. "I hear you play some tennis, right, Louie? Oh, you've met my wife, Rachel?"

Now the shoe was on the other foot. Louie nodded to Rachel, "Yes, we had a good match the other day at the club." His voice quavered a bit. "Uh, she's good, very good. Took me by surprise. Maybe another time?" He looked away from Rachel's glare to the glass wall. "Oh, I think Sarah needs me outside. Please excuse me." He pivoted and strolled off, nearly bumping his nose on the sliding glass door as his damp fingers slipped from the handle.

Sarah came silently from behind, startling them with her arms around their waists. "So, Yonny, darling, are you and Rachel enjoying yourself? Rachel, did you ever meet Louis when we were both in New York?"

She smiled shyly, then more slyly. "I came along a little later in

Yonny's New York career, you know, so I don't know what you and he were up to before I showed up." She glanced up at her husband, saw the traces of a wince. All she knew, all he had told her about Sarah, was that she was an old friend, since grade school, dated '*a little*,' he had said. *Maybe there's something else there*, she thought. *Maybe... well, whatever it was, or is, he's kept it to himself*. "Yes, Sarah, he and I had a good tennis match last week, spirited, you might call it. So we've managed to touch base, you might say."

Now it was Sarah's turn to be discomfited. "Oh. Well, he hasn't mentioned that. When, you say? Last week? You play a lot of tennis, then? I suppose he challenged you?" Rachel thought, *She's harvesting, collecting things about her husband, any woman can see that. I wonder...*

Sarah recovered, "Well, I hope you taught him a lesson, did you? At least gave him a run for his money?"

"I beat him. Challenged him, too, I suppose you could say."

Yonny smiled broadly, crowing, "She crushed him, Sarah. Or so she said. Could just be bragging, though."

Rachel smiled and said in an exaggerated drawl, "What d'you cowboys say down heah, '*Ain't braggin' if'n you kin do it?*' "

Her hostess laughed, "No, it isn't. Rachel, could you help me out on the terrace with the buffet, please? Yonny, you just run along and play with the little boys, okay?" She reached up on tiptoes to plant more than a casual kiss on his cheek. "Sorry, Rachel, but he's so cute, I can't help myself. Never could, right, dearest?"

As Rachel was pulled away, she glanced back at a blushing Yonny. *So there is something more. Now I understand, maybe, why Yonny didn't insist on seeing this old friend more in New York*. She didn't let the thought go as the two chatted, but as the evening went on, she relaxed and didn't let it bother her, meeting people, explaining who she was and where she came from, all that. At the door, Sarah held both Yonny's hands. "Do I have your permission to take Rachel to lunch this week? I think we might have some things to talk about."

Rachel covered Yonny's open mouth with a palm. "Yes, we might. And I would love it."

14

1981
San Antonio

***H**er lifeless body lay slumped in the back seat of the car. James Wilson looked over his shoulder one last time at her and laughed. Bobby Jackson rummaged through her purse and took out two envelopes, marked with their names. He opened his, looked at a cashier's check for $7,300 and sealed it back. He also found $200 in cash which he pocketed on the sly.*

Walking toward their pickup, neither one of them saw a woman fifty yards away watching from behind a large oak tree in her backyard. She took a picture of the blue truck with her Polaroid camera but the two men drove off before she could capture the license plate. She called the police and told them what she had seen, apologizing her eyesight wasn't good enough to see the numbers.

Bobby and James drove down to the Rose Room on Zarzamora to celebrate their newfound wealth. They bought a round of beer for everyone in the dingy bar. After his third beer, James couldn't keep his mouth shut, bragging about how he fucked and kilt a white woman. No one believed his story.

Sam showed up at Detective roll call hoping to get assigned to the Harrington homicide. After roll call he was told he would be riding with Tomas Acosta. He was also reminded to observe only and not speak unless spoken to. He went over to Homicide and found Acosta, greeted him and got himself a cup of Styrofoam coffee, anxious to get going. Acosta invited Sam into his office to review what information that had been gathered so far. They would be looking for a blue Ford pickup truck, plates unknown. Beyond that, the witness had said she saw two black men get into the truck before it sped away. That was it.

Acosta told Sam they would be driving out to China Grove to look for the truck and its occupants. Sam didn't understand. "China Grove?" he asked.

"Yeah, if they were in a pickup, they gotta be cowboys and there's some black cowboys working on the ranches out on 87."

Sam thought that was pretty asinine, but he was just there to observe, after all.

So they drove twenty minutes out to China Grove, wasting an hour driving around looking for the pickup. Finally, Sam suggested they pay a visit to Mr. Harrington, the dead woman's ex-husband. "He owns a fence company, probably has some trucks. Maybe a Ford pick-up?"

Acosta scowled at him, then agreed and turned their car around toward the north side of town. At Harrington's, they introduced themselves and had a brief, inconsequential interview, all of ten minutes. Walking back to their car, Sam looked around and spied a blue Ford pickup. He strode toward it to get the plate numbers and called them in, keeping his back turned to the lieutenant.

"Hey, Thompson! What are you doing? If you're pissing on the pavement I'll have to take you in!"

Sam turned and walked back to the idiot, thumbing back toward the truck. "Blue Ford pickup, plates registered at Harrington Fence Company. Don't you think we ought to ask Mr. Harrington where the truck was this weekend?"

The lieutenant scowled again, then relaxed. "Where do you want to go for lunch?"

"Lunch?" Sam was more than a little annoyed and puzzled, too, at the other's behavior. *Maybe he has some Colombo way of suddenly solving the case? Nah.*

Acosta wanted barbeque so they drove down Fredericksburg to a joint he knew. They took Acosta's time eating. On the way out, Tomas made sure they were comped on this one, telling Sam to go back and leave a tip for the waitress he had been ogling. As they were getting into their car, the radio squawked. The dispatcher gave them an address on Broadway for the deceased ex-Mrs. Harrington. *Finally we're getting something done*, thought Sam.

At the apartment, Tomas stooped down to pick up an envelope. Inside, in crude, sloppy handwriting in dull pencil was a note: *Call me about tha money. James Wilson*. A phone number was scrawled next to the writing.

On his own, Sam went back to the Plymouth and got on the radio to track down this James Wilson character. The dispatcher called back within a few minutes with a home address on Menchaca Street and some other pertinent information from his employer's records, Harrington Fence Company. Sam made sure Acosta heard this from the dispatcher's lips, not his. Another scowl, then, "Okay, Thompson, let's go."

They found James sitting on the front porch of a sad-looking cottage that had seen much better days. He was rocking placidly next to his mother who was knitting something when she wasn't consulting the family bible in her lap. Momma looked up at the two men in suits, one with a badge on his breast pocket, the other showing his. She turned to her son, then back to the policemen. "Misters, anything you gots to say to my boy you can say to me and to Our Lord Jesus who knows everything anyway."

Acosta replied, "Thank you, Ma'am. I'm sure he knows all. Ain't that right, James? Why don't we start with this envelope we found on your boss's ex-wife's doorstep this afternoon?"

James mumbled, "Don't know nuffin 'bout it."

"Maybe to set up a meeting to pick up your paychecks?"

"Don't know nuffin'," persisted James.

Acosta looked at Sam and said, "Well, it seems James, here, doesn't know anything about the murder of Mrs. Harrington…"

Mother interrupted him, berating her son. "Somebody got kilt? That Mr. Harrington's wife? She a nice lady. What you know about that, boy?"

"Nuffin, Momma. I tole 'em."

Sam started, "I think he does…"

"Hush, you. James, what you doin'?"

"Nuffin', Momma, nuffin'! Them motherfuckin'…"

"Do not blaspheme before the word of God, boy! Do not use that language while I hold the Good Book in my hands! The Lord will smite you with his rod of righteousness! If I catch you…"

Lieutenant Acosta took Sam by the elbow and turned to leave. He whispered, "When she gets through with her boy, we'll get a call. You come get him. He'll be ready to confess to anything."

Sam suddenly had a newfound respect for this idiot. Sure enough, half an hour or so after checking in at Headquarters, she called. Sam took his patrol car back out to collect poor James. He advised him that he was under arrest for capital murder and read him his rights; all the while, Momma was rocking and knitting and reading when she wasn't staring at her boy.

He handcuffed his prisoner and placed him securely in the middle of the back seat where he could see James' eyes and movement in the rear view mirror. About halfway back downtown, James asked, "What 'zackly do Capital Murder mean?"

"James, does the name DeWayne Gustus Foster mean anything to you?'

James' eyes grew wider, soon as big as saucers. "Yessir, dat's de nigger dat kilt that nurse, yeah?"

"Yeah."

James whispered, "But dey gonna fry his ass, yeah?"

Sam looked back over his shoulder, a slight smile crossing his face. "That's right, James."

Now thoroughly terrified, James croaked, "But, but, dat mean dey gonna fry *my* ass?"

"That's right, James."

Sam was on standby when Laura Harrington's family came down to Headquarters for a briefing. He wanted to meet them, so brought in a tray of coffees to the half dozen members. He settled in next to her brother, striking up a casual conversation while they waited for the Chief and Detective Acosta. Talk turned to the other's occupation, life insurance salesman. "Don't know if I could persuade people to buy a policy," chuckled Sam. "I have enough trouble persuading people to stop fighting or answer questions and I'm carrying one of these." He patted his weapon.

The brother nodded, "Yeah, it's hard at first. You start with friends and family, then cold calling…"

Sam's light bulb turned on. "Family? I guess so. Have you sold any family policies lately?"

"Well, sure. I sold Wilbur a policy on Laura not long before they divorced, maybe a year or so ago. A big one, three hundred thousand."

That was all Sam needed. Wilbur Harrington died in prison serving a life sentence for hiring out his ex-wife's murder.

15

1981
San Antonio

When Yonny and Rachel had moved to Texas, 'home', he called it, 'exile', she called it, he had worried about the reception she would receive, New York Jew, smart, approaching pushy, with a face and figure sure to stoke secessionist impulses. Where he was blindsided was the way his old girlfriends had reacted, those still single or now divorced, that is, jealousy or lost opportunity or what, he didn't know, would never understand, he was sure it was ordained somewhere in the Old Testament, something about the princesses and the severed heads of those not of the tribes.

Rachel had threatened several times those first few months to move back to New York, accompanied or not, if she had to put up with the looks she received and the slights she perceived at Temple. Only when Sarah took her to lunch at Club Giraud down on the River and spilled everything about her and him and the scene back in the day, did she begin to understand, to peel some of the layers back, get a glimpse behind the curtain.

The glimpses she cared most about were how Sarah and Yonny were high school and college sweethearts, she came to learn. How they had been second or third grade classmates, neither remembered exactly, but for sixth grade, proof was the class picture Sarah brought along. "Yonny remembers most of those names, he's so smart, you know. That's him, so cute in his buzz cut—we called them crew cuts—and that's me, all dressed up. Just like a fashion-obsessed mother would dress her little girl."

Rachel detected the bitterness. "Fashion?"

"Oh, yes, we own, or did own Langefelter's. Daddy still runs it, we hope Louis will take over someday."

"I love your store! Yonny never told me your family was involved. You have wonderful things there."

"Thank you, and yes, we do. It's been a wonderful thing, being in retail all my life. Opened a lot of doors, we've met the most fascinating people—by the way, please be my guest at our Bill Blass show next week? Bill himself will be there. Thursday at six, cocktails and dinner. Please?"

"I'd love to. Sarah, there's something else I'd like…"

"Tennis. I know. Sally told me before she went home the other night. I knew I could get it from the source. All of it. Every… sordid bit." She sighed softly, and with a wry twist of her mouth, "Louis is an extrovert. By that, I mean he's very friendly. With everyone."

Rachel understood.

16

1985
San Antonio

Sam sat by himself in the Dunkin' Donuts across Broadway from the Witte Museum, trying to have a quiet cup of coffee or two. 2:30 in the morning, not even halfway through the dogwatch shift. Sometimes on slow nights he'd come in and help make donuts, but not tonight. As he toyed with his spoon he glanced up at a familiar, if unwelcome at the moment, face. Lieutenant Cortez headed his way; Sam was sure he was going to get an earful for not being out cruising.

Instead, Juan eased into a chair and started a conversation, an almost pleasant one. "Quiet out there, huh? Plenty of time for a cup of coffee?" He stirred some sugar into his Styrofoam cup. "Any highlights of the evening?"

"Nope, not much going on tonight. Quiet, like you said." Sam glanced at his watch. "But you never know. Ought to be hitting the streets, see what I can rustle up."

"Rustling's still a crime, Sam. Keep me company a bit longer."

They talked, mostly cop stuff, but Cortez being Cortez, the conversation turned to his latest women, his new car, his clothes. "See this suit, Sam? Five hundred bucks, but got a little law enforcement discount, ya know what I mean?"

Oh, sure, Sam knew, either a gentle shakedown of some store owner or off some fence's rack. With Juan, could be either one, easy. No one knew of any rich elderly aunts in his family, but no one asked, either. "Nice, Juan, looks good on you. Wish I could wear 'em tailored like that. Can't—just too much muscle!"

That got a squeaky laugh out of the lieutenant. "Yeah, well, from what I've been hearing, you need all that beef. Just make sure you don't tangle with a bigger bull." He looked around the shop at several patrons obviously in bad need of coffee fixes, some loud, some dragging in silently. "Let's go outside, Sam, I want to talk to you."

This could be trouble, thought Sam. Cortez, besides his obviously expensive tastes, was in narcotics, so had connections, associations which sometimes caused comment in the department, sometimes whispering, sometimes grumbling. *But*, he thought, *got nothing better to do. Maybe he can get me some suits that fit*. "Okay, let me hit the head first."

When Sam came out, Juan was pointing down Broadway through the open window of his unmarked car. Sam followed a few blocks and eased in behind Cortez as the other came to a stop in the center turn lane near Funston. Cortez got out, Sam did the same, and they leaned against the still cool hood of Sam's car. "No, Sam, thought you might like to hear some of the bullshit going on over on my side."

"Besides Fontana?" Fontana was one of the local drug lords, used to do probably the biggest throughput of weed in the city. Last year, Cortez had orchestrated a dramatic arrest punctuated with several gun-shots, caught on camera by all three local news channels. Naturally, the detective got the interviews, the press, the citations, even though the dealer was back on the streets within hours, sprung by his shiny-suited attorney. He didn't last out there long, getting himself and three of his *vatos* popped at a West Side icehouse a few weeks later. Cortez was Juanito on the spot for that one, too. Sam had good reason to suspect both incidents were setups, that Cortez worked the first one for Fontana's benefit as a sham—no charges had ever been filed—but right away double-crossed him on the second. The vacuum got filled pretty damned quick by a new guy up from Mexico, Juan Ángel Algarve, Johnny Angel or just the Angel. *A killer angel, maybe*, thought Sam.

"That *pendejo*? Got too big for his *pantalones*, Sam. Pissed off some powerful people here and down there. And thanks for handling the mike, Sam. I owe you one." Cortez had insisted Sam come in off patrol to man dispatch the night of the arrest, keeping the lines open for his big event. He thought, somehow, someone was listening in, he didn't know how and didn't want to know.

"What about this other guy?"

"Algarve? Bad dude, man, don't mess with him. The wrong way, I mean."

"There's a right way to mess with a prick like that?"

"People are people, Sam." Juan reached in his shirt pocket for a smoke, offering one to Sam, who declined. "Suit yourself. Man, it's a pretty night, just a little too hot." He took the first drag, then, "I think you'll like what I'm gonna tell you, Sam, coming from all that rich Anglo shit back there in Alamo Heights."

"Sorry, Juan, not one of those guys."

"Yeah, and that's why you're gonna like this. You see, there's a guy up there, big name, big bucks, who decided he wanted a piece of the action. Wasn't gonna get his hands dirty, typical, so typical, but wanted a cut. He tried to get Fontana to go along, and when he wouldn't, well...," he drew his finger across his throat, making a *scrritchh* sound as he did.

"So who's this guy?"

"No names, Sam, no names." He looked down the street at the ButterKrust bakery humming away, lights burning brightly, the street filling with a yeasty aroma. "You might not know him anyway, and you don't need to. And he isn't an uptown Anglo, skin's nearly the same color as mine. Says he's Spanish, a Spaniard. Hmmph. Bullshit! Anyway, this rich guy looks around for someone else. One of his lawyers, Sullavan, you know him?"

"Yeah. Slimeball."

"That's the truth. Anyway this lawyer's a fixer, right? Know what I mean?" Sam nodded. "Yeah, one of those downtown, City Hall slick suit fixers. He's connected politically six ways to Sunday, does criminal defense, has a clientele, contacts. Lives up in Olmos Park, pals around with the high and mighty, country club and all that shit. Looks out for them, too. Mr. Rich has him look around for someone else."

"Angel?"

"Yeah, but back to Fontana. He was getting squeezed by the cartel, squeezed bad..."

"I thought he was making a shitload?"

"It's retail, Sam. Just like Sears, or Langefelter's, I like that place. Retail. It's a cash flow business. Inventory comes in, you gotta pay the man then move it. Takes money to get inventory and carry it plus he's got a big payroll, all his goons and hangers-on. And he couldn't say no to the cartels, say, '*Hold up delivery 'til next month 'til I sell this stuff already*' or, '*I'll gladly pay you next month for some kilos today.*' Doesn't work that way, Sam. The Mexicans are pushing stuff up here as fast as they can, want that cashola. So he had to take it or get put out of business, ya know what I mean?"

"So he needed a payday loan? Couldn't he just move it from one credit card to another like the rest of us stiffs?"

They laughed at that, then Juan started again, "We should be so lucky to get those big bucks, Sam. No, he didn't. That arrest was for his protection, Sam. I set it up so he could get some protective custody for a while to try to make it work, maybe even turn state's if it didn't. But he was stupid, arrogant, was smoking his own shit and figured it'd just be business as usual. It wasn't, obviously. After the arrest, I made a call to Icky Sullavan. Made a suggestion, Sam, that's all, a suggestion."

"To hook the Angel up with Mr. Rich?"

Cortez looked around the empty street and nodded.

"So Mr. Scuzbag Lawyer brings two partners to the table. What does Mr. Rich do?"

"He's the finance. He's the payday loan, like you call it, makes sure the cartel gets paid on time. Takes his cut, his vigorish. And Icky gets his fees, helps out with the laundry, too, I'm pretty sure. And moneybags also owns real estate. A lot of it. Gotta put the stuff someplace when it gets here, so he gets his piece there, too."

"Sounds pretty slick. So why don't we just bust 'em all?"

"That's not how it works, Sam. That's why I wanted to talk to you."

"No."

"Sam, listen. It's still a new organization, a new setup. And growing. We, he needs people, the right people in the right places. And, hell, Sam, everybody's doing it, or wants to."

As long as he had been on the force, Sam had remained resolutely straight, untouchable, naïve, even. A free cup of coffee here, a fried chicken dinner there, just getting comped for being a cop. Courtesies extended by a grateful public. He had kept his head down. Until now. "Everybody?"

"Not the real dumbasses, of course." Cortez rattled off a few names.

Sam whistled. "I never woulda thought. 'Specially Richard." He thought a few minutes, did some sums in his head, credit cards, mortgage, car payments. He rasped, "What are you talking about?"

Cortez lit himself a new cigarette. "Not much, Sam. It's an eyes and ears thing." He went on a few minutes, then, "Sam, I don't want you to do anything wrong, just some of those things. And there's money in it. Think it over. Okay, I'm done. See you around."

As he watched the detective speed away, Sam started to think it over.

17

1986
San Antonio

Over the years, Sarah and Rachel grew closer and closer. Rachel felt less and less the outsider as Sarah introduced her around, got her to serve on some volunteer boards with her, work this charity gala and that testimonial dinner.

Rachel couldn't quite put her finger on it, but there was something odd going on. Her situation, she understood—the obvious outsider, didn't grow up in the Country Club pool, didn't go to UT or SMU and go Greek with her kindergarten friends. And Jewish, too, that was always there, but she was being drawn into what passed for society, becoming accepted despite all that. But Sarah? She was an insider, her father and grandfather highly respected—*assimilated*, thought Rachel—a lifelong Alamo Heights person, even though she went to college up East and lived in New York those years. She seemed to be somehow less rooted as the years passed, something was working inside her that was suppressed, repressed, Rachel couldn't tell. And wasn't about to ask, not yet.

A few years later, Rachel announced she was pregnant. Not exactly a surprise either, they had been trying, but shock enough for both when she was told to expect a twosome. And of the female persuasion. Yonny's internal financial calculator began overheating immediately.

Naturally, Sarah was present for every moment, from decorating the nursery to labor and delivery to playing night nurse so Rachel could get some rest. One night after swaddling Rhea, or was it Leah—she turned the little one over to see her distinctive stork bite—Leah—Rachel thought, *She's pretty wonderful, the way she cares about everyone else. I hope she cares as much about herself. I can see why Yonny and she were so... close. But not close enough then, whatever happened to them, and no longer*. Her thoughts drifted to something else. *Now you're being totally irreverent, girl. Now we won't have to do Hanukah in New York. Too much trouble. Sorry, Mother, too bad, so sad!*

18

1993
San Antonio

A couple of years later, Sam left the SAPD and moved to Denton with a new wife. Up there, he did undercover narcotics for five years until his covers gradually eroded along with that marriage. Moving back to San Antonio, the department was happy to have him back on the force, given his record and his reputation as an officer who could make things happen, but could only take him on again as a patrolman. That suited Sam just fine, less paperwork, less office time, more time to drive, to observe, to reflect.

"Two—Five at Basse and McCullough. Olmos Club Apartments. Possible suicide."

"Ten-four, two-five," replied Sam.

The call was a long way up from Hildebrand Avenue, the northern boundary of Sam's district. Of the eight districts in the Two section, three were open, leaving five men to work all eight. On a normal workday it might have been okay, but there was a full moon and his natives were restless. Only 1900 and Sam had already made three disturbance calls and two accidents.

At apartment 213, he was met at the front door by a sobbing woman. "He's in the back bedroom," was all she could say.

"Okay," replied Sam. In a solemn voice, "Could you tell me what's happening?"

"Kenneth killed himself," said the woman through her tears.

"How are you related to Kenneth, please?"

"I'm his mother." *Some mother*, he thought. *What kind of mother lets her son get so depressed he kills himself?*

"What is your name, please, Ma'am?"

"Nancy." After a long drag on her cigarette, "Nancy Lousy Mother Collins."

It was at this point Nancy broke down and began to cry uncontrollably. Sam took her by the shoulders and led her inside to the living room, sitting her down on a worn sofa. Then he started down the hall toward the back bedroom. The air was thick with the stench of blood, of death. The closer he got to Kenneth's bedroom, the stronger the odor became. He choked down the bile, the urge to vomit his chicken fried steak from Earl Abel's, not an hour old.

As he stood in the doorway taking in the scene, he asked himself, *Why and how could someone do such a thing to themselves and their loved ones, the ones who would find this carnage?*

A shotgun was lying in his lap where it fell after its blast took the backside of the head off. Brains and blood splattered the headboard behind his limp body. A gaping hole in the back of his mouth was so large parts of blue-gray brain slithered down onto his red-and-white checked flannel shirt. Kenneth's eyes were still open wide as if the blast had frightened him. Sam halfway clucked at the irony that brought to mind.

Then the doorbell rang. Nancy had gathered her wits and strength to get off the sofa and answer the door. Sam heard the voice of his sergeant, "Babbling" Bill Braxton. She was upset that another person had come to ogle her son and told him to wait on the walkway.

Confronting Sam, she said, "Does that son of a bitch have to come in?" The crying started again.

"Yes, ma'am, but I'll get rid of him as soon as possible." He tried to comfort her, but continued, "There'll be at least one more to come and he will need to take photographs of the scene. Sorry, Ma'am."

A neighbor came to the door, asking what the matter was. "Nancy, Nancy, it's Donna. What happened?" Nancy couldn't talk, just fell into her neighbor's arms.

Sam asked Donna to take Nancy to her apartment next door. The dumbass asked why, so Sam took her by the hand and halfway dragged her down the hall to Kenneth's room.

"What's that horrendous odor?" she asked.

"You wanted to know why," he replied. "I'll let you know why. Would you want to stay in this place?" He turned her into the doorway to Kenneth's room.

Her first gasp was followed by a scream and more screaming. And more screaming. The horrific sight of the body was more than she could handle. She ran down the hall and out the door, Nancy close behind, screaming.

Babbling Bill stood sideways at the front door to let the women out, scratching his balls.

Finally, after all the photographs were taken, the shotgun tagged as evidence, Kenneth hauled off to the morgue, Sam sat down at the kitchen table for a talk with Nancy. "What's been going on with Kenneth?"

"For such a handsome and seemingly confident young man," Nancy began, "he was still very insecure. He's had three relationships this year and it's only September. Sharon was the first this year, met her at a New Year's Eve party. It was fast and furious. She's a gorgeous girl, but a little materialistic, well more than a little. The one carat diamond Kenneth bought her from Americus Diamond was beautiful, just not big enough for the former homecoming queen from MacArthur High some time back. They argued. She broke up. Said she'd be embarrassed to be seen with such a small diamond. Funny, she didn't mind leaving with it.

"Tore him up pretty bad. He started drinking and runnin' with some pretty slutty girls." Nancy lit her fourth Marlboro and continued. "Number two was a whore named Jayce." There was more than a little bitterness in her tone. "That lasted until one morning I caught her making breakfast wearing one of Kenneth's western shirts and apparently nothing else, she bent over to take the biscuits out of the oven and, well, let's just say, I caught a glimpse of the full moon." She laughed for the first time then took another long drag from her cigarette. "We had words. Not very nice ones. She left pretty soon."

She rose and went to the front doorway for some fresh air, maybe to get away from the scene. "This is Kenneth's apartment. I moved in with him. He makes good money." Sam let her ramble on a while, her audience of neighbors dwindling steadily as the novelty of the situation wore off. He was just about to quit the scene when he saw Nancy staring intensely at something or someone in the parking lot. "Susie. That's her."

"Susie?"

"Yeah, she was Kenneth's last, I mean, latest girlfriend. I liked her, she was so much better than those other sluts, that's for sure. I hoped it would work. I think I would have liked her as a daughter-in-law, we got along pretty well. But she had a temper—did she ever have a temper—and she's one of those who's got to be in control of things, all the time. I could stand it, pretty much ignore it, but Kenneth couldn't. He didn't like it. He'd push back on something, like where to go for dinner, then she'd blow up, lose her temper, they'd argue. They did that again over what stupid movie to watch on TV, she left in a storm of cussing. That was three days ago, she hasn't been back, not 'til now." She pointed to a blonde getting out of a Toyota and going round to the other side, retrieving what looked like flowers in the dim light. "Just like her. Come on back and try to make up. I think she really loved Kenneth, I think she did. I just wish she could have tried to control herself, not Kenneth."

Sam waited for the girl to mount the stairs and turn their direction. Susie was of average size, average looks. *More than average boobs, though. Probably more than average in the sack by that walk of hers. But that doesn't matter now, does it?* Her strawberry blonde hair just reached the shoulders of her western-style shirt, probably one of Kenneth's.

Nancy lost it, charging her, screaming, "You're the one! You're the reason my little boy's on his way down to the morgue! Why couldn't you come back last night or this morning? Why? He needed you!"

She stopped short, frozen as she processed Nancy's rants. The flowers slipped from her hands, the cheap florist's vase already shattered on the walkway floor, silently for all she was aware at that moment. Then she began crying uncontrollably, as uncontrollably as her temper had flared with Kenneth. Nancy ran to her, hugging, both women now alternately bawling and sobbing.

Sam watched a few minutes then turned toward the other stairway. At the first step, he turned to look back, then shook his head and ambled down the stairs.

That was when Sam decided he had had enough. Day after day, night after night, seeing what he'd seen, some of the worst things this side of a war zone, dealing with the worst of the worst. *What do they call it in guys that came back from Nam? PTSD? What's that mean again? P-T-S-D? Patrolman too... too shut down? Too shut down to give a shit any more? Out here or at home. You're tired, Sam, that's it. Just plain fa-tee-gayed.*

A few months later, he caught wind of a new opportunity, something a little different. One of his academy mates was the new Chief in

Alamo Heights, had persuaded City Council to let him hire a detective. Sam made a call, got the job and started the next week. He wouldn't get a full pension from San Antonio, but it was time.

TWO

Alamo Heights, Texas

1997

1

On the way to the Jonas house, Sam's memory wandered back to high school. He and Yonny had been friends, not close, mostly ran in overlapping circles, joined here and there through different buddies, Ricky Young, others. He smiled to himself as he remembered that time, *fall of their senior year, the big MacArthur game, when Coach Timms asked one of the guys who attended church regularly to say the prayer before taking the field. Tommy House was chosen to pray, the usual prayer to guard the players against injury and to be good sports. The tension in the locker room was building, the big bass drum right over our heads was pounding and booming, the players in our new bright gold jerseys with blue lettering getting pumped up and Tommy had to speak louder and louder, finally saying 'And one more thing, Lord, help us beat the hell out of the Brahmas!' As the team rumbled out from under the stands, the Muleskinners were shouting encouragement, clapping and hooting. One of them broke away from the line and grabbed Sam by the facemask. It was Yonny, yelling, 'Beat the shit out of Mac!' over and over. Sam finally broke off and grinned, giving him double thumbs up. Maybe they have a keg stashed somewhere. Smells like it.*

Over the years he hadn't seen Yonny so much, even after he heard Yonny had moved back from somewhere up East. Reunions, yes, and occasionally the 50-50, and football games, and after he had moved over to the AHPD, that one time he asked him to fix a ticket. *Just last year for his kid, wasn't it?*

That jolted him. This was different—he had never, not in all his years on the force, all three forces, had to tell a friend a loved one had died out there on the streets. Yeah, he had done that a lot, well, more than a few times on the SAPD, but with strangers, other people. The hardest part was showing the family or the girlfriend or boyfriend the body, just the face, but still… *You'd think the Medical Examiner would do it, or the guys who ran the morgue, but no, they left it to us cops, everything up to pulling back the sheets.*

And not here in sleepy Alamo Heights, not even once in four years.

At the door, he showed his badge to the peephole. As Rachel opened the door, Sam said, "Your husband and I went to Heights together, Ma'am. I need to talk to him, ummm, well, actually both of you."

Rachel went pale. "What is this about? Is there something wrong with Jeffrey? The girls?"

By this time, Yonny had shuffled to the door, fiddling with his pajama bottoms. He froze. "Sam?"

"Yeah, Yawny, Yonny, I mean." Sam looked around inside the house, looking for the dining room. He wanted them to be sitting straight up, not too comfortable, *because they're fixin' to be real uncomfortable*. He realized he was holding Rachel's hand. Looking down, then up at her, "Please, may we go into your dining room?"

The front door swung left directly into the living room with the dining room next on the left, up one step. Wordlessly, Rachel pulled Sam along, then had to steady her as she stumbled slightly atop the step.

Rachel half whispered, "Would you like some coffee, Officer?" She had more than enough experience dealing with cops, at least in New York, but now found herself totally at sea. Sensing her disquiet, Sam gently steered her to a chair on the long side of the table, pulling it out for her. He waved at her husband, "Yonny, please sit next to your wife."

Sam then sat at the head of the table, close enough to lay a hand over Rachel's. He needed to be close—sitting across from them could be, in his experience, confrontational, like an interrogation. He asked Rachel her name. That little step done, he felt a bit more at ease than with the strangers he had dealt with, but knew it was going to be rough on them. And him. "I'm afraid I have some bad news, and I know this is never easy. I'm obviously not here for coffee or to party." He heaved a breath, "Well, here it is. We, SAPD, actually, found… your son over in Olmos Park, the park itself. A buddy of mine at SAPD called because they found his wallet with his license, an Alamo Heights address, he asked me if I knew the family, would come by to talk to you."

Rachel blurted, "No, no, there must be some mistake!"

"That's why I'm here, actually. They found the ID, but I, well, they need a positive identification. I know what I'm fixin' to ask you is difficult, extremely difficult. I need you both to come with me to identify your son."

"Come with you where, Sam?" Yonny's voice was none too steady, quavering on his name.

Sam tried to never use the word *morgue*. "He's at the hospital, University Hospital."

Rachel broke in, "So he's going to be okay?" She slipped her hand over Sam's, squeezing it, *surprisingly strong*, thought Sam.

"At the Medical Center?" Yonny had calmed somewhat. "Not downtown?"

"Y'all will ride with me, don't worry, we'll get there. But we probably need to leave now, or pretty quick."

The parents went off to change clothes, put the dogs away and lock up, then joined Sam in his unmarked car parked out front. Along the way, Sam would have filled them in on as much as he cared to, as much as he wanted to, could do, but they just sat in silence in the back seat. It was about 25 minutes at that hour, steady, just long, it seemed to him, *but for sure for them*.

He pulled into the hospital drive, pulled out his light and set it on the roof. "Yonny, Rachel, this way." He led them straight through the ER where a security guard levered himself off his stool at a set of double doors. "Oh, Sam? Haven't seen you here in a while." The guard glanced back through the view window at the empty corridor beyond. "Going down there?" He pressed a button, then said softly, "Sorry, folks."

As Sam led the couple down a sterile-looking corridor, he flashed back to another visit, his first, *now fifteen years ago, maybe more? He had to take fingerprints from a corpse, a shooting victim, or was it a stabbing, he couldn't remember. When he got to the morgue, the attendants were scurrying around—it was a Saturday night—and one of them just waved him into the body room. The fourth tag checked out, so he slid open the drawer. Trying to avoid showing the face, he reached under the sheet for the left hand. It felt like a fish, limp, cold, clammy. Just then he heard a sound, a sound like Pssst! Shit, he thought, is there someone here? He looked around, saw no one, then shook his head and pulled out his card and pad. He took the lefthand prints, then went round to the right. Just then the sound came back,*

Pssst! He practically jumped out of his skin. Shit! Shit! Now he was downright scared. He hustled through the prints, flipped the sheet down and slammed the drawer shut. Just as he reached the door the sound came back. Pssst! He got out of that creepy place and nearly knocked down the attendant he had seen earlier. 'What's the problem, Officer?' Sam explained the weird noises. 'I think someone's alive in there!' The attendant fell back against the wall, laughing so hard. Now Sam was mad. 'What's so goddamned funny?' 'That's the bug spray. Just installed it. Sprays every thirty seconds.' The attendant could barely finish, laughing maniacally. Sam glared at him then slammed both doors against the wall and doubletimed it out of there.

He was barely aware he had traversed the corridor, then down an elevator, then another corridor when he came back, jolted by a nurse's harsh barking. "What do you want?"

"Oh, uh, Thompson, Alamo Heights Police. We're here for an identification." He fumbled in his back pocket for his wallet, then snapped it open to show her his badge.

"Name of the deceased?"

He closed on her and answered quietly; she nodded and slipped through the door. "Sorry, we may have to wait a bit. Over here," he waved to a plate glass window let into the wall a few feet to their left, a speaker set in the middle. A few minutes later an attendant backed in towing a gurney. Sam looked at Rachel. *She's fixin' to meet reality.*

The attendant leaned over the body to address the speaker. "All we need of you is to confirm this is," he reached over to the toe tag, "Jeffrey John Jonas, age sixteen." He reached to his left and pulled the sheet down to the shoulders.

Rachel gasped and turned her face into her husband's chest. Yonny looked for a moment, then nodded as he turned and buried his face in her hair.

"I'll take that as a yes. Officer?"

"Yep, that'll do."

"Okay, then. Thank you folks, sorry. Officer, you'll sign out up front?"

Sam nodded. He left them alone for a few minutes, then said softly, "Yonny, we ought to be going. You should be going home now."

On the drive back, Rachel, at least, opened up, wanting to know more. "What now, Officer, Sam, I mean?"

Over his shoulder he replied, “Routine examination, mostly toxicology. Drugs. Take some blood, some tissues, I’m no expert.”

Rachel cried, “They won’t cut him open, will they?” She turned to her husband, “They won’t, will they? Don’t let them cut my little Jeffy…” She held both hands to her face, wracking with sobs.

Sam turned halfway, “No, Yonny, not unless you want them to.”

“No.”

“Okay, then, they will be testing for drugs, then. Why? There were apparently no signs of obvious trauma, no cuts, bruises, just some scrapes where… where he must have fallen down. So, the next step is to check for drugs.”

“Drugs?”

“Yeah, Yonny. There’s plenty of that going on at the high school. Not like when we were there, not just beer drinking anymore.” He looked into the rearview mirror. “Yonny, was your boy doing drugs?”

“No, no way. No.” He swallowed hard, then, “No. Not that we know of, but… maybe some of his friends…?”

“Well, maybe it was his first time, that’s actually a pretty good explanation. Someone gave him something, we won’t know what until the toxicology report comes back, but it’s not unusual for a, a reaction, an allergic sort of thing. Right now, nothing for you or me to do. I’ll let you know when I know, promise.”

Rachel’s sobbing had subsided. “Sam, can we go by, drive us, well, the… where it happened?”

“No, Ma’am, and I’d rather you didn’t go by there. It’s still an active investigation scene, don’t want any, well, any tampering or fooling around with it. Please take my word for it. I’ll get you there when it’s okay.” By now, they were home.

2

Yonny helped Rachel out of the police car, then caught her as she stumbled, holding her trembling against him. He leaned into the open passenger's window and asked, "What now, Sam?"

"Just take it easy for tonight. As easy as you can, okay? I'll be by tomorrow to check on you."

"Thanks, Sam." He helped Rachel up the steps to the flagstone walk. At the door, she fumbled her house keys out of her purse, but could not steady her hands, so he pried them away gently and opened the door. *We forgot the alarm.* He led Rachel to the sofa in the living room and both collapsed against each other. Holding his hand to his brow, he croaked, "What do we do now, Rachel? What do we do?"

"Tell the girls tomorrow when they get home from Jenny's. Then tell your parents."

"What about yours?"

"I'm just not ready for that, not yet, Yonny. Don't make me do that, not yet."

They made their way to their room in silence, undressed in silence, slipped into the bed in silence. Not even a kiss. Neither could sleep, of course.

Why us? Why Jeffrey? This is... is something that happens to other people, other people who don't love their kids like we do, like Rachel and I do, have since the moment we knew they were coming? Where did we go...? Hold that thought, don't even think it. We haven't gone wrong, at least Rachel hasn't. Maybe I missed too many Little League games, maybe I missed too many... maybe I, we, missed too many signs. Maybe we just didn't get it, let too many things slide, didn't... He looked over at Rachel's lustrous jet hair, her head turned away from him, but he could see her jaws working, asking herself the same things he had just asked himself. He reached over and draped his arm over hers. She didn't move.

3

Sam drove back down the Boulevard into Olmos Park, turning right toward the blue lights eerily strobing the black treetops. The park was a sliver of live oaks and cedar elms and pecans and barbecue pits and picnic tables squeezed up against Olmos Creek on the west with McAllister Freeway towering above it and Devine Road on the east, a narrow peninsula of San Antonio separating the little cities of Olmos Park and Alamo Heights, the two a mere seven or eight thousand souls surrounded by a whole lot more. Back in the day, it was an okay spot for parking and beer drinking, but over the years had gotten dodgier, more dangerous, now the area's preferred spot for drug dealing and homosexual liaisons. He stopped a few yards away from two black-and-whites and got out, cursing his old knee injury as he bumped against the pillar. A young guy in a suit came up to him, barking, "Who are you? What do you think you're doing here? This is my crime scene!"

Sam just smiled inwardly as he whipped out his badge. "AHPD. Was asked to meet with the parents, tell them what was up." He looked around. "How long you been doing this?"

"Not too long." The other looked back a little sheepishly. "This is my first."

"Okay. Let me tell you how this is going to work. I'll help you, but you gotta share everything with me. Everything." Sam knew from his years on the force that the SAPD looked down on the little satellite cities' police. He needed to establish a little Alpha Male at the outset. As the other stiffened, then nodded, Sam continued before he could respond, "Okay, What have you found? Was the kid in a car? Did he fall out? Got tire tracks? Where was the body?"

"Over here. I'm guessing the body was tossed out of a car—see these footprints? One pair smaller, I bet went from the driver's side around, the other pair larger. Then back into the car, I'm guessing, then went that way," pointing toward St. Luke's spire, "got some dusty tire marks, but too dry to make anything of it."

Good work, for a kid, thought Sam. *But not good enough*. "Crime scene investigators coming out? Need pictures, maybe a tire mold. Called them?"

"No," responded the other, hesitatingly.

"Do it."

About that time a uniform came over. "Hey, Sam."

"Hey, yourself, Bill. Tell me about the body. Did anyone try to revive the kid?"

"By the time I got here, EMS had bundled him up. No, he was gone when they got here."

Sam turned back to the Homicide detective. "Any witnesses? This is kind of a strange place, what with the gays hanging out looking for each other."

The uniform replied for the other, "Two. Came driving in from Devine, nearly ran over the body. Shook up, pretty much. Didn't see anyone, no car, nothing." He looked around, then, quietly, "Don't think they want to talk, get involved. Names might show up in the paper, get me?"

"Got ya. Okay. Give me both your cards so I can get in touch. And copy me on your reports, okay? Who's the day investigator?"

Homicide gave him a name. "Know him. Good. Okay, guys, have at it."

As Sam walked back to his car, Officer Jackson caught up with him. "Sam, one other thing, wasn't sure our rookie back there was ready for it." He spoke quietly as Sam's eyebrows arched. They shook hands, Sam went home, not to sleep—*thoughts keep you awake.*

Next morning, he called Yonny's office. "Yawny, I need to come by and check Jeffrey's room—I need to search it. And alone, I can't have you there." Sam had called the SAPD day investigator, not learning anything new, but getting permission to be the one to search the kid's room. *Mutual courtesy sort of thing, good thing I still know who to call.*

"Really?" Sam could almost feel him stiffen, freeze across the phone line. "Uh, don't you need to have a warrant or something?"

"Trust me on this one, buddy." *Is he hiding something?*

After a silence, "Okay. When? No, wait a minute. Rachel's home until… until… probably noon. Can you do it at 12:30? I don't want her there. She's pretty raw, you know, she's…"

"I get you. 12:30 it is."

At the door, Sam wasted no time. *Can't let old times get in the way of the present.* "Have you touched anything up there?" He looked around, "His room is upstairs, yes?"

"Yeah, I mean, no, we haven't gone in much, not yet. Come on, I'll show you."

Sam followed him up the stair, pausing to admire the stained glass window at the landing overlooking the pool. Yonny almost smiled. "I made that, many moons ago, it was. My parents liked it, but when Jeffy was little, he thought it was fascinating…" He clutched at the handrail. "Let's go, Sam. Let's get this over with."

He didn't need much time; he had done dozens of these, it seemed, and knew where to look, which nook, which cranny to pry into, and failing to find anything, made a sniff pass. He crawled partway under the bed, then retreated and on rising, looked around one more time. *None of that death metal crap on the walls, almost too neat for a kid.*

He came back down the stairs and found Yonny standing at the kitchen counter, absentmindedly munching on some Fritos straight from the bag. "Want some?"

"No, not really. Did you or your wife clean up that room, move stuff around?" *Hide stuff?*

"Nope. Rachel wouldn't even go upstairs. I caught the girls peek-ing in, but shooed them away." He smiled weakly, "I think they want some of his things already, little vultures that they are."

"Good. That's the way it should be. I'm really not s'posed to tell you, but I think it's clean up there. You can tell your wife…"

"Rachel."

"Yeah, Rachel. But she's not to say anything to anyone. Tell her I could get in trouble. It's a good thing that it's clean up there, for you and her, but it makes my job, our job harder."

"Harder? How?"

"No obvious clues, nothing to go on. There wasn't much at the scene, either. Who did he go out with last night? We think he was with a boy and a girl, girl was driving, we're pretty sure."

"I… I don't really know, come to think of it. He walked up to the game, said he'd be out messing around with his friends after." He swallowed hard. "Used that same excuse with my parents, all the time, and usually found myself in some sort of jam."

"Me, too. They never knew where I was, either." Sam chuckled, then caught it. "Sorry, didn't mean anything by that, Yawny. Oh," he paused, torn between reveal and conceal, "one thing I sure wouldn't want to mention in front of your wife, not that I really need to say anything about it, but, well, your boy's fly was open when he was found, with his dick sticking out a little bit. Hadn't come or anything, but we did find, well, traces of lipstick. Kind of a light pink. That's all we've got on that score. Sorry."

Yonny let his head droop, then raised up, trying to suppress a weak, wavering grin. "At least he…"

"Yeah."

"Yeah." He looked at his watch, then said, "Got to get you out of here. Rachel may be on her way home. Thanks for coming, Sam. Keep me up, okay?"

4

***The** service was well-attended,* he thought. The cavernous Alamo Heights Methodist Church, aka the Methodome aka Vatican West, was about two-thirds full, the flowers were gorgeous and Reverend Tate's eulogy, delivered in his authoritative baritone, was heartfelt for the boy he had known so well, almost from birth. Yonny had bracketed Rachel with the twins, as much to insulate her from her mother as for their physical and moral support. *And Jeffy's acapella group was just right instead of the usual hymns, even though they broke down a couple of times. So did we...*

Afterwards the line into the reception snaked out into the hall, almost back to the doors into the transept. *And why not? Jeffrey was popular, sure to garner some Senior Superlative or whatever they do these days.* Looking past one elderly woman who had latched onto Rachel's hand with surprising tenacity, he noticed several clutches of girls, red-eyed or crying openly, hugging one another. *Pretty girls, too. Well, he was no slouch in that department, either.*

Principal Skinner jogged him back. "Ian, this is, well, it's a great loss for all of us. For the school, you see? He was such a fine representative, going off to, where? Had you all decided?"

"No, not yet. He liked UVA and Washington & Lee, we're, we were trying to discourage him from going farther north, to New York." He had been away when Skinner became principal, had been away long enough to not care, not give it another thought until he and Rachel came back from New York, then plunged headfirst into the Oh-Nine maelstrom. Hadn't changed all that much, except for the expectations dropped on them as parents, the competitive child-rearing bit, the...

He jerked back to the scene in the community hall to hear the principal intoning, "...should be an example for our students, the dangers of drugs, this plague..." Skinner's platitude was stopped short by a hand on his shoulder. Bob Sweeny said curtly and with finality, "No, Floyd, this one was one of our best. Our very best. Something terrible happened, some horrific mistake, but he wasn't one of those..."

He drifted away from the discussion, then started as a hand took his, then another moved over to his back, settling around his waist, gripping him tightly. "Hello, dearest," whispered a voice close to his ear. "I am so sorry for you and... your wife." He turned to look down at Sarah, as perfect as he had ever seen her, even in his dreams, those haunting dreams from thirty years ago. "These things should not happen, not to you, Sweetie. No, all that '*Bad things happen to good people*', that's all nonsense. I... I just hate to see you in pain, Yonny, I know that pain, the pain on your face. Plain for everyone to see, but no one can see it so clearly, as acutely as I do, now, this instant. You do know that, don't you?"

He drifted. She was still talking quietly to him, "...you do know that, don't you? Yonnybunny, Sweetie, did you hear me? I just said you are so lucky to have Rachel at your side, now, in such a difficult time for you, for the two of you." Now in her peremptory Princess-Who-Commands tone, "Acknowledge me, please?"

Yonny focused his eyes on her again, mumbling, "Yes, I heard you, and yes, you are right. Quite right. As always, Sarah." He smiled and looked over her petite form at the snaking line, an elderly woman next to her muttering something. "Sarah, hang around, okay? We could use some help. But there's a slew of people bunched up behind you."

"Of course I will." She turned to the fidgeter, "Oh, I'm so sorry, Mrs. Campbell! But you know how cute he is, it's so hard to break his spell, yes?"

That secured her escape and his rescue, and the line resumed its shuffling forward.

Finally the guy from Porter Loring stepped over to him, whispering quietly in his ear like he was Secret Service or something, "Time, Mister Jonas. We should be winding things up so we can get to Sunset."

Graveside was family and closest, closer friends only, still a crowd but so much easier than being under several hundred pairs of eyes at the church, each pair boring in on his back, the back of his neck, as they sat in black, marked as failures as parents, drug casualties themselves. Here, a beautiful South Texas day, an early break from the heat at

September's end, here under the spreading live oaks, things were better, much better. Rachel and her mother had gradually reduced the distance between themselves and were now huddling with the twins. He smiled at that. *Reconciliation. Like going home again. Hard to beat. And the girls, so brave, so grown up now, the hard way*. The identical soon-to-be-twelve-year-olds, handfuls for their mother, had been named Leah and Rhea by her in one of her "tradition" phases. It hadn't taken him long to shorten their collective names to LeahRhea, *rhymes with diarrhea,* he made sure to add in every introduction. Constant threats to excommunicate him from the family, throw him and his dogs and his collection of baseball cards out on the street, none of that had any effect. LeahRhea they were, and now and forever shall be. *God save the grooms at the double wedding!*

He flinched as a heavy weight alighted on his shoulder. He knew that weight, that hand, that paw, it belonged to his father-in-law, or rather his father-in-law belonged to it. Solomon Polsky was the type who spoke with his hands, dispensed justice rough and merciful alike with his hands, expressed his deepest emotions with his hands, usually waving them horizontally like the ebb and flow of the wash on an uncertain beach, no deeper than that. "Son," he said, in his thick, smoky, up-from-the-old-Lower-East-Side-now-totally-BBQ accent, "I wancha know I'm wit' you on this, all the way. Ya know dat, yeah?"

Solomon Polsky was worth millions and he and Rachel had a piece of that deal, but he still spoke, at least affected, the patois of his youth, *Ute,* he smiled inwardly, from the meaner streets of lower Manhattan. Except when in front of the bankers at Manny Hanny or the life company dulls, or his infrequent appearances at civic or charitable functions in Manhattan where he tended to speak a pretty damned polished version of something in between Cary Grant and Gary Cooper, 1939 versions, usually with a little of the old country thrown into the mix making for an unintentionally cosmopolitan air.

"Yeah, Solly, I know it and appreciate it, but Rachel knows it even more, needs it even more." He nodded to the distaff *klatsch,* "Nice to see her and Miriam speaking, calmly, I mean. A tough way to make that happen, though…"

"Tell me, Ian, tell me about this drug business. Do you mind talkin' about it? I don't wanna we should talk of it in front of the girls. Whaddya know?"

"Not much, at least not yet. An old friend, classmate of mine, is handling the investigation, he'll tell me everything he knows, I'm sure, but has to run some tests. Snorted something, he says he's seen more than a few of these reactions in a first-time user, but he may just be saying that. About the first time, I mean."

Another voice came from behind. He hadn't been aware of a presence behind him, another voice from the old Lower East Side depths. "So who got it for him? Who got him started on this crap? Who's his dealer? Does your cop friend know that? Does he know his shit from his shinola, I mean? You want I should talk to him?"

This was 'Uncle' Si, Simon Schlomsky, Solly's lifelong friend from the ghettoes of Łódź in the old country, came over together in '37 after another Polish pogrom, neither one of them with family or more than a few *zlotys,* just a couple of teenaged Yids on their way to the Promised Land. They made their way on the mean streets, hooking up with Meyer Lansky and the Jewish Mob, the *Undzer Shtik,* they called it when well into their ryes, but never really making it to the top. Lansky liked the two, used to introduce them saying, '*known each other before they were old enough to fuck'.* They were runners, enforcers, collectors, just middle management, so insisted Solly in one of his rare bouts of professed candor, never hitmen, never part of Murder, Incorporated.

When the war came, Solly enlisted in the Army and sure he could do better than just slog and carry a rifle, convinced his superiors to let him use his German and Yiddish and Polish as an interpreter. That got him into Camp Ritchie for intelligence training and then, in the 89th Division, way into Germany at war's end at the tip of Patton's spear, to the deathcamps. After the liberation of Ohrdruf, he caught the big shit for taking three SS guards outside the wire, one by one, handcuffed, kneecapping them before giving them the hollow right eye treatment. News of his exploits reached Patton just before his court-martial. After a brief audience with the general, the charges were dropped and his record cleared. He even got a Bronze Star out of the deal, for his interpreter service, not so much as executioner.

Si had been blinded in one eye in '40 by a shard from a slivovitz bottle in a bar fight, so had to sit it out, looking after things back home. When Lansky all but moved to Havana after the war, he and Solly started up a number of ventures in Queens, mainly, carwashes and bits of real estate here and there, but still doing odds and ends of mob bidness until the old crowd all died or went to jail for good.

"No, no, Uncle Si, no, I don't think so." He thought some more about it then, “I think they’ll do their job just fine, but it’s a small police department. It’s a small city, after all.”

“Small? Not so small. San Antone is pretty big, I thought.”

“Not San Antonio, Uncle. Alamo Heights. Its own city, own police. Surrounded by San Antonio, but all to ourselves.” He smiled, “We like it that way.”

“Suit yourself. Sol, you know we know guys can look into it. You want I should look into it?”

Solly dismissed the thought with his hands, but agreed with his eyes.

As the entourage folded itself into the waiting limousines for the ride back to the house, Uncle Si’s words exploded in his head like a roman candle, maybe a cherry bomb. He didn’t want the thought, but it just wouldn’t leave him—*Who got it for him? Who got him started? Who? Someone had to have given him the stuff, we think, but we really don’t know. I... there had to be someone else. Had to be. You’re just saying that, you don’t want to face the idea that he might have been the one, the dealer, even. No, not him. How can you be so sure? I can’t be and I won’t be, so I will be. There. That’s that. But who? Who got him started? Who?* He held that thought all the way home, then at the Porterhouses’ across the street that night, and for days and weeks and months to come.

5

Sam walked around the gravesite, eyes open, ears open, picking up on any gossip, small talk, careless talk. He saw two older guys talking to Yonny—didn't look Texan, not by their faces, their suits—*have to talk to Yonny about that.*

He strolled about some more, checking out the chicks—*didn't look like that in high school for us!* He was searching for something, anything, then remembered the pink lipstick. Immediately, he saw one girl, woman maybe, tall, thin, flatchested—*Pink lipstick! Damn!* He followed her toward a black Mercedes—*has some mud on it*—then stopped and turned away to not be too conspicuous, and seeing Bobby Andrews, asked who she was. *Married to that old guy, the one with the transmission shops.*

So much for that. Back to the dwindling crowd, looking for mannerisms, actions. Looking for someone with guilt on his or her face, *guilt being a mighty powerful thing, changes people's looks, actions*. Someone who didn't want to get too close to the casket, staying away from others, furtive glances. Half a dozen, more, young girls, all with pink lipstick, no help there.

Then something caught his eye. A girl, *built like a brick shithouse*, turned sharply away from a nerdy looking boy, huffing away. *Who is she? And him? Pink lipstick? She's gone now. Well, anything else*? He watched a stream of people passing before the family, then dispersing, only a few pausing for more than a brief comment.

Well, nothing more here. He drove back to his office.

6

The Porterhouses had offered to host a reception afterwards, Julie Porterhouse acquiescing in Rachel's request to limit it to just sixty or seventy of their mutual nearests and dearests, an acquiescence achieved only by Rachel's grabbing the lapels of Julie's Chanel suit until she finally got her point across, not entirely unrepresentative of their relationship.

Doug Porterhouse was a Heights classmate of Yonny's, went off to UT, pledged Fiji, made his C's, came home to the family insurance business as soon as he could. When he and Julie were married—*an arranged marriage, to be sure*, he always thought—the families blessed the budding dynasty as worthy of anything Florentine or Milanese, Medici or Borghese. Twenty some-odd years later, comfortable in their social stratum, club champion and clubwoman, the 20,000 acres old man Porterhouse had bought west of Cotulla in the Twenties finally produced something more than big bucks and mesquite and rattlers and flocks of whitewings, an enormous oil and gas find. It took less than two months from the lease signing for the trickledown to reach the third generation, and Doug first bought the postwar ranch across the street, then the German stone cottage next door, ending with the admittedly dilapidated house behind on its double lot. In a swoop he had assembled over an acre of absolutely primo building site and wasted no time scorching the earth and constructing a 10,000 square foot nouveau stucco Tuscan villa, replete with cherubim and seraphim and a plaster Venus or three.

Rachel came back from her first tour of the finished product needing a cold shower. "And to top off the whole gargantuan monstrosity, she showed me Daphne's room." Jeffrey and Daphne, the Porterhouses' only child, a sophomore then, blonde and preternaturally pneumatically buxom, had kindergartened at the old Methodist church on Broadway, matriculated together through Cambridge and the Junior

High, then went their separate ways a bit, as teenagers were wont to do. Yonny was sure Rachel resented Daphne's infidelity, but Jeffrey never made a big deal of it. *But he didn't play football, and she was a cheerleader, and ne'er the twain shall meet*, so he comforted himself with the thought that his son would be a heart surgeon or a CEO or a Supreme Court justice and Daphne would grow up to look like her mother, cankles and all. "And in the middle of this enormous room—Yonny, it's the size of our entire downstairs before we added on—in the middle of the deep pink carpet was carved a relief picture of her doing one of those clichéd cheers, back curved, big boobs out, heels kicking her butt, flawless teeth grinning idiotically at you. I said it was lovely and got out of there as quickly as I could. Do not let Leah and Rhea go up there, under any circumstances, understand?"

That night, exhausted, he waited for the hot water to build back up after wife and twins had depleted it to a subarctic nothingness, then took a quick lukewarm shower. Wrapped in his towel, he sat next to Rachel who apparently had been staring into space since he stepped into the bathroom, and embraced her. She snarled at him, "Don't even think about it! How can you think about that, now, at this time…?" She leaned back to look at him, then buried her head in his chest, whimpering, "Oh, Yonny, Yonny, I'm so sorry, so, so sorry. You didn't deserve that. Neither do I, none of us do. None of us do. Why? How will I go on? We, I mean?"

He held her tightly, whispering in her ear, "We'll make it. You saw the twins today, they're probably stronger than both of us put together. Let's us, you and me, try to be as strong, okay? I don't know what to do, or how to do it, but, well, we'll just have to muddle along, won't we? And we have our friends, and you have your family," he saw her wince, "yes, you do, if you would just let them be family. And I have mine. But we don't have Jeffy any more. Never will. We just have to face it."

She finally smiled weakly at him. "Sarah took me aside at the church, I thought she was going to jump on me for not having the service at the Temple, but, no, she just said you had asked her to help us out, so she and her maid, Audrey, is that her name, they would be coming over two or three times a week, she said, to help us out, maybe cook some, drive the girls, whatever. Yonny-poo," now with a little twinkle in her eye, "I thanked her, but asked her why and do you know what she said?" Not waiting for a reply, as was her habit, "She said it was because she loved you, always had and always will. You made quite an impression on the young lady all those years ago."

He knew there were no more secrets, not since the two women had lunched together back when, so he parried, "You know she dumped me, don't you? Says it was her father's doing, the religion bit, but I still don't believe her. She just got tired of me, that's what I thought at the time. Broke my heart. Changed my life. Ran me out of town, out of state, basically. And thus into your arms. So there." He allowed himself the first small smile of the day, "And how does that make you feel? Knowing a beautiful woman living not four or five blocks away says she still loves your husband?"

"Tells me I made the right choice, husband. The right choice for both of us. If there was a choice to be made. *Bashert.* And as I think about it, the right choice for her, too." She returned his smile, "Maybe we should… after all…"

"Up to you."

"We should."

Later that night, he started awake from a dream, a quiet nightmare, thinking, *I have to know who got him started. That's the key for me, if I'm ever going to get past this. I have to know*. He dozed into another fitful dream, *this time Ricky Young, it was 1970, summer, Ricky and I were at someone's apartment in Austin, we were double-dating, I was with a skinny girl from some small town in West Texas, had just come back after taking her into someone's bedroom and Ricky was doing his magic act. Which act consisted of holding up one finger in each hand, then putting his hands behind his back, then returning them with two fingers in one and none in the other, all to a thrumming, dum-da-de-dum-dum repeated over and over and over. The crowd loved it, drunks all, but finally his date, beautiful, Judy Collins with green eyes, not blue, came over and stopped the little act. 'That's enough, Ricky, that's enough for now. Come outside with me, I've got something for you.' Ricky's eyebrows waggled expectantly as he left the room. Suddenly I was on the balcony with them, walked through the wall, I guess, and she was handing Ricky a pointy cigarette. She turned to look at me and I'll never forget that face, beautiful, long honey-blonde hair parted in the middle, California-style, as she smiled, wickedly, I thought. Then they disappeared into the night, three stories down under the oaks.*

He woke, this time sweating, his tee shirt clinging to his back as he sat upright.

"Yonny?"

7

"Meet me at Jim's—fifteen minutes?" Sam hung up the phone. *This might be the toughest case ever, an old classmate, friends, all that.*

Sam looked across the table at his old buddy digging a blunt knife point into a packet of blackberry jam. *Strange how things work out, isn't it? A few months ago I would have gladly traded places with him. Hell, I guess I envied him, that life, that knockout of a wife of his, a knockout, yeah, those knockers, those kids...* He stopped himself short. *But, no, I guess not, sure hope not, having to go through this, having a hole as big as a forty-four magnum blown through his life, never had to go through that. But still, he had it pretty good, grew up here, had his lifelong friends, was popular, didn't have to adjust like I did, had money, some money, a rich girlfriend...*

He became aware of his tablemate staring back at him as he poked a corner of toast into his mouth.

"A penny for your thoughts, Sam? Maybe a Benjamin?"

"Hmmm? Oh, I was just thinking, just now. How, well, how you were always one of the good guys, shame to have this happen to you..." He swallowed, then stammered, "I, I mean, you had such a good—I shouldn't be saying this—a charmed life and all... Sorry, Yawny, I, well, it's just that..."

"Just that I seemed to have gotten a pretty good deal in life, Sam? Until now, of course?"

"Well, yeah."

"Trade ya."

Sam chuckled, that was all he could do. After a few moments' thinking, "No, you don't want to do that."

"No, I guess not." Yonny put down his coffee cup for the waitress to refill, waited for her to leave, then spoke softly in that amalgam of seriousness and mischief from the old days Sam now brought into recall, "Sambo, this may shock you, but as long as I can remember, I've been a depressive." He paused to let that sink in. "Yep, that's me. Since early adolescence maybe, thirteen, for sure, at least that's when we first tried some meds. Didn't work. Looking back, I was a melancholy yuppie, that's what we'd call me today. Only got worse through high school, really crested, or sank, I should say, about first semester of our senior year, I was close to doing some bad…"

Sam couldn't help himself, interrupting, "But you never looked that way. Class favorite, smart…"

Yonny held up a hand to stop him. "Yeah, I suppose so. But I was your basic duck on a pond, a still pond, a smooth surface…"

"Duck?"

He smiled back at his new favorite cop. "Yeah, a duck, Sam. Calm and unruffled, serene, even, on the surface but paddling like hell underneath to keep from sinking. It was close, Sam, really close, until Sarah and I hooked up, or I guess our orbits finally got close enough after knowing each other all our lives, for our mutual gravity to work on each other." He watered up a bit. "She saved me, Sam, rescued me, sorta like Jean Simmons rescued Marlon Brando…"

Seeing Sam's blank expression, he finished that thought, "Yeah, she was a Salvation Army worker, he was a gambler, a con, and she saved him. *Guys and Dolls*, the movie, '54 or '55. Rescued him. That's what Sarah did for me. I was being dragged down into the margins, to the edge of the cliff, a precipice, by the Black Dog, that's what Churchill called it, and she pulled me back, just in time, she did. And when it didn't work out, after a couple of years, less, well, then it was back downhill. But I fought it, fought it by going whole hog in college. Then worked a year or so, I was better, I guess, then back to school, but it never let go of me, I became more and more withdrawn, a loner, getting worse by the months or years. Then I met a girl in New York, she spiffed me up pretty good," he laughed quietly, "but, of course, with my luck, that bubble had to burst, but with my luck, Rachel came into my life the very moment Gloria—that was her name, Gloria—was leaving it."

Sam had nothing to offer, so after a couple more sips of coffee, Yonny resumed, quietly, "Ever since that day—night, it was at a fancy party—Rachel has carried me. Carried me on her back. She doesn't know that, please don't ever say anything, but without her, or out in the world by my lonesome, well…" His gaze drifted off past the line of booths beyond, not seeing anything all the way across the Broadway traffic. "So, that's me, Sam. If I seem detached or unfeeling or not showing the sort of grief—I never was good with grief, Sam, not even when I buried my Snoopy—that's just my armor, my cocoon—I am a Rock, I am an Island—Simon and Garfunkel, remember? That's me."

He rapped the side of his cup with his spoon, causing the waitress to dart his way. "Oh, sorry, just playing the drums. Or maybe the cowbell. But, while you're here?" He raised his cup. "So, Sam, that's me. What do you have for me today?"

"Well, not so much." He briefly summarized the paucity of evidence. "Just not much to go on, Yawny. Shouldn't we be bringing your wife into this? Not my business, but…"

"Not yet, not too much. I'll tell her what I've heard."

"Your call, then."

"Sam, how does this shit happen? How do they get started?"

"Friends."

"Really?"

"Yawny, it's not like the old days, drinking beer, getting drunk and throwing up." He smiled, "And sex, too."

"Yeah, well, we missed some of that, that's for sure. But, friends?"

"Uh, huh. Stuff is pretty easy to get, if you've got the money, and…"

"And we've got the money here in the Bubble." He laughed, then silenced himself abruptly. "Not funny."

"No, not funny, but it's not just here. It's all over town. The money talks, though. Some of the kids at the high school deal, but it's mostly street pushers. Doesn't matter, one gets some, shares with his friends."

Yonny leaned back, pushing his plate toward the center of the table. "I've been thinking, Sam, thinking about Ricky Young. Had a dream the other night. First time he had a joint. He had a really good-looking date, she gave it to him. Got him started, I guess." He looked away, then down at an empty plate. "I've often thought if I ever found that girl, I'd kill her for doing that." He snapped a plastic swizzle stick in two. "Strangle her with my own bare hands."

Sam replied evenly, "Agree with you. Wouldn't even arrest you." He had a spark of worry. "When did you see him last?"

"Ricky? Before the funeral? Oh, I guess, '72, no, '73, before I went off to Boston. Why?"

"I answered a call at a bar on Nakoma in June, maybe July of

'75." Sam laughed loudly, prompting some stares from the greyhairs around them. He quieted some, now leaned across the table, conspiratorially. "One of those hot and humid Saturday nights, always trouble, y' know? I was on the Northside, working in a new academy grad, showing him the difference between what they thought they learned in the classroom and what real life was like on the street."

He sipped on his fresh coffee. "Bill Johnson—the cadet. He seemed pretty smart, likable. I let him write a ticket or two and a report on a family disturbance call we made early that evening. Well, we were just fixin' to have some dinner at a Mexican food place when in comes a call for a violent disturbance at this bar out on Nakoma, you know, across San Pedro from the airport. By the time we got rolling, got another call from the dispatcher, two or three people had been stabbed. A possible DOA. I let Billy Boy hit the lights and siren and off we went.

"The place had been cleared out and all the patrons were milling around outside. I told Bill not to touch anything and definitely not to talk to the pushy news people who were bound to arrive soon. In fact, I positioned him in the front door to keep everyone out and not let them look inside."

He pushed back a little. "Am I going on too long? There's a good Ricky moment at the end."

"Keep going—I might get to like these stories of yours."

"Okay, then. You've been in more than a few bars, know the odor typical of most dives? Mostly beer and cigarettes?" Yonny smiled and nodded. "Well, this one was the same 'cept it also reeked of blood. Really distinctive, you don't forget it. Smells warm, alive, smells like meat, if that makes any sense. Two men and one woman were lying on the floor. She had apparently got in the way of a Buck knife trying to protect a friend. Dead. I walked around, keeping Billy Boy up on what I saw so he didn't have to look inside, add his puke to the scene, contaminate everything. Blood puddles, two large knives, including the Buck knife, on the floor, one large stain on the pool table. Pretty gruesome.

"Homicide took their time, but started taking photos of the scene when they finally got there. One of them told me to take the Buck knife out to my car and put it into an evidence bag, then lock it in the trunk. Well, when I opened the door and squeezed past Bill, the lights and news cameras came on. I tried to hide the knife, holding it by my side, when Gary DeLaune—Channel 12—shoved a microphone in my face and asked if that was a murder weapon and could they get a better camera shot?

"Stupid me obliged and held up the knife, a little blood still dripping from the blade. I looked up, blinking in the lights, and there was…" he shrugged, smiling broadly, "Ricky, jumping up and down, that white boy Afro of his jiggling, sticking out his tongue and pretending to wiggle his ears with his hands. I couldn't help it. I burst out laughing, then remembered I was on camera, and stifled it, a few seconds too late."

Sam waited for Yonny to stop laughing and finish cleaning up the coffee he had just spit out. "Gets better. Next morning I get a personal call from the Chief. Not pleasant. Included talk of unprofessional conduct and a possible suspension."

"And?"

"Nothing. Never heard another word about it. Except from DeLaune, every time I saw him." He laughed loudly again, then softer, "I think my Captain had my back, covered for me with the Chief."

"So you're, you were, a celebrity back then? Hey, nothing wrong with that."

"Yeah, right. But that was Ricky, right?"

"Yeah. Screwing around at some dive. Our, my and his and Joe's and the KA's favorite place in Austin, on the Drag, was the Pink Lizard. Talk about a dive! Worst place you ever saw. But what a great beer joint!"

"Those were the days."

"Were. Gone forever, now. But sounds just like him. Was he dealing then? I guess he was." Yonny's smile sagged into half a frown. "But today? Back to reality, Sam. Who are these pushers?"

Sam cocked an eyebrow. "Why? You know we can't prosecute them for overdoses, don't you?"

"Wasn't thinking prosecution, Sam." Just then his Motorola flip phone jingled. "Yes, Angela? Oh, right, I almost forgot. Be right there." He nudged it closed, then pointed at it. "Do not think you can escape it, at night or early in the morn… Gotta go, Sam. Thanks for the great Ricky story, sorta brings him back to life, doesn't it?" A pause, then, "Boy, is that ever a scary thought!" He nabbed the check. "Got this one, pal. Keep up the good work, okay?"

Sam watched his back recede toward the cashier. *Now what?*

8

He just didn't know what to do, how to deal with their loss, what was to become of their lives. And neither minister nor rabbi had the answers, not family either. He could only take so much advice, so many exhortations to look to God for relief, to use this to strengthen himself, to somehow make a new life, what doesn't kill you, all that stuff. Some busybodies had even had the gall to ask him if he was angry with Jeffy for doing this to him, to them. When Jeffy was little little, Solly gave him one of his rare wide, gap-toothed smiles and said, '*Saying from the old country, Ian, when a man has a son, he no longer needs a mirror.' He was right. How could I be mad at him, my reflection in life's mirror?*

Even that thought didn't help. It still felt like having his insides spilled out all over him, like a knife of ice plunged into his chest, deep. He tried to talk to Rachel as much as he could, but found himself bottled up inside. He could listen but just couldn't bring himself to talk, not much, at least. Not yet. With Sam, it was different. Nuts and bolts. Investigation. Facts. Leads. He could talk, ask questions, even knowing there weren't any answers, not yet. *Not yet.*

Patches pulled expectantly at her collar, then sat obediently after crossing Ciruela at the top of the hill, knowing the drill. He patted her neck and unhitched her leash, freeing her to do her laps around the cul-de-sac built a few years back on the old Texas Military Institute property. He followed her at his pace, stopping halfway in, realizing he was in the track's infield, the track he jogged around and around and around in those years before he went off to graduate school, pining and wondering over a lost love. *I didn't have the answers back then, I guess I'll never have the answers about Jeffy. Took me years to get over that, don't know if I'll ever get over this.*

He whistled and after a decent interval for a few last sniffs and snorts, Patches came bounding over. Leashing her up again, they turned back onto Ciruela, then right on Cardinal and over to St. Luke's, cutting across the parking lot down across the front lawn to the bridge over Olmos Creek. He stopped a while, gazing long at the death site across Devine Road. *How well did I know my son? Did I really, really know him? I didn't know anything about drugs or sex, never had more than the pro forma conversations, warnings, 'Don't do what I did'. What I did. About this same time Senior year, I was pretty close to doing some pretty stupid stuff. Maybe, maybe he just took the next step? But I was lucky, I sat next to Sarah in Sociology, sorta fell into her arms. And she knew my reputation, too. Do I know his? And the girl with the pink lipstick, did she tease him with the drugs? Get him to try it? And who was she? I'm ashamed I, we didn't know who he was with. Just don't know.* He shuddered at his thoughts. *And how many other families are asking themselves these same questions right now?*

Breaking away, he looked back upstream at last week's flood trash strewn about in the silt-stained branches, now surveying the pocked limestone cliffs, all of ten or twelve feet high, maybe fifteen, but a daunting challenge for a ten-year-old. *I guess I got my fascination with high places and my fear of falling from them when we used to clamber up and down those walls.* He had an evanescent memory of his younger self panicking, clutching for a handhold or a foothold to avoid a three foot fall. *Perspective. That's all it is. Perspective and another foot taller, that is. Time makes the cliffs smaller. Maybe time will make this new cliff smaller. Hasn't yet.* He took one last glance up at the cliff, then down at the turbid brown water below, thinking back in time. *Have to hold on, pull myself up. Can't slide down there. Can't slide down there, back into…*

He remembered something about driving the girls to school, maybe? *She couldn't take the looks in the hookup line anymore, was that it? That's another thing, concentration.* "Let's go, girl." Taking no chances, he led a disappointed pup back home.

The twins swirled around the living room, pretty little dervishes in plaid skirts, gathering books and sweaters and lunches and soccer bags as he opened the front door. "Mom! Mom! Daddy's back! He'll take us!"

Rachel gave him a look, tapping her watch.

"All right, already! Why aren't you guys strapped in? I'll get you there in time."

"It's not the bell, Daddy," whined Leah.

Rhea finished for her, "It's meeting our friends before school. All the girls get together, you know that."

"Oh, yeah, I remember. All the girls were waiting for me, too."

In chorus, "Yeah, right!"

Rachel finally smiled. "He was very popular back then. Just like Edward Brady."

"Mom!"

"That's what I've heard over the years, girls. Cute, too."

In spontaneous unison, "What happened to you, Daddy?"

"Enough. We're gone. Bus is leaving."

Rachel Polsky Jonas watched her entire life walk out the door, what was left of it.

Gathering up the breakfast dishes, she glanced through the French doors at the car and one of the girls clambering into the back, her long braid swinging back and forth. *Why they wanted braids today, well, maybe the other girls are doing it, so they had to? Pretty cute, though, we ought to do it more often.*

The dishes went into the sink. *I'll let Esmeralda deal with them when she gets here.* Idly flipping through the *Times* on the kitchen table, she noticed a revival of *Fiddler on the Roof* was playing at the Gershwin. She smiled again at the thought of her girls with their long braids. She had woven in some red ribbons *just like Nana did when she took me to see the play, at the Imperial, I think it was. My twelfth birthday, same age as the twins, I remember that. It had just opened, Nana said it was a tough ticket to get, I should feel special, and I did. I still have that picture somewhere, all dressed up with her, print dress flaring over my petticoat, white gloves, white frilly socks in my patent Mary Janes, my little purse at my side. My hair in a long braid, a flower, an orchid, I think, at my left ear. Mother didn't come with us, maybe she wasn't invited, maybe they just weren't talking then?*

We had wonderful seats, fifth row center, as they say. Nana made sure I understood what the play was about, about love and its difficulties and, she emphasized, oppression of the Jews by the Tsar's men although I thought the Constable was handsome. And tradition, even though she and Grandfather had left their Judaism far behind by then, and these were Russians or Ukrainians, whatever they were. And poor, too. I didn't understand that 'If I were a rich man' business back then. I thought everyone in New York was rich.

But I loved the daughters, so strong, willing to stand up to their poor father. Shprintze was about my age then, wore her hair in a long braid—that's why Nana did me up like that, I think—she didn't have much to say or sing, but was pretty. And Chava, just a little older, fell in love with a Gentile—and what a fuss that was! Maybe I knew then, maybe Fate was telling me something... Bashert, already, at that age?

And the music, I still cry over my favorite the way I rewrote it for myself:

'Are these the little girls I carried?
'Is..., was that my... little boy at play?
'I don't remember growing older,
'When... did... they?'

In her head she inflected the last line, scaling the notes upward like she remembered from that day thirty-something years ago. She went on, now aloud, eyes closed, keeping time with her hands, haltingly:

"*When did they get to be such beauties?*
When did... he... he grow to be so... so tall?
Wasn't it just yesterday when
They... were... small?"

She choked, opening her eyes. "Wasn't it just yesterday he was... still... here?" She laid her head down, sobbing.

"Señora Yonas? Esta todo okay?"

1972

"Yawny? You awake?"

I look at the kitchen wall phone, shaking my head. "Ricky, it's seven at night. Where are you?"

"I'm at..." Ricky struggles to remember, teasingly just on the verge of his consciousness, then receding, then grasping it. "Can you come get me? You're going over to Mike and Lynn's, right?"

"Yeah, just walking out the door. You got lucky."

I drive my Bug up and down and over the curves and swales of streets popping up in front of me as I navigate through Hyde Park, down 38th, left on Speedway. Then Ricky materializes curbside, waving frantically. I slam on the brakes, come spongily to a stop, and Ricky jumps in. 'Go!' he says, "Go!"

"What's the deal, R-man? She kick you out of bed?"

Ricky turns and gives me a big one on the shoulder. 'Shuddup,' he says, 'none of your goddamn business.' His eyes have that wild look they sometimes get when he was cooking up some stunt or prank or worse.

"Okay, okay! Geez!" I drive on, planning on cutting across on 26th to the interstate when Ricky grabs my wrist, "Here! Turn here," twisting the steering wheel.

I manage to correct the skid and we bounce onto Duval. "Shit, Ricky, what's the deal?"

"Nothing. Sorry. Here, over here on the left. I'll be right back." He gets out, then leans back through the window, "Come on in, why don't you?"

I follow him into the Craftsman-style house, over the creaking porch, through the equally creaky screen door. Ricky introduces me to a couple of guys, one fairly normal-looking, the other a pretty typical Austin freak. Mister Sort-of-clean-cut huddles with Ricky for a minute or so, then goes back to what he had been doing. I notice for the first time the skinny rubber hose around the guy's arm, then the little oil lamp, then the spoon and the sugar. "Want some?" he asks. "No, thanks, no," as I see the syringe dip into a load, then plunge into the forearm.

Ricky jerks me away, "Come on, we gotta go." Freaky hands Ricky a glowing joint. "Here," Ricky says, handing me the smoke, "here, Yawny, try it, you'll like it." Ricky's smile is the Cheshire Cat's, complete with a faint glow around him. Is that a tail twitching? I puff once and cough. "I don't do this shit, sorry. Don't like to smoke."

Mister Hypodermic says, jauntily, "Then this?" He points to the gigantic needle in his arm, blood spewing everywhere.

Then we're back in my car, driving south on 35, flying, pressing the VW to its absolute limit, the lights and guardrails and shiny markers on the lane stripes streaming by faster, ever faster…

Ricky taps me on my shoulder, "You're going thirty, man. You'll get us pulled over."

He awoke, jerking the covers off, getting one foot tangled, thrashing about until he freed it. *Hashish. It was hashish. The bastard slipped me that shit.*

"Sweetheart, I really think you need to go see Doctor Jenner, talk to him about these nightmares. Maybe get some sleeping pills. I need you to. Sleep in the guest bedroom for a while, please? I need to get some sleep, too, sometime."

9

Sam wheeled his Crown Vic into the long parking strip fronting the High School, looking for a visitor spot amidst the pickups and BMWs and Jeeps. He found one at the far end near the Auditorium—*makes sense, I guess*—then got himself straightened up for his parade in front of the kids spilling out of the main entry, flooding across the lawn under the oaks, onto the drive and the sidewalks and crossing Broadway. He hadn't been back, not since the first few years, but nothing had changed, not to his eyes. He opened the door for a teacher, young and attractive, and turned slightly to peruse her figure.

Inside, he automatically veered right to the office. "Hi, there. Sam Thompson here to see Bob, I mean, Mr. Sweeny." The student across the counter looked warily at him, then disappeared between some offices. In a moment, Bob Sweeny came loping out to meet him. "Sam! Goodness gracious, it *has* been a while, hasn't it?"

Sweeny, for an educator, now a disciplinarian, had always had a dramatic flair about him, amplified by his booming baritone. He had studied with Strasberg in New York in the early Fifties, palled around and partied with James Dean and Marlon Brando and others, came back to marry Francesca. Sam thought of that Jimmy Buffet song, the one that went "*some people claim there's a woman to blame…*" Back he came to the unenviable opportunity to attempt teaching Speech and Drama to successive waves of unappreciative, jaded highschoolers, himself included. *Damn, if we had known about his early days, we might have been more respectful. That was pretty cool of him…*

Bob had this way of looking down his nose through his glasses, pushing them up with his middle finger, a nose chiseled out of some sort of porous stone, not quite finished, Sam thought, *same way he did when Yawny and Ricky and I got called in to see him for the marbles gag. My first year at Heights, trying desperately to fit in, Ricky grabs me one morning before class, says he and Yawny need my help. Sure, I said, uhh, what kind of help? Just help us get these jars up the stairs. Quick! Each of us had two jugs full of marbles, a quart or more, we lugged them up the stairs in the North wing and over to the center stairway, crouching down against the second floor railing overlooking the front entrance. Below us, the Senior boys congregated around the school seal in the middle of the entry every morning, checking out the passing chicks, terrorizing any unwary freshman who stepped on the seal. Ricky nodded and we carefully tipped over the jugs and sent a thousand or so marbles down on the terrazzo steps below, bounding and hopping and jumping about as they flooded the floor below. We didn't wait to hear the thuds of bodies tripped up, the cursing, the calls to get the punks. Before first period ended, the summons to the office was delivered. Bob Sweeny tried mightily to contain his amusement, then said, "I'm writing you three up on special report. Understand?" We nodded solemnly, guiltily. Then he smiled tightly, "But I admire your initiative. They got what they deserve. Now get out of here and don't let me see you in this office again." We bolted.*

If anyone knew what was going on with the students, officially, Bob did. "Have a seat, Sam." He asked Sam about his life so far, the years on the force, the dramatic stuff, asked him a few more questions. "So, you're here about the Jonas boy?"

Sam nodded, saying something about how tough it was on the parents, how they didn't deserve this sort of thing when Bob cut him off, "Sam, no one deserves this, no matter how good or lousy they are as parents. But it happens, all too often and always unnecessarily, in my opinion. Think back to the Sixties, to your class, '68 was the last all we worried about was you guys getting drunk, stashing coolers, keg parties. Bad enough, you were. Next year, like night following day, marijuana took over. And not just the, well, the lower class, the troublemakers, the underachievers, you can think of any of those types back then. But not just those. Good kids, too"—he tossed off a few names Sam didn't know—"no, it hit the more affluent like a tsunami—they had the money, after all."

Sam caught up with him, "And a new breed of dealers, pushers, on and off campus. Worse, the menu changed from stems and seeds to stronger stuff, cocaine, ecstasy, terrible stuff. Peaked, crested about ten years ago, we think."

Sweeny leaned back, reflecting, "Maybe, maybe not so much. There's enough of it still going on to keep me busy. And your patrol-men, too. No, Sam, I don't think it will ever go away, might diminish some, but we're stuck with it." He leaned across his desk. "Now, the Jonas boy. You know Ian, one of our finest ever, Honors, National Merit, Ivy League, successful, involved with the school—his wife, Rachel, particularly." He paused to laugh lightly, "Even after that darned assembly he put on Senior year." Now more seriously, "I just can't imagine their son being involved in all this. And," now conspira-torially, "I don't think he was. I think this might have been a dare or a stunt of some sort, one that went tragically wrong somehow."

"Why would you say that?"

"Because Jeffrey was going to play the lead in the Senior play this spring. Curly, in *Oklahoma*, a major production for us. He was terrific in auditions and we'd just announced the choice when he died, that very afternoon, in fact. So, you see, he had a lot to look forward to, right? And another thing, Sam, since you left we've installed an honor code. One rule in there is no participation in extracurricular acti-vities if you get caught drinking or DWI, and especially using illegal drugs."

"So, why would he have risked that if he was doing the play?"

"Why, indeed, Sam? Why, indeed? That's your job to find out, isn't it?"

Sam slumped in his chair, quiet for more than a few moments. "Mr. Sweeny, who around him would have been using drugs, or dealing them? Can you tell me that? I need some leads, need 'em bad."

"Badly. You need them badly."

"Sure, but I'm serious. Straight arrow kid, great family, this honor code business, the play? Why?" He paused, then played a card. "He was with a girl, we know that, and another, probably a boy."

"And how is this? How do you know?"

Sam briefly replayed the scene in the park. He swallowed, then, "And the girl wore pink lipstick. I'm not going to tell you how we know that."

Sweeny pushed his glasses up his nose, *giving me the finger again*, thought Sam. "Hmmm. I don't know who he was going with, if he had a girlfriend. The two girls auditioning for the Laurey role, would have been Jeffrey's sweetheart in the play, they seemed pretty enthralled by him. Meredith Brady, she got the role, and Arabella

Goodman. I do know some of his friends were on the golf team, but he was one of those who got along with most everyone. He was working in the office here, helping out with some underclassmen issues, was really good at talking to some of those kids who were floundering about. Everyone who came in knew him, even if he didn't know them, at first. Just a great kid, Sam. Terrible."

"Why was he in here?"

"He had hurt his back on some hike or mountain climb last summer, in Colorado, I think. Couldn't play whatever sport he was trying to play, was left with an empty period. I asked him to come in, he was quite helpful. I really don't have any more. Wait, Sam, did you say something about the car, what kind?"

"We don't know. Best we can tell the tires weren't American, not Firestones or Goodyears, but that's all we know. Why?"

"Oh, we could have canvassed the lots to find one, easy enough."

I didn't think of that, but, I didn't know what kind, so… "Thanks. Good idea, but nothing there. Well, I need to get along. Here's my card, Sir, please call if you think of something else, okay?"

As he let the door close behind him, the bell rang. *Maybe I can catch Mrs. Thomas between classes*. He guessed she might still be in her old classroom in the south wing and sure enough, there she was, looking over some papers on her desk as her next gaggle of problems wandered in. He hung by the door, letting the kids stream by. She looked up and her frown instantly reversed itself into a smile. "Sam! Well, I'll be! How are you?"

He was engulfed in a hug along with a kiss on the cheek. "So good to see you!" She turned to her class, now a little self-consciously, "Class, Sam, here, was one of our best players ever! Reagan, Judson, Marshall, you boys could learn some things from him." Looking over his neatly pressed suit, she asked him, "But aren't you a cop, I mean, a police officer now?"

"Yes, Ma'am, Mrs. Thomas, but now I'm chief detective on the Heights police force." He was the only detective, but had learned a little puffery went a long way in front of a bunch of impressionable teenagers, second only to threats of bodily force. "Keeping y'all safe." He grinned sardonically. *Even you little peckerwoods peddling death.*

His thoughts were interrupted by the damned bell. "Well, Mrs. Thomas, I better get going." More quietly, as an aside, he asked,

"Could I come by tomorrow? Do you still have the team over on Saturdays?"

She patted him on the shoulder. "Noon, like always. I'll introduce you to some of the team. Now, shoo."

10

Rachel had gone back to work on a reduced schedule, just trying to keep busy, trying to let other thoughts occupy her. She spent a lot of time these days with her chair swiveled to her bay window on the twentieth floor, surveying downtown, the fragment of the top of the Alamo's façade she could just see among the other buildings, Hemisfair Park. *Not exactly Central Park or Fifth Avenue, but it has its charms, I suppose*. Focusing again, now on the green ribbon of the Riverwalk's cypress treetops enfilading itself sinuously around its horseshoe. *All those tourists down there, all of them, not a care in the world except for getting overcharged, or a parking ticket, or worrying about the baby's diaper change, all those things. All those things we used to think about, too, when we used to go down there. The River Parade's different. That I do like. So did Jeffy...*

Now she turned back to her desk. *Morrison v. Morrison. Tawdry, tawdry, tawdry. God, that woman had lousy taste in men.* She looked up from her papers, rubbing her eyes and leaning back in her chair. She couldn't help herself, couldn't stop thinking about Jeffrey, lately the way his goofy, gangly adolescence had slowly, finally begun morphing into a semblance of young adulthood, without the least sense of responsibility, of course. *He had that date with Sally's daughter—Cotillion or was it the Hayne party over at Jefferson?—was coming down with something, running a really high fever all morning. I called Sally and told her how sick he was, he'd have to cancel. She called me back, said Meredith was just devastated, the dress, her hair, her makeup, but mostly Jeffy, she was so excited he'd finally asked her out. Jeffy heard me, insisted he would be fine, took the phone from me and told her he was better, he would be there. He did look better, but I made him lie down all that afternoon before getting ready. The girls came chirping down the stairs, 'Mommy! Mommy! Jeffy looks so cute!' And so he did, in the tux he had already seemed to outgrow in the few days since I picked it up for him. He had that John Wayne sort of tilted shoulder saunter about him as he plucked the keys from his father's hand on the way out the door. He stopped to wave goodbye then threw up all over the BMW's hood! He tried so hard...*

Christine stuck her head in the doorway. "Conference call, remember?"

Rachel mused puckishly, *'God, what fools these mortals be!'* She wheeled her chair over closer to the windows. Dragooned into a particularly nasty divorce case, she insisted on keeping her distance from the more personal, so, so, sordid aspects, and, as she admitted to herself, away from some of the most distasteful personages she had yet encountered in all her transplanted years. She concentrated on the financials, the forensics she had been so adept at in prosecuting white collar crime in lower Manhattan. And she was good at it, so good that in a matter of a few weeks she had uncovered a massive web of fraud and deceit, of undivulged bank accounts and unauthorized transfers, of minks and Mercedes and Mouton by the case. *Oh, what a tangled web we weave when first we practice to deceive!*

Bob Flournoy, the managing partner, wasn't altogether pleased, grudgingly acknowledging her triumph when Rachel presented her dossier to his client, a wealthy older woman duped into marriage by a slick gigolo. He saw a thousand or more billable hours fly right out the window and at that moment began entertaining thoughts of chasing ambulances for a living.

Rachel stared out her window again, now at the deep lateral shadows playing across the streets in their implausible pattern, the prim Anglo-German rectilinearity subverted by the river's drunken meanderings. *Mr. Mondrian, meet Mr. Kandinsky*. The cream and green crown of the Tower Life Building was just beginning to glow against a pale cobalt blue-grey sky in the south; across the compact downtown precinct, the deco ziggurat of the Casino Club had already staked out its pastels against the deepening indigo of the eastern sky and the Tower's halo of bulbs was atwinkle.

Audrey was taking care of the twins until Yonny got home, thanks to Sarah, so she had some time to wrap up a case or two, get the files off her desk and off her mind. She leaned back in her chair, hiking up her skirt so she could pivot her stocking feet to the desk top. With her hands in her lap, she attempted to clear her mind of everything. That worked for about three minutes until Jeffy appeared to her like Banquo's ghost. He seemed to be trying to tell her something, something about the things that had happened to him, trying to mouth some words, maybe the names of those that had done this evil to him and her and his father and the twins. She started awake. *The twins. I don't know how they do it, carry on like they do, so strong. Some nights I can hear them crying in their room as they try to get to sleep, sure, but by morning they're in full pre-adolescent mode. We worried about them when we skipped their fourth grade that they'd be too young for the Junior School, but they've adjusted pretty well despite all this. There's a sweetness about their tweenage innocence, their undeserved victimhood, the double burden of a lost brother and the stigma of an overdose. But some of their new friends had experiences similar with close or extended family, this crap was so common now, so there were bonds being made there. And bless their hearts, their personalities, their looks, their intelligence, all those things made up some kind of armor against the mean girls. They never complain, well, not about matters life and death or their parents being so morose, plenty about clothes and hair and getting their first bras, sure.*

She smiled at that, then her eyes lit on the Fox Photo envelope. Shuffling through a fistful of 3 x 5's, she found the one she sought. *Yonny took these with his new camera, the twins and I were dressed up for that Mother-Daughter luncheon at the Argyle. Sarah invited us, found their dresses at Langefelter's, ordered mine to match, navy dresses buttoned up front, white Peter Pan collars, pleated skirts, patterned tights. Not my style, for sure, but the girls were pretty adorable, took my hands when we posed, I didn't even have to chase them down.* Still giggling at that, she scanned the photo again. *Do I really look so big?* She looked down. *Maybe I should go ahead and do something with them? What would Yonny think?*

Yonny. She sighed. *We are the blessed ones, Yonny and me, although he seldom drops his mask. I guess that's the way he deals with all this. I wonder how they see me, whether…*

Her cell phone interrupted her self-pitying reverie. "I'm worried about your husband, Rachel. He just doesn't seem himself, doesn't want to get out and about. I know how hard this has been on him, and you, of course, but, he's just so, so, different." Angela was Yonny's secretary, old school, part assistant, part mother hen. "He's just not himself. Hardly gives me any things to do. He just sits there, sometimes reading those spy novels…"

"What spy novels? He doesn't have any at home, not that I know of."

"Oh, I don't know. Those trashy paperbacks you see. All violence and shoot-em-ups." She lowered her voice, conspiratorially, "And wild women, too."

Rachel thanked her, hung up and slumped back in her chair. *What now?*

11

Sam had stopped by Satel's on the way home to buy a new polo shirt and pair of khakis. He figured he'd better keep up with the in crowd as best as he could, even if he thought Toffe's and Jimmy's prices were way too high. The polo he found on sale, which helped.

Next morning, he detoured to Dunkin' Donuts for a couple dozen fresh ones, mixed. He still knew a football team's basic food groups and hoped these would break whatever ice there might be. *After all, she blew my cover right off the bat.* He laughed out loud at that thought, startling the Indian or Paki behind the register. Smiling, he scooped up his boxes and headed out.

Back in his day, and long before, as far back in the '60's and maybe even '50's as anyone could remember, Nancy Thomas had hosted some of the football players and other students for an afternoon of pizzas and cokes. There they could feel comfortable, could talk about a lot, not near everything, of course, but their hostess was a sympathetic listener. The football players were coming straight from watching last night's game film at the stadium. The Mules had won big and the boys would be buoyant, rowdy, talkative.

Mrs. Thomas had somehow been given the moniker 'Rattlesnake Nancy' by some member of the class of 1967 but no one knew why and she steadfastly refused to tell, only breaking out in that throaty laugh she was famous for. So famous, in fact, Sam had never forgotten it, thirty years later. And he had never forgotten that episode one late Spring afternoon in '67, Junior year, hot, the class was drowsing in the warm unairconditioned classroom and she was doing her best to rouse them with her lecture on Tom Sawyer and Huck Finn. Sam was awake, had to be, sitting on the front row right in front of her. She was going on about the two boys and Jim, now saying, "And those two boys, Tom and Fuckleberry Hinn…" She froze, her eyes locked onto Sam's, afraid to look around the classroom to see if anyone else had caught her misstep. After a few seconds, she furtively glanced about as she launched back into her talk. After class, she detained Sam before he went to practice. "Sam Thompson, if you ever say anything about this…"

Sam gave her a huge smile. "About what, Mrs. Thomas? I didn't hear anything."

The rest of high school and for a year or so after, he had been her favorite. When Nancy opened the door, she greeted him with a big hug. "Well, Sam Thompson, how the heck are you? Big new detective in town, people might get the wrong idea about the innocent school-marm and the new sheriff!" Several boys had come behind him to the door, bearing pizzas. She let them all in, pressing a six-pack of Cokes on the last one in. Sam was a hit with his donuts, of course, easing his entry into the crowd on the patio. Enough so he could casually but incisively scan the group, listen keenly to the chatter, start to make some character judgments.

She sat down beside him. "So how's it going, Sam?"

"I've been busier than a one-legged man in a butt kicking contest," he joked.

"Well, that's good. It keeps you out of trouble, I hope?"

"No, well, maybe, being in the thick of it sometimes you forget you're… in the thick of it. And that's sorta why I wanted to come by." He lowered his voice, "It's about the Jonas boy." He explained his situation, how he needed some names of students who were into drugs, who were selling, who might have been involved in Jeffrey's death. "And not just the guys," he waved his hand around, "there was a girl involved, we think."

"The Jonas boy wasn't in my class, he was in AP, so I really didn't know him that well, other than Student Council and those things. I don't recall hearing about him and any girls, but I have to tell you, Sam, I'm really taken aback that you would want me to snitch on my students." She was silent a few moments, looking over her brood, then, "But, in the interest of keeping them alive after what happened to that poor Jonas boy, I'll tell you what I know. It probably isn't much."

She gave the detective several names. "Two of them are on this patio right now. Please don't arrest them. They're two of the best football players we have. But I'm pretty sure none of them are selling that horrible stuff. That I would have heard."

"Thanks, Mrs. Thomas…"

"Nancy, Sam. You're a grownup now, not back in my class."

He looked at her, realizing now how much she had given him and his friends all those years ago. "Okay, Nancy it is, then. Thanks. I'll be careful with them." He stood stiffly, rubbing his knee, catching the crowd's attention. "Edison, 1967. Kicked their butts, but I got blind-sided." He put his hands on his hips, then, "Doctor wanted to operate, but I played every down the rest of the season, both ways, never quit. Let that be a lesson to you. And GO MULES!"

He was followed to the door by applause. Nancy got on her tiptoes and gave him a peck. "Thank you, Sam. Come back anytime. I'm retiring after this year, but I'll still carry on." She turned toward the back of her house, let her gaze linger. "They're great kids, but, well, this is the Bubble, after all. They could use some life lessons." She gave him another quick kiss. "Bye."

12

The autumn morning had opened with a welcome chill, yet not nearly enough to subdue Patches' friskiness on their early morning walk. Later on, the sun infused the light mist with a sudden burst of warmth, clearing the sky instantly, it seemed, crystalline blue, *azul. As good as it gets, any time of year.*

Rachel had taken to calling Sarah 'Hazel' for the way she had taken command those first hardest days and weeks, doing dinners, driving the girls, doing their lunches, anything and everything. She had initially been a little suspicious, maybe even a tad jealous, maybe more than a tad, at the way the other fussed over her husband, his weight, his hair, any little thing. *Maybe a little too close, this beautiful old flame?* She had relented, relaxed with time, and in her own time, Sarah dialed it down, leaving their lives to them.

She had asked them to join her extended family for Thanksgiving dinner, sure to be a major production, and they were both happy to be invited, gratified in their own ways. Audrey let them in at the front door, enveloping Yonny in her vastness, pinching his cheeks and attempting to smooth his unruly hair. "So good to see you two agin! I been worryin' over you, tole Miss Sarah it was time we should be coming…" He hugged her back, giving her a peck on her cheek and amidst her fluttering they made their way outside. Walking hand-in-hand up the gentle manicured slope to the pool, Rachel did her usual quick survey. "Nice place they have here. Wouldn't want anything bad to happen to it."

"What does that mean?"

"Nothing. Just something Daddy used to say, I think he was always trying to ground me, keep me with my feet on the ground, that sort of thing. He has this, this, well, to use a word, eschatological sense of things."

Yonny held out his free hand, palm up.

"What?"

"Big word like that will cost you a dollar. Been jousting with Brooks again?" Yonny smiled at her. Brooks MacMullen was one of the V&E partners in Houston, the one who Rachel had worked most closely with the past few years. They had an ongoing vocabulary duel, even after she left the firm's San Antonio office, saying she just couldn't charge local clients the Houston scale, much less the national scale. Besides, Providence had another notion in hand for her, a less demanding role, of counsel to one of the local firms. *Goldilocksian*, she called it, just right. And when Jeffy went, it was just right.

She tilted her chin, peering sideways. "Of course. You're just jealous of our combined elocutionary prowess."

"Yeah, yeah, yeah. Try me some time." He claimed his twenty-odd years in the real estate business had left him with just eleven words out of his original hundred thousand—*Yes, No, HELLNO!, Damn!,* and George Carlin's seven dirty words you couldn't say on television.

Rachel shifted gears. "There's your girlfriend, dear. And I can see how you were smitten with that sex kitten." She smiled her vixen smile, "Poetry." Sarah was on the far side of the pool, holding court, her hands doing her talking for her, dressed casually but *trés chic,* as always. "You know I've been meeting with her parents, yes? I think I'm close to convincing them to leave their whole art collection to the museum." She had started taking her board membership more seriously, funneling her grief into her formidable powers of persuasion.

"All of it?" He waved to Sarah across the pool. "Don't do that."

"Why not?"

"Had lunch with Zach the other day, Tuesday, last week."

"Which Zach?"

"Silverberg. Your fellow tribesman."

"So?"

"So, he told me some things, locker room talk at Oak Hills…"

She interrupted, "Oak Hills? Why are they out there again? Seems so out of the way."

"Family was Jefferson, like Dad's. That side of town, grandparents were founding members back in the twenties, then his parents moved over here with the rest of the postwar exodus." He gave her a mock sneer, "And the Club wouldn't have Jews way back then."

"They do now."

"Yep, and it's your entire fault. You mesmerized the board members. Like Judith or, or…"

"Delilah?"

"No, Salome, that lewd dance you performed. Okay, so Zach says he was playing in a tennis tournament, the clubs challenging each other. Anyway, he was in the locker room afterwards, heard a familiar voice one row over, bragging about banging his girlfriends and looting his wife's trust fund to pay for them."

"Bragging?"

"Yeah. Pretty scummy. Guess who?"

Rachel shook her head. "Never liked the guy, you know that."

"Good judge of character."

"You're just jealous of him, over her, aren't you?" She turned, confronting him. "Aren't you?"

He looked over at Sarah who had been intercepted rounding the corner of the pool—*just has to hold court, just like always, has that magnetic personality, vivacious…*

She elbowed him. "Aren't you?"

He smiled impishly. "Maybe. And another thing, under your hat, dearest, if this were to get out…"

"Please!"

"Okay, stores are about to be sold out from under them—the parent company called Sol, he and the CEO go way back, it seems, old army pals, Patton, that special intelligence unit—to see if we would be interested in the real estate."

"And are we?"

He began steering her toward Sarah. "Yeah, sure. Sarah's father had, still has a really good eye, nope," he grinned as he ran his finger down her nose, "a nose for retail sites. So, yeah."

"Can the stores be saved?"

"Another story, another day. Here she comes."

"No." Rachel turned him about. "So she could be divorced?"

He shrugged, "Who knows? But, yes, if it came out. The girl-friends, all that, you see?"

"So, the art collection?"

"Yes. Don't take it away from her. Please?" With that, he turned to gather their approaching hostess in his arms for a heartfelt hug. Disengaging, "Rachel, didn't we bring other family members, shorter ones?"

"Oh, don't expect to see them anytime soon. Bruce's girls and

Daphne gathered them up and retreated to Arabella's room. They'll come out in time to pick at their dinners, grace us with a few weak smiles, then disappear again." Sarah beamed, "But that will be perfectly fine. The important people will be with me!"

She slipped her hand into the crook of his arm. "Come along, now, dearest, dearests. The boys are in the den, Yonny, Sweetie. Rachel, before I absolutely must chain myself to the ovens, I'd like to talk with you for a minute."

"Hey, you big slug! Gettouttathaway!"

"Make me, pussy!"

Yonny had wandered into the den and nearly mashed his nose on Doug Porterhouse's shoulder. Sarah, She Who Knows All, had heard that his and Julie's families were going out of town and decided it Just Would Not Do for them to be alone. He smiled, "Well, at least don't block the damned bar. Louie, did he bring anything decent?" He slipped a bottle from its brown cocoon, "For you, Laphroig. All yours, I don't drink the stuff. Oh, I will try a little of this. Yours, Doggie?" As the other nodded, Yonny continued, "Then I'll have a lot of it. Thanks. I want you to know I don't believe any of the bullshit these guys say about you. When's kickoff?"

Dinner was splendid, exhaustingly so, and the wine hardly helped him in his near existential struggle to maintain consciousness. He was more than ready to go and looked around for Rachel, finally finding her clustered with Julie, Sarah and her brother's wife. *Nice to know Rachel's not the only one with deranged sister-in-law syndrome*. He plucked his rose from the bush, pleading an enervating fatigue and too much turkey, or dressing, or Pinot Noir, or was it the Zinfandel? Kissing his hostess demurely, he hoped, he started for the door.

"Forgetting something, Sweetie?" Sarah laughed, "He was always like this, Rachel. Nothing new. Head screwed on tight?"

Yonny gazed blankly at her, then snapped his fingers. "The girls! Where are they?"

Julie said, "We'll bring them home with us. They're being initiated into big girl mysteries right now, I'm sure."

Rachel winced.

As soon as he closed the driver's door, Rachel started, "Did you notice Daphne? Pay her any attention?"

"Just my normal leering and ogling. Nothing special."

"Right. What did you notice?"

"This is a trick question, right?"

Rachel shook her head, and with a tinge of angry exasperation blurted, "Yonny, she is shrinking away. Julie says she's hardly eating anything. Misses one or two days of school every week—says she's sick."

"Since when, I mean, when did this start?"

"A week or two after… after Jeffy, I think."

"Hmmmm…"

His mind drifted away only to have Rachel jerk its leash. "You did notice her boobs, right?"

"Of course." He gave her a smug grin, then refocused on the Boulevard.

"No, really. She's a 36 now."

"Oh? I hadn't been keeping score. Front or back nine?"

"Sheesh." Rachel turned away, then back. "She was a 38. She's lost that much."

"That's a lot?"

"Please!"

"Okay, okay! So she's upset. So are we. I haven't noticed any diminution in our household." He reached across to her chest, pulling his hand back just ahead of the slap.

13

Sam still didn't have much to go on. He had put out the word to his patrolmen and the SAPD guys who patrolled the nearby districts to let him know if they brought in any kids for anything more serious than spraypainting or 40 in a 30. That pulled in more than a few over the next several weeks, but not much in the way of leads, much less actionable info.

Just as he was leaving one evening, a patrolman brought in a kid for being drunk or doped up, either, he knew because the walls of the small station were reverberating with shouting and cussing the officers up and down, threatening to have Daddy's lawyers come down on them *and it would be shit city for them and their whole pathetic little town, too*.

Sam ambled down the short hall to the interrogation room, same as the break room, and had just stopped to crane his neck around the door frame when a voice boomed at him from close range. "Sam! Sam Thompson, you ol' so and so!" He turned to see Texas Ranger Warren Lewis standing near on top of him, all 6 foot 6, 275 pounds of no bullshit lawman. Despite his bulk, he was a taut, angular figure, sort of a Jack Palance with more meat, white western double pocket shirt, star badge, khakis, boots, of course, and a spotless Stetson. And a bigass .44 Magnum strapped on. *An image fitting the man's reputation, that's for sure*, thought Sam.

He and Sam howdied and shook, Sam checking to make sure he still had all his fingers, then he glanced over his shoulder at a suddenly very quiet delinquent. With a hand, he shielded his whisper to the big man. Lewis grinned big time, hitched up his heavily buckled belt and sauntered into the next room, looming over a frightened teenager. "What the hell's going on here, Son? Sam, here, tells me you're not only being real uncooperative, you're being downright disrespectful of a duly authorized police"—it came out *po-leece*—"officer. Now, Son, that just ain't gonna do. Don't make me come over there and sit on your sorry punk chest, now."

He took a chair, turned it around and settled his bulk, crossing his arms over the top rail. "Okay, then. I'm not going to step in Officer"—he looked at a nametag—"Officer P'chernik's shit, whatever stupid shit you been up to. I come here to get some results. I want names. Who's dealing around here?"

Several questions and several stumbling, muttering answers later, he had what Sam wanted—names, several of them. "Well, Son, that'll do, for now it will. But don't cross Detective Thompson, y'hear? 'Cause if you do, I'll hear about it and I'll be back." He stood abruptly, twisted the chair in the air with one hand and slammed it back against the table in one fluid motion. The teenager wilted into an impossible posture, no doubt praying for him to leave.

Which he did, presently, with one last steely glare. Down the hall, he turned to Sam, smiling mischievously, "I was in town, just thought I'd drop in and see if you wanted to get some Meskin food at La Fonda?"

On the way out they approached Lester Ackermann, counselor to the trust fund set. Sam had never seen a two thousand dollar suit before and sure hadn't ever seen one go from crisply tailored to ill-fitting in a matter of moments. "Goddammit if it ain't li'l ol' Lesser." Ranger Lewis cracked eight very large knuckles a foot from the smaller man's face. "Your little boy's still in one piece, don't you worry none. I think he's waiting for his mammy to come suckle him. Might want to 'splain to him how things work out here in the real world. Let's go, Sam. The stench is about to spoil my appetite."

Sam made the call first thing next morning. "Yonny? Might have something for you. Available for lunch?"

He paused to listen, then, "Oh, well, sure, but… do I have to dress up?

"Oh, good. Whew! How about 11:45?

"Good. See you there."

He turned his Crown Vic off New Braunfels into the country club's main entrance and motored slowly up the grade to the portico. Seeing a half dozen cars waiting for the valets and dressed-up ladies exiting and congregating, he made an executive decision to swing around to the north side. *Looks like a new car dealership in Berlin*. He found a space next to the Burr Road exit and trudged up past the pool to the side entrance. *Damned Yonny didn't tell me I'd be climbing a bunch of stairs. Like fucking Everest. Damned knee!* After the third flight, Sam stopped to rub his knee and then opened the paneled oak door into a vestibule, then into the Men's Grill itself. *Probably an airlock to keep all their bullshit quiet.*

Yonny waved at him from the back corner overlooking the first tee. After negotiating his way between tables, Sam started to sit to his friend's right. "No, no, Sam, sit over here where you can see. You might see some of our classmates making fools of themselves. Golf's a great game for other people." He smiled, "Here's the menu. Westside Enchiladas are my favorite, meat gravy, grease just the proper tint of orange. Excellent."

Curtis had been waiting for him. "Mr. Jonas is right, and this is the first batch, just out of the oven."

Sam nodded and Yonny looked up, "Make it two, please, Curtis."

Over iced tea, the two bantered about this foursome and that one until their plates were set before them. His host was suddenly all business. "Sam, let's get down to the licklog on this. What do you have today?"

"Damn, these are really good enchiladas!" Sam smiled, pointing to a full mouth. Finished, he began, "Got a bit of a break yesterday for a change. You know we keep tabs on these creeps out around the High School—Junior High is San Antonio, their problem, glad I don't have that beat anymore. But the names and the M. O.'s change all the time, almost with the seasons. Some of 'em get beat up by competitors, a few get arrested or come to Jesus, some just move on, but if they're dealing, they've been blessed by the Angel…"

"The Angel?"

"Yeah, guy named Juan Ángel Algarve. He's the big cheese, *el queso grande*, in the business. Getting the stuff up here from Mexico, distributes it to his boys. He's good, real good, and plenty smart. And rich. Lots of business. Lots of little Gringo *cabrones* buying."

"Where do you find a guy like that?"

"And why do you ask?"

Yonny improvised, "Oh, uh, don't know, saw *Scarface* again, on cable the other night. Pacino, well, Tony Montana he was in the movie, had a mansion in the best part of Miami or the Gables, maybe. Is this guy living around here on his drugs money?" He smirked, "Nah, probably the Dominion, on some hilltop surrounded with concertina wire."

"Nope, wrong by miles. Lives on the West Side, on El Paso Street. Around the corner from where he grew up." Sam winked. "In the 'hood, get it? Nice house on the inside, I hear, but not all that fancy outside, except for the eight foot fence and the barbed wire and the Rottweilers. And the *vatos* marching around with MAC-10's, with silencers, even. Like Special Forces, even. Nasty bastards."

"Okay, what else about him? Go on, Sam."

Why the detail? "Well, he gets about three million a month of stuff, used to be weed, then cocaine got added, now some pills, and is real smart how he hides it. Part of the problem is some on the force are on his payroll, but that's a whole 'nother story. There's also some talk that a certain prominent Northsider—no names—warehouses it for him, finances it, too. Takes a big cut, for sure, but… Anyway, then he dribbles it out to some distributors who sell to the street guys. That's how it gets to 6900 Broadway, Yawny."

"So who's this Northside guy? Northside as in Alamo Heights or Terrell Hills or Olmos Park? And crooked cops?" He saw a look on Sam's face and tried to backtrack, "I mean, Sam, this is pretty fascinating shit, isn't it? Another gangster movie, or at least a book, right?"

"Maybe. You gonna write it?"

"I just might, if you'll feed me all your inside dope, I mean, info, that's what I mean."

They both enjoyed a smile, then Sam picked up the thread, "I'm not going to give you a name, but one of the lieutenants downtown, we figured he was in somebody's pocket—it wasn't an inheritance he was spending on cars and girls and really nice clothes, get me?" Yonny nodded. "So he decides to retire, we give him a keg party up at Raymond Russell. He's late—he always was—and this Rolls-Royce pulls up, stops, the driver gets out and comes 'round to open the back door. Out steps our Lieutenant So-and-So. We don't ask, he doesn't tell, but the vanity plates had three initials you might recognize. I'll leave it there."

There was a silence, a relaxing silence, then Yonny asked, "Mach ten's, you said? What are those?"

"Little submachine guns, like Uzis—you know what those are, right?" Not bothering with an answer, "Ugly little things, a box with a stubby tube sticking out, but deadly. They've been outlawed for years, but there's plenty of 'em still around. Some of the cartels favor 'em, easy to work and maintain, and there's lots of folks out there making knockoffs, expensive, but the gangs have the money."

"Hmmmm. Interesting. So, a lot of firepower in a small package?"

"You could say that. But why would you say that, Yawny?"

"Just curious, that's all. And silencers? Those things are legal? Where does one get one around here?"

"Why, Yawny, again, why? What are you thinking?"

"Nothing, Sam, just been reading too many James Bond stories, I guess." He dropped his jaw and tried to intone '*Bond, James Bond'* in Scots English. "I thought those things were just for spy missions and such."

"No, they're legal in Texas, so long as you jump through some hoops to get one, letting the Feds know who has 'em. Or buy from someone who doesn't care much about the rules. Some of the pawn guys will sell 'em that way, for a price, of course. And the bad guys don't bother with the regs at all, that's for sure."

"Isn't that nice. Back to the pushers. Who are they, again?"

"I didn't say, not yet. The main guys, so there's two brothers named Carter, longhairs, another couple of guys just go by nicknames, Gunner and Flounder. And there's another guy, a new guy, called Starter Boy. Guess that's what he does, gets 'em started."

"Just like Ricky's girlfriend, damn her."

"Yeah."

Yonny thought of something else and smiled. "Not Sportin' Life?"

"Who?"

"The cocaine dealer in *Porgy and Bess*. Called it 'happy dust'. The Devil incarnate."

Sam gave him a peevish look. "If you say so, Yawny."

"I do. You all done, Sam? I've got some appointments. Curtis?" Yonny motioned to the waiter who brought the ticket. He signed as he stood up. "Sam, you ready?"

Sam looked wistfully at his half-eaten order, ignored in the course of their conversation. "Yeah, I guess so." As he pushed back from the table, his host backed up and pointed at him. "Stay! Until you clean your plate! Curtis, please take care of Mr. Thompson. Anything he wants."

The two looked at each other. "Nawww!"

14

Rachel took a deep breath and released it. She picked up the wall phone and made the call. "Hi, Mother. Yes, it's me. I didn't see the message. No, it hasn't been a year, Mother. No, it hasn't! Is that you, Daddy?"

"Yeah, Sweetheart. Got your mother on the speaker here. How are the girls?"

"Girls are doing pretty well, all things considered, Daddy…, Mother. I just wish I had something good to say about us, Yonny and me."

"What's your cop friend sayin'?"

"Well, Daddy, they're still working on it, he's working with the San Antonio police. Not much to go on is what I hear." *But I really don't know, do I? Yonny and Sam talk all the time…* "But he's gone, doesn't really matter much anymore how it happened, does it?"

Miriam must have been behind her father, sounding muffled. "It most certainly does matter, Rachel! Someone did this to him, or is this just what you people do down there?"

Solly grunted, "Shaddap, Miriam! Plenty of that around here. Rachel, just last week the Aronowicz grandkid overdosed, so it's everywhere. What I want to know is who got him hooked. That's what your cop guy should be looking for. I want some people, Rachel, names. No one messes with our family…"

"Mother, Daddy, that's enough. I'm changing the subject. Manny sent me a nice note about his medical honor. You must be very proud, I am."

She could hear her mother mewling in the background. Solly apparently cut off the speaker, cutting her off as well. "Hush, Miriam. Just hush. I'm trying to talk wit' your daughter. Yeah, he looked really good up there, getting that medal around his neck and all."

"And Donny? What's up with them, I haven't talked to him

lately." *Or Esther, she smiled inwardly, sneering at us for having lost a child the way we did.* She sensed a hollow silence at the other end. "Daddy, Mother? Is everything okay up there?"

Miriam had taken the phone. "Your father doesn't want to talk about it. He just stomped out of the room. He, he's, well, we're worried about him. This casino business…, well, I don't really understand it, but it's all Esther's fault, in my opinion, and I'm entitled to my opinion, aren't I? Well, aren't I?"

Rachel sighed, "Yes, Mother, of course you are."

Miriam kept up her carping, "Nice of you to admit it after all these years. So, yes, Esther wanted to show off to her Jersey friends. Pushed Donny into that casino deal, then spent a fortune on the decorating. Thought she was a decorator, spent a fortune. No taste if you ask me, all her taste is in her mouth, if there. Spent wildly on a bunch of gaudy. Your father's investors had to pour a lot more money into it, but Donny still can't make it work. Spent too much, too damned much, losing money left and right. And all those other casinos, every bit as ugly, they're all doing terrible down there." She paused for breath, then, "It's not good, Rachel, not good at all. Your father's really worried. He's not himself at all. It's not good. Not good. Not good at all."

Rachel didn't really want to hear much more. "Mother, I hear you, but the girls are calling. I'll stay in touch, okay?" She steeled herself. "I love you, Mother."

The line had already gone dead.

15

Sam had just finished shuffling through three incident reports, all dealing with breaking and entering and theft of silver. *Just silver? Have to call, well, let's see, maybe Jack, see what's going on with silver prices. Sounds like a replay of the Seventies, every punk out there was looking to feed the meltdown market...* Just then his phone rang. Picking it up, he didn't even get to announce himself before a gruff voice growled at him, "Go stand by your fax machine. I'm sending you something. Don't let anybody see it." A cough, then, "And hold on to your balls."

He strode to the little comms closet as quickly as his bum knee would let him, getting there just as Alice, the dispatcher, was about to pull the first page. "I'll get that, Darlin', it's mine." He positioned his bulk between her and the sheaves piling up, then let her know it was all hers.

Taking his time back to his cubby of an office, he tried to straighten the papers without looking at them, knowing Max well enough to expect the worst. Sliding past two patrolmen, he closed his door, settled into his chair, adjusted his glasses and began to read.

Almost dropping the first page, he muttered, "Shit! Shee-yut!" He scanned the second and third pages, mostly reportese, blood work, statistics, procedures and such and turned back to the main event. *Subject: Male, age 16. Found nonresponsive on pavement in Olmos Park.* Running his finger down the page to the examiner's conclusion: *Ingestion nasally of a substantial quantity of Prussic Acid (Hydrogen Cyanide). Cause of death: Deprivation of oxygen due to interference with respiratory function.*

At the bottom was the examiner's opinion: *Intentionally introduced into subject by an unknown person with intent to murder subject.*

He took some deep breaths to calm down, to control his jittery nerves.

Picking up the phone, he dialed Max Espinoza at SAPD. "Took you goddamned long enough to call. Whaddya think?"

"Gee, Maxie, what do you expect me to think? Some kid from a great family up here gets poisoned? How does that happen? Have you seen this before?"

"Yeah, no, well, intentional overdosing, loading up some ultra-pure heroin, that sort of thing, but not very damned often. No, Sam, I never seen this stuff. Wouldn't have seen it if Maria Elena hadn't noticed some things on the cadaver." Sam had always recoiled at the c-word, too cold, too uncaring, too, well, too stiff. Espinoza continued, "Woulda just been another rich kid od'ing. Plenty of that, 'specially with the potent shit they're shipping up from Mexico these days. Keeping us really busy over in the Ten Section. Glad we don't own the Dominion yet, guarantee you that. County can keep it!"

Sam hadn't listened intently to the griping and just asked, "Maria Elena? What did she find?"

"Noticed some residue or something on the boy's lips, like some bubbles had dried out. Checked inside, found more on his cheeks, upper part of the mouth." He laughed, a low, guttural, ugly laugh. "I was watching her, damned if she didn't just stick her nose in there, jumped it back out pretty damn quick. '*Almonds'*, she said. She could see I didn't have a clue, so just said, '*Cyanide. Most unusual.*' Her 'zack words. That's why we call her the Snout, y'know."

"Hmmm. If she figured it out just like that, why take so long? Been a couple of months now."

"Because, you *pendejo* dimwit, it ain't anywhere near the usual thing, get me? They had to figure out what samples to take, more blood, piss, everything, then test it over and over. Not something the Med wanted to jump the gun on, you can understand that."

The Medical Examiner was noted for being conservative, cautious, even, often to the sheer frustration of those out in the field who knew damned well what their own lying eyes told them. "Yeah, that's him. So, what now?"

"Sam, I spoke to the Chief as soon as I seen this. I told him we should keep it quiet until we get somewhere with an investigation. Agree?"

"Yeah. Don't know how I can tell his parents."

"Figured that. Why I sat on it a couple of weeks down here, helpin' you out, right? So, I told him we should let you handle this.

We'll shuffle it around down here as long as we can, don't know how long that'll be, but you run with it."

Dazed, Sam muttered, "Sure. Thanks, I think."

"Yeah, well, you're the one who bailed out of the action down here to go uptown and take your siestas where nothing ever happens. It's all yours, baby. Call me when, not if, you need me." The receiver clicked off loudly.

Sam sighed as he sunk back into his chair. *Man, I could use a cigarette right now.* Opening his top drawer, he looked long at the pack of Marlboros. He had quit, cold turkey, when a physical showed a hazy spot on one lung, kept the unopened pack as a reminder and just for the sheer comfort of knowing it was there. *Eleven years ago, no, twelve. That long. Good for me.*

He shoved the drawer closed, swiveled around a couple of revolutions in his chair, then reversed course. Now looking at the report, he cradled his head in his hands. *Murder? You got to be kidding me. Now what? Now what do I do? Do I tell Yonny, his wife? Should I? What if he, he goes off in some way? Wouldn't put it past him?*

THREE

1

Time attempted to heal some of the family's wounds, did its best to at least blunt the hard, piercing, jagged shards of recent memory. And time had indeed made some progress since September, not nearly enough time, not nearly enough progress, but welcome nonetheless. Now they were coalescing into a family again, less a collective of damaged souls, the waking realization of their existential unity pulling them together. Yonny and Rachel actually were looking forward to the holidays for once, somehow free of the awkwardness of trying to manage celebrating two traditions at once, as if splitting their attention reduced their significance by half. This year, the twins elected to devote themselves to Hanukah, no doubt influenced by their new Jewish friends from Woodridge, all the while confident of all their other party invitations, especially Christmas Cotillion. So, there was a calm for the moment in the Jonas household, and if not exactly Matthew's great calm, maybe just a sense of composure, of stability, the quotidian gradually usurping the tragic. But, like Sam had said one day, *Fate, she was a fickle bitch,* and as likely to tease the lion as lie down with the lamb.

He heard the back door slam, all the way upstairs in his study he could hear it. *Cuidado, vato! Loca Nueva Jork Judia on a rampage, Cabrito!* He had a split-second decision to make—flight or fight—meet her on the stairs or duck out to the balcony, dangle and drop the few feet to the ground like he used to do in high school. Not any more, he couldn't, not with his knees, so it was the stairs. He beat her to the landing, jumping down on two feet to face her coming up.

"Hi."

With gray-green eyes incandescing, she started in on him, "Why, Yonny, why? Why did you do it?"

"Why did I do what it is I did? Or didn't? What are you talking about?"

"Your girlfriend! Sarah!"

"What about her?"

"What about her? How about I spell it out for you? D-I-V-O-R-C-E! Got it?"

He shook his head, almost imperceptibly, a bare shiver of recognition and something else. "So. She start it? Surely not him. He wouldn't give up all that."

"You know. You did it." Rachel had never used that tone, given him that look. "Why, Yonny? Why? Why did you do it?"

"Do what? Rachel, dammit, what are you talking about?"

"The pictures you sent, gave her father. Of Louis and some girl in New York, the ones you took when you were up there. You know damn well what I'm talking about."

"No, I damn well don't. Sit down. You're hysterical." He turned her about and walked her down to the kitchen. "Sit down or I'm walking out the front door."

Rachel saw something in her husband's eyes she'd never seen before, a glimpse past and future, full of fear and anger and something else, something darkly painful. She sat.

"Good. Now tell me what you're talking about. What pictures?"

She sighed as her head drooped toward hands clasped between legs. Looking up, "The pictures you took when you went up to talk with Daddy and the store people. Your new camera. You know what I'm talking about."

Solly had invited, summoned, more like it, Yonny to meet him and the top brass of the conglomerate that had bought Sarah's family's chain of fashion stores some years ago, now wanted to sell. Yonny unexpectedly ran into Louis at the airport, *on his way to meet some designers in Manhattan*, he said. There had been a few stories about him and 'designers', but nothing concrete, nothing like the locker room talk.

Sarah's father ran the stores but was ready to retire and hand them over to Louie. But neither were to attend this meeting. The big boys in New York were close with her daddy, ambivalent about Louis as far as he knew, but neither had anything to do with the decision to exit the retail business. Just a matter of dollars and cents, of margins and returns on investment and capital allocations. Just business, nothing personal. And nothing to do with Yonny's old romance with the daughter. Just business, but now Yonny had to submerge the personal, set it aside, pretend it and all that didn't matter. Now it was his job to come up with a number for the suits, a figure for the real estate, the improvements, the fixtures, the leaseholds, anything that couldn't be gutted and stripped out of the stores when the decision came down. The fates of the employees who worshipped the father and the whole store shtick weren't part of the deal, didn't count for anything, and he knew he would be tearing the heart out of someone close to him, very close then, very close now.

Rachel's firm had been retained as local counsel to represent the parent company, so he had to be careful. He couldn't share anything with Rachel aside from the obvious family real estate deal he was about to lay on the table, couldn't let her know about the other things running and working in his head.

When this all began percolating, he called one of his B-school classmates who knew the retail business, could grasp the opportunity he laid before him and had the sources of funds to act, all in confidence between old friends. Using the sales numbers and the financials for their due diligence, the two of them were working up a figure for the whole thing, stores, trademarks, inventory, everything. *Saving the stores. But for whom?*

"Again, what pictures? I'm waiting, Rachel. If you're accusing me of something, well, you're the lawyer, present your evidence." He reached for her hands, she jerked them away. "Okay, okay! Then just tell me what happened today. How did you hear about this?"

Rachel stared at him, her eyes hollow with grief for her closest, truest friend in town and fear for what she was sure her husband was thinking, intended. "Sarah dropped by my office…"

"She was there for the divorce?"

"Yes, met with Bob…"

Yonny interrupted again, "Flournoy? Really?"

"Yes, of course. With all that's at stake, he's the only choice, really, despite being the world's biggest jerk."

"That he is. So, he's her attorney now? Was her father with her?"

"Yes, and yes, he was. Why do you ask?"

"You said it—there's a lot at stake there. And her father was always pretty protective, if you get my drift."

Rachel couldn't suppress the slight smile, her lips even parting fleetingly. "So I've heard. Yes, probably for that but also for the trust funds…"

"Really?"

"Uh huh. Could get really nasty."

"So said Sarah? What else did she have to say?"

"Everything. An hour or so, and a whole box of Kleenex." Rachel had calmed herself, now was discussing the case with a confidante. "The pictures—Yonny?" He shook his head. "Okay, for now. So, apparently what Zach heard was the truth, not just some bullshitting male bragging. And the money, well, yes, seems to be true, too, but she doesn't know how bad it is. I can say that someone at the bank's trust department may be headed to jail."

As Yonny whistled, she went on, "And Louie? Just a typical male screwaround, Yonny. Some blonde bimbo here and one in New York."

"So, now what?"

"Oh, I think it'll be pretty cut and dried. She doesn't want to send him to prison or anything like that, but her father and Bob will hold the money sword over him sharp and close, you can count on that."

"I get you. I take it Louie won't be at the stores any more?"

"As soon as her father gets back to the office today."

Yonny smiled. "Good."

"What do you mean?"

"Umm, well, best make a clean break of it and for sure they won't want him around." He hoped that would suffice.

Of course it wouldn't. "Yonny, what are you talking about? Does this have to do with the stores, the real estate?"

He was cornered. "Indirectly, yes."

"Yonny?" She tensed up. "What are you saying?"

"I can't tell you."

"Why not?"

"You guys represent the parent, you're conflicted, you know that. I can't say, not anything about the real estate or anything else."

They lapsed into an increasingly uncomfortable silence. Rachel broke first. "It was the pictures, Yonny. Someone took them, sent them to her father. Then he hired himself a PI in New York and had his security guy—Wellington…"

"Witherington. Sally's father."

"That's right. Anyway, they tailed him, got more dirt, dumptrucks worth. Seems he thought he was invisible. So typical. And the girl here?"

Yonny leaned forward eagerly. "Yeah?"

She made a minor sneer. "One of the cosmetics girls at the store. At the mall. Can you believe it?"

"Oh, yeah, I can believe it. Who? Might need her name for my little black book."

Rachel shouted, "Not funny, Yonny! Not funny!" She bolted upright. "And from you, with your and Sarah's history?" She paused, absolutely radiating anger, "That's why, right?"

"Why what, R?"

"Why you sent those pictures. That's all I could think of while she was telling me everything—I missed a lot of it, I'm sure. So you could get Louis out of the picture, open the door to her bedroom, Yonny? That's it, isn't it, Yonny?" By now she was screeching, "Isn't it?"

"No. You know better, Rachel." He stood and hugged her tightly, resisting her ebbing attempts to wriggle free. "No. Listen to me."

He loosened his grip enough to lean back and look into her eyes, "No, Rachel, there'll never be another one for me, another you. She's the past, a fond, well, a very fond memory, tinged with pain, yeah. I'll never forget her, I admit, I confess, freely. But not now, not today, not with what we've gone through, what we're still going through. If you want me out, just say the word, but I'm not planning on going anywhere. Not down the street, not without you. I'm staying with you through the rest of our lives. Together, Rachel, together."

He released her, but she clung to him. They remained locked in place a good quarter hour.

1968

It's my birthday, my 18th. I'm wandering through a thicket, pushing branches aside, struggling to make some headway through the briars ripping my clothes and the vines tugging at my ankles. It's my birthday, why am I doing this?

Suddenly I break through into a bright blue sky sunlight. Blinking, I turn away from the blinding light back toward the thicket, no longer mesquite and huisache and prickly pear but a forest with grand trees, pines, firs, see it receding as a wave ebbs on a beach, replaced by a brilliantly verdant lawn, St. Augustine grass, I see.

I turn around and find myself facing a house, a familiar house, but whose? Hers. Of course. It's my birthday, she asked me to come by at seven. I look at my watch, remembering I don't wear one and then look back at the house changing colors, painted in riotous rambling blotches by the sunset off to my left.

My car, the white SS, is there waiting for me. But I'm not dressed for a date, am I? I touch a sleeve, seeing the Gant shirt she bought me at the store, asked me to wear tonight.

Now I'm ringing the bell. Opening the door is her father with that menacing smile he always wears whenever I come over. He dissolves obscurely into the shadows as she brushes by him, wearing a long-tailed white buttondown and cutoffs, her long dark hair streaming over her shoulders down onto her chest.

She takes me by the hand, leading me to my car. Now we're driving up the Austin Highway. The AM radio jumps from station to station, each point playing the same song, their song, Herb Alpert trying to sing 'This Guy's in Love with You'. I look over her way, her long hair swirling wildly, excitingly, up into the wind under an indigo sky punctuated with polka dot clouds. But my car isn't a convertible, it's a hardtop, right? I stare at her until she cries out, "Here! Pull in here!"

Now we're at the Teepee, in the restaurant in the front, the old-fashioned motor court of white concrete teepees in back stretching out into an impossible perspective. She snuggles closely to me as I take a bottle of beer from the waiter. But the waiter is Ricky Young, gargantuan, leering down at us. In the next instant we're on the highway again, Ricky at the wheel, the car slaloming around traffic cones atop the pavement.

Momentarily we're sitting on her front steps and now she's crying buckets because I'm going off to college tomorrow. But it's only June, I think, as I wipe a flooded cheek. I hug her closer, then kiss her.

Now we're on a sofa, side by side, close, very close, now skin to skin…

He awoke with a shudder.

2

"Any time, Yawny, any time, you know that, yeah?" Sam closed his office door as the other left. *Whew! Had to do some fancy sidestepping there. I just don't know how to tell him, or if I should, even. What will he do when he finds out? He better not find out from anyone else, and what about that wife of his?* He paused in his thoughts at Rachel's image popping up in his mind, then to another's, sitting next to him in class, maybe. *And Sarah Langefelter getting divorced? What kinda fucking idiot would do that to her? Running around on that beauty? Haven't seen her in years, I guess she's still beautiful, hasn't gone to pot, like some.* He leaned back in his chair and raised his right hand to shoulder level, making a cup, then did the same with the other. *Got a murder on the one hand, a divorce on the other. Anything else and I'll really be juggling old classmates.*

He made a note on his desk calendar to call Max at SAPD, see if he had anything new, remind him again to keep things quiet as long as he could. Leaning back again, thinking, *I wonder what she'll do? Some women go to pieces when their man goes catting around, some just... get even. But how? And how bad could it get? And where have I heard that before?*

1987

Sam was now in his second year as a Homicide Investigator, sometimes liked it better than patrol, sometimes not so much. At least the hours were better. He got the call, unit 24 was already there. Apparent homicide. Turning his unmarked car around, he sped down South New Braunfels into the Highlands neighborhoods. Making a couple of turns, he arrived at the scene where a patrol car was pointed at an angle into the curb. A stout officer was attempting to string some tape from one tree to another, dropping the roll as he saw Sam's car pull in behind.

Sam killed the motor and eased out. He pulled on his suit jacket and straightened his tie as he strode, authoritatively, he hoped, toward his man.

"Thanks for getting here so quick, Sir. They said you were a good guy, could help me out. This is my first one. Hell, it's my first day, Detective."

Sam checked the nametag. "Don't know about the good guy bit, Adams, but why don't you just tell me what you got here."

The stocky young man went pale. "Can't. You gotta see it for yourself."

They entered a modest ochre brick and siding house with an old-fashioned aluminum awning slung over a picture window. As they stepped across the threshold into a dim living room, Sam looked around. "Okay, all I know is it's a homicide. Show me."

"Looks like she shot two kids first, then herself."

"She? Does she have a name?"

The rookie gestured, "Here, talk to her."

For the first time Sam was aware of an older woman in the shadows, trembling, clutching some papers to her chest. The rookie wasn't going to be much help, so Sam approached the woman. Gruffly, "Who are you and what's this all about?"

She looked up at him and started, haltingly at first, "I got the letter this morning. I didn't open it for an hour or so, figured it'd be the same whining, poor pitiful me, all that stuff I've heard over and over and over. She should've just kicked his sorry butt out the door. But, no, she had to..." Her voice dropped away. "Shoulda called police earlier..." Now the trembling had given way to tears as she slumped onto a sofa.

Sam turned, looking for the patrolman, but Adams was already reaching out to guide him into the back. Whispering, "She's no use. Come see with me. Back here."

Sam was led into a bedroom. A rather large, dark-haired woman in a nightgown and robe reclined on the bed, propped up against the headboard, an apparent gunshot wound to the right temple, one arm hanging down limply, a pistol on the floor. Next to her, a little girl of two or three in pink teddy bear pajamas, gunshot to the head. Sam looked first to the obvious—the wounds—then back to the little one. Her hands were still clasped around her mother's arm. He turned away sharply, having seen all he needed to see, all he wanted to see. He croaked, "Where's the other one? Show me."

The junior officer couldn't speak, turning so Sam couldn't see the tear trickling down his cheek. He motioned and led Sam into another bedroom where a young man, fifteen or sixteen, Sam guessed, was lying relaxed on the bed. Looking closer, he saw fresh blood mingling with the maroon of his letter jacket, already seeping into the white winged foot embroidered on his chest.

He just stood there, hands on his hips. Finally he turned and said, "Let's go talk to the lady."

Back in the living room, Sam took over the questioning. "Ma'am, why are you here, again?"

"I'm Darlene's aunt. She's my sister's girl. She sent me this letter. She..."

Sam shushed her with a hand and took the letter, handling it carefully. It was eight or ten pages long, in a neat cursive. Seems the mother had seen her husband with another woman more than once—that shit happens, thought Sam—but she didn't want to confront him, to hear the truth from him. She wasn't afraid, she wrote, just didn't want to face the truth.

Reading on, she didn't want to leave her husband, she loved him so much. Sam skimmed through several more pages, glancing at some parts, ignoring others, then stopped short. The woman was writing, '...when I told Bobby, he got real upset. He knows her daughter, couldn't face her in school anymore....' He kept on reading, knowing this could only get worse. When he reached one part, he looked around for a chair and sat down. The little girl had asked her mother, '...Mommy, am I going to see Jesus soon? Yes, my darling, I told her, we are...' At that, Sam had to stop for what seemed an eternity.

Finally, he read the last paragraphs. 'So I'm going to Reed's pawnshop when it opens tomorrow and pawn my wedding ring for a gun. I'll leave the ticket on the counter if you want it. I will mail this first thing, you should get it by 10. By that time I will have done it. I love you, Aunt Grace. Goodbye.' The letter was signed in the same neat cursive, no trembling hand or tear stains.

The aunt had been prattling on to Adams and Sam was now

paying attention to her for the first time. "...No good, I tole her that. She jes' didn't want to do nothing about it. The children, she said. Well, look at them now. But if I had jes' opened that letter when I got it...'

Sam rose and cupped his big paw atop her bony shoulder. "Don't blame yourself, Ma'am. She would've done it sometime, or maybe shot him. That's what this," shaking the letter, "tells me."

He asked the patrolman if he had called for the ambulance. The other nodded. "Good. Looks like I've got a report to write." He stopped at the door to talk to the Crime Scene guys just arriving and handed one the letter with a brief explanation. On his way out, he saw a man was trying to slip under the yellow police tape. Sam called out as he approached, "What are you doing? That tape's there for a reason."

"This is my house."

Sam flipped his badge. "I don't think you want to go in there and I'm not going to let you."

The man wasn't deterred, asking coldly, "Are they all dead?"

"Why are you asking it like that?"

"I got a call at the shop, said there was a big scene at the house, some sort of shooting."

Controlling himself, just, Sam hissed, "Nice of you to take an interest now, after you've been fucking around, not worrying about the consequences. You're the cause of it, what happened in there."

"That's none of your fucking business."

Sam's stare just bored right through him. "Oh? Murder is my business." With that, his right hand collided with the other's face, staggering him. Sam grabbed him by the arm and towed him back into the house, shoving him inside, waiting to see the look on his face.

When the husband stumbled back into the living room, Sam saw what he wanted to see, turned around and left.

At lunch, Sam just sat and stared at his tacos. *Why? How could it get so bad that you'd kill your own children? Your life gets so screwed up? I can see killing yourself, but the kids? Who could do that? Could Sarah? She needs someone, maybe Yawny's wife. Maybe Yawny. I'll talk to him about it.*

Back in his office, he tried to focus, going over some reports, pretty trivial stuff, a bicycle stolen over on Rosemary, some outstanding warrants on a speeder, nothing near as confounding as what he was dealing with, this Jonas kid thing.

Enough to drive a man to drink. Sam had given up the booze years ago, just gave it up, none of that AA stuff. Just gave it up after the Saturday night in Denton his wife found him collapsed at the front door, passed out cold, his key in the lock. She thought he had the DT's, he was shaking so hard, but it was just a North Texas Blue Norther chilling him to the bone. It was enough, that and her threats to leave him once and for all. Sitting in church that next morning, still hammered, he made his choice.

But like his cigarettes, he kept a bottle in a drawer, just to look at it warning him to stay away. Eight years just sitting there, seal unbroken, untouched. Eight years. He reached down and picked it up.

3

Christine opened the office door, closing it behind her. Quietly, "It's Mrs. Goodman. She called, wants to know if you're free for lunch?"

Rachel looked up, then at her clock. Taking off her glasses, she thought a moment, then stacked her papers in their folder. "Sure, why not? Tell her… here, I'll go with you."

The morning's rain had cleansed the downtown air and scrubbed the streets and the Riverwalk paving. *A beautiful day. Hope she's able to enjoy it.* She thought of just walking over the block and a half, but decided to drive, remembering she had to run by Hanley-Wood to pick up some gifts for her tennis team.

Sarah was just walking in as Rachel pulled up and whistled at her. Taking the valet's stub, she trotted over to embrace her friend and turned her into the entry. Club Giraud wasn't too crowded that early; the ladies had a room practically to themselves, which enabled Sarah to vent, telling Rachel how distraught she had been, how she couldn't sleep, how betrayed she felt.

"You were betrayed, Sarah. No other way to look at it. A cheap, tawdry, altogether typically stupid male brains-in-his-crotch thing. I'm sorry, but it's just that simple."

"No, it isn't, it never is and you know it. I've been wracking my brain. I can come up with a dozen, two dozen things, three dozen things about me he could have, should have found annoying, but this?"

"Sarah, it's over. I hate to be such a bitch, to be so blunt, but it's over. Has he called, asked to see you?"

Haltingly, the other began in a whisper, "Yes. He came back two nights ago, said he was sorry, wanted me to take him back…"

"I hope you told the schmuck no, hell, no?"

"I tried."

"Sarah, what tried? You did or you didn't." Rachel hated herself for being so hard on her, but she could tell a battered woman, emotionally if not physically, knew she had to use some tough love. And it was love. Beyond just religion, Sarah was her only true kindred spirit down here, had a similarly unhappy upbringing, never-ending problems with The Mother. And then there was Yonny…

"I tried, Rachel, I tried!" She was on the verge of breaking down amid a room by now populated by the city's worst gossips and shrews.

Rachel leaned over, took a hand. "Slowly now, girl. Get yourself together. Take your time."

Sarah just barely avoided hyperventilating, then managed to continue, "I tried, I really tried. And, Rachel, I told him no. I told him to get out and never step foot in the house again. I told him to go off with his blonde bimbos and never come back and if he didn't, I'd, I'd…"

"That's okay, Sarah, that's okay." Rachel was impressed, no, stunned at her friend's sudden gumption. "And that was that? He slunk out like the weasel he was, he is?"

Sarah teetered on the brink. "No."

"No? What did he do?"

"He… he grabbed me by my wrists and dragged me to the maid's room and… and…"

"Raped you!" Rachel hit the emphasis through her husky whisper.

"No, I, well, yes, yes, he did… I didn't want it, Rachel, I really didn't. Maybe I was wearing something, maybe I shouldn't have invited him in…"

Rachel was on fire now, didn't care a damn for the other ladies in the room. Still whispering, "Maybe nothing, Sarah. He raped you. That's a crime. A vicious crime, especially when it's him that's made you so, so… so vulnerable. You have to tell the police. You have to."

"But, the divorce, the children? If he goes to jail, what about them?"

"He may go to jail anyway when your father gets through with him."

Sarah was silent, but Rachel was grateful she was more composed, at least outwardly. The waiter came along to inquire about things until Rachel drove him hastily back with a look that could have fried bacon. On Mars. "Listen, Sarah, the very least you have to do, you absolutely must do, is get a restraining order. I'll take care of that this afternoon with Bob. The DA will ask questions, but you know her, another one of your high school people, I'll go talk to her." She paused, tapping a long fingernail, "And go see Jill Schulberg this afternoon, right after lunch." The two shared the same Ob/Gyn. "Right now. Tell her you need a blood test right away. Right away! This instant!"

"A blood te… Oh, my God, Rachel, I hadn't thought of that."

"Well, I just did. Let me do your thinking for you, at least on a few of these things, okay? I want to, and you need some help. Just admit it and let me help you. And, Sarah, one more thing, very important. Don't let Bob Flournoy in your house, not if you're alone. Don't meet with him anywhere but his office or your father's office. In fact, make him go there. Yes, yes, your father's office. He needs to know about these things anyway."

Sarah gave her a look. "Bob, too?"

"He has a reputation. Trust me. But he's the right attorney for you, no question. Just be careful." She snapped her fingers at the waiter, signed the ticket. "Now go, Sarah. Go straight to Jill's. Do not pass *GO*. And remember, everything will work out in the end, it will. Doesn't seem like it now, but it will. Go."

Under the canopy, Sarah turned to her friend, smiling for the first time. "Thank you, Rachel, you've been so helpful." As her Mercedes was delivered and she settled into the driver's seat, she called out, "And thank Yonny, too. He's been a lot of help, too. He's given me so much time, every day, it seems. He's the kindest person, but you know that. Bye."

Even before the valet brought her Suburban around, she knew where she was going. *To see Sam Thompson. And then my husband.*

4

The neon 'POLICE' sign cantilevered out over the side alley, practically crying out for a misty night with a couple of '56 DeSoto squad cars and a passel of the usual *noir* suspects below its buzzing, sparking yellow-green light.

And that was the only distinctive feature of City Hall. The rest of the building was architecturally undemanding, at best, just bland, emanating a bureaucratic ennui. Which ennui was shattered as a raven-haired tempest barged through the door and down the one corridor, official notices and lost dog flyers aflutter in her wake. She turned the corner to the police dispatcher's window. "I need to see Sam Thompson, right now. Right now!"

The dispatcher might have been shocked if this were the first time a wronged woman had shown up like this. But it wasn't, and she wasn't.

"Who's asking?"

"Rachel Jonas."

"Oh. I'm so sorry about your boy. My niece and him were friends, well, friendly, like." She disappeared around a corner.

"Rachel? Sorry, had a little question, umm, business to finish up. What's up? What can I do for you?"

"It's not about us. Not today. It's about Sarah Goodman. May we speak confidentially?"

Sam ushered her into his cramped office, offering her a chair. He settled in behind his desk, covering up some reports and closing two folders. "Now, then, Mrs. Jonas, ummm, Rachel, what can I do for you?" He had been at this business long enough to recognize a volcanic temper, to sense the seething, roiling magma just beneath the surface, the prickly tingling on his cheeks a sure sign of things to come. He braced himself.

It didn't take long. In a torrent of anger, Rachel let loose, "Like I said, it's about your friend Sarah Langefelter, Goodman, now. You remember her from high school, surely? And that she and my husband were boyfriend and girlfriend back then? Weren't they pretty close?"

"Maybe. It's been a long time."

"Well, they were, and pretty close, from what I know, but that's not why I'm here. Sarah's getting a divorce. Did you know *that*?"

Sam responded defensively, "Yeah, I heard something about that. Word gets around here, y'know? And am I s'posed to do something about it? If I had to get the lowdown on every divorce or cheater in this town, I wouldn't ever get anything done. So what does that have to do with me," waving his hands around aggressively, "and us?"

Rachel relaxed her jaw, he could see, then she continued, "Yes, so she's getting a divorce. Scumbag of a husband carrying on with several women. And other things… It could get really, really messy, you see? Really messy. Anyway, he came to her house a couple of nights ago and…, I'm violating a friend's trust, here…, he forced himself on her."

Sam's face twisted in disgust. "That's pretty damned crappy."

"You think so? Now, I don't know if you know, but I'm an attorney. But I don't do criminal defense, so I'm not as up to date on that sort of thing as I should be, not Texas law. I could go back downtown and look it up, but I thought since it occurred here, I might as well get started here. So, what is the law in this great state?"

Sam bought some time, saying calmly, "I'm not an expert on it either, don't think it's any different from other kinds of rape, but I could be wrong. Haven't dealt with it in years. Lemme see." He thumbed through his rolodex, then picked up the telephone. "John Cantu, please. Sam Thompson, Alamo Heights PD. Oh, I see. Yes, please, as soon as he can. Here's the number.

"Let's give him a minute. He owes me some favors, so he'll get back to me pretty quick. So, let's do this right." He pulled out an incident report form, retrieving a pen from under his papers. "Okay. Complainant? S-a-r…"

"No, Sam, not yet. Put that away. This is an informal inquiry. I just…"

Sam picked up the beeping phone. "Juanito, vato! Como esta Lydia la Latina loca?" He listened a few moments, then made a lemon sucking face. "Yeah, I get you, but she's still too good for you, you know that, don't you?" He paused, listening some more, then turned away. Quietly, "Well, yeah, we're, we're, well, it'll work itself out." Turning back, "But enough of that. I got a case here, a potential case, need the law on it. Ex-husband," he looked at Rachel, "soon to be ex-husband, I mean, been out of the house, comes back, jumps his wife…" He had started to say what he would usually say, but it somehow didn't fit the Sarah of memory. "Yeah, her attorney thinks it's rape, but…"

Rachel couldn't make out the other end of the line. Sam turned to her, asking, "Did she let him in?" She nodded, then started to object as Sam stifled her with a hand, pointing to the phone. He shook his head. "Not that easy?" He listened quite a bit more, then said goodbye.

"Don't tell me. You won't go after him!"

"What he said was, well…, it's complicated."

"It always is with you men!" Rachel's cheeks were reddening up again. "Of course. What she was wearing, how she was acting. Or is it worse? His woman, his chattel? Really?"

"Settle down. The law's pretty clear and says there's no difference between spousal and other rapes. That's pretty new, why I wasn't sure, but there's still some prejudice against the wife, and it's a '*he said, she said*' type of deal, especially if she let him in."

"She said she opened the door and was talking with him when he grabbed her."

"Again, her story against his. Did he threaten her?"

Rachel was close to her boiling point. "If you call being dragged to a bedroom like some caveman's prize, yes! Don't tell me you won't charge him! Don't you have any balls?" She stared at the ceiling. "Was Mother right, after all? Cowboy country?"

"Don't know about the cowboys, but mine are just fine, Ma'am, thank you very much. I'm just telling you what Johnny said. Hard to make a case, very hard. If he hasn't, hadn't been physically abusive beforehand, almost impossible to make something stick given what you've told me." He paused, admiring the view. "What do you want me to do?"

Rachel slumped against the back of the plastic chair. "Oh, I don't know… Of course I do! A restraining order! Keep that sleazoid away from her and her kids, if we can. Allison, Allison Walker, wasn't she one of your classmates? She can issue it. I bet she'd be happy to do so."

"Maybe, maybe not." Some memories stirred. "But I'll still need Sarah to make the complaint."

"Well, I could do it on her behalf, right?"

"I'm not the lawyer, but doesn't she have to okay it regardless?"

"Yes. Yes, she does, but I'll get to work on that."

Rachel rose, stretching to her left as she did, her sweater tightening around its obstructions. Sam followed her every move with his eyes. At the door, she turned. "Sam, I apologize for being rude, if I was. I just got pretty worked up over this."

"Understood." He started to rise, to be the gentleman and escort her out, but realized he had an erection, a sizeable one. He weighed his options and elected to stay put, rising just to desktop level. "I don't have much to tell you about your son, sorry. Nothing that could bring him back, that's for sure. Just not much to go on, sorry."

Rachel murmured, "I know. Thank you just the same." She turned and stepped through the portal so he wouldn't see her tears.

5

Angela looked up as the door flew open. "Mrs. Jonas? Rachel?"

"Is he in?" She didn't wait for an answer and half-pushed, half-kicked open the door to Yonny's office. She paused only long enough to slam it closed before she started in on him. "Really, Yonny, really? How often is it you talk to your old girlfriend? You just can't shed her, can you? Can't give her up? Why, Yonny, why do you do this to me? Why? If you think you can just run off with her and leave me and the twins behind, you've got another thing coming! And have you stopped to think for a damned minute the effect, the impact on her divorce case? Which, if you're too dense to understand basic family law, will take months to resolve. And in the meantime if you two run off together, there goes her case. Boom! He skates, takes everything he's taken, waltzes off scot-free, probably even gets the kids, the trashy bastard. And why? Because you just can't control your goddamned post-teenage hormones!"

He knew well enough to wait until she exhausted her breath, then began calmly, "R, you're wrong. She calls me once, sometimes twice a day, for this advice or that opinion. I help her wherever, whenever I can. But I also…" he held up his hand, "if you want me to tell you the truth, then shut up!" Satisfied with her silence, he continued, "So, yes, I listen. That's it, the long and the short. And I've given her some damned good advice about what to do with that conniving twit. That's it. Care to apologize for your outburst, your unfounded accusations? Damn it, Rachel, you can really be such a bitch sometimes… "

His words struck her back as she stormed out.

6

Sam was enjoying himself down on the field at halftime, one of fifty or sixty football alums being honored at the playoff game, the Mules' first in forty years, ten years before his time. Some teammates he hadn't seen in years, including Benny Proctor whose ass he had kicked in practice—*thirty years ago already? I had forgotten about that, but he hadn't, says his father has never let him forget it. Too bad.* The group joshed and jostled then broke up, the players making their ways back into the stands.

Sam had planned to sit up near the top of the stands with some of his fellow linemen, but his knee had other ideas. As he stopped halfway up to massage it, he spied Rachel and Yonny sitting off to one side, a little apart from the rest of the crowd. He called out to Yonny who waved him over and stood, gesturing him to sit next to Rachel, between the two. Sam thought that was a tad odd, but said his hellos and took a seat. *Not looking at each other?* In between cheers and Rick Shaw's booming voice over the PA, Sam tiptoed through twin tensions, one created by his knowledge, the other by what he saw, or felt, between the others.

Rachel broke the silence, "Sam, is this, what happened to Jeffy, is it common?"

Sam hoped he could avoid saying what he knew he couldn't say, or wasn't ready to say. "More with PCP and some of the other crazy drugs out there, but, well, we get a few calls every month, more for crack than powder. Almost all of them can be treated if…"

"If what, Sam?"

He swiveled to his left to face Yonny, "Well, if they can be helped in time. Not left like your boy was."

Now back to Rachel who said, "That's what bothers me so much, Sam. Surely he was with someone he knew, probably knew pretty well, we would think, and they just left him? Left him there on the pavement?" She choked, "To die?"

Sam put his arm around her, pulled her close. "I know. I've asked myself the same thing. That's why, or what I'm looking for, the others." *She feels good against me, those big boobs and all. I wonder what she's like in bed.* He snapped out of it, turning to Yonny. "Still don't have anything, Yawny, sorry. But you," turning back to Rachel, "and you don't have anything to be ashamed of, I don't think. There's enough of this going around, like I said, lots of families just like yours in the same boat. Or close."

"Not much comfort," snuffled Rachel, sitting up straight again.

"No, but you have company, that's what I'm trying to say. Drugs take money, especially if someone gets addicted, and there's money around here. Actually, I'm surprised there isn't more of it, with all the money these kids have. But it's not just the money, it's the peer pressure, the one kid who's always getting into some trouble, taking risks, doing stupid stuff, he tries some dope, then gets his friends to try it, and so on. Pretty soon he's a dealer…"

"Like Ricky."

"Yeah, Yawny, like Ricky. And if he's one of the cool guys, then it's cool for the next one to try it. Like I said, with all that, it's surprising so many kids don't try the stuff. I'm betting, well, I'm of the opinion that your boy wasn't using, not regularly, I mean. You knew about the school play?"

Rachel snuffled some more, "Jeffy came home right away to tell us that afternoon, the day he…" Sam let her catch her breath and she continued, "That's why it just doesn't make sense. That and, well, just the way Jeffy was. He wasn't one of those. I'm sure of that."

Sam leaned back so he could see each of them more easily. "My older sister, when she was still married to a sergeant, lived on Fort Sam, was sending my niece to Cole. But even Cole had a drug problem, even with all the security, the MP's, everything, so after her freshman year, she sent her to Heights. I told her not to, that Heights was no better and how it took me a while to adjust, to fit in. But, no… Off she went and by the end of a semester, she was already into that shit." Sam's voice grated bitterly. "She didn't even graduate, got busted several times, finally she and some scuzz boyfriend did some breaking and entering to feed their habit. She's doing ten in Gatesville, gets out in a few years…"

Yonny could see how Sam was affected. "Some people…"

Sam waved him off. "I tried everything to help her, even arrested a couple of her dipwad boyfriends. Roughed one of 'em up pretty good —I was off duty when I did it—he didn't bother her anymore, but it wasn't enough. I guess she had that addictive personality, the drugs took over…"

"Like Ricky Young, again."

"Yeah, like Ricky."

Rachel piped up, "Ricky? That's the one whose funeral you went to when we were still in New York?"

Yonny nodded, "That's the one. Really sad." He looked away, watching the colors move across the field, then turned back. "Sam, what can we do? Is there anything we, Rachel and I, can do? For others, I mean? Mutual support organizations, that sort of thing?"

"There are, I'm sure. Let me check around for you."

"Thanks, but I'm thinking maybe something more direct, maybe we can do more good one-on-one?" Yonny sought out Rachel's eyes, but her face was fixed forward. "Anyone at risk, someone we might know, someone we could help, Rachel and I?"

Rachel darted her eyes back, "How, Yawny? Get down on our knees and confess to being the worst parents ever, beg them to not be the same?"

"Quiet down, Rachel!" rasped Yonny as heads turned in the seats below. He took advantage of a long kickoff run by one of the Mules to clap and cheer. Still clapping, he leaned over, "No, Rachel, no. But we have been through something, an experience that might help others. That's all I'm saying."

"And all I'm saying is I'm sick of being stared at, whispered about behind my back, people saying '*She's from New York, what do you expect?*' I'm sick of it, Yonny!" She paused, caught her breath and continued, "I'm still expecting to see Jeffy come slouching down the stairs every morning to inhale his breakfast. I still want to have to stop him so I can tuck in his shirttail in the back before he goes to school. I still want him to surprise me with who his next date is, to call her mother and laugh about our wayward children, or worry about him and her if I don't know her family. Damn it, Sam, I still want to cringe every time I hear tires squealing on the Boulevard on a Saturday night! I still want all that but I don't have it any more. I want it back, Sam, I want it back. And now, Yonny, somehow it's going to help to tell that to someone else? Someone who…" That was all for her. She slumped forward, chin on fists.

Yonny looked at Sam and shrugged his shoulders. "Still think it's a good idea. Maybe we can…"

He was interrupted by someone calling Sam's name. A younger woman in scrubs under her parka came up the aisle to their right. "Sam! Did I miss it? I had to stay over my shift, we had a car wreck. Did I miss it?" She stopped short when she saw Rachel sitting close to her husband, his arm over her shoulders. "Sam?"

He stood and pointed to Rachel. "Rachel Jonas, her husband Yonny. It's their son's investigation I've been working on. Rachel, Yonny, meet my wife Linda. She's an ER nurse at Northeast Baptist. Explains her clothes."

He was relieved when he saw her relax and say sweetly, "Oh, so nice to meet you. Sam talks a lot about you two and your boy. Actually, he hardly talks about anything else." This last carried a bit of grit mixed with the sugar. "So sorry for your loss. We see too many of those, well… we do."

Rachel mumbled, "Thank you." Then she turned to her husband and said tersely, "Yonny, we should go. The girls will be home soon."

Yonny stepped around Sam and stooped over Rachel, lifting her. They shuffled off without a wave.

Linda stared at Sam. "Well, so they're the famous parents of the famous dead boy? It's kinda good to see other people have problems, right?"

7

Rachel had had enough, enough of the daily reminders of Jeffy, who would never come back, and maybe just of her husband, who she wasn't sure she knew anymore. So, despite the motherish terrors she was sure awaited her, she caught a flight to La Guardia. After two days of those motherish terrors she decamped across town to her grandmother's apartment on Amsterdam. Nana was much more simpatico, more understanding of her need for a little time, for a little peace and quiet.

A light drizzle clings to everything, the curbs, the newspaper boxes, the black London Fog trenchcoat walking toward Lexington Avenue. Clutching his collar closer, the wearer times his steps as a town car turns the corner, then stops. A well-dressed man helps his well-dressed companion out, the figure hangs back. The passenger closes the door, the black cloak quickens its pace.

The doorman exchanges pleasantries as he opens the right-hand leaf into the lobby. He starts as someone comes up behind him. Trench-coat man smoothly pulls a longbarreled gun from a side pocket, pressing it to the other's temple. Turning sharply into the entryway, he slams the doorman's head against the wall. Then shows the pistol.

Quickly now through the vestibule, matching his steps to the couple ahead of him. Without stopping he raises the pistol and shoots, twice apiece, then once more, head shots into each of the bodies sprawled on the floor.

Drawing the brim of his fedora down and wheeling sharply, he points his gun at the doorman. Through the vestibule to the entry saying, "Don't say a goddamned thing..." Then on the sidewalk, turning north, half-turning once just to keep the doorman honest.

Rachel sobbed over the phone; it was after three, Texas time. Yonny tried to make out her muffled wailings. “Terrible, Yonny, it’s terrible! It’s… Donny. He’s gone, dead.” Several minutes passed, Yonny straining to make sense of the rustlings in the silence. “Mother, well, she’s off the wall, really, really bad. And Daddy, he’s… he’s scared. I can tell, he doesn’t want to let on, but he’s at least worried.” She was quiet again. “It has to be that casino down in Jersey, which means it’s his old mob business. I can’t get him to talk about it.”

She lapsed into another silence, then collected herself. “I need you, Yonny, I really do.”

He went to get his OAG in his study. Flipping through it, he said, “Earliest we can get there is… four. You do want me to bring the girls, yes?”

“Of course. They have to come.”

“All right, I’ll call the school tomorrow morning.”

“Hurry, Yonny, hurry.”

8

"Yeah, thanks, Yawny. Appreciate the call and give your wife my sympathies, she's been, well, y'all have been through a lot. Let me know if I can help out down here. Yeah, right, okay, see you when you get back." He swiveled his chair around and let his head droop between his knees, massaging his temples. *Man, I need the break. This damned kid thing has just about taken over my life. And just about ruined it.*

Sam and his wife were on the rocks, and this drug, now murder business hadn't helped a bit, not one damned bit. Things hadn't been so bad, not for long. Four years coming up, but Linda wanted children, wanted them right away, her age and all. Sam was game, too, even at his age, had been more than willing, but they had not been able to conceive, not so far. Linda thought it was her, had several difficult sessions, expensive ones with expensive specialists. Nothing had turned up with her plumbing. Ironically, for a guy who had been around a lot, it turned out to be Sam's problem, the result of his run-in with five black thugs and a hammer almost twenty years earlier. At least there was a sense of relief from not knowing who or what.

Their pastor had been very supportive, was probably the glue that had kept them together for months when he and she had been doubting, questioning. A year and a half or so ago, he brought them into his study after church one brilliant, bright Sunday morning with good news, he said. *"God has delivered unto me, and unto you, a message, a solution, not exactly a virgin birth, but serviceable just the same."* He chuckled slightly at this last, then, *"Just yesterday, as I was writing my sermon, no, well, more like wrestling with the demons keeping me from finishing it, a miracle occurred. Through that very threshold,"* pointing behind them, *"came our miracle. A young woman, not a regular, but her mother is, she walks in with Mom and confesses to her sins. She's three months pregnant, not quite sure who the father is—she's only sixteen, you see, was arguing with her mother about an abortion. I tried not to preach,"* he smiled, seeing their grins, *"just explained to her what a sin is the taking of an innocent unborn life, a life that had not even had the chance, the opportunity, to draw breath, squint against the bright lights, open its little mouth and let loose a roar, 'Here I am, world! You'd better get ready for me!'*

"I think that last little bit did the trick. I brought them down into prayer, and lo and behold, when we arose, she was a changed child. She looked at her mother and said, 'I'll do it, Mommy, I will.' To me she turned and said, 'Do you have someone? If I'm gonna do it, I want to see who'll be... be taking care of him, or her.'

"Of course I was thinking of you two, but before I could get past even a nod, she said, 'Good. Let them know, then. And Preacher,' she changed again, like a chameleon, 'don't think for a goddamn minute all your Jesus stuff and your shaggy whiteboy God had anything to do with this. Just made me want to make sure it, the baby, will be loved.' She turned toward her mother, scowling, 'Not like me.'

"She bolted from the room, just like that. 'She's a hard case,' said her mother. 'I've tried, Lord knows I've tried, but...' She sighed the sigh of the weary and oppressed. 'Lucy jes' grew up too fast, got too pretty and all womanlike before her time, before she knew what all that did to men...'

"I consoled her, or tried to, but Dear God, I do hereby confess I did try to get her out of there as quick as I could. So, now you know. Yes, the girl is a hard case, I'm sure, but something tells me she'll go through with it. Now I'm going to let you go talk with Brother Raymond. There's a sh—... a load of paperwork to go through, but it'll get done. God means for it to get done, that was the sign from yesterday. Just think about it and give us your answer, if y'all are ready for this, I mean. Now, please join me in prayer."

The next six months were the smoothest sailing in any of Sam's marriages, he thought, blissful, even. And even when Linda insisted on shopping for baby stuff, he went along without protesting too much unless the Cowboys were on. Even when he started having second thoughts, cold feet, he never let on, kept it to himself, he could see how much it meant to her. After all, she was a lot younger, still a good-looking woman, could find another man easy, one with working equipment if he let her down on this. And they met with the mother-to-be several times, finding her not nearly the hard case they expected. If anything, she cozied up to Linda like the loving mother she never had, or claimed she never had.

So, the shock when they first were allowed into her hospital room to see her cradling a healthy pink baby boy and she tells them she's keeping him, so they can just run right along. No sorry, no excuses, no nothing. Just get out of their lives.

Sam wiped a tear from each eye. *A year ago, was it? And neither of us has recovered yet, not fully, not me, at least*. But he submerged much of it in his work, plenty of stress there, plenty enough to keep him from remembering, not all the time, at least. And plenty enough to keep him working the hours, keep him from home, from facing her. *She, well, she took it really hard. But so did I. I still do. You walk in expecting to be holding this little thing on your chest and what? Get out!* He stopped that train of thought, abruptly jerking his head to the ceiling, cracking sounds popping from his neck. *That's it. I, we, lost a son, just like Yonny and Rachel. We both lost our sons. That's it. Maybe that's why…*

His phone interrupted him. It was some lady whose poodle had been stolen, she was sure, *and could he send some people out to look for it?* He didn't have the heart to tell her a coyote had probably got to it first, but sure, he would tell his patrolmen to be on the lookout. She kept on with her prattling about Precious Pooh, or whatever its name was, as he cradled the receiver with his shoulder and opened the bottom drawer. He twisted the cap off, leaned over to take a sniff, then capped it again and closed the drawer. "Yes, Ma'am, we'll get right on it. You keep calling for him, okay? It's a she? Okay, keep calling for her. 'Bye."

The drawer opened itself.

9

Donny's services were held at Esther's sister's synagogue across the Jersey line in Pennsylvania. Miriam had objected mightily—*too far, too long, why not here in Queens even if it had to be Conservative?*—but it wasn't her decision. Just one more aspect of her son's life that Esther had usurped, taken over. Friends, business, where he lived and how he dressed, now even unto death.

On the drive down the Turnpike with Manny and Rebekah, her brother shared the latest on their mother. "She's losing it, Rachel, you've seen it, admit it, you'll see it even more today, from now on. Maybe early Alzheimer's, maybe, well, maybe some other form of dementia. Stuart Rudofsky over at Mount Sinai—you remember Stewie, he sure remembers you—says it's too early to be definitive, but it's coming, Sis."

To Rachel, her mother hadn't changed, was as difficult as ever, still the same. *Just another straw being placed on my back. Great, just great. First Jeffy, then Donny and now Mother? And my husband?*

Yonny saw her jaws work, clenching and releasing, over and over, her brows knitting, thought of holding her close, then thought better of it.

He vaguely recalled the synagogue, Beth Shalom, from architectural history class years before. One of Frank Lloyd Wright's late designs, it reminded him of a Mongol's cap, earflaps along the edge, a roof tapering to a peak like some sort of Samurai's helmet crest. Closer, he noted the six points—menorah points?—ascending the ridges toward the peak, the use of Fiberglas for the sloping roof panels.

Inside, the sanctuary was reasonably full. Miriam was wedged securely between Rachel and Solomon, fidgeting and muttering the entire service. *That bitch Esther. This should never have happened.*

These horrible people! Solly tried squeezing her knee repeatedly, then simply shrugged at Rachel.

She wasn't discomfited, had been away too long to care what others thought, didn't know most of these people anyway, just annoyed at her mother more than anything. From time to time she stole glances at her girls beside her, caught them jerking toward this or that muffled grandmotherly outburst, uncomprehending concern on their faces. Then she turned to Yonny. *He's staring straight ahead, avoiding me. What's wrong with him, with us…?* Miriam rumbled something about the decorating just as they stood to leave. *Finally!*

At the reception afterwards back home in Forest Hills, Rachel steeled herself for a confrontation when she saw her grandmother and her mother squaring off. Unexpectedly, blessedly, the friction and the anger just weren't there, *not today, at least*. Nana was still sharp at 91, probably saw her daughter's condition more clearly than anyone, probably mustered more compassion and understanding in the next two hours than over the past forty or fifty years.

In a lull, Solomon came over to Yonny, turning him about and taking him into the sunroom at the rear of the house. "We gotta talk about these stores, Ian. Stooky, that's Merrill Raab, he's ready to do the deal, ready to go. Got it all teed up with his board. 'Cept I gotta tell him yes or no, you see? And I can't tell him yes and then turn around and tell him we ain't got the money. So tell me what you're doin' wit' that buddy of yours."

"Solly, is this what we should be discussing, I mean, at this time, with all this, Donny and all?" For the first time, Yonny saw something in his father-in-law's eyes that wasn't opaque, granite-like. Something that just might have been fear. "Solly," he began quietly, "is this mob business? I don't know what else to call it, but is it? I never asked, didn't want to know, but is it? Because if it is…"

Solomon grunted, "Yeah. Some of it is."

"You worried?"

"No."

"True?"

"Yeah, well, some."

He was unsure how to proceed, how far to push the older man. He had made a point all these years of avoiding the obvious, keeping as far from the money spigots in New York as possible, letting the lawyers up there handle the closings, the fundings and transfers, everything. For all he knew, for all his rationalizing, the various and anonymous limited partnerships and trusts that were their partners were pension funds or widows'-and-orphans' benefits or family offices. *Well, maybe not that kind of family. Didn't want to know, never wanted to know, even though you knew pretty damned well, Yonny. Just found the deals, ran the properties, made the numbers work and that was plenty fine with me.*

"Did the… mob… Donny?"

The older man just looked down, another first.

"So, yeah. You know that's pretty scary to me, for Rachel and the kids…"

Solomon bristled, "You think I don't know? You think I don't care?"

"Shhh, Solly, shhhh. Of course you do. But Rachel, the kids? Any threat?"

"Before now, no, not at all. But with Donny gone, you gotta be the point, kid. Your name on the line. When you left New York, you basically disappeared. You've just been my guy down there. Now, if we're gonna get the stores—and believe me, they want them—well, it's on you. You see, Donny got… whacked… 'cause of no discipline, too high a profile, too glitzy, that damned Esther. Not enough discipline on my part, too. They don't like that, don't like it at all."

He gestured to a chair and pulled another closer to the windows. "You see, our… associates… have financial advisors, too, y'know, say they need more deals like this, not just real estate. And they dress nice, too, unnerstand? And so do their wives and girlfriends. They're already talking about Paris and, and, what's that fashion place in Italy, Mellanno?" By now Solly was lapsing deeper and deeper into his roots, each sentence descending a dozen cross streets, traversing the years. Pretty soon he'd be more Yiddish than English, then Polish, maybe even some *szurzhyk. Hard enough to understand him normally.*

He continued, "Never wanted you in this, this deep. Yeah, I wanted you to come to work here, help keep Donny straight and all, but not this, none of this. That's why I let Rachel go to Texas with you." He stifled an objection with a paw. "Figured you couldn't screw up too bad down there, not like Donny." He sighed, "What's done is done. Ashes to ashes. Gotta go on living. Harder on you, 'specially Rachel, with all this death. Not easy on me, neither, or her mother, who's another tale of woe. Least I seen it before. My father, my brothers…"

"Solly?"

"Yeah, my kid sister Anna, too." He looked up and motioned to a waiter. "Another rye and soda." He quieted down until his drink came, but was fidgeting, almost palsied. He took a sip and carried on, "Y'know, everyone says the Nazis were the worst, and they was monsters after I left, sure, and when I found 'em at the end of the war, too," now thinking back to those days in Łódź in the Thirties, "but the Poles was just as damned bad. Some of 'em come to our quarter, in their black uniforms, smartasses they was, grab old Moise, the rag man, by the *payots*," he gestured to his temple, "the sidecurls, drag him into the street, make him lick their boots—he must have been eighty—then they plug him,"—pointing again to his temple, pulling his imaginary trigger—"then went looking for more. Simon and me, well, we was hotbloods, well, hotheads, maybe, we went to warn my family—he didn't have none, was an orphan, lived from place to place —well, two of 'em come in our building, start up to our floor and…"

He stopped to pull out his handkerchief, resting it on the bridge of his nose a good while. When he was able to resume, haltingly, sighing, "We didn't have no guns, Jews wasn't allowed, but we had our knives, and, well, we got 'em. Don't ask me how. Was this broom closet behind, under the stair, we stuffed 'em in there, then run back upstairs."

Solomon Polsky was now in a different realm, as real to him at this moment as it was sixty years before. "We was coming down the stairs, Father and me brothers and Anna, when the rest of 'em come in. Five of 'em, in their pretty uniforms. Then I recognize one of 'em from school, Wladislaw, it was, think he'll help, but no. One of these guys notices the blood coming out under the closet door, opens it, their friends fall out. Then they starts shooting. My father, my brothers. Si and I jump on 'em, roll two of 'em out the doors onto the street. Kill 'em. Slit their throats like they was pigs." His face was screwed up in sheer, dark hatred. "Then the others come out, shooting wild, pulling Anna along. We start after them but have to duck down. They jump into a truck, keep shooting at us and drive off.

"Then we hear the police sirens—they wasn't no friends, neither, just as bad. I start to run again after Anna but Si pulls me into the alley, away from the bullets just missing us, and we run."

He slumped in his chair, his bulk now seemingly deflated, flaccid. "We run all the way to America, Yonny, Ian, boy. We run away and left Anna. She was eleven, almost twelve, looked just like your little girls. And I left her, never saw her again. Never saw her again, don't know what happened to her. Probably..."

He straightened, then slumped back again. "Got leave after the war to look for her in the camps, but the damn Reds were even worse than the Poles and the Nazis." He clutched his handkerchief again, burying his face in it. "Not s'posed to break down in front of a son-in-law," he offered weakly. Now abruptly standing, "And that's why I won't let anything happen to my Rachel and her girls. You have my word." He clamped his hand onto Yonny's. "My word."

All Yonny could do was stammer, "Sol, Solomon, Sir, I appreciate this..."

"No, you don't. You don't got no fuckin' idea. But you make this happen, good and all, and you'll be fine. We'll all be fine."

Great. No pressure here. How did I get into this? Why did I get into this? Thinking I could pull this off? Be honest with yourself, Ian. Sarah? History? Is that what this is all about?

He started as Rachel interrupted his ruminations. "Daddy?" A bit cooler, "Yonny? Daddy, are you two talking about Donny?" She saw something in her husband's eyes. "The stores? Don't tell me it's about Sarah!"

As Solomon gaped at his daughter, Yonny said softly, "Sol, please let your child, here, in on what we're up against. I'm checking on the girls." He spun unsteadily on one heel and was gone.

10

The secretary stole the occasional glance at the big good-looking guy in a nice suit whose glances at her neckline sometimes crossed hers. *She's playing with me, making me wait half an hour out here, but I don't mind, nothing wrong with the view.*

The intercom buzzed and a voice laden with small gravels came through, "Lupe? If he's still here, let him in, please."

The District Attorney had a pretty nice office, decorated politician-style, photos of her with local and some national movers and shakers, diplomas from Southwest Texas and St. Mary's shoved off to a corner. *What counts, for a politician, I guess,* mused Sam as he raised a hand in greeting.

She barely looked up from her papers, waving to a seat opposite. "Okay, Sam, what is it this time?"

"Rape."

"Rape? Is that the big deal you said? Don't you cops ever follow procedures, file a complaint? I don't see one here," waving at stacks and strews of files and forms, "so why are *you* here?"

Allison Walker, Esq. and Sam Thompson clashed almost from the day each took up their respective positions, despite knowing each other pretty damned well in high school. Sam had been surprised at her reaction to him when they worked their first case together. He thought maybe it was because he was a dropout cop and she had just passed the bar, or maybe because he had made fun of her clothes, her hair, way back when, harmlessly like friends will do, he always thought. *Or maybe it was that one time in the back seat?*

He was brought back with a sharp comment. "Sam? Do we have something here or not? If not, get your sorry ass out of here, okay?"

She was smiling, *but then, she always smiled when she sunk the icepick in the ol' cerebellum.*

"Yeah, yeah, okay. I'm going to keep this on a confidential level, you'll see why." Walker frowned, but he kept on, "Just wait, okay? Alright, there's a divorce up in our part of town. I'm told it could be pretty messy. But," he tried to form his words precisely, never his strong suit, "there is an allegation of… forcible intercourse. The husband forced himself on the wife…"

"Has she brought charges?"

"No, not yet, at least."

"So come back when she does. Or better yet, follow procedures next time, okay? Is that it? And don't screw this one up if you do come back."

Sam had almost forgotten the Mansfield case, a double murder, her foulup with the evidence and the perp's accusation of Sam's use of excessive force. *So I popped the guy a few times, so what? She made like I screwed up the whole thing when she messed up the evidence, needed a fall guy. Me.* "Don't worry, Pookie,"—he knew she hated the nickname—"it won't be me this time. But I need a restraining order. Is that too goddamned much to ask?"

She leaned across the desk, pointing her finger at him. "Normally, for you, yes." Relaxing back into her chair, steepling her fingers, "Okay, I'll play. For now. Who are we talking about?"

"Sarah Langefelter, Goodman, now."

Allison's face wrinkled up like a Shar Pei's. "I figured. The dirt gets shoveled around, y'know?" Now she was smiling broadly, all friendly-like. "Well, isn't that just too damned bad, Sam? That rich stuck-up Jew? Her and her fancy clothes, perfect hair, perfect fingernails, fancy new car, all that stuff? Thought she was some hot stuff, Spur, yearbook editor and all?"

Sam now recalled that date. *Chaps uniforms were a lot easier to get off than the fancier Spurs' getups, at least I figured they were, never had that opportunity.* "I don't remember her that way, not at all. She was always pretty nice to me."

"Not to me, Sam. And parading around with Yonny Jonas like they were royalty?" If an Anglo girl's face could tan instantly, hers did, blood darkening it up. "Well, well, well. What goes around. So she's got problems? Too goddamned bad, just too goddamned bad." She stood and rounded the corner of her desk, pointing to the door.

"Fill out the paperwork, Sam, I'll get you a TRO. But the rape charge? She probably got what was coming to her. Get out of here."

11

The twins squabbled and sulked up until the very moment they buckled their seatbelts and accepted their Cokes and snacks from the stewardess. He had sprung for first class as a sort of small token of appreciation for their impeccable manners and behavior while all about them were losing their heads back in Queens. Looking across the aisle at them peeling open their cookies and peanuts, he couldn't help thinking, *like giving glass beads to the natives*. He smiled, then turned his head to the window and gave himself a gift, a deep sleep.

Once home, he made a point not to pester Sam Thompson as he had the last few months, non-stop. *We both need some time away from each other, from the case, the investigation. Okay. A few days.*

Craning his head into the stairwell, he whistled; in no time, girls and dogs came bounding down the stairs in search of their favorites from Teka Molina—bean cup, guacamole cup, two puffy bean-and-cheese tacos, their customary doses of basic nutrition. Before the girls could finish arranging their plates, the kitchen phone rang.

Rhea head faked her sister to reach it first. "Hello? Oh. Yes. May I say who is calling, please? One moment, then. Dad, for you. It's Mrs. Goodman." She handed him the phone with a shrug then dashed across to the counter where Patches was threatening a taco.

"Hi, Sarah, what's up? No, no, nothing wrong with…" he squinted at one girl disappearing into the dining room, "Rhea, no, nothing. I think she was disappointed it wasn't a certain young man they're pursuing."

A chorus of '*Dad! Please!*' rang through the void.

"Yes, that's what it is. Who? Edward Brady, Sally's boy. Which one? Both, they're identicals, you know."

He listened a minute or two then, "Well, no, I don't think… well, okay," he lowered his voice, "but wouldn't it be better in the daytime?

"Okay, after they go to bed, then. But I can't leave them here alone for long."

He hung up the phone quietly and loosed a long, gentle sigh.

It occurred to him that he hadn't made this walk in *what, almost thirty years, no, twenty-nine? Not since I walked her home after our graduation party.* He smiled to himself. *It was four or five in the morning. Has it really been that long? Means another reunion coming up. Time…*

A car came speeding behind him on the Boulevard, then roared away, startling him for just a moment, then again as a police car came careening around the curve, siren wailing. *Great, just great. Witnesses.*

A few minutes later he was at her front door. Sarah opened it, taking his hand and walking him into the living room. He had been here, at parties and dinners and such, but the place, the setting never failed to remind him of those halcyon days of senior year, the whole world spread wide before him, her, their friends. And the gnawing sense of impending loss, knowing the calendar was turning and reeling ineluctably toward destinies beyond knowing as all would be flung fluttering into the gusts of change, of new lives. He marveled even today that the feeling persisted, and seeing Sarah again, every time, only brought it back so very vividly.

"Well, Sweetie, what do you think?"

"Hmmm? Sorry, just daydreaming. Think about what?"

"Where to start? What will I have to do to get this place ready to sell?"

"Sell? Why?"

"It's much too big for… for the three of us. And too expensive. The taxes are horrendous. And the water bill for the pool and the lawn, well… And I just don't see myself doing much entertaining again, sadly. Daddy wants me to find something smaller, more manageable." She looked up at him, the stress of the past weeks obviously having affected her, but not dimming her luminous gray-green eyes. "He thinks as much to get rid of the memories as anything."

"He may be right. And what does your mother say?"

"The usual. I can't do anything right, I'm such a disappointment, all that stuff. She's not being very helpful."

"Sounds like Rachel's mother. Without the dementia, I hope?"

Her voice quavering a bit, "Sometimes I think… well, you can guess what I think, you always could. Come, let's walk through the place."

It took a bit less than an hour. The house was an early postwar contemporary, not a typical ranchburger, but a long, low, rambling California architect's design, custom built and fitted out inside. The air conditioning system was surprisingly archaic, though, even for a fifty-year-old house, and was due for replacement anyway. The rest of the interior could use a few cosmetic upgrades, and the electrical service was on the light side, but that was about it.

"I'll have to come back another day to look at the outside and the foundation."

"Okay with me. Glass of wine, Yonny?"

"Just a tetch. I don't like leaving the girls alone."

"That's what I love about you, you and Rachel. How much you love your children, would do anything for them, just like me. Among other things."

"Among other things?"

She set her glass aside on the end table and took Yonny's nearest hand in both hers. "I was so happy back then to hear you were making the move home from New York, the same time as we were. And so delighted to know Rachel was due just a little before I was." Jeffrey and her Arabella were two months apart; if anything, daughter was even more beautiful than mother, *if that were humanly possible*, he thought, as he felt a web closing around him.

The two couples hadn't interacted very much, hardly at all, those few overlapping years in the city, Sarah living up in the Seventies, Rachel and Yonny homesteading lower down in the loft building he and some friends had rehabbed. And synagogues were different, friends were different and the pain had never really subsided, flaring each time they met. He had avoided her, to be truthful, it was just not comfortable. Not just for him, for both of them, or so he imagined at the time.

"And why weren't Jeffy and Arabella ever a couple?"

Sarah had been running a finger idly over his hand, now looked up. "You know why."

"Not sure I do, unless…"

"Unless. Except. Because. All the reasons why." Her eyes watered. "Daddy and Louie discouraged it, but you need to know, Rachel needs to know, that she wanted to, so much, so many times. She was so, so disappointed she didn't get the role in the play, she said she wanted people to say they're in love." That brought forth a small giggle, then another, "And she was so jealous of Daphne when the Porterhouses moved in across the street from you. She wanted to sing with Jeffy to each other from their balconies, all Romeo and Juliet." Remembering something, she paused to recover a breath. Suddenly more serious now, "Daddy was all about the Jewish thing, saw what we went through, maybe even realized what he put you through, just didn't want her getting serious about someone who wasn't Jewish, just like back then. He saw how we were, you know, I think it scared him, it scared him a lot. A lot. Louie was just jealous. Didn't want your boy, or you, hanging around." She sighed, "He knew all about us, of course, not that it mattered much."

"It did matter much, Sarah. It mattered a lot."

She looked deeply into those same bright blue eyes from long ago. "I know it did, Yonny, I know it did. I know it does, now, even all these years later." She turned her head, shuddering slightly as she did. "Something happened, just this week. Something, well, I was sitting on the floor in the den, trying to separate out my books from his when Arabella came in with my Olmos."

"The perfect yearbook, the perfect editor, the perfect year."

"1968? It was a terrible year, Yonny, horrible, you know that. Except where we were concerned, blissfully unawares, so much in love."

"True." He tried not to flinch from the pain. "The Olmos was still pretty perfect, though. So was its editor."

"Thank you, but… Anyway, Arie comes in and sits down on the floor with me and opens the yearbook—she had marked a page—and says, '*Mommy, is there any chance you and Jeffy's daddy could ever, well, could ever get together? Again, I mean?*' "

"I laughed, giggled, really, '*Only over Rachel's dead body. No, that wasn't very nice. No, Sweetie, he is very happily married to her and she's probably my closest friend in the whole wide world. And they've been through so, so much.*' "

'*So have we, Mommy.*'

"Yonny, I was having real trouble keeping it together, but I managed to respond, '*Yes, we have, but I'm not about to see another family torn apart. Not by me.*' I looked at her, '*Why are you asking, Sweetie?*' "

'*Because I read what he wrote in your yearbook, Mommy. Mommy, he really loved you.*'

That did it; the floodgates opened. She threw her arms around his neck, burying her head in his chest. He dropped his face to the lush crown of her head. *Her scent, just like it was back then.* He let her cry on a while, then gently raised her up. "I have to go, Sarah."

"No, please?"

"Yes, I really do. I've left the girls too long. Probably having a junior high orgy by now. You remember those, don't you?"

She slapped his chest gently. "You know better."

"Yes, I do, unfortunately."

She leaned against him, then retreated with a long sigh. "Yes, I suppose you should go. I've kept you far too long."

They rose and walked straight to the front door. He reached for the lever, was about turn it when she stayed his hand. "No, no, Yonny, please don't go. I, I'm so sorry, so sorry…"

"What about, Sarah?"

"How I hurt you back then. I know I did, I knew I was, but…"

"You explained it all, Sarah. Your father and all, but I knew better, all this time I've known better. You just got tired of me, wearied of me, we were just too far away from each other, Dallas to Boston, to make it work, to keep it going, all those things. I thought you had just gotten lazy with our memories, let them slip, I just sort of fell out of your heart, ebbed away out of your life." He leaned down, a head taller than her, and gently cupped his hands to her wet cheeks. "It just wasn't ever going to work out. I could tell, your tone over the phone had changed, your letters weren't the same. I knew what was coming. And was powerless to stop it. That was always my curse, Sarah. I could make girls fall in love with me," he laughed hoarsely and quietly, "it was just that I couldn't keep them in love with me. That's actually how I met Rachel, on the rebound. Thank my lucky stars it's worked so far. Now I've got to go. I'll call, come by tomorrow to look around outside."

"No, please?" She began to pull up her tee shirt, one of those sequin-decorated French things. He stopped her, but not before she had pulled it above her bra. He looked down on a perfect pair, thought about it for just a moment, then leaned over to kiss the top of each one, pulling her shirt back down as he stood straight.

He pulled her close, then let his gaze drift upward through the glass walls to the live oaks beyond shimmering with the light from the pool dancing amidst the voids of their tangled branchings. "I've always had this image, Sarah," not looking down, "of this, well, I guess, this river, the River of Life, or Time, you could call it, if we wanted to get all pretentious about it. Wide and dark with a strong current like the rippling muscles of a racehorse, ropy like that, contained within its banks. And we move, all of us, in the river, not on our own, sometimes touching, more often just carried along. Sometimes, some of us are rocks, boulders, obstinate, defying the flow, for a time at least, mostly we're just flotsam afloat in the current at the river's whim, at its pace, not our own, whatever we might imagine that to be." He looked down at her, "You were a boulder once and you caught this forlorn bit of debris and held him, held him tight, so tightly, for a while. All too briefly, then the current shifted and the river swept him away. And I think at that point the river swept you away, yes?"

"Yes, yes, it did."

"Yes, it did, both of us and the current has tossed us about ever since, disconnected, bobbing about in its turbulence, life's turbulence. We can't fight the current, Sarah, if we try, we'll tire and drown. That's what happens. So let's not fight it, okay?" He kissed her lightly on the forehead. "That's it, Sarah. I'll be back." He opened the door and slipped from her grasp. "And I won't forget you. I never have and I never will." Then he disappeared across the driveway.

The walk home was a lot longer, down her street and up under the oaks on La Jara, then over. He walked slowly, contemplatively, reprising thirty years in those few blocks. *Do I still want her after all these years? Have I ever stopped wanting her? Is it just her, so pretty, so sexy and... seductive? What? And Rachel? Good God, who am I? Is this what happens to people like us, we just, just fly apart?*

Next morning, he bumbled about with the twins' breakfasts and just managed to get them to the Junior High before first bell. After fiddling about at his office with several files, signing some checks, the usual humdrum, he turned and stared at the telephone. Jerking abruptly to pick it up, he dialed a number. "I can come by in half an hour, would that work?"

"Angela, I've got some things to do, then lunch. What else do I have?"

"Just those engineers at four. Promise not to tell them how to do their work again, okay?"

"Who, me?"
"Uh, huh."

Parking half a block down the street, he looked both ways—*incognito, right, Yawny?*—and jogged up the steps, twirling his finger at the bell, then ringing it. Sarah opened the door, taking him by the hand. "Welcome back, stranger, long time no see." She rose up on tiptoes to give him a small kiss on the cheek, then pushed him gently away. "So, where do you want to start today?"

Yonny stifled a thought and more than a twinge. "Outside. I'll take a look at the foundation, the roof, what I can see of it. Make sure there aren't any drainage issues, those sorts of things." He tapped his clipboard. "Making a list."

"Okay, then. Start out back?"

He followed her, admiring the view—khaki shorts, slender legs, narrow waist, the full head of mahogany hair. *Down, boy.* The inspection didn't take too long, a couple of minor stairstep cracks, to be expected in a house of this age in these soils, some downspout issues, overhanging oak branches. "Pretty clean bill of health, Sarah. Nothing you need to worry about right now. Who's listing it for you?"

"Sally, who else? Starts next week, once I get my act together on the inside. Would you like some coffee before you go?"

He nodded and sat on a stool by the kitchen table, watching her, watching her every move.

Everything set and working, she turned around and began, "Yonny, I'm so, so sorry about last night. I made such a…" The look on his face stopped her.

He awoke from a light and dreamless sleep. Sarah's head rested on his bare chest, bobbing lightly with his breathing. He looked at the ceiling a good fifteen minutes or so, then gently lifted her head and turned her onto the pillow next to him. Dressing in haste, as quietly as he could, he slipped down the hall. Locking the front door from the inside, he pulled it gently closed, muting the click of the lock.

As he pulled into the parking garage, his radio, set to KONO, started with Billy Joel's *She's Always a Woman*. He sat there, sat through the whole song, his head sagging against the steering wheel. *Yes, she is. He wrote that song for her. For both of them.*

Angela was off to lunch, he guessed. *She left me a message on my chair. Her way of marking it urgent. Arnie. Well, he'll just have to wait.*

"Took you long enough, Sweetie. I thought you might have abandoned me." Sarah stood in the doorway wearing a pink robe, her hair wrapped in a towel.

He had just started to take a step inside when she stopped him with a palm to his chest. "No, Yonny, no. Never again. I can't have you in this house alone with me. Not ever again." She saw the pain of surprise in his face. "You know why, Yonny. I wouldn't be able to stop myself. Not where you're concerned. And we can't have that, as much as we might want it. I'm not going to betray your Rachel. And certainly not going to betray you. So, just stay there and listen to me, please?"

She snugged the robe around her. "Yonny, did you think of me over the years? I know you've told me, but did you really, really think of me? You know I thought of you."

"Every day, Sarah, when I could stand to. When I could handle it."

"Me, too. I'm going to… this is terrible… I thought of you often and fondly, and sometimes more than just fondly. Yonny, on my wedding night…" She folded her arms and looked away. "And many more times after that. You?"

All he could do was nod.

"I thought so. I, well, I hoped so, all those years. I dreamt of you, you know, should know, would have given a Queen's ransom," she smiled slyly, "well, a Princess's ransom, after all, just to…" She dropped her head, then more gravely, "But when I heard you were getting married, it was a blow, a real blow. You were single so long. Why was that, Yonny?"

"You."

She frowned, saying simply, "I'm sorry, so sorry…"

"I wasn't exactly a hermit all that time, Sarah. And I did meet someone, and still sometimes wonder how it would have worked out. But that blew up spectacularly…"

"Yes, Rachel told me all about it. Your story is so dramatic, so romantic…"

"So was ours, Sarah."

Sarah just looked at him, then stroked his cheek and started again,

"Well, you were single a long time. I guess I was living a fantasy life alongside my real life, thinking somehow I would someday be free, free to be with you, that you would always be there, free, just waiting there for me when I needed you, whenever I was ready for you. But when we, Rachel and I, got pregnant, that was it. You made me grow up, Sweetie, made me, helped me to face life, the life I made, was making."

She released her palm. "Does any of this make any sense? Any sense at all?"

Yonny made the slightest of nods, so she continued, "Good. And when I finally got you alone, got you where I wanted you, last night, this morning—I was so happy to see you this morning, I could hardly contain myself—and when we…well, when we were one, as if we were fused together forever and always, holding you so tight, I realized something, something very important, so vital."

He croaked, "What was that, Sarah?"

"That I had freed myself from the past, our past. That all the longing and fantasizing and dull pain all those years, it was all swept away. And at that moment, or maybe when I woke up and you were gone," she made the merest of mock frowns, "I realized I, and I hope you, had everything we needed, ever wanted from each other. That we were now secret intimates, two lovers bound together forever, yet freed to go our own ways, freed of the burdens of not knowing, not being able to touch, no, well, knowing even though we could not be together, we *would* be together always, two kindred spirits. Two kindred spirits who knew each other for what we were, are, and accepted each other, and…"

She sighed. "I suppose that sounds like one of those silly romance novels I read at the beach. But it's not some idle fantasy, Yonny, it's the real thing. We are free to love others, well, you have Rachel and your girls, and I have my children, love them with all our hearts and souls, sure, but free to love each other. I will love you until I die, you rascal, you." She beamed up at him. "*Bashert.*"

"Hmmm?"

"Bashert. Yiddish, of course. Means destiny, also means soul mate. That's it! Soul mates, that's what we are, free to live in each other's hearts, hidden away somewhere behind the love for our families, safe, secure, in perp… in perpet… perpetually." She laughed lightly, then, and more seriously, "And one more thing, Yonny, and I never knew how important this was, but I know I can always trust you, completely, totally. I trusted you so much back then, trusted you to do the right thing by me, to protect me and comfort me, not take advantage of me, infatuated with you like I was." She giggled, then caught herself. "I only now remember that. Except for you, I've lost that trust, and I doubt if I'll ever regain it, not with any other man, any other than you. Bashert."

She took his hands. "Cat got your tongue, or just couldn't get a word in edgewise?"

He stood mute, then replied slowly, "Both, I guess. You said exactly what I came here to say, just so much better than I ever could. Captured me completely." He tried to muffle the catch in his throat with a small cough. "Thank you."

"We always did think alike."

"Yes, we did."

Sarah reached herself up to give him one more kiss, one last long, passionate kiss. Drained, she nestled against his chest until her breathing quieted. Looking up, "Yonny, I suppose we were just children back then, but I did love you so. I did, and I always will. I can't seem to say that too much, but it's true. And you?"

"Yes."

"Then we can let each other go because we do love each other so. That's a strange way of… well, of looking at life, isn't it? No, go, get out of here…" The lilting song of her laughter finished her sentence.

He sat for a moment in the car, trying to remember every last thing she said, every word, archiving it into memory. A sense of melancholy permeated him until a warm golden glow began suffusing within his chest. *Rachel.*

12

Something was eating at Sam, something that eluded him whenever his thoughts came close to the phantasm in his head. Something that gave him a bit of a chill even if he couldn't name it, even tried put a mental finger on it. Something that couldn't be, but just might be. Whatever it was, it was inside someone else's head, a place he didn't know how to reach. He thought of someone who might help, someone the department had hooked him up with after that nurse was stabbed and left for days to die in that field. That had really torn him up and for the first time in his career, his life, he had accepted help.

"Dr. Wolens, Sam Thompson, I worked with you after the DeWayne Gustus Foster case back in the '80's, you may not remember…

"You do? Well, thanks, I appreciate that. What I'm calling about is a friend of mine who's lost a child, a son, to a…," he paused, checking himself, "a drug overdose, all sudden like."

Sam cooled his heels a while in Wolens' waiting room until the door opened and a tall, very attractive woman stepped through, trailed by the doctor who gave him a furtive nod and finger salute. He escorted her through the entry into the elevator lobby, arm around her shapely waist. Sam strained to make sense of their muted conversation, then gave up.

"Officer Thompson—oh, no, I see, Detective Thompson. Congratulations on your promotion and… Alamo Heights? Keeping our sister city safe in these trying times?"

"Doing my best, Doc. Wouldn't be here if it were all peaches and cream, though." He squinted at the goatee, then, "I don't want to take too much of your time…"

"Of course. Come along, please. Magdalena, hold my calls, and stall Mrs. Shapiro a few minutes if…" The doctor smiled at her expression. "Yes, yes, I know, my dear, Canute stemming the tide. I, we'll do our best, won't we, Sam?"

His office was generic medical, the usual splay of diplomas and certificates on the walls, several pictures of the doctor posing with Spurs players and some woman Sam hoped wasn't his wife, for his sake. He looked around and opted for a chair over the couch; not wanting to linger longer, he launched into an abbreviated version of the case, then sat back.

Doctor Wolens looked out his window at Methodist, then turned back. "You see, Officer, Detective, rather, Thompson, Sam, neither you nor I nor anyone who hasn't actually experienced this type of loss, so magnified by the boy's youth and promise, none of us can truly comprehend any specific case. All we can do, my profession, that is, is to collect our observations over time. With enough of these observations we can construct certain theories…"

Sam felt a yawn coming on, stifled it. *This guy…*

Unaware, Wolens droned on a bit more in jargonish, then asked him, "Are you familiar with the name Dr. Elizabeth Kübler-Ross?"

Sam jerked, not sure whether he had drifted off, then shook his head.

"Yes, then, Dr. Kübler-Ross is a psychiatrist from Switzerland originally, now living over here, although she seems to have gotten off on a weird track—mediums, spirituality, that sort of bunk. But, in the sixties, she came out with what she called '*the five stages of grief*', which became, first, a useful model for our profession, then, as so often happens, adopted wholesale into popular culture and taken as gospel although no subsequent research has substantiated any of her hypothesis. But it still is useful, whether empirically proven or no. I find it a simple, clear model—I used that word, right?—a model that helps families, loved ones, others to deal with loss, simply because it is so clear and so simple."

He paused to tap the ashes from his pipe into his wastebasket, then began filling it. "Oh, I'm sorry, do you mind?"

Sam grinned. "Just so long as it doesn't smell like weed."

They both laughed as Wolens finished packing the tobacco, then lit up. Leaning back in his chair, "Ah, yes, where were we? The five stages. Let me give you them in the order Dr. Kübler-Ross stipulated: Denial, Anger, Bargaining, Depression, Acceptance. Think of your observations of your friend. I won't confuse you with any of our profession's gobbledygook, just think how he may or may not fit in."

Sam gave it a few moments' thought. "Denial, sure, he and his wife didn't want to believe it, at first. Even after they saw the body, don't think it really sunk in 'til later. Anger, dunno, not so much, but can't tell with him? Same thing with bargaining, but, well, he and I trade information, mostly my information. Does that count?" Wolens shrugged, so Sam continued, "Depression, yeah, that's really why I called, but he says he's been depressed all his life, mostly. Effect on him, hard to say, he keeps things pretty close. And hasn't brought her into it, his wife Rachel, not with me, so can't say about her. Finally, what was it?"

Wolens intoned, "Acceptance."

"Yeah, acceptance—he's pretty cool, well, pretty cold about it, when you get right down to it…."

The psychologist leaned first one way, then the other against the arms of his chair, trying to get comfortable with something not so comforting. "Cool? Cold?"

"Mmm, yeah, I guess so…"

"He was, he and his wife were upset, troubled, distraught at seeing their boy?"

"Sure…"

"Then he's calmed down, got 'cool' with it all?"

"Wouldn't say that."

"But is calmer?" Sam nodded back at the pipe. "And the depression? All his life? Really?"

"So he said."

"Detective, this is most troubling. You see, most of the… characters… we deal with, you and I, are possessed of or by something—anger, greed, the residue of past abuse or neglect, sometimes present, sometimes just the intense need to fit in with a crowd, usually a street gang, maybe a country club. Dangerous enough?"

"Yep."

"But it's the quiet ones, the ones in whom the emotions, the painful pasts, are submerged, sublimated is our buzzword, somewhere under that quiet surface is a drive, a resolve, a steely resolve, to act on a suppressed desire. Or worse, an inner demon, sometimes a whole tribe of demons tormenting them, prodding them, enraging them inside. It all builds up. These types, sometimes there is no safe outlet. Then the pressure cooker explodes one day. You said he keeps things close. Follow me on this?" Sam nodded, Wolens nodded back. "Tell me, and I don't expect you to have the answer, does the man in question have sexual issues?"

"He has the prettiest wife in town, for her age, that's for sure. And built like..." Sam caught himself, laughing nervously, "Now you'll think I have issues!"

"We all do, Detective, we all do!" Wolens threw up his hands in mock despair, then dodged away from some falling ashes. "No, sexual frustration is a powerful element in these types. But we'll set that aside, for now. Obviously this death, his, their loss, is preying on him..." His intercom squawked at him. "My next appointment, but just let me say, keep close tabs on this man. He could be displaying every indication of, well, you'll know what I mean by this, a cold-blooded, remorseless killer, vengeance being his driving force. Perhaps not today, not tomorrow, but the seed, the first hints seem to be there. I say this only because I have seen it many, many more times than I would like. It may be nothing, but, well, safe than sorry, you see?"

He rose and escorted Sam to the door. "And where might I see this wife of his?"

Sam glanced down at his notes, the 'stages', Wolens had called them, *maybe Linda and I, well, maybe we...* He jammed on the brakes just in time to avoid a rear-ender, then thought of turning his flashers on to get him through the intersection at Fredericksburg and Medical. *Last damned time I'll come out to the Medical Center at rush hour*. As he sat fuming quietly, he thought back on Dr. Wolens' words—*Cold, cool...*

He let his memory drift.

1978

It was a beautiful summer's morning, albeit already stiflingly hot. Not particularly busy on his shift, but it was a Sunday, after all. Churchgoers were about the only ones on the streets. The emergency tone on the radio broke Sam out of his trance.

'50 Mingo Road for a shooting with 2 hits. 2-5.'

He replied, '2-5 on the way.'

With emergency lights on and siren blaring, he made his way to a large lot he was familiar with, having passed it several times on every shift. He had seen bikers hanging out there on occasion.

There was only one house on the place, old and tired, in need of repair. He pulled up to the house and knocked on the door. Twice. No answer. The door was open so he walked in, service revolver at the ready, looking in each room for a victim. Seeing none, he walked out the back door into an unkempt back yard, weeds and trash everywhere.

He walked around the house just in time to see his section Sergeant helping a little girl of ten or eleven out of his patrol car. Sam holstered his pistol as he greeted Sergeant Barrientos and looked at the girl. "And who might you be, young lady?"

"My name is Mandy and I live here," she answered. "Are you looking for my Mama and Sister?" She began to cry.

Sam bent down to hug little Mandy. "Yes, Baby, I am. Can you tell me what happened?"

She placed her little hand into his and began leading him across to a sad, sandy part of the yard. There was blood, a lot of it, in two distinct puddles approximately three feet apart. She pointed to one and through her tears managed to say, "That's where he shot Mama." Then pointing to the other, "That's where he shot Sister."

Despite her sobbing, Sam could make out what she said. He bent down to hug her again. After a long pause, he asked her where 'he' might have taken Mama and her sister.

"He dropped them in the well," she cried. "I ran to the 'partments when he shot at me... b-b-but he missed."

"How do you know where he put them?"

"When he stopped shooting, I got down in the high grass and watched him." Now her little voice had more than a little child's anger in it, more like a grownup's. She showed Sam where the well was, covered with trash and dead branches.

"You've been a lot of help, Mandy, like a big girl. Would you like an ice cream cone?"

She giggled 'yes' and Sam motioned to the sergeant that they should leave.

Once they were safely away, Sam began removing the debris from the well. When it was all clear, he cupped his eyes so he could see better into the darkness. It took about two minutes before he could make out what appeared to be legs twenty feet or so below him. He sucked in a long breath and called Susie Wells, the dispatcher, told her what he had. She immediately dispatched the Fire Department to the scene to pull the bodies up and out of the well.

Two more officers arrived with an ambulance and fire truck close behind. As they were bringing the bodies up, a car, a civilian car, drove in the long driveway. Sam went to meet whoever it was to ask them to leave and certainly not to come any closer.

In the car were Mandy's grandparents. The grandmother asked, "What's going on?" then began crying. She knew it couldn't be good. The two older folks got out of the car and just sat in the grass, trembling, crying in extreme emotional pain.

Sam explained what had happened, hard as it was.

They told him they should have come up from the Valley the night before but their daughter had told them he was asleep and would be sober by the morning, she hoped. So they told her they would come up right after early church Sunday morning\. Their tears were flowing uncontrollably.

Mama and baby sister were being loaded into a hearse while the grandparents spoke briefly to the representative from Mission Park, Grandma asking if he thought the baby was comfortable. Mandy had been returned to them. They all stood with arms around each other and watched the hearse drive away, all crying.

Sam gave them some space and time; he had neither the desire nor the stomach to have to sit down and compose a report on this one. Finally, he turned to the grandfather. "What's the name, his name, that is?"

Mandy surprised them all by blurting, "Frank Wilson. He's got a white tee shirt on and blue jeans. His hair is blonde and kinda shaggy. He's on his motorcycle."

A few hours later as Sam was back at Headquarters still trying to fill out a report, an officer across town notified Susie that he had the suspect in custody and was en route with him to Homicide.

Sam met them outside the back door. When the suspect was hauled out of the back seat, Sam glared at him, "Did you look that little baby in the eye when you shot her?"

The other's eyes were cold, blank. "Fuck you."

Sam started toward him when a voice rang out from behind, "Sam! Don't!" It was the Chief.

By now Sam had gotten himself ensnared in the Loop 410 traffic tangle. *I wanted to kill that sorry bastard, right there, I wanted to. That cold, cold stare, no feelings, no nothing. Certainly not remorse...*

Shit, Doc! Yonny?

13

Driving to work, just like every other morning, he eased up to the light at Patterson, the new Central Market they made out of the old HEB and the French café staring at one another across Broadway. *Where Dick's Hobby Shop was before that, I could ride my bike there to see what Mr. Elvey had and back, not like today. No helmet, no nothing...* He was brought back by a familiar set of chords from his British Invasion CD, idly drifting in and out of the lyrics:

> *... trying to find her*
> *She's not there*
>
> *... the way she looked*
> *she acts and the color of her hair*
> *...soft and cool... eyes were clear and bright*
> *But she's not there*

He was brought back by a discordance of car horns in every register, jamming the gearshift into first and bolting away.

Her hair, her voice, her eyes, those eyes. But she's not there, here. Where? Who?

As he turned onto Houston Street from Broadway, a different thought took him. *Instead of moaning on about that girl, why didn't you help Ricky? Help him when he really needed it, he asked himself. Because, Self, I was a thousand miles away that whole time, came home for the occasional holiday, Mom's birthday, some Christmases, that was it. That's why. I didn't know... And that was then, this is now. So the girl still matters, this girl, this time. The girl with pink lipstick. Is she the one? Does she have green eyes, too?*

14

Sam's cramped little office had just gotten a lot stuffier, closed in, oppressive and almost claustrophobic, the faded green walls not adding much in the way of an antidote of cheeriness. Across the desk from him, Yonny was quiet a good while, Sam honoring his silence. Finally, he croaked, "Why, Sam? Why would a pusher sell that shit?"

Sam looked at a different person slumped in the office chair. "They don't, Yawny. Bad for business, y'know? Don't usually kill off their customers, well, they are, y'know, but not like this. Not to mention leaving your fingerprints, sorta, all over a murder victim. Doesn't make any sense, does it?"

"None of this does, Sam."

"No, I guess not. So, now we, well, SAPD, has a murder investigation on their hands. Knowing them, this one would be well down Max Espinoza's's pile on his desk at Homicide if they didn't let me run with it, for a while, at least." He looked across the desk. "I've done these before. I'll do my best, trust me."

Yonny brightened, but only slightly. "Thanks, Sam. That would be a big help for Rachel and me."

Sam just stared down at the toxicology report he had read at least twenty times before. Two or three times he glanced up at the other across from him, focused on the wall, unmoving. Then Yonny startled him by jerking back his way. "Sam, how do we find out? How do we find this scumbag pusher? And what are we going to do to him when we find him?"

Sam was more than a little alarmed at this last. "Do to him? What we do with every jerk we pull in off the street. Read him his rights and wait for his lawyer to come threaten us with a lawsuit. Works every time, the bigger the perp, the better the lawyer. Let him out on bail, try to make a case. It's not easy, Yawny, not at all. Not at all." He drummed his fingers on the desktop, then continued, "You know, when Ricky got shot—hard to believe it's been nearly twenty years ago now —I followed the case with a buddy on the Austin force. It took them six months to catch the guy, then he got no-billed at the grand jury…"

Yonny interrupted, "No-billed? What does that mean? He got off?"

"Yep, but it's pretty unusual, very unusual. Something happened up there, because if the DA wants an indictment, he can almost always get one. Maybe some political pressure, maybe some witness paid off, if there was one, or more likely someone recruited some witnesses and an alibi. With Ricky and the numbers he was doing, either one wouldn't surprise me."

"How big was he, Sam? I wasn't around those years, up East."

"Couldn't give you numbers or anything, but he was pretty big-time, I heard. Austin was a huge market then, is now, too, the University kids and all the hippies who never left." Sam leaned over, then back against his chair. "I went to Robby Coleman's bachelor's party in Houston, probably '77 or '78, yeah, '78. We were at one of those high dollar titty bars with a bunch of guys, Ricky was there, Tick Munger, too…"

"Not my favorite."

"Not mine, either. Talk about a, a jerk. Anyway, we're there having a big time and I'm sitting a couple of seats from Ricky and he won't even look at me, much less talk to me. Well, didn't bother me too much, well, yeah, it did, being old friends from way back, but I managed." He winked at Yonny, "Had other things to look at, you know?

"So I get up to go take a piss, Munger comes in and gets right next to me, kinda creeped me out, but I ask him, '*What's the deal with Ricky?*' He looks at me like I'm some sort of dumbass and says, *'He's the biggest weed dealer in Austin. That big. And he knows you're a cop now. So why would he want talk to some asshole cop?'* "

"Oooohhh."

"Yeah. I had a reputation on the force as a brawler back then, more than a little truth behind it, but I managed to restrain myself. Just. So, Ricky had hit the big time. Austin cops said the flow was over a million a year. Anyway, the guy who shot him got arrested for another murder a couple of years later, drug-related, and got off again. Must have had some powerful people behind him, looks like it."

"So he got off, just like that?"

"Uh, huh. Then got himself blown away in another deal. My Austin buddy said he was buried on some ranch out to Fredericksburg. *Buried like some old dog*, he said. What goes around?"

His friend sat back flexing his fingers together, then relaxing, then flexing them again, over and over. Then he sighed, "So, Ricky never got any justice. Maybe like you say the police or the DA up there were crooked…"

"They are down here, too. Some of 'em."

"So maybe we shouldn't be relying on the cops at all."

"I'm a cop."

Yonny stammered, "I, I mean… the San Antonio police, that's what I mean, not you."

"Thanks."

He grinned back, "*De nada.*"

"Yonny, let them, let me handle this. There's nothing you can do about it that we can't do a zillion times better. Okay? Listen, you have more things to worry about, starting with telling that wife of yours. And don't get any ideas, okay?" Sam was alarmed now. With a little bitterness in his voice, "You sound just like his father. I visited him and Mrs. Young not long after the funeral. He was slouched in his chair, might have been drinking. Started in on me about the Austin police, how stupid and incompetent they were, how they just didn't give a shit, how all cops were like that, just didn't give a shit."

Sam let loose a gale of laughter. "And there I was, towering over him in my uniform! I guess he just got all worked up about it. Can't really blame him. I don't think he or his wife really knew what bad shit Ricky was up to, or couldn't face it. But, when you lose a son like that…"

He caught himself, squaring his chair toward Yonny. "Sorry, I didn't mean to…"

"I know, Sam. I know how they felt, and I know what you meant to say. Don't sweat it. We're past that now, I think, I hope. I've got, I have, well, I know, knew my son and I was sure he was an innocent, a victim, and now I know it for sure. That doesn't make it any easier, knowing he was murdered, does it?"

"No, I s'pose not."

"No, it doesn't. You see, if it were the typical accidental… unintended… overdose… Damn, it's hard to say that word, still… But if it were, then, that would be it. The pain would still be there, realizing you'll never see…" He looked off to the wall calendar again, stared at the bluebonnets awhile, then started again, "I was ready to beat the crap, well, no, I would've tarred and feathered him, figuratively, I mean." He saw the quizzical look across the desk. "No, not really, just identify him, the pusher, I mean, stalk him, pester him, you see? Let everyone know who was dealing that death stuff, maybe hound him out of town. At least into San Antonio," he smiled slightly, "but now?" His brow furrowed, then relaxed. "Do you read your Bible, Sambo?" Not waiting for an answer, "Neither do I. Or didn't. Started looking through it—only one in our house is the Hebrew version in English, not the New Testament, the sequel, Rachel calls it. You know an eye for an eye?"

Sam had listened impassively all this time, wondering where his friend was going with all this, but now had to interject, "Us, Yonny. The po-leece. Not you." He narrowed his eyes to make his point. "Not you. We'll handle this."

Yonny went on, ignoring him. "It's in, in Numbers, I think. I came across it the other night, not thinking of murder, just death, death of a child." He reached for his wallet and pulled out a little slip of paper. " '*The revenger of blood himself shall slay the murderer; when he meeteth him, he shall slay him.*' It goes on, '*Moreover ye shall take no satisfaction for the life of a murderer which is guilty of death, but he shall surely be put to death.*' That's what it says, Sam. So, what do we do?"

Caught wrongfooted, Sam could only grasp at the last. "Put to death, it says. Lethal injection here in the Great State of Texas, after a fair trial before a jury of his peers…"

Yonny glared back at him. "Just like with Ricky in Austin, Sam?"

15

Yonny pulled up to the terminal, the old one, American, weaving around a Yellow and a minibus unloading a flight crew. There was Rachel, dressed almost formally among the tourists and local schlubs. He jumped out and sprinted around the car to her, giving her a quick kiss, leaving her with her arms in the air as he reached down for her luggage. Plopping her bags in the trunk, he lost the race to open her car door. He smiled tautly as he tucked her skirt against her thigh and closed the door quietly.

Not a word, all the way home. Fourteen minutes of stiff silence. In the driveway, he killed the engine and turned to her. "Rachel, I have something to tell you."

She leaned back against her door and started, icily, "Let me guess. You and Sarah?"

"No, not Sarah." He thought about something Sam had said, *guilt is a mighty powerful emotion, shows on people's faces*. "Something important. Very important. About Jeffy. You might want to hold your breath."

She tilted her head with a quizzical look but for some reason didn't respond as she would have… *a few months ago.*

"Talked to Sam, he told me…"

She interrupted eagerly, "They found the pusher? The one…"

"Please, Rachel. More than that, much more." He turned to face the blue-and-white propeller on the steering wheel. Without turning, "It was murder, Rachel. Somebody poisoned him. Put something, well, they know what it was, hydrogen cyanide, into the other stuff. It… it choked him to death, and not quickly, either."

Now he turned to his wife. "That's it. Don't know much else right now."

"That's enough." Rachel turned sharply away from him, then jerked back to face him. "Yonny, I, I…" She leaned over and kissed him passionately, then wrapped her arms around him. "Yonny, Yonny, oh, Yonny, why? Why? Who could do that to our boy?"

"I don't know, not yet, Rachel, but I'm going to find out. And when I do…"

Alarmed, she pulled back. "Yonny, don't do anything, anything, well, nothing you shouldn't do. Let Sam take care of it. Please? That's his job, the law's job. Don't do anything stupid, I'm begging you. After all we've been through? Promise me that, please? Please?"

He took her face in his hands, kissing her lightly and pulling away as she sought more. "Promise."

She knew he was lying, knew something was working inside him. *He'd never…*

They walked up the flagstone path to the door. "Yonny, how did they know it was cyanide? That's spy movie stuff." She shivered, realizing something horrific. "And Nazis! That's deathcamp stuff! Not here?"

"You're right." He stopped, setting her big case down to switch arms. "Rachel, you have to pack lighter, okay? My arm's just about pulled out of its socket. The cyanide? One of the technicians examined his mouth, saw traces and flecks of foam. Sam calls her the Snout, she has a keen sense of smell. Anyway, she sniffed a whiff of almonds. That alerted the toxicology analysts, and sure enough, there was a residual dosage, or presence, don't know. Enough to kill him. Apparently doesn't take all that much."

"Where would someone get it? Some pusher?"

"Don't know. Sam says a pusher wouldn't have done it, killing customers is bad for business, what with enough of them OD'ing without being poisoned, well, of course they're being poisoned, but you know what he means."

Rachel gritted her teeth. "I have to tell Mother and Daddy right away."

"Yeah, you do, but no one else. Not the girls, for sure. I'm not telling Mom and Dad or anyone. Sam's going to try to keep it quiet down at the SAPD, maybe out of the papers, if he can. It's not something that would really help things now."

Rachel laid a hand on his arm as he was about to resume schlepping. "It would help, Yonny, it would help here. Think about it, how people couldn't blame us for being such dismal failures as parents. They do, you know."

"You think about it, R. The only thing that changes is the poisoning. He still was snorting coke. That makes us failures just the same."

"Maybe you're right. No sense in getting people stirred up, I guess."

"No."

"But I still have to call my parents."

"Yes, you do, but consider the stress they're under, just like us. I don't know if your mother could stand it, much more of this. And your father, with his history?"

The babysitter met them at the door, her slender legs silhouetted against the light glimmering through her thin skirt. *Enough of that, Yawny. Enough. Don't even start.* The doorway soon filled with two more girls, two barking dogs and one insouciant cat slipping through them all. *Home again, home again, jiggedy-jig.*

Earl Abel's fried chicken made it a surprisingly festive dinner, the twins bubbling and burbling on this boy and that girl; at least the parents' façades held up against the silent landslide tumbling down all about them. After, Rachel pleaded fatigue and retired to the bedroom, sitting on the bed, then leaning back against her pile of pillows. *Why? I can't talk to Yonny about this, he'll just dismiss it, but because I'm a Jew? No, can't be, not here. Yes, there are some people here... No, not here. But I know the stories, every Jewish child growing up in New York knows them, I've seen the tattooed numbers, the photographs of the skeletal figures, Daddy's story, Nana pointing to the old country family portrait, her... her... him... his sons... all gone.*

She finally picked up the phone and dialed.

"I'm... I'm actually calling to... to tell you something about, well, umm," she stammered a bit, "it's, it's about Jeffy."

Solly let out a gruff growl, "Yeah?"

"Yes, Daddy. It, well, the test reports for the... drugs came back, Yonny talked to our friend Sam yesterday."

"That cop doing any good down there? You know I can get Bill Bratton himself down there, just you and Ian say the word!"

"Daddy, please. They're doing as well as they can down here. But about Jeffy, he," she sputtered out the words, "it wasn't an accident. He was... murdered. Someone laced, spiked cocaine with cyanide. They think it shut down his respiratory system, he choked to death."

That was as much as she could say, leaning back, letting the phone hang down, not even attempting to acknowledge her parents' screaming.

Finally, "Sorry, Mother, Daddy. I had to, I had to catch my breath. Sorry. That's all we know now. Don't know how he got it, where, from who, or who he was with…"

"When they killed him? How do they not know any of that?"

"Daddy, I told you, right after. There was a car and two sets of footprints. But not good enough to identify anyone. They, our detective friend, did give Yonny some names of the pushers around the high school, one of them sounded like a fish, Fluker, Flounder, that's it. And another, Gunther, something like that. And some bigger fish, Angel, I think, or maybe I'm thinking of an angelfish. No, no, that's the guy's name, he's the contact with the Mexicans smuggling stuff up here. But they wouldn't have done it, he doesn't think. Is pretty positive about that."

"Murder, huh?"

"Yes, Daddy…"

Her mother screeched, "So they still kill Jews down there?"

"Mother, what's that? No! Absolutely not! This isn't the Wild West, not anymore."

"You don't be so sure, such a smarty! You're the one who wanted to move down there with those wild people, those cowboys and those, those, goyim! Get away from your mother as fast as you could! Disgraceful! And ano…

"Mother, stop it! Just stop it! Isn't there anything you can't make worse?" She caught herself, "I'm sorry, Mother, so sorry. I shouldn't have said that, but we're, we're so strained down here." Into a silence on the other end, she said, "So that's what we know, now. Not much more to say. How are you two doing?"

"Yeah, yeah, everything's fine. We're good. You got the problems down there, let us know if we can help. Bye, now."

She could hear Miriam squawking in the background, *could imagine Solly trying to corral her, get her away from the phone. Corral her? I'm a cowgirl myself now, I guess*. She hung up.

Solomon set the handset back in its cradle, then picked it up again. "Si, Solly. I want we should talk about my grandson again. Yeah. Yeah. Yeah, it's important. Just tell Letty it's important. Get over here as soon as you can? Yeah, thanks."

He shuffled to the window overlooking the front lawn. *So some creep killed my grandson, my little boy?* He shuddered. *If it's them, the gloves are off. They're off. That's it.* He reflected a bit more soberly. *No, they wouldn't have done that. Not their M.O. No, not them, someone else. Someone down there. Someone down there. Some asshole down there. Some punk, some pusher. Down there.*

The passengers filed and fidgeted their way out of the gate, two mothers stopping to set up their strollers, blocking the way for most. One figure, dark glasses, black suit, white shirt, black tie, a gray straw fedora with a wide silk band like Sinatra used to wear in the '50's and '60's, watched with some amusement. One toddler started fussing, then arching his back and screaming, resisting being straitjacketed into strollerdom. The man, his features tanned and angular, leaned over and smiled at the wailing urchin who abruptly quieted and sunk into his cushion, wide-eyed. He tipped his hat to the weary mother and moved along toward the terminal.

He took his time down the ramp from the satellite terminal, then surveyed the baggage claim area. *Quaint*, he thought. *And they call this an airport?*

The cabbie took the ten and was waved off when he started to make change. At the Doubletree, he kicked off his shoes and hung up his coat, then loosened his tie and embraced the air conditioning. *December, and it's almost 90? Gimmeabreak.* He looked at his watch, then laid back on the bed. *Early, yet. Calls can wait.*

16

He didn't have an address, didn't think he'd need one, not from Sam's description. Down El Paso Street, a dry, dusty, desiccated street framed by arid lawns and peeling pickets and listless houses, threadbare in their tarpaper and peeling bevels and aluminum-foiled windows. Withered pecan and hackberry leaves congregated in scruffy pockets in the gutters or swirled across the street in their self-absorbed whorls, typical West Side, *Alto Mexico* to an Anglo's eyes.

On the left corner coming up, an ice house, sad and tumbledown in the flaking stucco shell of an old gas station. Several dark-eyed men in baseball caps and Jalisco straws lounged around small picnic-style tables nursing their longnecks, some arguing, some watching a small TV on the bar. To the right, a couple of lowriders, spinners still spinning, a clot of young men idling and smoking, turning as a squad to stare at him. A little further down the dusty way he spied barbed wire—*the Devil's rope, they called it in the Great War*—wreathing its way atop a tall chainlink fence. He sped up, trying to be as inconspicuous as a sandy-haired Gringo in a loud black BMW could be. For once he regretted not tinting the windows to blackness. *A little opacity would be comforting right now.* As he passed a wrought iron gate attended each side by two cigarette smokers, a big black and tan dog peeking around one's stool, he made some mental notes. *That's four. How many at night? Have to check.*

He kept on another two blocks, these better, much prettier, all pastels and brighter colors, *Tia Marias* tending neat yards or porch-sitting with their Chihuahuas. Then he turned right and right again on San Fernando to check out the back. Sure enough, the compound spanned the block front to back, demarcated by corrugated panels interrupted by another wrought iron gate. *This one ajar? No, chained loosely. File that, Yawny.* The corner was delineated by a creosoted pole with a camera pointed right at him. He chilled at the sight until he realized there was no blinking red dot. *Not on during the day? Hmmm. When does it go on? Have to check*. Glancing back over his shoulder, he spied its brother, but still didn't see anyone manning the parapets. *Maybe...*

Enough for now, he thought, *don't want someone writing down my plates or fingering me to the bad guys. Have to come back a few more times, though. Maybe I can find some aerials somewhere?*

At the enchilada red library he began looking through the newspaper archives for articles about the Angel. A big shootout back in the late eighties showed up right away in the database, so he requested that microfiche and another with a story about the redoubt.

The reader was hard to use, at least with his dexterity, running past the spot several times, finally zeroing in on the shootout. He had forgotten most of this, how the ambush went off, the Angel getting a grazing shot to the butt, a couple of his boys shot up, but no surprise to many, no drugs were found at the compound. He spent a few nights in the pokey and came out free as a bird, accompanied by several high priced lawyers and flacks. Yonny peered at the photographs, one after the other, an ordinary looking guy, not tall, beer belly hanging over a dinner plate-sized belt buckle, wearing the Full Cleveland, dark polyester leisure suit, white belt, white shoes. This one must have been after his release, grinning triumphantly. *And that's his wife?* Same size, same shape, teased cloud of jet black hair, grotesque makeup.

He started to pull that sheet when he saw a familiar face in the background. *Sam? I'll have to ask him about it, he's been holding out on me?* Next were the photos of the compound, including aerials from the news helicopters. *Bingo. Not too good, but good enough.* He pressed *Print*.

Montanio's 50-50 bar was quiet at this time of day, three in the afternoon, only four patrons at the bar slumped insensate over their beers and shots. Every once in a while one would mutter something, triggering a cascade of profanity in two and a half languages. Yonny took up a defensive position in the back, facing the door. Soon enough, said doorway was engulfed by a mass and its shadow. He whistled to Sam. Sam took off his aviators and nodded, making sure to brush the barflies' backs on his way over, then leaned across the bar to say something to the waitress.

"What are you trying to say, Yawny, hmmm?"

"Curiosity, Sam, that's all."

"Curiosity gets you dead on the West Side if you're an Anglo in the wrong place at the wrong time on the wrong night, okay, Yawny?" Sam veered away from the point. "And why were you looking for his place? You sure seemed to go to a lot of trouble."

Yonny beat a strategic retreat. He looked around at the long bar, at Elvis in the window, at the bandbox, then through the windows at the few cars passing at this hour. He might have stepped out of bounds, but with what was working in his mind, he had some needs. *To know who was fish, who was foul.*

He grinned at that bit of wit, then looked back to Sam's unrelenting scowl. *Okay, no defense like a good offense.* "Yeah, guilty of curiosity, Sam. Can you blame me? Huh, can you? Someone kills your only son, takes him away from his family, and you just sit by while the killer runs free, struts around preening his lunch out of his moustache, nibbling the crumbs? Huh?"

Sam had faced down far worse than this guy. "Huh? I'll give you 'Huh'! Three of my best friends got it from the Angel's thugs. One of them was just sitting in his car, he turns and Boom! That was it. Wife and three kids. Boom! That's the way it is with these guys."

'Sam, I understand that. I get it. But you said it yourself, cops down here are crooked, just like with Ricky in Austin. Even if you and I could figure this mess all out, how do I know I, we, Rachel and I and the girls can ever see justice for Jeffy if this is the way your world works?"

"Maxie, the other guys I'm working with are good, they're straight. But overworked, big time. You'll get justice, just let us handle it. Just don't do something stupid like ring the Angel's doorbell and say, *'My friend, Mister Magnum here, wishes a word with the fucker who killed my son.'"* He smiled slightly, "That actually happened once, some of our other guys answered the call, not me. Not a drug deal, in fact, wrong house. Really wrong house for the guy ringing the doorbell." He made a pistol gesture and shrugged.

"Not my style, Sam."

"Good."

"One other thing, Sam." He reached into the outside pocket of his Mules windbreaker, extracting a single sheet. "Got this out of the

Light's archives. Señor Algarve leaving the Bexar County jail after the big shootout. I guess all these guys are on his payroll."

"Lawyers. That one's Raul Campeon. Slimy as they come. And this one…"

"No, Sam, I was thinking about this guy in the background." He pointed to a less distinct face in a suit two ranks behind the entourage. "Here," pulling out a magnifier from another pocket, "maybe this will help?"

Sam shot him a look of repressed violence. "No need, Yawny. That's me."

"Why? What were you doing?"

Sam sighed as he leaned back. He remained silent.

"It's okay with me, Sam. I've got all day." He took out his flip phone and pressed the *off* button. "No one will bother us."

In the dim light in the corner, Sam held up two fingers. The waitress hadn't decided which of the two she'd like to go home with more, so she made every move count. "One Miller Lite and a little Gentleman Jack, Sam, one Rolling Rock for you, Sir."

Both watched her flounce away, struggling to stifle their laughs. "If she only knew," whispered Yonny.

"If." Sam knocked back the shot and took a long draw off his bottle, suddenly subdued by domestic thoughts. "If."

"You were about to say, Sam? Unless you don't want to share. I'll get this one." He tilted sideways to get at his wallet until Sam motioned him to stop. "Okay, I'm here, listening."

Sam shook his head. "Yeah, Yonny, I was, was in his pocket. On the payroll. Little things here and there, mainly kept an open mike on a separate walkie-talkie so he could hear what was going down, all over town. Did it for a few years, actually. My wife—my second wife, man—was a spending bitch. It was all I could do to keep from drowning in debt. Juggling three credit cards, paying one with another one. The Angel's money got me even, then she split on me, the bitch."

"Sorry to hear that, Sam. Disappointed just the same, though."

"Well, fuck you very much, you… you goddamned pussy, you. Everything easy for you. Never…"

"Sam, Sam, easy. Don't get carried away, okay? Just that, well, knowing you like I do now, I would never had thought it. That's all. Then what?"

Sam held his breath, then let it out explosively, startling the other.

"Scared you? Good. Remember that. Well, not so long after that I let the Angel know I was out of there."

"Out of there?"

"Yeah. Got myself a new wife, she wanted to move back to Denton, where she was from."

"He let you go? Just like that?"

"Yeah."

"Okaaay." Now Yonny realized he really was in someone else's world, and he wasn't at all sure he had booked this excursion.

Sam had some more beer, then turned to look at some noisy newcomers. Tick Munger strolled in like he owned the joint, straight to their table. "No shit! Look, the odd couple!" He turned to two ratty-looking pals and started, "A cop and a Jewlover walk into a bar, see? And they sit down at a table…" He turned back to Yonny just as a massive fist crashed into the right side of his face. He went down in a heap, was still.

Sam looked at the other creeps and flashed his badge. "Get him out of here." He sat down as if nothing happened. "Anyway, yeah, Denton. Worked undercover, five years almost. Then came back here when that didn't work out. That marriage, I mean. And I was straight, Yonny, I mean it. Just patrol, that's it. Then up here, four years now."

"That's good, Sam. I forgive you."

Sam smoldered, "I don't need your fucking forgiveness…"

"Easy, Sam, easy. I don't want to end up on the floor," looking down at a small blood spatter, "like Tickypoo. Great left jab, by the way. Remind me to duck." He smiled generously, raising his longneck, reaching it toward the Lite.

Sam growled, "You're a real asshole, you know that?"

They clinked bottles together.

17

Murder had brought Rachel and her husband close, at least closer than they had been in weeks, months. *What would have happened if Jeffy weren't gone? Would we have been sniping at each other like before? Would I have gotten so worked up over Sarah? Would I have been so suspicious of him, of everything? Donny, well, Donny would be gone, too. Oh, well. Que sera, sera. At least I have Yonny, don't I? Don't I?*

Tonight was the Christmas season's installment of *Las Muchachas Locas*, the party club she had been asked to join once some of the locals had figured her out, just a group of wives and wannabes, a nice excuse to get together, drink Margaritas, chitchat. And their husbands, of course, wouldn't do to give them their own nice excuse to get together without adequate wifely supervision, but as the evening wound down, few gave them another thought.

It had taken her quite a while to work herself up to go. *Better I go than have to answer questions tomorrow and all week. And Yonny, too, not let them get to flapping their jaws about another Jonas family crisis. As if they have any right to know where I was, why we didn't come, what's going in this impending wreck of a life…* Once at Corrine Perez's vast house, Rachel had hooked up with Sally and Martha, just chatting Oh-Nine things, how the chilluns were doing in college, how LeahRhea were taking the Junior High by storm, those sorts of things. With glances and turned backs, they wove themselves a little cocoon in a corner beneath a huge Longhorn mount, free to chat without shouting over the din in the living room next door.

"Meredith says to say hello, Rachel. You know close she was to… to Jeffy."

Rachel thought her friend was about to open the sluices, so she reached out to her, saying, "Sally, I want to thank you again for her sweet note with the picture of the two of them together at the coast.

It's on my nightstand, you know? And we were so looking forward to seeing them together on stage… Oh, look! Sarah! Sarah!"

She beckoned and a clearly self-conscious Sarah Goodman came over to join their little clutch. "Thanks, Rachel, Sally, Martha, it was getting a little uncomfortable in there. Everyone wanted to talk but made clear they didn't want to talk too long, especially, well, you know…"

Martha, twice divorced, laughed. "Worse than the lawyers, telling the kids, splitting up everything. Been there, done that. Don't worry, Hon, it'll blow over." She grimaced, "But not 'til you've been abandoned, betrayed, shunned for a good while. Believe me, I know. Best bet is to get yourself a new husband, quick. Like me. But not too quick. Haste makes waste, you know? I do, unfortunately." She looked her over and up and down with her trademark gimlet eye. "You won't have any problem, girl, not looking like that. Love the scarf. Hermes? Oh, speaking of third edition husbands, here comes Ralphie. He'll join us to gossip if we let him, so I'll take him safely away. Bye, my dears!"

As she swished away, Sally stood and made much the same case, saying, innocently or pointedly, Rachel couldn't tell, "I need to see what trouble George is getting himself into. Bye-bye."

Sarah watched them leave and turned to Rachel. "They don't want me around."

"You're beautiful, they aren't."

"Thanks, but I don't feel so…"

Rachel squeezed her hand. "That wasn't so much a compliment as it was a threat assessment. Trust me, you don't have much competition in the beauty department. Present company excepted, of course. Come along, let's bedazzle 'em!" She smiled broadly, unforced for once. "Well, at least bewilder them."

18

Sam was having a really hard time concentrating on what she was saying. Rachel's thin ribbed sweater clung to every curve and swelling, and every curve was swelling with every breath, every movement. He tried his best to keep his eyes level as she went on, "So, that's it, Sam. Sarah's signed this, but won't press a rape complaint. I've tried and tried with her, but she just won't do it. And she's probably right. It would hit her children pretty hard and she's afraid they'd not understand and blame her. So, this is…"

1979

He escorted the two strippers from his squad car into the station, motioning them to sit down on the hard chairs lined against the wall. Trying not to stare as they made themselves the centers of attention, he spoke briefly with the officer on the duty desk. The officer craned his neck around Sam's bulk and drew back grinning. "Sam, use the first room. But I'm going to turn on the cameras, okay?"

He played the gentleman to the two women, one pretty young, probably just out of high school, if that, the other a bit more... seasoned. Satisfied with their comfort, he took his position across the desk from them, not taking his eyes off them even as he pulled an incident report form out of a drawer. "So, ladies, you were hitchhiking home from Dante's Inferno? Why in the world would you do that?"

The older dancer leaned forward suggestively, her bosoms pressing against her blouse, threatening an imminent escape. "Because, Sweetheart, her car wouldn't start and it was three in the morning, so what were we going to do?"

Sam made his entries. "Then a carload of Hispanics..."

"Meskins, darlin', Meskins."

"Hispanics will do just fine for my reports, Ma'am. So they picked you up and drove up Broadway, correct?"

The younger girl nodded.

"Then they began harassing you?"

Senior Sister replied, mischievously, "They were attempting to take some liberties with us, Officer. We objected, naturally."

"Uh, huh. By sticking a fingernail in one of them's eye?"

"Just a poke. He took it the wrong way, that's all."

"And what else before I got there?"

The younger woman piped up, "They started grabbing our tits."

Sam kept his head down, studiously avoiding the evidence, writing, 'Assailants began fondling complainants' breasts...'

At that, the older stripper stood and uncaged her goods. "Chickens have breasts. These are tits!"

"Sam? Are you all there? My eyes are up here, you know."

Rachel nearly tripped down the stairs going down to Broadway, so engrossed in her thoughts she was. *Now to drop by Sarah's, give her a copy of the TRO, sit with her a while. It isn't going to be easy on her. And me? Helping Sarah out, wherever I can, dealing with the twins' coming of age, and Yonny... How about me? Who's helping me?*

She looked in the rearview mirror to check her hair, noticing her eyes didn't look quite so horrid today, not as bad as weeks before. *I'll have to thank Sarah—she told me to lighten up on the makeup, said I was beginning to look like an old woman trying to look young again. 'You're one of the lucky ones, Rachel', she said, 'you're much prettier without any makeup.' Lying through her teeth, of course, but sweet.*

And Yonny noticed, said he liked it. She felt a twinge down there. *Mmmm.*

An hour later, she turned onto Broadway, heading back to work. She smiled at her session with Sam. *He sure had his eyes glued to my chest.* Musing as she looked down, *I guess this top is a bit flimsy. Shouldn't have taken off my jacket, but that little hole of an office of his got so hot and stuffy.* Seeing a big truck lumbering along ahead, she flicked her blinker to move to the right lane. Idly smoothing some lint from the wales of her sweater, she brushed a nipple with a fingernail, prompting a tingling, a mix of pain and pleasure.

Just then her left erupted in honks and shouts. Two guys loomed over her in a Lone Star Beer truck, the passenger leaning out the window, laughing and banging on the door. She smiled and flipped them the bird just as their heads jerked forward, faces frozen.

She left the sounds of tearing metal and tinkling glass behind, glancing in the left side mirror. *A cop car. How nice.*

19

Sally hailed Rachel from her minivan. "Rachel, Rachel, your girls look so cute! Where did you find their outfits? You always find the prettiest things!"

Rachel smiled tolerantly. Sally was one of her oldest, or longest-standing friends, another one of her husband's high school friends, a rare non-girlfriend, family friends three generations. And thereby not a threat, or much of one. She was tenacious to a fault and monotonously obsessed with the goings-on in the Bubble, who was going broke, whose affair had petered out, all the important things in life. But she was as supportive a friend as Rachel had in her difficult times—*except, of course, for Sarah*, she smiled inwardly and somewhat grimly.

"Thanks, Sweetie. But that Edward of yours better not break their little hearts! He's the older man, remember?"

"Trust me, he won't. Not if I have anything to say about it. And where are you guys going skiing? Over Christmas break? I didn't think you two were skiers."

"Skiing? No, no such luck. Not that I know of. Why?"

"Oh, I saw Yonny at Oshman's the other day, buying some ski clothes. You know, windbreaker, turtleneck sweater, ski pants. And a pullover ski mask. All black, too, quite stylish, he was."

"Always. Oh, my, look at the time. I'm going to be late." She turned the steering wheel.

"Were you trying to surprise us?"

"Surprise?" Yonny instantly knew to be on the defensive. "About what?"

"It's your surprise, silly. What is it? A little birdie told me we're going skiing. Where? Anyone else coming with us?"

"Skiing? No. Remember my dislocated knee? Way back in my dissolute youth?"

Rachel had indeed forgotten the story, how his friends had left him behind atop Ajax, a worse than novice skier. He took a prodigious fall and when he finally got himself together to stand, his left leg had taken a right turn at the knee into two vertical axes, high and low. Before he could comprehend how badly it hurt and how serious it probably was, he shifted his weight and everything popped back into place with a resounding crack. Thus had endeth his skiing career.

"Oh, that's right. So what's with the ski clothes?"

Yonny had anticipated this line, was ready. "Stuff was on sale. I had just gone in for a new pair of Nikes. Lost my head, but the price was right."

"Well, Sally thought you looked dashing."

"Well, she would. Never has had anything bad to say about me, even at my worst. She's a saint, if you ask me."

"That she is. Are all your saints so boring, though? No girls gone wild among them?"

"That's sorta the basic profile, Rachel. Piety, sobriety, distinct absence of notoriety."

"And you two never dated?"

"Love her to death, but have you looked at her?"

20

He gave thanks, praise, even, for the weather, South Texas' idea of an Advent evening, damp, cold, well, at least in the low 40's, a spitting sky. *Not too many folks out and about. Good. Maybe his boys are hunkered down, too*. He parked the black BMW 535i around a corner a block and a half away, praying it would be fairly intact when he returned. *If I return*.

He checked and re-checked his gear, the long military-style knife and his pistol, screwing the noise suppressor tight, flipping the cylinder, *six*, and put it back in the holster for the umpteenth time. *Okay, then. Showtime*. He pulled the black ski mask over his face.

He made his way through the shadows, from street to sidewalk and back, staying in the dark where he could. The city hadn't caught up with the needs of the West Side, so two of the streetlights were conveniently dark. *Or maybe his guys shot them out, to keep it dark? Well, if they did, it's damned nice of...*

Waking himself with his groans, his eyes struggled to adjust to the points of light punctuating the darkness. His hands were on the steering wheel, his car was in the driveway, the front porch lights were on. He looked in the rearview mirror back at the Porterhouses' place, all ablaze for Christmas. Then he became acutely aware of a sharp, slicing pain atop his head, and with his first move came the throbbing. *What happened? How did I...* Then he remembered his plan. *Down the street in the dark, slipping through the slack in the back gates, under the chain, then...* He dropped his hands from the wheel, his right touching something cold and wet. It was his knife, and the wet was blood, he could tell that, even in the dark, could feel it slippery and slimy on his palm. *So I did it. I got the bastard. Good, got what he deserved. But...* He felt something else in his left. He squinted at it, a small piece of notepaper, the top ripped off, 'FLOUNDER' written on it. He started to scratch his head, then felt the blood on his hand. *No. Gotta get back into the house without waking everybody.*

He reached for the door handle, then froze as a pair of bright lights came careening around the corner from the Boulevard. Sweeping past him, the car skidded its way into the circular drive across the street. Hunkered down behind the headrest, he saw in the side view mirror a head of long blonde hair appear above a white ragtop, then the full Daphne rushing to the side of the mansion, stopping to tug on her skirt, then disappearing around the side. *Sneaking out, were we?* The car, a vintage Corvette, a '67 by the side vents, left a bit more sedately.

Forcing himself to wait quietly, searching both houses for lights or movement, he finally slipped out of his car and up the driveway. He had left the bottom leaf of the Dutch door unlocked and slipped in, defeating the alarm. He carefully bowlegged his way up the stair to the guest bedroom and shed his clothes as quickly as he could, tucking them into a laundry bag. He checked his pistol, smelled gunpowder, then the cylinder, all shells punched. Stuffing it into its hiding place where nobody would look, he hurried to the bathroom to clean up and then slipped into bed. *Good thing I've been snoring and yammering in my sleep, got banished, for now.*

Sam had been called out late that night about some punks breaking and entering over on Patterson, the same gang he had been after for some time. He went out to Central Park Mall to meet his patrolmen who had chased and collared three suspects, their Cutlass stuffed with CD players and stereos. *Open and shut.* "Dale, Brett, take 'em in and book 'em. I'll call County and reserve a room, you get 'em on down there."

Now way past wide awake, he was hungry. He swung over to Jim's for an early breakfast. Acknowledging the "*Hi, Sam!*" from Tisha, he eased into a booth at the back, began warming his hands around the hot coffee she had followed him with and ordered from habit. Like the seasoned professional he was, he took his time. Finally finished with his Rustler's Roundup, he sipped the last of his coffee, looking the place over one last time for omens of potential mayhem amidst the formica and naugahyde and then headed home.

Driving south on Jones Maltsberger, he saw a figure coming along the left curb. Closer, he saw it was in a jogging outfit, black pants and white jacket. He slowed to a stop. The jogger stopped opposite him, hands on his thighs, bending over slightly. He waved weakly at Sam, who rolled down his window and leaned out slightly. "You okay? Kinda late to be out here. Or early, maybe?"

"No, no, I'm fine," replied the other in a distinct and bold accent Sam couldn't place. "Just my morning run. Can't take the sunshine, got these skin cancers here." By now he had straightened and was pointing to indistinct blotches on both sides of his face. "So, I'm good. Almost done."

"Where you going? Need a lift?"

He almost recoiled at that. What's that about? Sam decided to get out of the car. As he did, the man backed up, stepping over the curb. "Is there a problem, Sir?" Going by the book, "I need to see some ID, please."

Now the jogger smiled and abruptly reached inside his jacket. For just a moment, Sam had focused on the jacket's coarse seams, then instinctively went for his service pistol. Not quickly enough. He found himself looking down the barrel of a short-barrelled .38.

"Hands on top of your head. Now!" Sam complied. The mystery man smiled again, then flipped the pistol grip toward Sam. "Here, hold this a sec." He fished around in his jacket, finally pulling out a wallet. Opening it, he thrust it under Sam's nose. "Pistol, please?'

Sam saw the badge, '*Miami-Dade County*' across the top. Below was a name, *F. Wolszyk, Detective*. He gave the piece back, grip first, courtesy between policemen, noticing it lacked the normal heft. "Sorry, Detective Woll, Woles…"

"Voychek. Frank Voychek. Now let me see yours." Sam whipped out his wallet. "Alamo Heights, huh? That little burg back there?" He arched a thrice-scarred eyebrow. "Sam Thompson, huh?" He smiled as he handed it back. "Your instincts were good, Detective Thompson, but you would've been dead, dead, dead. Never, ever let a suspect reach into his clothes without drawing a bead on his forehead. And being ready to pull the trigger. They teach you that in this Alamo Heights place?"

"Did at San Antonio, where I started." *He's right. I'm getting careless. Losing my edge?* "Guess I assumed you…"

"Assume will make an ass out of you and me, friend. It's okay, just work on your technique."

"Yes, I will. Ummm, you carry empty?"

Mr. Miami chuckled, "Seemed to work just as good as loaded in getting your attention. No, tonight it's just for show. And you know it's too easy to make a mistake, to pull the trigger and wish you hadn't, right?"

Sam mumbled, "Actually, I've never shot anyone, better than twenty years now."

"Then you can sleep at night. Me, not so much. Another reason for being out here at this hour." The jogger bored in on Sam with a cold, even cruel stare amplified by his hawk-like features. "They don't go away, the memories."

Now Sam wanted to change the subject and asked, "You here on official business? Got a case here?"

"No, just visiting my daughter and grandchildren. She and her husband are Air Force doctors at that, what's that place way over there?" He waved to the west.

"Wilford Hall?"

"Yeah, that's it. They wanted me to stay with them, but three little kids, you know? So I'm up at the Doubletree other side of the freeway. Ran all the way down through your park down there, found myself on that, what is it, a dam or something? Halfway across before I figured that out, so I turned around. Still got eight or nine miles in, or will, if you'll let me go."

"Sure you don't want a lift? Cup of coffee, talk some shop? Say, you don't sound Miami, not that I really know what that sounds like."

"Brooklyn, pal, Brooklyn born and bred. Got out of the NYPD as soon as I could draw my pension, then followed the sun. Mistake," pointing to his face again, "but my daughter says I'll be all right. No, thanks for the offer, but I'll just get on with my run." He turned and began striding, then jogging with a wave over his shoulder.

I've forgotten what the beat can be like. You sure meet all kinds. He headed home.

21

"Mr. Jonas? It's that Detective Thompson from the police department."

He looked up from the plans table. "Okay, thanks, Angela. Put it in here. And close the door, please?" Settling into his chair, he took a couple of deep breaths, then picked up the phone. "Yeah, Sam? What's up? Got anything new?"

"New, yeah, but not so much about your son. Can we get together this morning, talk about it?"

"Ummm, not this morning, or today, really." He rubbed the knot on his head. "Have several balls I'm juggling right now. Day after tomorrow, maybe?" Yonny hoped he made a convincing liar.

"No, well, we'll just go over it now. I was out late last night on a case, got a call from one of my old buddies downtown, knew I was working the drug scene up here, same guy who told me about your son. Said I might want to get dressed and go down to El Paso Street, something big had gone down."

"El Paso Street?"

"Uh, huh. The Angel's place. You know what I'm talkin' about. So, curiosity getting this cat, I went on down there, hell, I was already dressed and wide awake anyway. Blue lights everywhere, Fire was just finishing putting out a blaze in the back. Big, big scene. I worked my way in, saw Maxie Espinoza, asked him what the hell had happened.

"He pulled me into the house. Back wall had burned off, the main fire was the garage in back. Took me past five or six sheets on the ground into a bedroom. I recognized the Angel even though his face was a pulp. His wife, I guess, she was a mess, too, slit top to bottom, or bottom to top. Pretty damned gross, even for me, nearly puked."

"Sounds lovely."

"Yeah, I guess you had to be there." *Should be talking face-to-face with him. But he couldn't have done this. No way?* "Funny thing —the boys recovered a couple dozen or so slugs already, no cartridges scattered around, means a revolver, not an automatic, not a Uzi or a MAC 10, the usual instrument—but we're guessing most were from a . 38, but some look to be .357 magnum."

"Two guys, gunmen?"

"Figures to be, but can't tell—no tracks, no prints. Could be just two pieces used by the same shooter. Or just the same one, don't know yet. And the way he, or they, got in, well, had to be a pro."

"A pro? Like a hitman or a James Bond?"

"Yeah. Someone in one of the cartels was probably pissed. Might have been skimming, maybe late paying. Maybe just new competition muscling in. Happens. If that's so, we can expect more, soon."

"Hmmm?"

"Gang war, Yonny. Heads will roll, I mean it. Will keep my buds at SAPD busy, that's for sure. Let's just hope it doesn't spread to the Northside." *Leave it there, Sam. Wasn't him, couldn't be, not the way it went down. No way he could do something like that, no way. But if he did do it, I should thank him for it. No more ball and chain. Free at last, Great God Almighty, free at last!* He chuckled. *Yeah, free.*

Yonny hung up, shaken. *I did all that? Yeah, got a knock on the head in the process. Wait, two guns?*

22

Over the next few weeks he changed his daily routine from early morning walks with Patches to longer walks right after work, at dusk, timing them by the sun's sinking. And instead of down through the basin, now up to the high school and around, maybe down to Sunset Ridge and up Brees for the cardio, then back. Three or four, sometimes five miles. Back in time to help with dinner, commune with the tweeners, hold Rachel close at least once or twice a night.

He wasn't quite sure what he was looking for but figured he'd know it when he saw it. The first several nights, there was nothing that looked pusher-ish, and what action there was seemed innocent—band practice, some Girl Scouts one night, plenty of joggers and strollers and dogs for Patches to bray at when she wasn't sniffing their butts.

They stuck with it for a week or so. As Patches strained at her leash in anticipation of seeing the same squirrel again, they careened around the Mule Stall corner at a half trot just as a shiny pickup wheeled into a slot. Popping up onto the sidewalk as they passed, he caught a wave of weed and a glimpse of a head of stringy hair nodding in and out of a greenish gray cloud. As casually as he could, he turned his head and kept on, finally slowing the dog about fifty yards out. He stopped behind an old hemlock tree on the corner three blocks down and let Patches flop around in a bed of jasmine as he maneuvered into position behind the trunk.

He didn't have long to wait. A white Mercedes, a C-series, stopped four or five spaces away from the truck. A few moments later, a figure in jeans and a blue shirt—he couldn't tell if it was a boy or a girl—sidled away from the car and slipped through the pickup's passenger door. Not a minute later, the figure—it was a girl, he thought—slipped back to her car, swiveling her blonde head left and right as she went. *Yeah, dope deal going down. That's my guy. Need another look.*

"C'mon, Patches, let's go." Crossing the street, he heard something behind him, a steering rack whining softly as it was turned. He quickstepped to the curb and slowed to let the new car, a Jeep, decide what to do, whether to stop or keep going. *He's not sure,* thought Yonny, *slowing down, now picking it up, no, now slowing down. Let's get out of his way.* He startled Patches into a jog and passed both vehicles from behind without a look. Around the corner, he crouched at the edge of the ligustrums, just able to see between the leaves. The little drama played itself out again, but this time he got a better look inside under the dome light, the same halo of long stringy hair straggling down onto sloped shoulders. Then the light went out, then, seconds later, on and off again. *That's my boy, I'll betcha.*

He caught a faint flood of light out of the corner of his eye and stood up, making like he was tying a poop bag, and resumed their walk. One car, then another had turned off Broadway, passing them, continuing on. *Not customers. Okay.*

"Let's go home, girl."

After another week and a half of intermittent surveillance, Yonny decided it was time. Walking briskly up to the high school as the light faded from a fiery gold to a dusty rose through the perforated live oak forest behind him, he let Patches have a bit more leash and she took it, winding around the nearest "No Parking" sign. As he stopped to unscramble her, lifting first one leg, then the other from the leash, he scanned Castano back to Broadway. *No one behind us*. Now from the other direction came a bright yellow late model Corvette pulling in six or seven spaces from the corner. *That's not so good. Hmmm. Maybe not tonight. Well, we'll just see what we can see.* The father-pup pair resumed their walk. Someone was inside the Corvette, smoking. *Weed, no doubt.* Passing the car, he caught a quick glimpse of the driver's face in the side mirror, fanning smoke away frantically. *Teddie Berger? That car? Crap, whatever precious wants, precious gets, I guess.*

Picking up the pace, he and the dog hopped onto the sidewalk at the Mule Stall corner. There he is, just like before, just like Sam said. *Can't be too smart if the local cops know all about your habits. Okay, then, let's just mosey on by.*

He leaned down to unhook Patches' leash, looking over his shoulder back into the pickup's cab as he did. *Looks like he's asleep, maybe smoking too much of what he's been selling*? Patches darted down Vanderhoeven after some imagined cat, racing past a black-clad jogger without a glance. Yonny sidestepped back to the passenger side, below the window, slipped on the latex gloves and then gently opened the door. He expected some sort of response, angry, most likely, maybe even a gun, but encountered nothing but a soft moaning. He slipped into the seat. *He looks like his description. Flat, shallow chest, thin stringy hair, short arms, yep, Flounder-like.*

Flounder roused himself to look blearily at his guest. "What… what do you… who…"

"Hey, man, it's okay. I came for the stuff, man. The coke. You got it?"

"You not… not…" He jerked back to face forward, then puked his hamburger and French fries all over the windshield, barely started on their digestion, gross stuff, streaming down the glass, ketchup and all. His head rocked back over the top of the seat, hitting the rear window and bouncing back as he moaned and mewled.

Yonny opened the switchblade and pressed it against the other's greasy neck. He could see the vein or artery, or whichever blood vessel it was, just pulsing away. Flounder didn't flinch a bit, just kept moaning and muttering, his eyelids fluttering. "What's the deal, Flounder?"

"Ahummahmm… Stuff, man."

"What stuff?"

"Guy gave me… Shot… Arm…"

Yonny looked him over, then down at his feet at a small plastic bag, all white inside. "That stuff?'

"Ahmm, uh, no, ahummm."

"Then tell me how Jeffy Jonas got his. You sold it to him, didn't you?"

Flounder's eyes flickered for the first time as he jerked his head toward the voice. He felt the blade for the first time, too, and now his eyes grew wide. "What… no, no, man, no I didn't sell him that shit. Never did… with him… not…"

"Then you know who I'm talking about?"

"Mmm… yeah… high… school… yeah… friends… with… oh hahmmm… oh, man, I'm dizzy, gonna puke…" He retched several more times, then drooped back. "Man, what's happenin'…"

Yonny pressed the point a little harder. "Who, Flounder, who'd you sell to? You know I'm talking about the boy found OD'd in Olmos Park last fall. You do know, don't you?"

"Umm, yah… Olmos… Park… yeah… ummmm." His head fell

forward to the steering wheel, then bounced back up. "Help me… yah…"

"I'll help you, Flounder, just tell me who you sold to that night. Who'd you sell to?" Yonny was getting impatient with the freak and knew he had to get moving. "Who?"

"Tur… Tur… Bur…" He shook and spasmed as if in a seizure, then rocked his head back. "Turd… ahhh… ahhh…"

"Turdbur?"

He turned his head, "Yah, Tur…," then was rocked again.

Yonny looked at his watch, timing the other's pulse. He couldn't track it. *Four, five to the second? Jesus!* He picked up the knife again and pressed it gently against the blood vessel. The tip rocked in and out, rapid-fire. Just then, Flounder arched his back and went all stiff. A gurgle was followed by a bloody belch from his quivering mouth and then his head fell heavily onto the steering wheel, setting off the horn. Yonny pushed it to one side, silencing the horn as quickly as he could.

He stepped out of the truck and closed the door quietly. *Okay then, TurdBur? Shit! TurdBurger. Teddie Berger. Shit! Just waiting around the corner for his stuff. Sure. Well, maybe we can get two birds tonight. A twofer*. Going around to the driver's side and opening the door, he retrieved the plastic baggie at the unfortunate Flounder's feet. Whistling for Patches, he waited thirty seconds for her to come back into view from down toward Fair Oaks Place, then let her trail him around the corner.

Still there. Probably pretty well stoked by now. He went straight to the passenger's side, opened the door with a gloved hand and jumped in, surprising the hell out of a still lucid teenager. Turdburger, Teddie, or Theodore Berger coughed up a cloud. Yonny said pleasantly, as calmly as he could, "Your friend around the corner wanted you to have this." He tossed the baggie into the boy's lap. "Tell me, Turdie, sorry, Teddie, tell me about Jeffy. Jeffrey Jonas. You do know who I am, don't you?"

He could see fear chilling Teddie's body as it crept up from his gut. "Uh, yes, Sir, yes, sure, you're Jeffrey's dad. I'm so sorry about that, terrible…"

"Save it, Turdie. Why'd you do it? Why'd you give him that shit? You juiced it yourself?"

"Sir, I didn't do…"

"I'm just curious, son," lowering his voice hoping to lower the other's defenses, "how did you get that stuff? Your parents are doctors, right?" The other nodded jerkily. "So, did they give it to you?"

Teddie answered snippily, "Oh, no, Sir. I made it myself. Prussic acid."

"Really?"

"Yes, Sir. AP Chemistry, I have a free lab period in the afternoon. I learned how to do it, got the cafeteria ladies to save the apple seeds…"

"Apple seeds?"

"Yes, Sir, but it takes a lot. Took me about ten cups to get it right, to get enough to…" The young man realized his nerdy pride had gotten the best of him. "Sorry, Sir, I… I…"

Yonny flicked the switchblade open. Slipping the tip into one nostril, "Relax, kid, I just want the truth. It's all a parent can hope for, once it's done and over. So, tell me, why? Or was there someone else? Maybe with you, too?"

The other looked cross-eyed at the blade slowly razoring its way upward. "Please, Sir, it was an accident. I didn't know he would… would die like that."

"So you gave him that coke and cyanide cocktail. First time? I need to know, Teddie."

"Yes, Sir, first time, at least with me, uhhh, by me… uh, my stuff. First time. But it wasn't my idea."

"Never is. Whose?"

"Sir, please, Sir, let me go, please?" He wheezed, "I didn't mean it…"

A pungent odor enveloped the cozy quarters of the sportscar. "Had asparagus tonight, Teddie? That's so gross. What will you tell Mommy and Daddy when you come home with wet pants?"

"Sir, please, let me go. Please?" He was whining now, like he did as a child on the playground at Cambridge when he kept pestering Jeffy and his friends to let him play big boy games.

"Okay, Teddie, we're almost done here. Whose idea was it, if it wasn't yours?"

"It was hers, Sir. She wanted to get him to like it so they could maybe go out together. Said he, Jeffrey, hadn't paid any attention to her in years, said she was pretty damned mad about it." He gulped a bit, "Said she wanted to show him a lesson, give him a lesson, something like that."

"She?"

Teddie now tasted a weak trickling of blood, trembling fear. “Please, Sir, please?” in a trilling, high-pitched, quavering voice.

“Who, Teddie, who, and then we’re done. And we won’t tell anyone about this, will we?” He jerked the blade slightly, “Will we?”

“No, Sir, no, no, Sir. It was… well, it was…”

“Who, Teddie? Chemistry? You want to be a doctor, right?” A slight nod. “Well, then, you know some anatomy, you know how I can slip this blade right up through your sinuses and into your brain, right? And slosh it around in there?”

“Please!” The word came out in a squeaky rushing glissando. “Please? It was… it was Daphne. Said she wanted to get him to do it with her, the coke, Sir, said she’d give him a blowjob if he’d do it.”

“And?”

“And, well, she started on him, but then he… he… he started jumping all around, I got scared, I jumped out of the back seat…”

“Back seat?”

“Yeah, her car, her Mercedes. I was in back, she was going on him in the passenger seat. So I jumped out and started pulling and she started pushing and we got him out and, well, I pushed him down on the ground…”

“And left him there? You left him there? Just like that? To die? Didn’t get help? Really?” He scowled at the scared young man. “I should kill you right here and now for that, just that.”

Teddie cringed, trying to back away from the stiletto. “Sorry, Sir, it was all happening so fast, we couldn’t believe it, we didn’t know what to do…” He began gasping, straining to catch a breath.

Yonny calmed somewhat, “And then?”

“We left. As fast as we could. I had her drop me off a few blocks away, then I walked home.” He wheezed a hoarse whistling sound. “That’s all, Sir. I’m really sorry, Sir, really sorry.” He wheezed again, then began some choking sounds.

Reaching into the front pocket of his khakis, he withdrew an inhaler, popping off the cover. Before he could use it, Yonny snatched it away, holding it over the dashboard. He let the boy see nothing but a stone face, no emotion at all. Then, quietly, “Daphne Porterhouse? Really?”

“Yes, Sir. She said… she wanted him.”

“To add to her trophies, I’m sure.” He let the other see him relax, soften his features, unknot his brow, loosen his tightened lips. “Thanks, Teddie, Theodore, I appreciate your telling me this. It will really help me, help my wife understand what happened. You see, having him die so young was bad enough, but not knowing how he passed his last moments, well…"

Teddie choked some more, then struggled for a breath. "Please, Sir, please, I need it… I'm so sorry, Sir… please?"

"And you wanted her, but Jeffy was her first choice? Gave him that stuff? Got him out of the way? That's murder, kid."

Teddie made a weak lunge for the inhaler, thrust back into his seat by a forearm pinning him in place. "Need this, do you? Is this how Jeffy died, gasping and choking?" He moved to within a few inches of the boy's russeting face. "Is that the way it was?"

"Yes, Sir…" One rale followed another. "Yes, Sir, I suppose so…" His eyes pleaded, "I need that, Sir, I can't breathe!"

"Neither could Jeffy, could he? Did his lungs fail him? Or did he just pass out when you shoved him out of the car?"

The boy was writhing, squirming side to side under the unyielding weight of Yonny's arm. "I need it…" His voice was feeble now, trying to slip through a tightening throat. "Please?"

"Just a little longer, Teddie, just a little longer. I want you to feel, to experience what Jeffy did. I want you to feel it, feel what it means to be on the edge of death, of dying. Like Jeffy. Just like Jeffy."

He held the boy down as he jerked this way and that, twisting, trying to free his lungs to breathe, lapsing into one spasm after another. Then he went limp, his face a mottled blue.

Yonny held him in position for a minute or so, releasing the boy to collapse against the window. He felt for a pulse. None. Looking at the inhaler, he slipped it into his pocket. He picked up the plastic bag, casually tossing the contents about the body, then folded it carefully, concealing it in his hand.

"What are you looking at, Patches?" The dog had been whining softly outside the car window all this time. They walked an extra mile, down around La Jara and back, plenty of distance to discreetly dispose of his little cargoes in somebody's tomorrow's garbage. Home, Rachel started in on him immediately, "I was worried sick about you two! You've been gone almost two hours! What have you been doing?"

"Walking. Stopped to say hi to some guys I know from Kiwanis. Then I let Patches off her leash to chase a cat, had to wait until she was sure it wasn't ever coming back to this part of town, ever, then home. That's it."

"You let Patches off her leash? She could've been run over! Where?"

"La Jara. No traffic. I was careful."

LeahRhea tumbled in, chiming in unison, "Now can we eat, please?"

23

Sam walked through his front door headed straight for the kitchen. "You're late. Again." Linda didn't even turn. "You got lucky, I was just about to throw it out."

He leaned a hand flat on the kitchen countertop, thought of a kiss on her cheek, then said simply, "Thanks, Sweets. Sorry, but this Jonas case…"

Linda turned sharply, snapping, "I'm sick of your cases, Sam! Sick of them, sick of them! That's all you do, is work on them or talk about them when you get home, in your sleep, even. Enough!" She caught a breath, took another, then, "Sam, just go somewhere until you're done with them, okay? At least done with your high school thing, okay? That, or get back to normal. And lay off the booze! You promised!" Cooler now, "That's it, Sam. That's the way it has to be."

He watched her walk down the hall, watched her close the bedroom door behind her. *Fine! That's how she wants it, fine! Martinez has a spare bedroom now that he's on his own. Maybe I'll bunk at his place for a while. Sure as hell beats coming home to this every night.*

Sam kept on fulminating in his mind, angel on one shoulder cautioning him, devil on the other urging him to bolt. He was leaning toward li'l Lucifer when his walkie-talkie crackled, *'All units to the high school, Castano. Two DOA's.'* He reached over to dial it down, then looked at his dinner. Rising abruptly from his chair, he listened to the little devil saying, *She ain't much of a cook, either.* He scraped and rinsed his plate and gathered his things.

Three patrol cars were angled in at the Mule Stall, blocking a Ford 150 pickup. *Shiny, dealer plates, new.* Another car was alongside a late model Corvette. *Typical Alamo Heights motor pool*, thought Sam. Lights in his rearview mirror caught his eye. *TV reporters. Damn! Not ready yet*. He jerked his Crown Vic backwards and spun it broadside, stopping the TV truck dead.

The driver started yelling at Sam. He stepped out of his car and sauntered over, opening his jacket to show his sidearm. The driver stopped his yelling, but an attractive Latina stepped aggressively toward him. Wearing tight khaki pants under a purple quilted parka zipped against the whipping breeze, she reminded him of a grape on a stalk. *A pretty grape, give her that*. "Excuse me, excuse me, who's in charge here?"

Sam decided to string her along. "No one, Ma'am."

"What do you mean?"

"Never mind. Sam Thompson, AHPD. Listen, I know what you want, but I need some time here before I can tell you what's up." Pointing to the officers spooling out yellow tape, "Please stay behind those lines, okay, so I don't have to take you down to the station?"

"I'm a journalist! I'm a professional, unlike…" She caught herself, just. "I have a right to get this story! For the people!"

"For your ratings, you mean. Tell you what. You be a good little girl and I'll give you the first interview. Get set up over there, so you can get the pickup. Deal?"

She turned in a snit and barked out instructions to her crew.

Sam wheeled around and headed for the pickup. He was soon sorry he did, very sorry. The stench of vomit was overwhelming, even from a few feet away. He regretted attempting Linda's attempt at cooking.

"Great stuff, huh, Sam?"

"Yeah, Gary, just great. I think I'll check out the other car, okay?" That one was better, much better. *Just a kid, do I know this kid? Never seen him down at the station. Looks familiar, though, doesn't he?* "Dale, what you got on this one here?"

"Can't tell. Got cocaine all over his lap, but don't see any on his nose. Definitely had been smoking dope, smells it, big time, all over." He handed over a wallet. "Theodore Berger, age 17. Lives, did, on Parklane over in Olmos Park. That's it. Plates check out, registered to a David Berger, same address."

"Daddy's car? Out for some thrills, wrong place, wrong time?"

"Maybe. Oh, Sam, out of the way. EMS."

He stepped out of the way of the stretcher bearers, nodding to one of them. Turning back to his patrolman, "Called the parents?"

"Yes, Sir. Left a message, asked Alice to keep trying."

Apparently she had gotten through. A black Mercedes S500 stopped with juddering brakes. It sat there, engine running, for several minutes. As the emergency crew strapped down the body, both doors opened and a couple dressed for a gala came rushing up. Sam stepped into their path, holding up both hands in stop signs. "David? Sam Thompson, Alamo Heights Police. Was a couple of classes behind you."

"I don't, well, I, what happened? Is that Teddie?"

"Yes, but…"

"Sam, you said? Sorry, but I don't remember. I have to see my boy. He's…"

Sam interrupted, "Yeah. Here, come on into the ambulance. You, Ma'am, please stay put, please?"

"Officer, I am a doctor. My husband is a doctor. We need to see him, so please stand aside."

Whoa! "Yes, Ma'am! Please come over to this side, the TV people are over there, can't see you get in."

He helped Doctor Mother Berger over the bumper and left the doors just ajar. *Crap. Back to Vomitville.*

The other had already been covered on a stretcher. "Sam, got nothing, here. Plenty of baggies, mostly weed, some more coke. You know who he was?"

"How, man? I haven't seen him yet. Jacquelyn, can we get a peek?"

"You buyin'?"

Sam laughed. "Sure, Darlin', whatever you want."

Big white guy and petite black woman squared off for a moment, then, simultaneously, "Nawww!"

When she stopped laughing, she said, "Here you go, but hurry. Too many eyes."

Sam pulled the sheet down about a foot or so. "Damn! The Flounder."

The patrolman held out a wallet. "Robert Cavendish Flournoy, Fourth, says this." Sam took a quick look then handed it back. "Log it."

Hands on hips, he stood still, searching the scene, scenes. The mercury vapor streetlamps gave off an eerie greenish-yellow light, softening the shadows in an unnatural way, in an indistinct fog. He flipped open his flashlight, peering under the truck, then into the cab as long as he could stand the stench, then to the other side. Nothing, no signs of struggles. No casings. *What happened here, to him?*

Before he could don his gloves and start scraping the vile puke off the windshield, a voice rang out from the Castano side. "Sam, is it? Come here, please?"

It was the Berger mother, so he half-jogged over. "Yes, Ma'am?"

Briskly, "Apologies for my rudeness. You can understand, I hope. It appears our son died from an acute asthma attack. He has suffered from childhood with chronic asthma. Here, write this down for your report." She rattled off a bunch of medical jargon, stopping from time to time to spell something for Sam. "There." Now her voice was pleading, not peremptory. "Please, if you would, no mention of any drugs, drug use, no marijuana or cocaine. Please?"

Sam responded quietly, "Ma'am, Doctor, you know I can't do that. But, but…," he held his hands up to stifle her, "unless there's violence, which I don't see, there's no need for any of that to get public. This is our city, our records, I, we have plenty of say how the County looks at it."

"County? Oh, you mean its medical examiners. Their participation will not be required. My husband and I will prepare the necessary papers, sign same." Now her voice was clipped, her diction precise, as polished as her long red nails. "We are more than qualified. No need for anyone else's participation, understood?"

"I'll have to talk to the Chief, not sure…"

She cut him off, "Of course. David and I will be in his office first thing. Will there be anything else?"

"No, no, that'll do." He considered his options. "But I do need to see the body before it is taken, where?"

"No. And none of your business."

"Yes, it is my business." He stared down at her. "Unless you and your husband want to be our guests overnight for interfering with an investigation. You'd see the Chief first thing when he gets there at six."

Her dark eyes narrowed, then relaxed in capitulation. "Very well, but make it quick."

"Your wish, Ma'am." Sam clambered into the crowded ambulance, gestured to the medic to uncover the body down to the waist. Quickly, as promised, he looked for needle tracks, found none, forced open the mouth, didn't want to find anything, then noticed a small stripe of congealed blood below one nostril. "Light? Magnifier?"

"Officer Thomas? Must you? I must…"

"Take him out." Sam had had just about enough of this family. "Take him out!" One of his men grappled the doctor, who resisted briefly then wilted. Sam looked back. "Okay, okay! But stay put and shaddup!"

Now he took his time, peering up into the right nare—he remembered the word from the examiner's lecture at the academy, thought it a funny one at the time—and followed a small trail of blood as far as he could. He poked his pen up there, to much parental agitation, then pulled it back. "Something went up there. Something very thin and very, very sharp, like a scalpel, a surgeon's scalpel. Would you fine doctors know anything about that? Either of you surgeons?"

Doctor Daddy mumbled, "No, radiologist, she's a pediatrician."

"Yeah, but all doctors have scalpels, right? Like getting a box of crayons for the first day of school, yeah?" One of the medics tapped his watch for Sam's benefit, so he closed, "Don't go anywhere. Don't try to book a flight to Aruba or wherever doctors go. Very stupid, and I'm sure y'all aren't stupid. Now these guys have work to do."

He herded the parents out and jumped down, instantly regretting the jolt to his knee, then slammed the doors. He left the doctors behind, limping toward his car when the Latina confronted him. "Our deal, Detective. First interview?"

Sam bent over to rub his knee. "Okay, but short, okay?"

She smiled, "We'll see."

It took a while to set her scene, the lighting, the way her makeup looked, the cameraman moving his tripod so the breeze blew her hair away behind her, not onto her lipstick. Finally, she cued the lights. "This is Cassandra Elvira Benavides reporting from the Alamo Heights High School campus on the Northside where two young men have been found dead in their cars a few feet away from each other. Apparently these deaths were drug-related, and I have Detective Sam Thompson of the Alamo Heights Police with us in an exclusive Channel Five Eyewitness News interview." She turned to Sam with a shake of her long wavy hair. "Detective Thompson, please tell our viewers what you've found at the scene."

Sam leaned over slightly, taking hold of the microphone. "Well, Cassandra—it is Cassandra? First, no names, not until we've notified the next of kin." He hoped she had been checking her nails, not prowling around the Berger scene. "It's too early to tell the cause of death, but something drug-related cannot be ruled out. Neither can violence or natural causes, for that matter. And if it was drugs that caused this, it's just another senseless tragedy. Think of the families affected. I can't emphasize enough the need for parents to know, to really know…" The reporter was trying to pull the microphone back to her side, Sam holding it tightly. "To know what their children are doing, to look for the signs…" she pulled again, he resisted, "of drug use. And don't think that smoking marijuana is harmless. Learn to say, *just say no*."

This time he released his grip, the mike almost hitting Cassandra's nose on the rebound. "Thank you, Detective." She glared at him. "And what are the next steps in your investigation?"

"We are canvassing the scene thoroughly according to our search protocols"—Sam loved spouting the handbook jargon for the know-nothing reporter types—"and we will know more in a few hours." He looked at his watch, "Probably around, oh, I'd say 11:30 or so."

"That long?" Cassy was definitely pissed at being gigged like this.

"Quality can't be rushed, Miss Benavides."

Flustered, she had just enough field experience to not call him out on live TV for being a sexist pig. "Of course, Detective, of course." Turning to her cameraman, she intoned gravely, "We will follow up with the Alamo Heights police and report back to you. Over to you, Brent and Maria."

As soon as the lights dimmed, she turned on him like a rabid vixen. "Don't ever make me look stupid like that, ever again, or I'll, we'll…"

Sam reached over to relocate some errant windswept strands. She recoiled as if snakebit. He leered, "Have time for a cocktail, Miss?"

As she turned away in a huff, her high heels clattering on the pavement, he glanced over at a grinning camera crew. He winked.

24

Next morning, Yonny padded his way across the kitchen where Rachel was tending a pan of bacon. "Shouldn't do that, R. You know your rules. Yahweh will be pissed."

She smiled wanly back at him. "As if She has not visited sufficient sorrow and lamentation upon us aforehand?"

"All Biblical, are we? This early?" He reached in for a kiss.

She brushed her lips against his. "Seems appropriate."

"Yeah, it does. Sure does." He opened the refrigerator, taking out some eggs and milk and then some orange juice. "French toast?"

She nodded, so he went to work after pouring himself some coffee. They had but a few moments of tranquility before the twins came bounding down the stairs, their soccer cleats click-clacking across the floor, the sound of Pop-Tarts erupting from the toaster, Patches and Sluggo, the Boston Terrier, sniffing and snuffling, finally, the tortoise-shell Princess Eloise strolling in regally, tail held high. To cap the pandæmonium, three sharp honks from outside. The twins grabbed their juice boxes and pastries and dashed out, trailed by barking dogs.

After the door slammed, Yonny turned to his wife. "They are become Shivas, destroyers of peace and quiet."

"That they are. Get the paper, please?"

Yonny flipped to the sports pages to read about the latest Spurs smack-down, this time Philly at the hands of Robinson and Duncan, the new kid. He had just lifted his cup to his lips when Rachel gasped, "Oh, my God! I can't believe this!"

"Believe what?"

"Last night, around the high school. Two people found dead in their cars."

"Murdered, you think?"

"That, or, well, let's see… possible drug overdoses. Probable drug overdoses."

"Who were they? Names?"

She gasped, "Bob Flournoy's son! And, yes, here it is, Theodore Berger. Isn't she a doctor?"

"So is her husband, a radiologist. A good one, too, I hear. He went to Heights with us, too, a couple or three years ahead of us."

She read through the balance of the article. "Sam is quoted here. Not very happy. '*Too much of this going on. Causes too much crime, and now death.*' "

"Hear, hear!"

She squinted at him over the top of the paper. "You were up there last night, weren't you?"

"Are you suggesting something?"

"No…"

"Patches and I went up there so I could let her run on the practice field."

"I thought you said she ran loose on La Jara."

"She did." He could see the quizzical look quite clearly. "Both. Are you trying to get at something?"

"No, it's just…"

"That I might have had something to do with all this? That I might have killed them?"

Her wrists flopped to the tabletop, taking the paper with them. "Yonny, why in the world would you say that?"

"Because I did, well, no, I was there, sorta helped them was all I did."

Rachel was speechless, her mouth a perfect O.

"R, here's what happened." He related the incident with Flounder, then Teddy. "You see, once Sam told me it was murder, I, well, I… Rachel, now I want revenge. Just like I'd like revenge of some sort on that girl who got that old friend of mine started on drugs. I had to find out, Rachel. Maybe that explains the way I've been."

He pushed his plate away, settling his fists on the table. "Flournoy's boy was a creep, a slug, a slacker. I planned to use a knife to force him to tell what he knew, torture him if I had to, then kill him, maybe. Dead men tell no tales." He gave her a sardonic smile. "But when I got there, he was already in bad shape. Said someone did something to him. He was convulsing and vomiting—it was pretty terrible—and died. Before he died, though, I managed to get a name out of him.

Teddie Berger. Do you remember what Jeffy and his friends called him?"

She shook her head.

"Turdburger."

Wrinkling her nose in synaesthesia, "That's terrible."

"Yeah. Kids. Anyway, Teddie was right around the corner, waiting for this guy. So, I, well, I persuaded him to tell what he knew. The knife helped. He was the one who doctored the coke, all right. Why? Why deliberately kill one of his friends?"

"Why?"

"Love, dearest, or at least jealousy." His slight smile evaporated. "Seems there was a girl he was interested in, but she was interested in Jeffy, not him. She had snubbed him, Jeffy, for years, but all of a sudden wanted him now, before he went off to college. So I guess it was Teddie's idea to get rid of his rival. Said this girl wanted Jeffy to do some cocaine with him, wanted to have sex with Jeffy, not him, so he got the stuff, fixed it." He swallowed hard, "Sam told me, right off the bat, the day after, that Jeffy was found with pink lipstick on his…"

"Penis? Oh, God!"

"Yeah, my sentiments exactly."

"Did he tell you who this girl was? And what happened to him, Teddie?"

"Teddie had been smoking grass and when I interrogated him," he smirked, "he started wheezing and coughing. An asthma attack. He had an inhaler, but I took it away from him, and I, well, I put a little pressure on his chest, and, well, he choked to death. Just like Jeffy."

Rachel's voice was flat, impassive. "Poetic justice, but what about the girl?"

"The girl?" He let the word hang in the air. "Daphne Porterhouse."

"Daphne?" Her eyes darted through the French doors to the house across the street. "That pumped up little slut?"

"Now, now."

"Now, now, my ass! Her airhead of a mother lording it over me all these years, '*Daphne this, Daphne that!*' And now this? I could strangle her!"

"Who? Daphne or Julie?"

She almost choked. "Yonny, tell me you wouldn't…"

He stared at her, stone-faced.

"You would?"

Yonny murmured, "Telling you all this was a mistake, right?"

"Mmm, hmmm." Rachel covered his hands with hers, could only stare across the table at someone she thought she knew, now a different person unfolding before her like a rosebud, the closed outer sheath finally yielding to some darker emergent forces within.

"You're my wife. You can't testify against me, now can you?"

"Can't be forced to testify."

"Typical lawyer, picking hairs."

"Splitting hairs, you mean. No, I can't testify against you." She folded her hands in prayer against the bridge of her nose, then looked over her fingertips. "And I won't testify against you." She took a deep breath, letting it out in a hissing sigh through clenched teeth, "So do it."

"So will I, Milady MacBeth, so will I."

25

Rachel folded down the top of Yonny's sports section as she reached over to take his plate. "Nothing about this, right?"

Before she went upstairs to change for tennis, she turned on the little television in the corner, pushing aside a box of dog biscuits and a pair of headbands, identical, of course. Rinsing her hands, she turned abruptly at a familiar voice, then the other way at the telephone. Stepping over to the other wall, she answered, "Jonas residence, head of household speaking." Ignoring the cry of '*What?*' from the dining room, "Oh, Sam, hi. I, we just turned on the TV. Did you know from across the room without my glasses you look just like your cousin Fred. You know, the actor? Sound like him, too. Yes, of course, that's a compliment."

She paused, listening, then responded, "Terrible, just terrible. The paper said it was drugs? Here, wait a sec, would you? Let me get Yonnyboy in here on speaker."

She punched a button then cradled the receiver. "Yonny, it's Sam."

He had already leaned his forearms onto the counter, peering at the interview. '*...if it was drugs that caused this, just another senseless tragedy. Think of the families affected... I can't emphasize enough the need for parents to know, to really know...*' Without turning, "Tell Sam he has a bit of a country twang, last syllable gets a little twangy. Oh, yeah, Sam. Still sounds good." He went over to his wife and wrapped his arms around her waist, then higher. She didn't resist. "So, what's the deal, Sam?"

"Hiya, Yawny. You're just jealous I'm on TV and you're not. Okay, pretty ugly, one of them, guy nicknamed the Flounder..."

Rachel interrupted, "His father is a partner at my law firm, Bob Flournoy. I'm really surprised."

"You wouldn't be if you knew him like we know him. Sorry Mrs., Rachel, he was a real creep. One of my predecessors had taken it upon himself to play—what was that character's name, Popeye something or the other—play the hardass, get rough with some of the slimeballs hanging around the High School, even Cambridge. Knocked one of them around so hard he got himself indicted for assault and use of undue force. Got off, the jury thought the pusher was a total loser, but his father, your law partner, got a restraining order keeping us away from his precious little boy. All we could do was watch him, follow him around, park where he might be doing some business. Daddy objected to even that, so we just pass by every now and then. Not very good, even for police work."

Yonny did his best as an innocent. "So he was one of the ones you were talking about, about Jeffy, that is?"

"Oh, yeah. But I don't think he would have poisoned your boy, not good for business, like I said."

Rachel leaned over. "But he could have given someone the stuff, they could have doct—umm, fixed it up?"

"Sure. Anything is possible." The other end was quiet five seconds or so, then. "Yawny, Rachel, tell me the truth. Do you know anything about this?"

Before Rachel could silence him, Yonny said, "No, not anything more than what you've told me so far. But I was up there last night, right around sundown, didn't see anything unusual."

As his wife shot him a recriminating look, Sam asked in a level tone, "Yonny, what did you see?"

"Like I said, nothing unusual. I had Patches with me, she likes to run free on the practice field. I clean up after her, Sam, promise. So she ran and ran, quite a bit, then we came home. After walking down Castano to LaJara, then back up the hill, if you must know. Up at the High School, I only saw one car, a really nice Corvette, bright yellow, came up just as we were leaving, but the windows were up, it was getting dark, I couldn't see whoever was inside. That's it."

"Is it?"

"Sure, it is, Sam. What are you saying?"

"Oh, nothing. Just doing my job, suspicious cop, you know how that goes."

Rachel and Yonny looked at each other. She silenced her husband with a hand. "Sam, what else? The papers said this was an overdose, overdoses?"

A whistling sigh came from the phone. "Okay, I'm going to tell you some things, but don't, repeat, don't say anything about this to anyone. Let me close my door." Returning to his squeaky chair, "I'm betting this Flounder kid od'd on methamphetamine. We don't think he ever dealt meth, just weed and coke, maybe ecstasy. Won't know how much 'til we get the toxicology results, but it looked like he had shot up gallons of that crap."

"How so, Sam?" Rachel had relaxed, now wanted to steer the conversation away.

"I've seen bunches of these. Old, young—thirteen, even—you can tell. Funny, no track marks, no rubber hose, no bruises. Shoes still on, too."

Yonny smiled at Rachel. "Shoes?"

"C'mon, Yawny, where you been? Like heroin users. Once they collapse all the veins in their arms, they go between the toes next."

"Okay. What then?"

Rachel interrupted her husband, "And the Berger boy? He was brilliant, such a nice family. What happened to him?"

"Choked to death."

Looking at each other, both exclaimed, "What?"

"Choked to death. Talked to the parents right before I taped my latest fifteen minutes of fame. She was on call, got the page, they came straight over. Kid was an asthmatic. Mom and Dad did an impromptu postmortem. Let me see here," a silence except for the swishing of some papers, "*Sudden asphyxic asthma. Bronchospasm. Cause of death constriction of the airways, death within minutes if sufficiently acute*. We haven't released that, so don't say anything. He had apparently smoked a bushel of weed, too, not real smart with his condition, don't say anything about that, for sure."

Nods in unison, "Okay."

Sam continued in measured tones, "Something else. We looked through his pockets, the car seats, found what his mother said was the cover to an asthma inhaler, but looked up and down for the thing, couldn't find it anywhere, even outside. Also, this morning the examiner reported he had a long bruise across his chest."

Rachel hushed Yonny. "What does he think that is?"

"Like a steel pipe, maybe a forearm, a strong man's forearm."

Before she could stop him, Yonny laughed, "Rules me out. Oh, hell, that wasn't very funny, was it?"

"No, it isn't. Not funny at all. The kid's dead, you shouldn't be making jokes."

"Right. Sorry." Husband smiled broadly at wife, who covered her mouth.

They could sense Sam's budding anger. "And the inhaler? My guess I someone was hassling the kid, took it from him, then leaned on him 'til he croaked. And took the thing with him."

Rachel smiled grimly. "Or her, Sam."

"What do you mean?"

"Could have been a girl? But no, I guess not, maybe not with that bruise. But there are some pretty athletic girls out there, Sam. Equal opportunity, all that."

Don't try that feminist shit on me, changing the argument. "Yeah, but not likely."

"Maybe his dealer, maybe he hadn't paid up or something?" Yonny paused. "Just trying to be helpful."

"Uh, huh, right. No, I doubt it was his dealer, Flounder himself, probably. Not with a baggie of coke spilled all over his lap. No, not likely. And another thing, someone had shoved a blade of some sort up his nose."

"Ooooh…"

Rachel moved closer to the phone, shouldering Yonny aside. "I need to give Evelyn a call. That's Teddie's mother, we've worked together in the Sisterhood. I'll wait a few days, I guess, but she's going through the same…"

Sam had another thought. "Weren't your… son and him, Theodore, friends?"

Just then, the front door slammed and the house erupted in barks and shouts signaling an end to adult conversation. "Shhh, girls! Daddy and I are on the phone! Sam, we'll have to catch up with you later, okay? Let us know if we can do anything."

She clicked off, smiling broadly at her husband.

That night, Rachel called her father, hoping to avoid her mother if she could. "Daddy, can you keep Mother away from the phone? I, we've got some new information on Jeffy's death."

"Yeah, let me close the door here." A few moments later, "Okay, then. What you got?"

"Turns out there was a girl involved…"

"A girl?"

"Yes, Daddy. She's the one who wanted Jeffy to try the cocaine. If it weren't for her, Jeffy would still be… with us."

"I don't get it. What'd she do? The poison?"

"No, there was another boy who did that. They were together with Jeffy. That boy is dead. Daddy, don't breathe a word of this, but Yonny, well, he didn't exactly kill him, but he, well, he helped it happen." She choked quietly, then whispered, "Daddy, he made it happen. He had a knife…"

Solomon murmured incredulously, "Ian? My son-in-law?"

"Yes, Daddy. I've learned a lot about him I never knew, never, ever guessed. So much, Daddy, so much. He took it on himself to find out who was involved, forced this kid to confess, then…, well, he got him to tell about this girl. She wanted to date Jeffy, was, well, anyway, she's the one. The one who persuaded him to do the cocaine, the poisoned stuff. Now Yonny and I can finally be sure Jeffy didn't do any of that before this, so she has to be the one who got him started."

"So the kid is dead. Who's this girl?"

"Our neighbor's daughter, just across the street. Daphne Porterhouse. Oh, Daddy, you'll never know what this means to us, to know what happened to Jeffy and why and who was there when he died. And now we, well, we…"

"Uh, here comes your mother. Good for you. We'll talk."

Rachel looked at the phone. *Daddy?*

26

In all the drama surrounding a young man's death, the acquisition of Langefelter's had moved along at its own pace. Once he had spelled out the deal to his friend Arnie, Yonny had stepped back and let the latter run with it, with the lawyers, the corporate formation, the investment summary for his investors and such. He and Arnie separated the real estate from the operations, quickly negotiated leases for the stores, each getting what he wanted and needed: Yonny, the anchor tenants to keep the retail centers populated, Arnie, a large slug of subordinated capital raised almost effortlessly. And Yonny had other reasons to keep things separate, reasons he wasn't going to share with his friend, reasons his pal was better off not knowing. Now it was time to bring the management in, namely, Sarah's father. Arnie flew in from Dallas one afternoon, was picked up by Yonny and over to the mall they went, a five minute drive.

"Does he know why we're coming? Has corporate managed to keep it quiet?"

"We'll find out both."

"So…, what did you tell him?"

"That I, the Polsky Organization, that is, was interested in a couple of development parcels and one retail center, just a real estate deal. I had to re-introduce myself, he seems to manage, or prefers, to forget me every few years."

"Why?"

"His daughter and I were pretty damned close, a long time ago, now. And I am not one of your Chosen, am I, right?"

Arnold Rothstein just shook his head. "I get it. All too well. Same happened to me. Dad, well, Mother, really, wouldn't let me keep on going with a *shiksa*." He looked away, then back. "She was beautiful, a cheerleader at Highland Park, we were, like you said, pretty damned close. Wasn't meant to be, I thought at the time."

"The bad side of *Bashert*."

"Bashert? Where'd you get that, goy boy?"

"You haven't met my Rachel yet. I've been keeping her under wraps until this deal is done, but I think I can introduce you now. You'll understand."

"Yeah? Holding out, are you?"

Yonny turned, a big smile splitting his face, "Yeah."

He turned back to the wheel as they started up the ramp. "Do you still see the beautiful blonde cheerleader—I assume she was blonde, still is?"

"Oh, yes, pretty frequently. And yes, blonde. Natural back then, can't say now."

"Won't say. Here we are."

Before they reached the store's entry, Yonny stopped his friend. "When you see her, your old girlfriend, how does it feel? What do you feel, seeing her again, seeing her with someone else who has her instead of you?"

"Like getting skewered in the chest with a hot poker. Like drinking acid. Every damned time, it just won't go away."

"Did it, did it affect your marriages, I should say, your divorces?"

"Guess."

"Don't need to."

"And you've been single six or seven years, now, you haven't tried…?"

"Six years this time. And, no, not my style, old friend. And…" He paused, swallowing hard, "Why so inquisitive about my love life?"

Yonny stepped aside to let past a group of ladies who lunch, or maybe lunch ladies, by their look. "Oh, nothing. Just curious, you know, the religious persecution bit. Here we are."

After keeping them waiting a bit, Nathan Langefelter's secretary ushered them in. While not an overly large office, it was impressively accoutered with photographs, plaques, awards and other paraphernalia appropriate to a very highly regarded pillar of the community. Yonny was a bit cowed, but Arnie took it all in stride. "This is a nice letter Stanley wrote you, Mr. Langefelter. And a better picture of LBJ than you usually see, that late in life."

"May I help you two? Something about real estate, one of you said?"

Yonny hastily introduced Arnie, then himself using his proper name.

Ignoring Yonny for the moment, "Your father is Arnold, Senior, or was, rather?"

"Yes, Sir, Arnold, Junior, actually, I'm the Third."

"I was very sorry to hear of his passing. Please do give my regards to Diana. So you're in real estate now?"

"No, he is." He pointed to Yonny. "He and I are here because the two of us are buying Langefelter's, lock, stock and barrel. Including the real estate."

Mr. Langefelter was no more startled by his friend than was Yonny, who tried to speak, "You see…"

"Sorry, Yawny, I don't want to waste his time. Yes, we have an agreement with Consolidated, just doing our due diligence, dotting i's and crossing t's. It's a bit simpler than most of the deals I do, same for him."

Langefelter stabbed at his intercom. "Louise, get Merrill Raab on the line. Immediately!"

"Don't bother, Sir." Yonny had regained his voice, but more, the heady rush of having gained the upper hand for once, just once after all the years. "It's a done deal. My father-in-law and Mr. Raab shook hands, agreed on the number, and it's done. My group, the Polsky Organization, has the real estate under contract, and Arnie, here, likewise for the operations and inventory and trademarks. It's done, Sir, we're just here as a courtesy."

Arnie followed, "And as part of that courtesy, we have a proposal for you. I urge you to take it seriously." He took a folder from his briefcase and slid it across the desk.

Yonny, trying mightily not to gloat, said, "I urge you to accept it, Mr. Langefelter. Strongly. For Sarah."

"For… Sarah?" The older man squinted over his reading glasses. "Of course. You're…" He snapped his fingers twice and pointed at him. "You're that Ian boy who went with my Sarah in high school?"

"Yes, Sir, and you're the father who broke us up and caused us both such grief. Oh, yes, she did marry a Jewish boy, didn't she? Look where that got her. Hope you're happy." He turned to Arnie. "I think he has everything he needs. Please, Sir, take this, us, seriously and get on the bus with us. Please?"

As the two younger men reached the door, Langefelter called out, "One moment. You," pointing a gnarled finger at Yonny, "I want you to tell me something. That's an order!"

"Sorry, Sir, we give the orders now. But I'll listen. What is it?"

"Are you the one who sent me those photographs? Of Louis, I mean?"

Yonny showed him the merest cryptic crease of a smile. "Time to go, Arnold Threesticks, time to go."

Arnie decided to make an impromptu inventory appraisal as they meandered their way through the colorful store, *couture* here, shoes there, the Gucci boutique off to one side. In menswear he stopped to finger the surgeon's cuffs on a double-breasted suit, then scrutinized his new partner. "You're still wearing those preppie things? Not one of these Italian jobs?"

Shaking his head, Yonny countered, "Rachel wants me to, but I keep telling her Armani is an Italian curse word, words plural, that is. Nope, not me. No fashion risks taken here."

Rothstein smiled as he riffed some ties displayed on a table, then turning abruptly, blurted, "So that's why?"

Yonny adopted his best pretense of innocence. "Why what, Arnie?"

"Your sudden interest in my love life."

"Yes and no. Yes, his daughter and I went through the same thing. I used to experience the same pain over and over, each time I saw her. But," he checked himself, his gaze drifting toward the Turnbull & Asser collection, turning away slightly, "it passes. She manages to ease it, never can heal it, but just being around her helps a lot."

"You're lucky."

Yonny faced his friend. "So are you. You'll meet San Antonio's most beautiful women of the Book tonight. And sometimes the most difficult, to which I can attest. Both. Consider yourself warned."

Rachel had told Sarah a little white lie or two to get her out of the house and out in public. '*Dinner at the Argyle with several friends, low pressure, Yonny has some people in from Dallas, thought we'd get some people together, thought you'd like to meet them.*' "Okay, Yonster, she's going to come. I may have to go over there and dress her myself, but she'll come. So, who is this mystery guest? A classmate? I didn't meet him at a reunion all these years?"

"Between your baby schedule and his divorce schedule, we just haven't intersected."

"Divorce schedule?"

"Yep. Made a couple of unfortunate choices. He's one of my group that sat on the back row, absolutely brilliant. But," he laughed, "Arnie never said a word, unless he got called to open the day's case. Once or twice, but that was it. Adamant about it, although rumor had it that speaking up in class was worth half your grade. Didn't matter, he graduated with distinction."

"As did you, if I recall your braggadocio correctly?"

"As did I, yes. Anyway, he went out to San Francisco, venture capital, for about ten years, I think, then came back to Dallas, investing his family's and several other high value families' money. His family was originally in retail, sold their stores to Sanger-Harris, I think, then invested in other retailers, there and around the state, other things. I knew he coveted Langefelter's ever since he tried and failed to get Neiman's, so it was an easy sell. It's his history, though, that's so interesting. His grandfather was Arnold Rothstein, the first Arnold. Heard of him? You should have."

"If you say that, it has to be because of Daddy. A gangster?"

"Not only a gangster, he's the one who fixed the 1919 World Series. The Black Sox scandal. Remember that movie, *Eight Men Out*? And better, Fitzgerald wrote him into *The Great Gatsby*. Meyer Wolfsheim, remember?"

"No."

"How about Nathan Detroit, the gambler, *Guys and Dolls*? Frank Sinatra, one of your favorites? Get it now?"

"No, I don't. And this gangster, you're going to fix him up with Sarah, your girlfriend? Really, Yonnypup, really? A gangster? A serially divorced gangster?" This time, her words were bathed in honey laced with more than a few traces of iron filings and carborundum. "Really?"

"Really. He's as straight as they come, a perfect gentleman. Great guy. You'll like him, but don't try to steal him, okay?"

At the Argyle, after a brief walk around the antebellum structure and up to the little-used third level to catch the views, Rachel, Arnie and Yonny were back on the ground floor, standing by Finley's pulpit, just chatting. Yonny was giving his guest a bit of the place's history when

Sarah walked in. Rachel looked at Arnie's gape-mouthed stare, then at her husband. He just winked.

At dinner, Rachel and her husband were mere spectators. If Arnie had normally been more than a bit laconic in school, not so tonight. He and Sarah started by playing '*What a small world*', their retail and religious realms having overlapped, mutual friends, all that. *She is in her element*, he thought, *has a captive audience and boy, can she talk!*

And one Arnold Rothstein the Third was a most willing captive, the very exemplar of Stockholm Syndrome. Rachel stole several amused glances toward her husband, returned in kind. She slipped her hand under the table, searching out his, soon rewarded with a firm squeeze.

When the girls went off to the powder room, Arnie turned to his host with a look of the gravest concern. "Do I, we tell her? What will she say? More, you know her, what will she do? Does she make scenes? Run off crying? Pull the tablecloth off the table?"

"She's been through a lot, Arnie, a lot, okay? A very bad deal. So, she's pretty vulnerable, fragile, even. On the other hand, don't think for a minute her mother hasn't already left her a nasty message with the news, blaming it all on her for knowing me. So, yes, I think you should tell her."

"Me? She's your old girlfriend. Why me? Why not you? It's the two of us, right? Partners?" The last came out pleadingly.

"One, she's your new girlfriend. Two, I still can't say anything in front of Rachel, nor can you. Her firm represents Consolidated here. Three, *what you mean, partners, Kemosabe?*"

"Here they come. What do I do?"

"We're going home a bit early. Babysitter issues, okay? I'll suggest she drive you home, but first show you around some more, tell you the history. She's been very involved in this place and the foundation it supports. She'll be happy to do it. And then, just as you're about to kiss her good night for the sixth or seventh time, you tell her. Just make sure you let her know we've asked her father to stay on, in between all the panting, that is. Okay, now, shush. And we do have a curfew, so you know."

Rachel snuggled as close as the BMW's seats allowed. "You are the very devil, do you know that?"

"A very lucky devil, wouldn't you say?"

"I would." She leaned over, bringing a kiss.

Later that night, as he walked back into the bedroom, there was Rachel laying on the bed, her crossed ankles the only demure thing about her. "Hiya, sailor. Want a date?"

"Maybe, maybe not." He squinted at her form then let out a mock sigh, "Yeah, I guess so." As Rachel giggled, he finished, "But don't keep me up too late. I've got to get up early for my flight to New York."

"I promise." She crossed her arms and her fingers over her breasts. "Sort of."

On his flight he reflected on the last few months, not just on a lost son, but all the cards Fate had dealt him, all seemingly piled one atop the other, randomly, chaotically, *52 pickup*, the twins' favorite game. Jeffrey, of course, though some clarity prevailed now he knew who and how, even if he couldn't really come to grips with why. Closure, some might say, but not quite complete, not quite yet. *No, not just yet.* And Sarah, somehow thirty years of suppressed longing had crested, washed them up on the shore of their passion and receded to a calm, placid surface, secure and comfortable somewhere inside.

Even structuring the Langefelter's deal with Arnie, doing his normal due diligence and valuation of the real estate, his specialty, even the back-and-forth with Consolidated, all those had been the easy parts. And putting Sarah's father in his place after all these years, finally being the one lording it over the other's future, that was immensely gratifying, if evanescent. But all along, he kept asking himself, *why are you doing this, Ian? Not just because it's a big deal, your biggest ever, but because of your past, right? A past you just still haven't been able to shake? Trying to keep someone from getting hurt, someone you still love deep down in your heart of hearts? Too late now, Yonny, old boy, too late. Now comes the main event. Better be ready.*

"Are you sure you know what you're doin', Ian?" Solomon's nerves were jangling, palpably, understandable given what he had been through and who they were about to meet, to confront, maybe. "You haven't given me much to work wit' and I'm tellin' you we can't screw up here."

"Relax, Solly, Sir. The politicians call it plausible deniability. I've deliberately withheld what you don't need to know. If I do screw up, you can say you didn't know what that idiot son-in-law of yours down in Roy Rogers country was up to. Not you. Let me just leave it at that."

"This ain't no game..."

"No, it's not, and neither is having a son, a brother-in-law killed, is it?" He stifled the older man with a wave. "Sorry, Solly, we do it my way or not at all."

They were being driven through Queens to meet the Jewish Godfather, the autocratic head of the crime network whose tendrils and tentacles still had a touch on his father-in-law. The once leafy streets were now forbidding, shorn of the soft comfort of a canopy still awaiting spring. At length they pulled up to a set of gates in a brick and stone entry, a large Tudor mansion visible beyond the hedges lining the drive. Two rather menacing sorts took up positions either side of the towncar. Two more were just visible inside *and those aren't rakes they're carrying. Oh, well. This is it.*

"Straight out of *The Godfather*, right?"

Solly nodded toward the driver. "Don't joke."

Inside, instead of the cobwebs and organ music he half expected, or maybe Gay Nineties bordello, the house was furnished rather stylishly, even tastefully. Biedermeiers here, a Majorelle there, all very nice, like the Serapis on the floor and several Impressionists he didn't have time to misidentify before two of the hoplites showed them into a large library, told them to wait. Yonny cruised the shelves, found them populated by selected volumes, not some wholesale or estate sale inventory. Heavy on history, nineteenth and twentieth century, in several languages.

His self-guided tour was interrupted by a bustle at the other end of the room. In came their host, he surmised, based on the retinue in his wake. This one grasped Solomon by the shoulders—*jeez, is he going to genuflect?*—then seated himself behind a massive Empire desk. Yonny looked over the seated figure—*if Herr Goebbels ever needed a model for his anti-Semitic propaganda cartoons, here he is, a corpulent, malevolent, hooknosed Jewish gangster. I wasn't nervous before, but now?*

Their host, one Imre Gollancz, spoke up in an accent probably Hungarian, abraded by years of American slang yet still formal, almost Oxbridge in syntax. "This would be your young man, Solly? I certainly hope he proves superior to the other."

As he stepped forward to the edge of the desk, Yonny could feel, sense Solomon's cringe. "That's me, Sir. Ian Jonas, his Rachel's husband." He stretched his hand across three feet of desk.

Gollancz ignored his hand and turned to a figure seated behind and to his left, an austere fellow with a downturn of a frown etched onto a pinched face. "Irwin, please listen very carefully to what this lad has to say. Solly," not turning his way, "this had best be good. Very, very good. If there is one thing I detest more than losing money, it is the wasting of my precious time. So tell us."

Yonny tried to adapt to the other's style. "Yes, then, you are familiar with Langefelter's, the company we propose to purchase? I believe you also know the seller's chief executive, Mr. Raab?"

"I asked you not to waste my time, young man. Please get on with your proposal."

"Very well, then. We are cutting Langefelter's in two. The real estate, including several very valuable development parcels, is to be..."

Gollancz pounded a hefty fist on the desk, startling all. "No!" he thundered. "We are buying..."

"No, you're not." Yonny leaned against the desk, his curled knuckles whitening against the green leather top. "This is my deal now and we're going to do it my way." Shunning the gangster, he stepped over to 'Irwin' and handed him a single sheet. "The top line shows the forecasted net sales figures. Next you see the base rent figures, projected ten years, of course. Below, five percent of sales, and below that the total rent plus percentage of sales. Finally, the net return on investment to the real estate entity."

He left the advisor and returned to Gollancz. "The real estate will be held in a private real estate investment trust chartered in Luxembourg." He had picked up that little twist from Arnie, now trotted it out as some street cred for the green eyeshade type. "For tax purposes, obviously." Gollancz raised an eyebrow at his man who nodded back. "A friendly local bank has offered exceptionally generous leverage and terms based on the tenants' credit. The Polsky Organization will have its customary twenty percent ownership, with your ownership in an entity registered wherever you like, Bermuda, the Caymans, Switzerland."

Irwin stood and limped over to the boss, showing him the spreadsheet and whispering rather animatedly.

Yonny waited patiently as the two carried on a conversation in more whispers and gestures, then continued as the two looked up at him, "You see the percentage rents, yes? That's your vigorish, if you like. But I will not have your organization as an owner in the stores themselves. There are people, persons involved there whom I will not allow to be affected by your other business interests, if I may use that term, delicately, of course?"

"You may. Irwin, this percentage rent business, what portion of the stores' net profits would that represent?"

"Including the base rent, approximately twenty percent, more if margins decrease, less if margins improve."

Gollancz, now to Yonny, "And if your stores fail?"

"We own the real estate. It's not quite that simple, but you and we own it, in a senior position."

The other leaned across the desk, fists bunched tightly together. "You are aware I have killed men in the line of our… other business interests, as you term them, so delicately, as you do?"

Yonny replied evenly, "So? You're not going to kill me. Or even scare me. You want this deal too much. And I damned sure am not Donny." He paused to control his rage and fear, then rasped, "And you have no idea what I've done, do you?"

Solly nearly tumbled down, catching himself against a chair.

"Hmmmm." Gollancz steepled his fingers and leaned back in his chair, swiveling back and forth. Finally, he turned to Sol. "Solomon, this one, I approve of him. May we have him up here, here in our organization?"

Solly summoned what courage he had left in him. "No, Imre, no. He belongs down there. He and my daughter and their girls have their lives down there. And I mean no disrespect, he don't, he doesn't belong up here, not with our kind."

"But surely we may solicit his advice? I am told," he waved at his financial man, "that this is a most ingenious solution to several other… vexing issues with which we are at present grappling, the federal taxation issue most prominent among them." He turned to Yonny, "You are aware of what we are about here, my good fellow, these games afoot in the financial sphere?"

"An osmotic filter."

The gangster laughed, "Yes, yes, precisely! I must use that expression in our discussions with the other fam… organizations. Cloudy wine in, clean wine out! Yes! Precisely and succinctly told, young fellow." He looked at the ornate clock on his desk. "The time! Irwin, you will make the necessary arrangements? Bring in our solicitors at the earliest, yes?"

Yonny had scarcely the chance to inhale when Gollancz trundled around his desk, taking him by the arm. "There is one other matter, my good man." He whispered in Yonny's ear.

"I see no reason that can't be managed. And like we say back home, sounds like a road trip. Might Rachel and I join you?"

He almost stumbled from the swat on his shoulders as the other brayed, "Of course, of course! Now, I must send you off. Solly, thank you for bringing us this opportunity. Far, far better than this late unpleasantness, yes?"

A docile Solomon just nodded.

"Please, Solly, do not think for one moment I called that move. The Franceschis and D'Urbinos were behind this. Their anger was unquenchable, by blood only. You and your family shall remain safe, on this you have my word." He bowed, Solly responded, then they embraced. "I am very, very sorry, please know that."

Gollancz walked them to the door. "Young man, my old friend Solomon mentioned your wife and girls." He raised a shaggy eyebrow. "Does memory deceive or does he not also have a grandson down there in Texas?"

"He did."

"Did? Something has happened to him?"

"He was murdered."

"Murdered? Solly, why did you not tell me of this? We, well, you know as well as I, we do not countenance such, certainly not to innocent family members."

Sol leaned over and whispered in his ear.

Brightening, Gollancz simply said, "Good." He stood still a few moments staring at the medallion at his feet, then, "I am so very sorry to hear of this. It is a terrible thing for a father to bury a son. So said Croesus in his wisdom and his suffering." He stared a moment at Yonny, letting him know he knew. "I have done the very same and know… Well. Off with you two, now. Get to work!" He spun rather ponderously and was gone.

Approaching the car, Solly smiled as he asked, "Ian, Yonny, Son, you want to piss your pants right here in the driveway or can you hold it until we reach the house?"

27

"Yonnybonny, come on, now, I don't want to have to spend any more time over there than I absolutely have to, so come on. And check the fire before we go—we don't want to burn the place down, new drapes and all."

He paused at the step up into the den, then strode over to the stair. "Just a minute, Sweets, I left something for Doggie up in my study."

"What?"

"You'll see. Soon enough."

"Make it quick, then."

He reached into his cigar boxes, found what he wanted and came back downstairs as quickly as he could. "Here, his birthday present." He held up a 1957 Topps baseball card, José Valdivielso, number 246. "From when there were Senators, not clowns, in Washington." Every year for the last eight or ten, Yonny had been disgorging treasures, one card at a time, from the several thousand he had bought from little Doggie back in 1959 for ten bucks, then protected from Doug's father by the simple stratagem of merging them into his own stash of ten thousand as soon as he got them home. He credited his present day detached negotiating style to the experience of standing down the older man at the doorstep. "You want 'em? Go find 'em. Sir." His father and Mister Porterhouse didn't speak for months, maybe a year, not even at Rotary. Later in life, his father thanked him, *'Larry wanted to put me up for the Order, but I didn't really have the money back then for your sisters to be duchesses, so that was the last I heard about that.'*

"Grand, just grand. You little boys."

He smiled, tweaked her rear and got in a quick ear nibble in the same move. "Yep, that's us. Keeps us young."

"Immature, you mean." Rachel was delighted to see his impish smirk for the first time in months, it seemed, since…

They strolled across the street, he in his preppie holdout bulky tweed sport coat and bowtie, she in a clingy dark green silk wrap thing under the obligatory mink jacket, just a little something from her nuclear arsenal guaranteed to prompt late-night Armageddons when certain wives got certain husbands home. Rachel and Julie exchanged air kisses at the precise, divinely-ordained one centimeter spacing then the couple waded into the maelstrom that passed for the rituals of society in the Bubble.

Two hours and several Silver Oaks later, a hubbub in the rear gallery caught everyone's attention, as intended. In swept Julie and Daphne, the latter resplendent in her cheerleader's outfit, fresh from the basketball game, dewy forehead adding to the allure, the former basking in reflected glory. *Seems restored to her original dimensions, too*, thought Yonny. "Now, now, she needs to go upstairs to shower and change. She has a big date with Johnny Buckingham!" The very mention of the handsome quarterback's name drew appreciative *oohs* and *ahhs* from certain quarters, a poke in the ribs from Rachel. Off flounced *la jeune fille* up the stairs, close enough to the railing to prompt some oglers below to wonder if she wasn't wearing any underwear?

Yonny sidled up to Julie, she still flush from her moment of triumph before her congregation, whispering in her ear, "I have the goodie, Juicy. Where should I put it, Sweetheart?" He palmed the baseball card so she could see, slyly inviting her into his conspiracy. "Maybe his bathroom?"

"Yes, yes, that's great!" She clapped her hands a little too exuberantly, drawing some looks, then hushed. "Top of the stairs, left door, just next to Daphne's. Yes, that will be perfect! I'll need to get the video camera for that!"

"Okay, then, I'll get on it."

About then, Doug Porterhouse wove his way their direction across the vast family room. "You two planning to run off on me? And her?" He leered at Rachel, then lurched over to clutch her about the waist. "Fair trade, I would say. When do we start, beautiful?"

"2050, handsome, not a moment before. Just make sure you're still vertical, then I'm all yours."

That was enough for Doug to digest, the arithmetic beyond his current state, so he wandered off. Yonny had cocked an ear to the floor above to the sound of a shower. He smiled at the two women, "You girls sort out the details. I have places to go and things to do."

He set his wineglass down on a side table and slipped upstairs, unnoticed, so he hoped. He made a brief show of admiring the formerly living creatures adorning the upstairs gallery before slipping into the upstairs master, then cracked open the door into Doggie's bathroom. It looked like the men's room at the Westin's ballroom, if that were large enough to have a steam room at one end. He rummaged through the drawers until he found a can of Edge. Foaming an arrow pointing down at the countertop, he propped José below, upside down just for the hell of it. He slipped back into the gallery, then went left instead of right. On went the latex gutting gloves, pulled up over his jacket's sleeves and the surgeon's booties over his Weejuns. He turned the knob.

Rachel watched her husband disappear, then turned at a familiar voice.

"Rachel, Rachel! I've been looking for you!" Sarah was sidestepping her way through the crowd toward her. "I, well, I have some news!"

At that very moment Rachel was T-boned by two pairs of bored wives. She thought quickly, and gathering Sarah's hand, led her new entourage onto the terrace. "Okay, Sarah, you're positively giddy! What is it, as if I don't know?"

Ignoring the others, "It's Arnie!" She raised her left hand and if a ring finger could flounce, this one did under the weight of one of Cartier's more generously endowed creations. "Isn't it beautiful?"

"It is, and so are you. He's a lucky man. Girls, what do you think?"

The others lowed and mooed appreciatively, but Rachel could see relief swelling in their eyes, their features, a vast relief at the neutralization of a most formidable threat.

It was Martha, as usual, who had the upper hand. "Sarah, girl, didn't I tell you not to be hasty?" With a huge smile splitting her face followed by a cackle, "Unless the rock is a really, really big one?" She lifted the other's hand, appraising the bauble. "Does this one have a brother?"

At the door, he looked down the hall, then stepped out, quickly removing his disposables and stuffing them into a brown paper bag tucked into an inside pocket. He reached back into the room to lock the door from the inside, using a Kleenex to cover his prints and then muffle a small sneeze. He smoothed his hair and descended the back stairs into the service hallway, slipping into the guest bath. He waited a bit, flushed the toilet, then re-entered the gala. A few steps along, Doug Porterhouse grabbed him from behind. "Where the hell you been, Yawny? Screwing the caterers?"

He froze momentarily, then relaxed, seeing his host's loose features and watery eyes. "Yep, Doggie, all of them. All in a row. You ought to try it some time."

The other roared, then leaned unsteadily forward to wink at him, "Just Josefina, she's enough. Get it?"

"Come on, you good ol' boy, let's get you another drink." He steered his host over to one of the bars, passing Rachel on the way. "When do I have to get the twins?"

She looked at her watch. "Oh, another five or ten minutes or so. You can cavort with your playmate a little bit longer."

Doggie gave her an extended wink, then careened toward the bar. Yonny split off to talk to several friends, then headed to the front door, stopping to let Julie know he'd be back in ten or fifteen.

When all was quiet upstairs, a figure in black emerged from behind ballgowns and cocktail dresses in the closet. Quickly and lightly stepping to the windows, it slipped out onto the shelf then shinnied its way down a drainpipe to the ground, disappearing between garage and fence to the street beyond.

Back home Yonny placed the brown bag in the fireplace, stoking the embers a bit, and piled some kindling atop it. He turned the gas up about a quarter. That done, he stepped through a sliding glass door and walked to the far end of the pool. Slipping on a pair of latex examination gloves, he emptied the cylinder and dropped pistol and silencer into plastic bags full of muriatic acid, then went back into the house to turn off the fire. Satisfied the bagful had been reduced to ashes, he poked the remains and went back outside and retrieved the bags, placing them carefully in a plastic tub on the front seat of the BMW. Driving toward Olmos Park on the Boulevard, he stopped along the curve where no houses faced the street. He dumped the bags in the holes he had dug amid the brush thirty feet from the street, then covered them over with soil and leaves and trash with the rotten board he had set aside. Back in the car, he stripped off the fresh pair of latex gloves and rolled them into a wad, tossing them and the shells into the still roiling creek at the low water crossing as he drove through.

A few minutes later and the girls were buckled into their seatbelts along with their friend Margaret, the three merrily chittering away. At the house he said, “You girls, go get ready for bed. I’m going to get your mother.” He walked across the street past a loudly idling Corvette in the circular drive and back into the frenzy, socialized a few minutes, then extricated Rachel.

“I thought you’d never get back and I would just die in that house.”

At their door, he smiled and kissed her gently. Just then came the first screams.

28

Sam arrived to chaos. AHPD only had four patrolmen on a shift and every one was already on location. Dale had shut down the valet operation and was casing the street for escapees. Jerry and Daniel were herding the guests into one or two rooms, trying to keep them quiet; Brett was watching the back and the caterers. The Chief was upstairs with Doggie and Julie, so Sam headed his way.

He wasn't surprised by the scene. Julie was lying on her side on the vast bed, bawling, of course. *Can't blame her, not one bit. Poor thing. I always liked her, even if she never had much to do with me.* Doggie was comatose, it seemed, but popped up out of his chair when he saw Sam.

"Sam, thank God you're here. You heard?"

"Yeah, I heard. I'm very, very sorry to hear this, Doug, Julie, very sorry. I'll do what I can, call me any time." He patted Julie on the shoulder; she reached up to squeeze his hand, then commenced crying again.

Doug began, "Sam, I guess you'll want to see…"

The Chief interrupted him. "Mr. Porterhouse, you just stay here with your wife, please? No need for you to look at her again, not right now, okay?"

Doggie nodded and sat beside Julie as Sam trailed out into the gallery. "Here, this room. Watch your step around these markers. And brace yourself."

He did, but sure could have used some more bracing. "Damn!" was all he could say. A spreading pool of blood had already begun to congeal into a maroon halo around the girl's blonde tresses. The Chief said quietly, "Sam, tell me what you see."

Sam slipped on his latex gloves, knelt down and used his pen as a pointer, brushing aside some hair. He reamed a dime-sized hole in the temple. "Large caliber, .38, .357. No recoil, it doesn't look like it, maybe had a foot on her neck. Otherwise we would have had a bit of splash over this way? Close, but not much powder spread." He peered closer at a couple of bits of nubby grey stuff, wondering what they were, then stood abruptly.

"Looking for this, Sam?" Standing by the four poster bed, the Chief held a dark pink pillow sham gingerly by its corners. "Whoever did this was fastidious, that's for sure."

Sam stepped over to the bed. Circling a fifty-cent piece's worth of black and gray, he looked up, "Confirms it was a silencer, probably held this tight up against her, makes sense. And back here," surveying an irregular red scab punctuated with a black dot, edges singed, "yep, that's it. Muffled the shot some more, blotted up the splash, didn't get on his clothes. Smart, but he must have had time."

Returning to the body, with a light touch he lifted her head just enough to see a hole in the carpet, trying to ignore the shredded exit. "Magnum, my guess. Had some power." He gently returned her to the floor, then noticed a matted swatch of hair, darkened a bit. He rubbed his gloved finger gently over her scalp, picking up some dried blood. "Popped her with the pistol butt. That's how he got her down."

He gazed at a pretty face, glazed green eyes already dulling. "Didn't bother to close her eyes, of course, so she saw it coming, saw her assailant. Means he was here long enough for her to come to. Creepy. And these bonds? Even creepier. Where's the closet?"

He stepped into the bedroom-sized closet, recognized the three bathrobes whose sashes were now binding up a dead girl. Then he noticed something else. "Chief, come here. See these fancy dresses? Kinda crumpled on the backside, like someone pushed them aside. Maybe whoever did this was hiding in here, waiting on her. Maybe."

Back in the bedroom, kneeling on the carpet, he couldn't see any impressions at first. *Good carpet will do that, rebound pretty quick.* He followed what he thought might be tracks to the windows. *Maybe that, maybe there.* His knees creaking as he stood, he looked across the room to the bathroom. "There, Chief. See the carpet? In this light you can see the tracks her legs made. Let's get some pictures, okay? What else we got?"

"Over here, Sam. Windows unlatched." The Chief pointed to a bank of casements.

"Yeah." He opened one leaf with a handkerchief and looked down. "Whoowee! Pretty steep climb. If it was one."

Just then the crew from the SAPD started in. Sam waved and

said, "Hi, guys. Careful there. Okay, need prints on all the surfaces. Maxie, come in here, willya, I want to show you something."

In the closet, he said quietly, "I've got some suspicions…"

Espinoza replied, "Lemme guess. Inside job? One of the swell types downstairs? Let's hope they don't start dancin'. Pretty scary thought, fifty-somethin' Anglos gettin' down."

Sam laughed lightly. "Yeah, it is, isn't it? But, look here. These dresses. If someone was standing, hiding back there, think you can find some fibers, something?"

"No, but I'll give it a try, just for you, man. Old time's sake. Now get out of our way and let the pros do their thang."

He went downstairs to start interviewing the cloistered guests; every one of them had a babysitter they absolutely had to get home or had Labs or Cavaliers to let out. Some were friendly, some not, some remembered him, some didn't, and most didn't even know he was on the force. *And I really don't like some of the looks. Jeez. This is gonna take hours. And need to track down anyone who left early.*

Sam noticed Yonny sitting across the room with his wife and another couple. He tapped one his men on the back and whispered something, then pointed. Stepping outside onto the terrace, he waited a few minutes, then heard, "What, Sam? Tell me really what happened, can you?"

He turned and sized up the other. *Dressed like a college professor, cool, calm. Yes or no?* He was beginning an answer when Rachel came through the French doors after her husband.

"Sam, here, was about to tell me what happened up there, what's going on down here."

Sam cleared his throat. "We got the call, two of our cars were here within sixty seconds, but that doesn't mean much in a case like this. Okay. Doggie and his wife went to check on their daughter, she was taking way too long, the boyfriend was getting impatient. Door was locked, but Doggie had a key, opened it and there she was."

"And?" Rachel stepped from behind her husband. "What? What was it?"

"The girl was gagged and bound. Naked, just got out of the shower, looks like. A sock in her mouth, some bathrobe belts tied around her and well, well, she was twisted up in the same pose as the carpet."

Rachel gasped. "No!"

So she's been up there before? "Yeah, 'fraid so. Like she was doing her last cheer. No more, though. Bullet hole right here," he pointed to his temple, "point blank, it seems. Pretty neat, once you've seen a bunch of these."

Yonny started, "Neat? Like some professional?"

"Mmmm, don't know. Why do you ask?"

"Umm, don't know, myself. Neat, you said. Plus someone had tied her up."

Seems a bit nervous. Why? Time for the hammer. "You were up there, weren't you? What were you doing?"

"Like I told your officer, putting Doggie's present where Julie said. It's still up there. Your guy saw it." He laughed, "Every year he jumps up and down, gets all red-faced, says I stole his stuff, I'm a thief, all that stuff. '*Possession is ten-tenths of the laws*', I always say."

"That's it?"

"That's it, Sam."

"But you left, so said Julie. Where were…"

"Stop right there, Sam."

"Ma'am, Rachel?"

"Are you questioning him, Detective? Or me?" Her voice was steel-edged, cold. She crossed her arms over her chest.

There goes the view. "Not formally, no. You know that." Now his voice took on more than an edge of anger. "And I'm not arresting him, either, so you can take off the lawyer hat. Just trying to figure out what happened, how it happened. You should know how that works. You two, of all people, ought to want to help out here. I guess not. Now, excuse me, willya, I've got some more work to do."

29

Finally, around one, the guests were released, two by two. Rachel and several others stayed upstairs with Julie, managing to keep her from interfering with EMS when they brought the body down the stairs and out of the house. "Julie, you'll see her again and she'll look like her old self. Trust me, that's the way it was with Jeffy." Rachel swallowed, then, "I honestly don't know what's worse, Julie, seeing her like you did, just for that one moment, or having to identify him in that horrible, sterile place, such a, a strange place to see our boy. So cold…" For a moment, roles reversed as Julie patted her on the shoulder. But only for a moment before she began bawling again.

Doug wandered downstairs, seeking out Yonny, doing his best to avoid the stares, replying minimally to the words and gestures of the remaining sequestered guests. He saw his neighbor and gestured outside. On the terrace, they embraced and Doug began, haltingly, "I know I shouldn't ask you this, but, well, you've just done this, well, how do we do this?"

"The services, Doggy? Rachel can help Julie with that. It's not all that much work, with the women at the church taking care of a lot of it. Don't worry about that." He took the other by the shoulders, "The rest of it? I'm not much help, still haven't got past it. We're lucky, still have the twins…," pausing, "sorry, but you still have family, all of them here, and you'll learn to just muddle through it all like we've tried to. Doggie, let's sit down."

He led him to the wall at the edge of the terrace overlooking the manicured gardens. "Here." Taking a deep breath, "The first really hard thing, well, after this, after the first shock, I should say, is oddly enough, writing the obituary. What do you say about a life cut short? A beautiful young life cut short?" He sighed, dramatically, he hoped.

"Doggie, our Jeffy was murdered, too. We've managed to keep that quiet, Sam has for us. You hadn't heard that, had you?"

Porterhouse was visibly shocked, his sad eyes lighting up, but could only manage a shake, *No*.

"Yeah, murder."

"Who did it? Do you guys know?" came a rasping whisper.

"Not sure, but the Berger boy was involved. Theodore, Teddie."

"Shit! That nerdy little prick? How?"

"Poison. Apparently he did a lot of drugs, had scored some cocaine, there was poison in it. Cyanide, like the spy movies. Jeffy snorted it, choked to death. Not pretty. Hell of a way to go."

"How…?"

"He confessed. At least to being there when… Right before he died. To someone, well, someone who told someone else."

"The cops?"

"Not exactly, but they found out when they did their tests."

By now, Doug had set aside the night's tragedy in fascination, if only for the moment. "Damn!"

"Yeah, right. Damn!"

The other started to ask the obvious, but Yonny cut him off. "Someone I know, someone I trust, Doggie. Someone we both know. Someone I can't name, won't name. Even Sam doesn't know. Don't tell him, okay?"

"But why kill him? And why kill Daphne, for God's sake? What had she done? Teddie's killer wanted revenge, right?" He tried to shake the cobwebs. "No, wait, that doesn't work. That would have been you, right?"

"Might have been, if I had known about it. But I didn't, had no reason to suspect, even think about the kid. No, I didn't hear about it until later, just a couple of weeks ago. Not saying how."

"Maybe someone pushing drugs?"

"Not necessarily. Maybe."

Yonny's cold glare sent a chill through Doug's chest. "But, then, I think, maybe Daffy…" He gulped and shivered, "He had been hanging around here, helping her with her trig and, what else, oh, yeah, chemistry. And for the SAT, her second try. He was a really smart nerd, wasn't he?"

"Was."

"You don't think Daphne was, was…" He flared, "You're not suggesting Daphne had anything to do with it, Jeffy, I mean, are you?"

Yonny let his head rock back. “Oh, hell no, Doggie! Not a chance! She couldn’t have done anything like that. No way!” He moved closer, draped an arm over the other’s shoulder. “But if Teddie told her about it, what he had done, well, then she could have been in danger.”

“But he’s dead, a couple of months ago. How could he…”

“He didn’t. Obviously. That means someone else was involved, someone who was there when Jeffy died, wanted to make sure no one squealed on him. So, first, Teddie. Now, Daphne.”

“Who?”

“No idea. I’ve been working with Sam, working on my own, too, trying to figure all this out. Nothing. Haven’t a clue, I just don’t know shit. But Doug,” now in a conspiratorial tone, “I only tell you this to help you through it. Not that there’s much difference in our case, he was still doing drugs. First time, we think, hope, maybe, but that doesn’t matter anymore, does it?”

Doug processed all of this in a mental fog, a haze of shock and alcohol. “So, you think the Berger kid and someone else killed Jeffy? Why?”

“Don’t know. Maybe just a prank that went wrong. Don’t know.”

“Yeah?”

“Don’t know, Doggie, just don’t know. Wish I did, though. Main thing, you see, is to direct yourself to this other person, whoever it is, was. That’s what I had to do, that’s just about all what keeps me sane. Got to get your mind off your tragedy, get it going in a positive direction. Focus. Make it your mission in life. Justice for Daphne.” He looked down at the brick pattern, then up again. “That’s all I’ve got, Doggie. All I’ve got. And I’m still on my mission, see? I still have to find this other person and then maybe I’ll find Daphne’s killer, too. Maybe we both will.”

“I get you now. You had me pretty confused for a while there. So, work with Sam?”

“You know him, too, you don’t need me there. But give yourself a few days after the funeral, then go sit down with him, talk to him. He’s been great, by the way, good investigator and even better listener. He’ll be happy to help, but please, keep what I said under your hat, okay?”

“Sure, okay, and thanks for everything. I think I’m feeling a bit better already.” He frowned, “Maybe not…”

“That’s just the Scotch wearing off. You’re getting there. You’ll get there, trust me.”

Finally back home, Rachel came downstairs after checking on the girls. "Well?"

"Mmmm, had a little talk with Doggie."

She arched an eyebrow apprehensively. "About?"

"Just trying to help him through this." He paused, then, slyly, "Gave him some ideas, like Teddie Berger…"

"Stop right there. You told him about Teddie? Are you totally nuts?"

"No, not at all. Merely planting a false trail, a red herring. Told him there must have been a third person involved, that I figure Teddie told Daphne and this third person killed them both to keep them quiet. Told him he should talk to Sam."

Rachel shook her head. "Yonny, why? This isn't a game, you know. You know that? Pretty soon Doug will blab it, well, all he has to do is whisper it to Julie and it'll be all over town. All over. And Sam? You don't think he's smart enough to figure it out? Trace it back, connect the dots?"

"Of course he will, and come up short. But to make it sporting, I told Doggie that Teddie had confessed to being there, one of the people there when Jeffy died. A deathbed confession, just as he was dying. To someone, someone I made out like I knew, but couldn't tell him. Now, Sam will hear that, although I swore Doggie to secrecy, and will be on me like a ton of D'Hanis bricks." He smiled at that. "And all I say is, '*Sam, you know the Johnny Cash version of that old honky-tonk song, Long Black Veil? Well, when I was at the high school that night, Sam, I sorta ran across a couple in a car, hot and heavy. And they were married, but to other people, you know how that goes around here, yeah? Not long ago the man called me, told me he saw what happened, saw someone in the car with Teddie who got out and ran away. He checked on the boy, just about dead, got the story. He panicked and bolted with his girlfriend. Kept it quiet for obvious reasons, two of them. Adultery, not to mention the betrayal of friends and, what's the term, Failure to Render Aid? That's how I know, and that's why I can't tell.*' "

"You're getting worse by the minute. What's this black veil business?"

"The song. Johnny's character is falsely accused of murder, has an airtight alibi, but keeps his mouth shut and hangs for it. Why? Because when the murder was done, he was, quote, *'in the arms of my best friend's wife*', unquote. And she walks the hills in a long black veil, mourning her lover and his honor. That's why."

"That's why? You've staked our lives, our children's lives on some stupid redneck song? One last chance, Yonny, tell me why!"

"You saw Sam tonight, heard him. He suspects something. I've probably said more than a few things to justify his suspicions. You didn't help by cutting him off at his… knees, did you?" That made Rachel nod a bit sheepishly. "Okay, then. He knows I was up there. He also can figure out whose lipstick was on Jeffy's, well, on Jeffy. So, I, we, have to assume he won't let up. This story, what happens to me if he questions me, arrests me, even?"

Rachel thought about that. "You don't lie, not exactly, no, you tell your story and you stick with it. No one to say otherwise, right?" Her husband nodded and she went on, "So long as you don't reveal any names, obviously." She raised another eyebrow. "Even if they're fake. And whatever you say, don't say you told me any names—that would blow any defense of confidentiality."

"Why? You're my lawyer, right? And my wife?"

"Right, but it won't be what you said but the fact that you said it. Would stink to high heaven with a jury and a sharp prosecutor. And attorney-client privilege only goes so far, same as spousal. If somehow I get put on the stand, I can't lie. I'm an officer of the court."

"Oh." He scratched his head. "Then what?"

"You're playing jury roulette. If they don't believe you…" She drew her finger across her throat. "Or maybe refuse to answer, contempt of court, although if you tell your little story dramatically enough, use your song, maybe not even that." She folded her arms under her bra. "Wait a minute, Yonnybo, were there really people there, screwing?"

"Can't say. Won't say. On advice of counsel." He patted his lips with his fingers. "And there's one other thing…"

"What now?"

"Sam was on the big drug guy's payroll ten or fifteen years ago. He admitted it. So I have a little leverage now. But I don't want to use it—might tear up another life, don't want to do that."

"Then don't."

Rachel turned to him, placing a hand on his chest. "Yonny? You're not asleep, are you?" No response. "Geez, you could sleep through a tornado. So annoying."

"I'm awake, R. Wide awake. Have you a proper reason for disturbing me, Milady? Other than pestering me about this business?"

"Pestering for now, Yonnypuppy. Cooperate now, I just might cooperate later." She batted her lashes coquettishly. "But I need to understand why you would do something so stupid."

"Time will tell if I'm so stupid, I don't think so, but, like I said, we need something to throw him off the scent. Look at it this way. He has all the time in the world to put the pieces together. And I'm not going to chance that he can or can't. At some point, he's going to figure out some sort of connection from Daphne back to Teddie—two sets of footprints, he said, right?" He sighed, then, "And don't forget the pink lipstick—he can't possibly miss that connection to Jeffy. So he figures that Daphne and Teddie are the two, forget motives, all your rules of evidence, all that. He, well, something I haven't told you, might explain some things. We had a mutual friend, guy named Ricky Young, we were still in New York when he was murdered, remember?"

"Vaguely. Your drug-dealing best friend? You mentioned him not so long ago, somewhere?"

"Excellent! Two gold stars for my favorite pupil." He brushed away some strands of hair, kissed her lightly on her forehead. "Yeah, he dealt drugs big time, apparently. But earlier at UT, he and I were partying and his date gave him his first joint. Boom! It was downhill for him from there. And Sam and I, when we've been talking about Jeffy and his investigation, we've been reminiscing about high school, life in general since. Makes sense we'd talk about Ricky, the drug connection." He shrugged a sigh. "So, I've talked about the girl who got him started, saying, all bullshit, of course, that if I could ever find her, I'd kill her. We've laughed a lot at that. But he will come back to it, I know he will. And then he'll come after me. Pink lipstick on private parts. Say, what color was that tonight?"

She slapped his chest. "Forget it, Casanova. So this couple. Big secret. Not bad, Sherlock, not half bad. But you better get your story straight and stick to it. Why would you make it such a big deal anyway, protecting them, I mean?"

"Big money. Big, brutal, complicated, ugly divorces. Children are friends of our girls. Think of the fallout, the way LeahRhea would be treated if two families' worth of kids knew their daddy was the snitch. And both were, still are good friends of mine. That admission alone would set the social set to chittering volcanically, that's for sure."

"I'd like to see that, personally."

"Sure you would. But won't happen. Long black veil, remember?" He tilted back to focus on her. "I was a cooperative witness, wasn't I?"

Rachel smiled as she pulled closer. "Most cooperative."

30

Sam was trying to sort it all out over the last couple of days. He closed his office door and unplugged his phone. *Three deaths, two of them murders in a couple of months or so, the other probably murder, too. This shit just doesn't happen here, not in this sleepy burg where nothing ever happens. Seven thousand people, all of 'em boring as cow patties. Nothing happens here. Sure, right.*

He looked through his notes. *Looks like forced entry through the windows, yeah, but Yawny was up there, too. No one heard anything, not much powder, so it was a silencer, so had to be a pro. Or was it? A silencer? Didn't he and I talk about that? Jesse Sepulveda, maybe?* He picked up the phone and called the pawnbroker. "Jesse, Sam, here. No, no, got nothing on you now, just need some help. Looking for silencers, got a hit job over here."

Sepulveda's laugh came through loud and clear. "In the Heights, *vato*? A hit job? You're kiddin' me, man, right? That's some crazy shit for them Anglos over there. And why should I help you, huh? You gonna 'splain that to me, you dirty fuckin' cop?" Another rasping laugh crested and faded followed by a low confidential tone, "But, here, out of the goodness of my heart, I'll give you somethin'. 'Bout a few months ago some white boy come in here, bought a .357, threaded barrel, really nice piece, Sam. Made the big bucks on that one, yeah? Then he wanted a silencer. And a switchblade, too. I asked him if these weapons were to be used for criminal purposes. He said no, I figured that would do for background."

The phone went quiet for a few moments. "Sam, 'cause I like your sorry ass, don't know why, I'll give you somethin' else. The dude was an amateur."

"How so?"

"Fake beard, sunglasses, Yankees cap pulled down real low. Real nervous, lookin' around all the time. Paid cash, small bills." His chuckling just came through. "Lot of 'em. Took the bus, I watched him. No fuckin' way he was a pro, I'm tellin' you that true. Now, don't go threatenin' me, Sam, you owe me some favors, remember? Now you owe me some more. Why don't you start with that *cabron* Espinoza, okay? Okay?"

"*Gracias, amigo*, I think. I'll see what I can do. He'll know what I'm talkin' about?"

"Yeah. Bye. Don't bother visitin'."

He went down to Jacala on St. Mary's for lunch, to get away from the station, the town, the situation. Over his enchilada plate, he kept thinking, noodling. *But that Berger kid, he's dead, he was known to hang out with her, right? Yeah, saw them at the Jonas boy's funeral, that's who he was. Weren't they fighting or something? And that Flounder guy, dead. Same day, night, together? Drugs, sure. Leads to the Jonas kid? Someone said someone was out that night, in the dark. Who was it? Who? Oh, right, Yawny. That bruise?*

And what about Doggie's house? Yonny had been upstairs, seems to have an alibi, but the timing? After she gets home, he goes up there. How long would she need to take a shower? Was he up there before or after her shower? Or during? Then he leaves, then comes back? How long was he gone? Long enough to hide a gun? He was clean when I saw him. He took a sip of his iced tea, held the glass up, squinting through the sepia at the waiter who had always reminded him of Dracula, Bela Lugosi. *With his obsession about his kid, bugging me all the time? I guess I'll have to bring him in for questioning, after all. His wife can be his lawyer, if he wants, she wants, more likely. Fine with me. She can be a bitch if she wants, seen worse. And what's this damned baseball card business again?*

Now in his car, he just couldn't let it go. *Back to basics, Sam, back to basics. Any prints? Footprints? Nada, nuthin'. Bullet went right through her into the flooring, stuck in plywood below lightweight concrete, tough enough to leave it pretty well deformed. You know SA's ballistics guys won't get right on it, not going to jump for me, do me any favors. Well. And no security cameras, not even an alarm on the upstairs windows. And those windows? Woulda taken a pro, hell, an acrobat, to get up there and jimmy them open like they were. Or were they? Maybe from the inside, just to make it look like someone got in from outside?*

No, probably a pro. A hitman. But why? She hadn't paid off her doper? Maybe... maybe her father had some issues with someone. Maybe Doggie owed someone some big money. Vegas, maybe? I'll have to check that out. Maybe like those Mexican drug guys seeing the oil money coming out of Carrizo and Alice... Kidnapping went wrong? Tied up like that, how would they get her out with all those people around? Why would they even try? Maybe something with the guys bankrolling the dealers here? Don't go there, boy, unless you're dead positive about it. Didn't you learn anything downtown?

Back at the station, Dale Potchernik was waiting for him. "Sam, might have something for you on that girl's murder. I was cruising when some kids came out of the brush over on the Boulevard, down off La Jara. Had tripped over a soft spot in the woods, found a gun in a bag of water, they thought. Lucky it leaked out when they opened it—swimming pool acid, said Gene, when I brought it in." He unwrapped a bundle and laid a pistol carefully on Sam's desk. "Pretty rough shape. Looks like it's spent some time rusting up in that stuff, won't be able to get anything much from ballistics." Dale took a Bic from his pocket and pointed. "Numbers filed off before it got dunked, I bet."

Sam poked his pen in the barrel and lifted it gently, gingerly. "What do you think, Dale? .357 or .38? Can't read the stamping here," tapping a fingernail on the barrel. "And got himself a threaded barrel—we need to get back out there and look for a silencer. I'll bet it's there, bet you a hundred bucks. Let's go, before it corrodes worse. You drive. Where's the metal detector?"

A few minutes later, Dale was scanning the leaf-strewn ground while Sam looked for footprints. "Bingo, Sam. Something here." The patrolman put his folding shovel to work and almost immediately hit something hard. A few more scoops and up came a four-inch-long cylinder in a clear baggie leaking an acrid liquid from the small hole made by the shovel point. "I didn't take your bet, remember, Sam?"

After entering the weapons into evidence, Sam signed them right back out. On the way over to Blanco Road, he couldn't help thinking this was too easy. *Circumstantial evidence, Sam, old boy, that's all it is. That, and a conspiracy of coincidences that probably only exists in your head. Time, Sam, time. Their son gets murdered by juiced drugs.*

I investigate. I tell Yonny everything I know. The drug chain. Juan Ángel Algarve? Dead. Flounder? Dead. Then the Berger kid, dead. Finally, this cheerleader queen, Doggie's girl. Dead. Not enough. I told him about Algarve, but... He thought a bit more. *Flounder, I might have mentioned him, but he was just one of several, though. None of the others have shown up dead or beat up. Have no idea where the Berger kid and the girl fit in, 'cept that one thing that went on at the funeral. And the coke on his lap, that, too. Maybe he was the one...? And now they're both dead. Ain't gonna blab no mo'...*

The drab pawnshop sat in the middle of a forlorn strip of auto parts, thrift and nail shops and empty storefronts, next to an *Abogado*. *Convenient*, thought Sam. He looked up at the faux Mansard front, paint peeling, corrugated coming loose entirely in a couple of spots. *Jesse sure doesn't put much into the decorating besides the number six rebar on the windows. Not that he ever had any style...* He pushed his way through the door, brushing aside the little bell up on the jamb. "Hello? Selling security systems."

A short Hispanic with randomly stringy hair under a greasy Oilers cap came from behind a counter full of firearms. "I told you not to come visitin', asshole. What do you want, man?"

Sam looked around the cluttered pawnshop. "Getting a better quality of product in here, Jesse, hell of a lot better since last time I arrested you. Must have a taller fence around the place, right?"

Sepulveda shouted, "Fuck you, Gringo!" with a broad grin between mustache and soul patch. Placing a finger to his lips, he came forward and gave Sam a hug. Whispering, "*Momento*," he turned to a CD player and cued up some *narcocorrido*, loud. Still whispering, "Okay, now, whachugot? That Anglo hit thing?"

Sam nodded and took the evidence bags from his pockets. "Over here?" Sepulveda nodded back and Sam carefully opened the bags. "No touch, *amigo*, no touch. Seen these?"

"Shit, yeah, man. That's my .357, know it by the grip, man, see, modified Python. Great piece, like I said. What's gone on with it?" He leaned over to sniff it, recoiling instantly. "Whew! Can't even smell if it's gone off. Just junk, now."

"Acid."

"Hitman, Sam. A pro. Knows how to cover up evidence. Acid, man."

"What about the numbers filed off? Before it went in the bag?"

Jesse shrugged, palms up. "Hey, man, I don't know nuthin' about that. I just takes 'em in as-is, where-is." He darted his eyes conspiratorially. "Trust me on that."

"Right. But you said the guy who bought it was an amateur, a dude, you said."

"Yeah, and I'll bet you *buñuelos* to Benjamins this is the gun, but you ain't gettin' nuthin' from this pile of shit now. Nooo… You remember that Harrington bastard? You worked that case, didn't you?" Not acknowledging Sam's nod, "Yeah, Harrington bought one of those guns from me, but he was smart enough not to pull the trigger, gave it to that dumb nigger Wilson. That dumbass shoulda fried. Same thing here. *Señor* amateur dude buys it, gives it to the guy he pays to do the job. Maybe not the smartest operator, not if you found this pretty quick, but the amateur didn't do it. You'll have to find the trigger, then get him to talk. But you know all that." He pointed to the pistol then turned to the CD player, switching it off. "Sorry that don't work for you, friend. It's an AIWA, don't get no better. Wasn't the music, was it, man?" He smiled at Sam and waved him out.

On the way back, Sam replayed the pawnbroker's assessment. *Maybe he's right, maybe not. Nothing says Yonny couldn't have done it. Well, just the little matter of shooting someone in the head, tied up like a calf, those big green eyes looking up at him… But… Maybe he's right. Someone smart enough to plan this could do it Jesse's way. And Yawny's plenty smart. Back to basics, Sam, back to basics. Pool acid? Yonny has a pool. Hasn't had me there since high school, graduation night party, the stuck-up bastard. Hold on, Sam, getting mad? No. Not smart. Okay, he has a pool, so he has some muriatic acid lying around. So what?*

He pulled through the McDonald's drive-in, using what passed for willpower these days to limit himself to a large coffee. Parking off to one side of the lot, he grinned at a mother with one on the hip and two in tow. He stirred in a couple of creams and some sugars, still thinking, still working the case. *Start from the beginning. Teddie Berger. Daphne Porterhouse. Right, those two, now I know who they are, saw their dead faces, saw them at the funeral, having a little spat, weren't they? Right.* He made a vise for his temples with one hand, squeezing. *At the park, two sets of footprints, one large, one smaller. Boy and girl. Teddie and Daphne. Girl was driving, most likely. Girl left pink lipstick on the boy's pecker. Damn! Have to bother Doggie and Julie again, search through her makeup. Why didn't I think of that then? Because there wasn't a connection then, dingbat, not at that time. Okay, okay, easy now, back to basics. First Teddie, then Daphne. Teddie had some cocaine, we know that, smart kid, coulda done the poison, too, maybe? And Daphne was there, giving him a blow job? Driving the car? So she's part of it. You're repeating yourself, Sam.*

But why would he do that shit? Motive? Let's say he did, then someone fingered him to... who? No, makes no sense. Leave that, Sam, basics. Then, six, seven weeks later, Daphne. Teddie, then Daphne. Teddie told on Daphne? Told the person who set this up, told him she was there? That person now knew about Daphne, whacked her. No, no, no, don't need another perp. Too complicated. Run the whole thing backwards, Sam. Daphne to Teddie to cocaine to... Jeffrey Jonas? If the Berger boy did poison him, then there's only one person left in your little puzzle. Only one. But how did he know? The bruise, the nose? That's how. It's him. Has to be. Or maybe there was someone else, after all?

Or maybe the Berger kid was the target in the first place, maybe his pusher did it, didn't want the kid ratting on him about something. He wouldn't have known about it, the stuff just went up the Jonas boy's nose first, instead of the other kid's. Then the other one, Teddie, tries to 'splain to a hysterical girl with a prick in her mouth, they panic and run off? That actually makes sense for a change. He smiled inwardly. *So that can't be right. Or... As good as anything I've got. Except Yonny. Motive, revenge. Knowledge? Good Christ, Sam, this is getting more fubar by the thought.*

He walked into the station from the back, took a wad of messages from Alice without looking, not a word. *A buried pistol, may or may not be the one—had to be, with the silencer—someone would have had to know about that little patch, a pro wouldn't have ditched it, not there, not that close. Close.* He shut his eyes and drew a mental line from Doggie's and Yawny's houses to Dick Friedrich and on up into Olmos Park. *Yep. The Boulevard, only way. No, could've gone to the end of the street then over to Devine? Out of the way, a lot slower, had to be pretty quick. Nope, down the Boulevard, past the Little League fields, then over to, where does that little Merrill girl live, Mandalay, is that what I heard?* He scratched a note to call her parents, find out when Yonny picked up his girls. *So, La Jara. Or is it the Boulevard in that stretch? Takes it easy, maybe, no, probably planned it in advance, then goes and gets his girls, comes back. Didn't punch a time clock and none of those people were paying attention, so...*

He slammed his file down, liberating a cloud of dust and doughnut and eraser crumbs. *And now I'm going to have Doggie and that wife of his all over my butt, same as Yonny. Worse. Hmmm. Maybe if Yonny eases up on me, maybe that means he's settled things. What did that Doctor Wolens say? Acceptance? Yeah. If he drops out of all this, that means he did it, or had it done, or maybe is just exhausted... I'm exhausted. Oh, shit, I don't know. And Linda is on my case, big time. Shit!* He leaned back, took out a cigar from a drawer. *Against regulations, but what the hell.* Lacing his fingers behind his head, chewing on the butt clenched in his jaws and the case clamped onto his brain, he tried to relax. *Sometimes you gotta let it go, Sam. Let it take you where it wants to take you, where it's gonna go. But one thing you've learned, after all these years knowing them, all of them, thinking you know them, you never really know what goes on with people, these people, behind their façades.*

He tossed the cigar into his wastebasket, then looked down. *Jack, you still there?*

That night crept along slowly, no sleep for him, not so far. Sam was trying his best not to fidget in bed, trying not to add to Linda's irritation, but thoughts ran rampant tonight, pounding through his head like that hammer years ago. *Why this Daphne chick? What had she done? Just going down on a boy, how many others did she do like that? Just got caught up in something else? But if it was a pro? Why? Okay, Sam, options, think through your options. A pro? Why would a pro tie her up like that, like the carpet picture? A pro would've got in and out, quick-like, popped her quick. Or maybe some kinko, some pervert. Maybe a kinky pro perv. Examiner will check her for semen anyway, we'll find out. And the pillow, pretty careful, pro-like.* He sighed quietly. *Shit, this is going nowhere.*

Or someone in the house? Yonny, sure. Maybe one of the caterers. Coulda been. Coulda been someone planted on the staff. There was that back stair to the kitchen...

Try something else, Sam. Think outside the box. You're sure, absolutely sure whoever killed the Berger kid killed Daphne, or had it done? What if, well, maybe he told Daphne he, or he and someone else had spiked that shit. She didn't know, why would she? Kinda hard to give a dead boy a BJ. And she's got a lot of money, she coulda hired someone to snuff the nerdy little prick herself. Probably out of her allowance. She's no skinny thing herself, maybe she... Isn't that what Rachel was saying? Gotta check my notes tomorrow. He squinted his closed eyes, trying desperately to bring a picture into focus.

Or maybe she just knew too much about something else entirely, no connection to the Jonas boy dying? Some sex thing? Rape? Incest, maybe...? Hmmmm....

Sam sat up in bed. *Ricky! Yonny yaks on and on about that girl got him started. Obsessed, already. Daphne? She's the one? Got him started? So, Yonny again. But how would he know? Kids talking, maybe, what else?* He reached over as smoothly as he could to his notepad, scribbled on it in the faint light. *Daphne. Why?*

He rolled over and tried to sleep.

31

"Is that you, Yonny? Cutting it rather close, aren't you? We need to be as close up front as we can, so everyone gets a good look at last year's news. I'm all done with the shower."

He started into their bedroom when the phone rang. He quick-timed it to the kitchen and grabbed the handset. "Hello?"

"Yawny, Sam."

"Hey, Sam, what's up? Anything new for Doggie? How terrible this is for them. It really brings it back home, the memories, that is. I thought we had pretty much regained lost ground, then this."

"Yeah, it's pretty bad, for everyone." Sam listened intently to his friend, chasing every tone, pause, word, trying to find a crack. *No luck. Cold, cool.* "But, as always happens in these deals, it only gets worse."

"How, Sam? How could it get any worse?"

"Okay, I'm going to tell you how. New information I've just finished collecting." He spoke at length and waited for the response.

"No way."

"Way. Wouldn't have thought it, not in a million years."

"Same here. You sure?"

"No, just allegations, rumors, really. Still pretty ugly, so don't say anything. If it doesn't pan out and he gets trashed in public…"

"Gotcha. Don't have to worry about me. Wouldn't do that to him or Juicy. Not for anything, with what they're going through, just like us, I get it, I really get it."

Rachel called out from the bedroom, "Yonny, who's that? Is it about Jeffy?"

"It's Sam, but it's about Daphne. Nothing much new. Sam, gotta go. I'll see you in a bit at the service?"

He hung up the kitchen phone just as Rachel walked in. She bored in on him, “What is it? Tell me, right now. This minute. What did Sam say?” With furrowed brows, “Is he… is he onto you, us, you think?”

“No, I don’t think so. Not right now.”

“So what, then? Tell me!”

Yonny bumped his head against the wall a couple of times, then stared sideways at her. “Promise? Not a peep?”

She made a gesture. “Cross my cleavage and hope to die.”

“Hmmm.” He savored the thought, then, “Several of our, their friends were questioned, like we were, have… have made allegations about Doug and Daphne, based on comments made by their children, rumors…, maybe she was… was pregnant… and…”

“No!”

“That’s what I said.”

“No. Won’t believe it, whatever, however sick it sounds. Not him. About as much sexual impulse as a eunuch.”

“He thinks, thought you’re pretty cute.”

“That’s different, how could he help himself? You can’t.”

“Still can’t.” He smiled mischievously, placing his hands either side of her waist, perching them atop her hips. *And an alibi now, no, a scapegoat, to boot. Maybe, maybe Sam starts in on Doggie, forgets about me? For sure poor Doggie isn’t going to add any clarity to the situation, not after what I laid on him. And his is the really hot story, not an OD or asthma but a bullet to a girl’s head and this sex thing? Can’t be. Maybe I say to Sam, forget about us, concentrate on Daphne. Maybe I go ahead and tell him about the Berger kid, say that was the end of it for me, for Rachel and me. Tell him that was closure enough for us. Hell, Doggie will have to tell him some time. Maybe I have to admit to being there with Teddie, hearing him. Doesn’t mean I had to know anything about Daphne, just Teddie. That’s it, it was Teddie, he wanted Jeffy out of the picture, Daphne didn’t know anything about it, he never told me the girl’s name, and he’s dead, can’t contradict me, she’s dead, I can say whatever I want. So why would I have… No way can he connect me with Daphne. No way. But… doesn’t he know about her and Jeffy? No, only I do. I’m the only one the kid told about it. And Rachel. Shouldn’t have brought her into this.*

But Sam knows about Ricky’s girlfriend, shouldn’t have made such a big deal out of that story. But I didn’t know it would have been a girl… Yes, you did. Right from the start, the pink lipstick. Right. Like you were trying to get set up to get caught all along… All that shit you told Doggie, maybe Rachel’s right, I am el stupido.

He turned Rachel around and swatted her rear. "Go get even more beautiful, Beautiful. I need to get cleaned up myself." As he watched her swaying hips, he was caught in a sudden chill. *Do they still do lie detectors? I couldn't pass one. No way. I'll ask R. I'm not going to worry about that, not now.* Suppressing a slight trembling, he had another thought. *So, I tell the truth.*

Time, Yonster, time. That's what this needs. Time to let our story get stale, old news. So what do I do now? What did I tell Rachel when we first heard? About Jeffy, I mean? That all we could do was try to muddle along, muddle through? That's what we have to do. We're not through with this, not nearly through with it. Now, it's almost worse. All I could think about was revenge. Revenge kept me from grieving, overpowered grief, took my focus off Jeffy and put it on... Now the big question is answered. Who got him started. Now there's nothing to take me, us away from Jeffy. All this pusher and girl stuff, that was just a bunch of brush covering a big hole, hiding a deep well. Now I've thrown all that off and I'm staring into that well. A deep, dark well. I've been here before, I've stared long and hard down into that well, that impenetrable darkness. That darkness rising up out of that hole to take me. And I already know I can't take my eyes away...

"Yonnybunny, are you coming?"

32

Sam hung up, still in his own muddle. *Maybe that'll smoke him out, maybe not. We'll see. Not sure I want to know any more, sure as hell don't care anymore. Maybe I just give him the benefit of the doubt, the tiebreaker. Spot him one dead boy. One real fine dead boy.* He pitched forward on his elbows, rubbing his temples. *And if he goes to the Chief with my hookup with the Angel? I'm out of a job. And another marriage. Crap, that was stupid, Sam, telling him that. But, he's a friend, right? Wouldn't do that. Would he?*

He leaned back and swiveled to his right, staring at a blank puke green wall. *Cold case, that's it. That's all. And one more life to get on with. Mine.*

His bottom drawer opened as if on its own. *Ol' Black Jack's back.* Gazing at it a long while, he started to toe the drawer closed, then stopped. He reached down just as his phone rang. Sam stared at the quart through three rings. "Yeah? I… Detective Thompson here."

"Yo, Sam. Maxie."

"Yo, yourself."

"Whassamatter, man?"

"Oh, I don't know, just tired, I guess. All hell's broke loose up here and I'm right in the shit middle of it. These people are just plain wearing me out."

"I got you on that, old friend. Lotsa bad shit goin' down in the Heights these days. You know, Sam, this kind of stuff didn't happen 'til you got there, right?"

"Screw you."

"Ri-i-ight. Okay, since we're still on speakin' terms, I got somethin' for you."

Sam brightened for the first time all day, maybe several days. "Oh, yeah? Gimme, gimme! I need some breaks on these cases." He sat through a few seconds of silence, then half-whispered, “Maxie? What is it?”

“It’s on the Angel deal, the shoot-em-up. Couple weeks ago, one of the beat guys noticed a plastic bag, one of those white H-E-B things, sorta stuck behind one of the sheetmetal fence panels, barely seen it, had some leaves blown over it. We had cleaned up the scene real good, you know, so he was curious, thought maybe we missed somethin’. Looked like it maybe been there a while, and he could see somethin’ dark inside. He said it didn’t smell like dog crap,” a hoarse laugh came through, quickly stifled, “so he nudged it open with a stick. It was a piece, a .38.”

“You found slugs, didn’t you? Casings, too?”

“Uh, huh, plenty of ’em. Matched, some of ’em did.”

“Ballistics took its own damned sweet time if you’re just now finding that out.”

“No, we had to check it for prints first, you know that. Found some, but didn’t find no matches with the usual suspects, so… Well, we expanded our search. Brought in the FBI, DEA, everything. Couldn’t give it to ballistics ’til we checked it out completely.”

“And you did, right?”

“Right.”

Something gnawed at Sam, sending a tremor down the back of his neck, leaching across his shoulder blades. “And?”

“You, Sam. Your prints on the barrel and cylinder. Grip and trigger been wiped real clean, like with acetone or somethin’. Just yours on the steel, man.” The phone went quiet, ominously, until Max rasped, “What can you tell me, Sam?”

Sam froze, unresponsive, as his mind raced, struggling to recall something hiding in the wandering gray wisps in his skull, hiding behind blocks and curtains and wiggly things in there.

“Sam? Sam, am I gonna have to come up there? Do I have to bring my cuffs with me?”

33

He couldn't help comparing the funerals, the congregations, the mounds and sprays of flowers. *A good measure of relative social standing, I suppose. Well, Jeffrey's wasn't half bad, just not this big. And think of the big bucks Doggie just saved, not having to put on the wedding Julie would've demanded. You'll go to Hell for that, Ian Jonas, that was most unkind. True, but true, too. So what? After what I've done? So what?*

A movement across the grave caught his eye. It was Sam, staring at him intently, not paying attention to the minister or anything or anyone else.

Yonny winked.

END

About the Authors

James E. (Jimmy) Loyd and David B. Matheson are 1968 graduates of Alamo Heights High School in San Antonio. After going their very separate ways, they reconnected at a reunion where the tale told here was hatched.

Jimmy Loyd is a recovering architect and retired real estate executive, hardly apprenticeships to becoming an author of any kind of fiction. But one day he decided to write his first novel. With a rough idea of a subject, ending World War One without Versailles and Bolshevism, he sat down at the keyboard. Before long he found himself simply taking dictation from his characters as the storyline grew, and three volumes and thirteen hundred pages later, his Great War Won trilogy was complete. He must have done something right; the trilogy was nominated for the Historical Novel Society's Best Indie Book of 2016. Not done with writing, and thinking he just might have learned something about the craft, he conceived of this memoir/mystery set in Alamo Heights, his hometown. The character Ian (Yonny) Jonas, while mostly fictional, draws on some elements from his life.

A San Antonio native, he spent twenty-five years away from home then returned after marrying his high school sweetheart. They live with their three dogs in their old neighborhood. He can be found at jloyd24@gmail.com or on Facebook.

David Matheson grew up in a military family on bases around the world, the son of a Sergeant Major in the United States Army. He moved to Alamo Heights in time for his sophomore year, and went on

David B. Matheson

to a nearly twenty year career in law enforcement, first on the San Antonio Police Department, then in north Texas on undercover narcotics details. Some of his experiences in law enforcement can only be described as hilariously terrifying, while others are as gritty and brutal as can ever be found on the mean streets. His character, Sam Thompson (his undercover name), is closely modeled on his life and experiences. Several of his stories enliven our book, sometimes with altered names and places for obvious reasons, but always true in spirit and pretty darned faithful to the facts. David can be reached at dmatheson573 @gmail.com or followed on Facebook.

This twosome is collaborating on a new work, a compendium of some of those tales from the streets and the beats. Tentatively titled Out of the Blue, we hope to publish this book in early 2018.

Finally, Ricky Young (not his real name) deserves a credit here. Now deceased nearly forty years, his encounter in college with a beautiful temptress bearing marijuana is the symbolic theme running through this book. A dear friend to both, his murder was our closest and deepest personal brush with the tragedies of the drug epidemic of the 1970's.

81622244R00154

Made in the USA
Lexington, KY
18 February 2018

A SHARED CHRISTIAN LIFE

BEN WITHERINGTON III

Abingdon Press
Nashville

A SHARED CHRISTIAN LIFE

This book is printed on acid-free paper.

Cataloging-in-Publication Data has been requested from the Library of Congress.

ISBN 978-1-4267-5317-6

All scripture quotations, unless noted otherwise, are the author's translation.

12 13 14 15 16 17 18 19 20 21—10 9 8 7 6 5 4 3 2 1
MANUFACTURED IN THE UNITED STATES OF AMERICA

For Steve Harper upon his retirement. A good friend, a good brother, the first John Wesley Fellow (and the first to retire). I can't wait to see how a tireless servant of the Lord manages to retire. May the Lord bless you and keep you and make his face to shine upon you until you have a holy sun tan!

Contents

FORWARD CHRISTIAN SOLDIERS

John Wesley was getting aggravated with his Moravian friends because of their "do-nothing" tendencies when it came to grace. They were having some heated discussions in London about the means of grace, and there were some Moravians even arguing that "grace happens" according to God's preordained plan and that there was nothing we humans could do to prod God into giving it sooner or later—no spiritual exercises, no fasting, no earnest praying, no taking of the sacraments—NOTHING.

Wesley was completely dissatisfied with their answer that they must just sit in their chairs and wait for the grace of God to descend from above like waiting for God to send the rain (which in London seemed to appear more frequently than grace in these Moravians' views). Finally, Wesley threw up his hands and basically said to the Moravians, "You should wait *actively* for the grace of God! Go take the Eucharist!" These words came naturally to a man who did his best to take Holy Communion every single day of his life, if possible. He had also urged "constant communion" on his followers, on the theory that we always could use more grace and presence of God in our lives.

This little story, which is a true story, speaks volumes about John Wesley's approach to what we today call "spiritual formation." In many ways, it stands at odds with some of the models of spiritual formation we hear so much about in our era—models that promote extreme introspection, individual isolation and individualistic seeking, spiritual athleticism of various kinds, and even spiritual navel-gazing of a sort. Sometimes when reading some of this literature, it seems almost as if ordinary Christians are being told "get thee to a nunnery" if you want to be truly spiritually formed.

What has happened in the age of narcissism and "me first" is that spiritual formation exercises and inventories have all too often taken on the character and ethos of our age, including the radical individualism of the culture. When you take a spiritual inventory that keeps asking questions about your *feelings* about God or how close you personally *feel* to God, there is a good reason to become uneasy. The language and praxis of psychology and psychological counseling have crept into the discussions of spiritual formation as if emotions were some sort of good guide or gauge to the state of someone's soul or his or her relationship with God. But in fact, this is often far from the truth.

Your visceral feelings are, more often than not, subject to the whims of your health, your circumstances, how much sleep you've had, whether you've taken your medicine or not, whether you are employed or not, and a thousand other such factors. Feelings, as Eugene Peterson once said, are remarkably unreliable guides to the state of your relationship with God, and are indeed seldom very reliable as guides to the state of your relationship with others.

Think for a minute about the Great Commandment—love God wholeheartedly and neighbor as self. I remember a day when my wife had a migraine headache and we had company coming. She felt terrible but there she was being a gracious hostess and no one but me knew that she was loving our guests *in spite of how she felt*. Don't get me wrong; I have nothing against feelings. I am just saying they are not very good litmus tests of where we stand with God. Just because, at a given moment, I don't have warm fuzzy feelings about God doesn't mean that I am, or sense that I am, distant from God! For example, *love* in the Bible is an action word. It is your ethic, what you do and how you act toward God, others, and self. It is not really meant as a feeling. Doing loving deeds is what the Great Commandment is about. I am rather certain that the greatest loving deed of all time, Jesus' dying on the cross for all of us, was not accompanied by warm fuzzy feelings. On the contrary, the story in the Garden of Gethsemane suggests that Jesus faced that prospect with icy dread.

The concern of this little book is to help us get away from certain unhelpful models of spiritual formation and practice our faith in ways that head in a more Wesleyan direction. There are two concerns I want to stress. First, the primary form of spiritual formation in the Wesleyan mode focuses on activities, and more specifically on *group* activities, and even more specifically on the activities of the *body of Christ* gathered—activities like worship, shared teaching or Bible study sessions, fellowship meals and times, taking Holy Communion, and doing works of piety and charity undertaken together. In addition, these activities are meant to edify us but also celebrate God's presence with us.

I believe that *primary* spiritual formation happens during the times two or more are gathered, Christ is present as well, and we are all caught up in love and wonder and praise. For example, for a Wesleyan, congregational singing and praying are primary means of spiritual formation, as opposed to someone singing to himself or herself in the shower or in his or her prayer closet. Praying the Lord's Prayer together is a means of grace. Saying the Apostle's Creed together is a means of grace. Singing the hymns is a means of grace.

Second, spiritual formation in the Wesleyan tradition is not primarily an individual's lonely personal quest for spiritual transcendence and growing closer to God. It is not primarily about looking inward so much as it is about looking outward at creation, at other creatures, and at the Creator. *It is not about becoming more self-centered, more self-focused; indeed it is about becoming more self-forgetful.* It's about knowing God, and in that quest, *as a by-product,* one comes to know one's self. It's not about taking Socrates' advice to "know thyself," much less taking the advice "to thine own self be true." There is an important distinction Wesley makes between mere emotions and religious affections, and we will need to explore the differences in due course. Religious affections are different from emotions because they are inspired by the spirit of God, not by normal physical factors or human interactions.

Too often in spiritual formation literature certain kinds of extreme monastic models of piety are held up to the ordinary Christian's eye, which, apart from sporadic spiritual retreats, she or he could never live up to or into. Who exactly is capable of "praying without ceasing," if by praying one is referring to specific spoken or unspoken petitions to God? If you are not a cloistered monk or a hermit with someone else providing you with food, shelter, and clothing, and with no family responsibilities, this sort of spiritual athleticism is beyond the scope of the life of the everyday or normal Christian. My concern in this study is to talk about spirituality for the *normal* Christian life, to talk about ordinary spiritual formation as well as extraordinary spiritual formation. This book is for ordinary people caught up in the normal weekly cycle of work, rest, play, worship, family time, and other mundane activities. It is for those who want to grow in Christ and in their Christian maturity without having to become monks or spiritual Olympians.

This book has arisen out of some frustration with a good deal of the literature I have seen, which has adopted and adapted certain ascetical and medieval monastic models and forms of spiritual formation, baptized them for normal modern Christians, and called them good—indeed called them necessary if one wants to be a "spiritual" Christian. Like ambitious New Year's resolutions, having impossible expectations leads, in the end, to spiritual frustration, feelings of inadequacy and guilt, and little real progress in one's Christian life. And besides, as Bob Dylan once said, "The times they are a-changin'."

I was at the monastery of Gethsemani near Bardstown, Kentucky, where Thomas Merton once was a monk. I was sitting quietly in the gift shop, waiting for my mother to finish shopping (that Gethsemani fudge is pretty delicious). Sitting next to me was a monk who was so ancient I assumed he had arrived when the monastery had been built, decades and decades ago. I also knew that the Trappist monks were famous for taking a vow of silence, talking to no other human beings but devoting themselves to things like silent prayer, fasting, and working in the garden. The Trappists were, so to speak, trapped in a very quiet place. So I resisted the urge to say something to this brother in Christ.

As you might imagine, I nearly jumped out of my skin when this ancient monk began to strike up a conversation with me out of the blue! In fact he talked a blue streak about Thomas Merton and how he himself had arrived at the monastery before Merton, with only a little prompting and questioning from me. He informed me, "We're not as silent as we used to be." Clearly not! Spiritual formation and practice is not necessarily all about silence, individual quiet times, and a hermitlike withdrawal from society.

My point is this: I would like to offer in this book a workable model of spirituality in a Wesleyan mode for the normal Christian life—a model that does not put people on unnecessary guilt trips and does not encourage them to indulge in spiritual navel-gazing or focusing on mere visceral feelings. To do this, the book is divided into two major parts: collective practices that spiritually form us, and more individual practices, with the emphasis on the former. *Modern Western Christians don't need encouragement to be more individualistic and self-centered. To the contrary, they need more encouragement to be integral parts of the body of Christ working and serving together.*

In a day and time when mainline Christianity is often seeing declining membership, at least in the West, it is time to do a rethink and a rewind on the subject of spiritual formation. We can't just keep walking down the road to Emmaus forever and think such retreats will cure all our ills. As valuable as retreats are—and indeed they are valuable and formative—they are not the stuff of day-to-day Christlike formation. It's time to take the road less traveled. But the good news is that it involves our journeying together, not alone. Won't you join in the journey? I promise it will lead somewhere and to Someone.

Finally, to help you understand the logical order of this book, we will begin with the primary activity of all Christians when they gather together—namely worship. It is in worship that we begin to be formed in the image of Christ and hear about imitating Christ and other spiritual practices. Indeed it is in worship that we place ourselves before God, admire his Son, and learn how to become his followers. After dealing with worship we will talk about the actual beginning of spiritual formation in a person's life—namely the new birth. This will be followed by a discussion of sanctification and imitation of Christ. Once we have carefully located spiritual formation within the larger subject of salvation, then we will be better positioned to discuss various spiritual disciplines and practices that can fit into a normal Christian life.

PART ONE

Spirituality as Life in the Body of Christ

CHAPTER ONE

LOVING AND WORSHIPING GOD WHOLEHEARTEDLY

Religion is the spirit of a sound mind; and, consequently, stands in direct opposition to madness of every kind. But I mean, it has religion for its object; it is conversant about religion. And so the enthusiast is generally talking of religion, of God, or of the things of God, but talking in such a manner that every reasonable Christian may discern the disorder of his mind. Enthusiasm in general may then be described in some such manner as this: a religious madness arising from some falsely imagined influence or inspiration of God; at least, from imputing something to God which ought not to be imputed to Him, or expecting something from God which ought not to be expected from Him. —John Wesley, sermon "The Nature of Enthusiasm"[1]

One of the great problems in the twenty-first-century church is the problem of time. This is all the more a problem during an economically difficult time. People have to work—work hard to find and then keep a job—to provide for their families or to pay off their college education. When they are not busy doing such things, they are resting or occasionally having a bit of fun with family or friends. And frankly, there are not a lot of hours in the week for *religion* of whatever sort.

And so it is, that when the spiritual gurus call persons to extreme spiritual athleticism ("drop everything and come to my seminar"), or alternatively serve up pablum in some sort of "chicken soup for the soul," it is no wonder that the Christian public gets confused about what the normal Christian life should look like.

Is spirituality like some sort of hothouse flower that requires a self-contained environment where "heat" is the constant requirement just to produce any sort of growth at all? Is it some sort of human self-help program? Is it all about deep introspection and intense feelings about God? Is it only the seeking after some sort of cathartic religion experience? In short, folks get discouraged because they feel like they either don't have the time or don't have the energy, or don't have spiritually what it takes to do spiritual formation. And this is unfortunate but normal.

John Wesley certainly had some thoughts about this whole matter, and one of the interesting things about Wesley is that he did not think one size of spiritual formation fits all. In fact, he set up groups—societies, classes, and bands, three different levels of spiritual commitment—to help persons at different stages in their spiritual growth learn to draw closer to God. And while on the one hand Wesley was all in favor of Christians having a deep and abiding love for God and neighbor, and manifesting the love and joy and peace as the fruit of the Spirit in their lives, on the other hand, John Wesley was not a fan of what was called "enthusiasm" in his era, by which was meant religious fanaticism. As the quotation from Wesley at the beginning of this chapter shows, his view was that true religion, true "enthusiasm" in the positive sense, was the spirit of a sound and rational mind, not the spirit of someone who had taken leave of his or her senses. It was also not about a Christian *needing* to go through some "dark night of the soul" experience, or even some extreme ecstatic experience, in order to truly commune with God. What Wesley goes on to stress in his sermon is that false enthusiasm is *seeking the ends without the means,* seeking something from God directly that God, in fact, regularly and normally gives through the communal life in Christ. Here's how he puts it at the end of this sermon:

Beware, lastly, of imagining you shall obtain the end without using the means conducive to it. God can give the end without any means at all; but you have no reason to think He will. Therefore constantly and carefully use all those means which He has appointed to be the ordinary channels of His grace. Use every means which either reason or Scripture recommends, as conducive (through the free love of God in Christ) either to the obtaining or increasing any of the gifts of God. Thus expect a daily growth in that pure and holy religion which the world always did, and always will, call "enthusiasm;" but which, to all who are saved from real enthusiasm, from merely nominal Christianity is "the wisdom of God, and the power of God;" the glorious image of the Most High; "righteousness and peace;" a "fountain of living water, springing up into everlasting life!"

What then are the ordinary channels of God's grace? Although they include things like prayer and Bible reading that we can do on our own (which we will discuss later), Wesley is talking about things we do together—participating in the weekly worship of God, and if possible in the sacraments with the body of Christ, and participating in the weekly study of God's word. In Wesley's own day it also meant attending the group meetings as well.

For a start, the normal Christian life involves doing one's best to observe the Lord's Day every single week. It involves coming prepared each week to wholeheartedly get caught up with the congregation in love and wonder and praise of God in Christ. We will say more about this, but participation in learning about God through Sunday school, Bible study, or small-group learning with fellow travelers—fellow Christians—is equally important.

The Christian life involves both education and transformation, both learning and loving, both fellowship and worship, both being lifted up in spirit and being enlightened in mind. The normal Christian life needs balance not only between work and rest and play; it also must include worship and learning. To some degree the Christian faith is something caught through participation in worship; to some degree it is something taught through Christian education. And in our biblically illiterate age, we need large doses of both. Let's start with worship, and more specifically singing, as a means of spiritual formation.

WORSHIP THE WESLEYAN WAY

John Wesley, a man who had rules for almost everything, had some interesting rules about singing in a manner that glorified God and edified one's fellow worshipers, which he published in 1761. Here is what he said:

1. Sing all. See that you join with the congregation as frequently as you can. Let not a slight degree of weakness or weariness hinder you. If it is a cross to you, take it up and you will find a blessing.

2. Sing lustily, and with a good courage. Beware of singing as if you were half dead, or half asleep; but lift up your voice with strength. Be no more afraid of your voice now, nor more ashamed of it being heard, then when you sang the songs of Satan.

3. Sing modestly. Do not bawl, as to be heard above, or distinct from, the rest of the congregation, that you may not destroy the harmony; but strive to unite your voices together, so as to make one clear melodious sound.

4. Sing in time. Whatever time is sung, be sure to keep with it. Do not run before, not stay behind it; but attend closely to the leading voices, and move therewith as exactly as you can. And take care you sing not too slow. This drawling way naturally steals on all who are lazy; and it is high time to drive it out from among us, and sing all our tunes just as quick as we did at first.

5. Above all, sing spiritually. Have an eye to God in every word you sing. Aim at pleasing Him more than yourself, or any

other creature. In order to do this, attend strictly to the sense of what you sing, and see that your heart is not carried away with the sound, but offered to God continually; so shall your singing be such as the Lord will approve of here, and reward when he cometh in the clouds of heaven.[1]

Almost every element in Christian worship is and should be focused on God. In other words, it should be *theocentric,* God-centered. The interesting thing about church music is that while it is in praise of God and primarily directed to God, the congregation is *not,* according to Paul, merely performing for an audience of one. Ephesians 5:18-20 preserves the balance correctly: "Be filled with the Spirit, as you sing psalms and hymns and spiritual songs *among yourselves,* singing and making melody to the Lord in your hearts, giving thanks to God the Father at all times." What Paul has in mind is: (1) while singing is a thank offering to God and its content should be in praise of God, it is also an act of spiritual formation of others—we are to sing songs of praise to one another for the purpose of spiritually forming one another. The phrase "in your hearts" is not meant to suggest one is only singing internally. If that were the case, others would not be edified. The phrase means singing to the Lord wholeheartedly or in a heart-felt way. (2) What is ruled out both by Paul and in Wesley's rules is *singing for the entertainment of others.* Church music is not intended to be the performance of the few for the "couch potatoes for Jesus" in the pews. In fact, the emphasis both in the New Testament and in Wesley is on *congregational singing.*

It is not surprising that in a narcissistic consumer culture, people have come to judge the merits of worship by its music and preaching *as entertainment.* This self-centered approach has had numerous bad outcomes. For one thing, people decide *where* they will worship with this consumer mentality: "I will go where I can get the most out of it." They pick a worship service like they pick a car or a movie. They never even ask, "Where would the Lord have me go to best serve him and edify God's people?"

Part of the problem lies in not knowing the proper function of the elements of true Spirit-filled worship.

The function of music in a worship service is not merely to rev up the troops, nor is it mainly to set the mood. Music reaches people at noncognitive levels, at affective dimensions of our personalities, and the goal of worship, including congregational singing, is that our whole person—mind, spirit, emotions, and will—is caught up in love and wonder and praise of God. When this kind of worship happens, we become self-forgetful, and then, being wide open to God's Spirit, we become shaped and formed in ways that lead to growth and Christian maturity. Let us examine a little more closely what Wesley says about singing.

Notice Wesley says at the outset, "See that you join in the congregational singing as often as possible." Christian worship is not an *American Idol* contest, and you should not be afraid to sing, even if you don't think you have much talent for it. The idea is to make a joyful noise unto the Lord and get caught up with the congregation in loving and praising God with one's whole heart. Singing should be done in a self-forgetful, not a self-indulgent, way. The emphasis on singing in one accord is part of the process of *consciously* uniting one's self with the rest of the congregation in this act of praise. We must listen to one another and if possible harmonize with one another. It is one of the ways to both create and further solidify the unity of a particular body of believers. Indeed the rules for singing are much like the New Testament rules for Christian living—seek to be in harmony and in one accord (or even one chord) with one another.

The last paragraph of Wesley's rules on singing is the most important. Wesley asks us to sing spiritually, not neglecting the meaning of the words; *thus, meaning what we sing and singing what we mean.* Think of yourself as tuning up for the heavenly choir, practicing here for the glorification of God what we will do there in the afterlife. Corrie ten Boom once said that she imagined Bach up in heaven being given the opportunity to direct the heavenly choir. The point is that worshiping here is already participating with the saints and acting "in concert" with them. It is sometimes said that Methodism was born in song. This is a bit of an exaggeration, but it was certainly carried along by singing, because of the efforts of Charles Wesley and Isaac Watts and others, and to this day singing is a crucial means of conveying our faith and forming our spirits.

While I was doing my PhD at the University of Durham in England, most weekends I was asked to preach somewhere in the Durham and Darlington circuits. There was one little chapel way out near Pity Me (yes, that's the name of a small coal mining village outside of Durham) that I preached at a couple of times in a three-year span. The second time I preached there it had been a while since the first visit, and quite naturally I was preaching out of my sermon barrel, not having a lot of time to write new sermons. At the end of the worship service one elderly lady came up to me and said, "You certainly like that hymn by Saint Francis, don't you, because we sang that the last time you were here." Now as it happens, I only had one sermon in which that was a hymn I had selected to sing. The old lady, being the good Methodist she was, remembered I had chosen that hymn before; but what she didn't remember was that unintentionally I had managed to preach the very same sermon twice in that church! This was a good humbling experience for a young Methodist preacher.

BODY LIFE

In the Methodist tradition, there has always been an awareness of how the grace and spirit of God often transform people when they are sharing together in inspiring worship. Francis Asbury, when he was praising the large camp meetings that took place in early nineteenth-century America, called it "fishing with a big net" not only because such large worship services are good tools for evangelism, but also because in a large group people unconsciously relax and let their guard down, perhaps feeling there is safety in numbers. And what happens when one relaxes and lets one's guard down in the presence of God, in the presence of God's Spirit, is that life can be suddenly and wonderfully changed. There is no spiritual formula or formation more important at the beginning of the Christian life than the new birth, conversion itself, and Asbury was quite certain that this could most easily happen in large groups. He once exulted, "Camp meetings, camp meetings—Glory, glory!"

Asbury knew as well that such large-group meetings were also meant to revive the flagging zeal of all Christians. Postconversion spiritual growth and formation most easily happened in the collective, when the church met as the body of Christ and experienced life in that body. And herein lies an important point: the body of Christ cannot directly minister to you in a hands-on way unless you actively participate in its gatherings. As the book of Hebrews exhorts, we must not neglect the gathering of ourselves together. Even the metaphor of the body helps us see this.

I need my hands to tie my shoes. My feet cannot do it for me, nor can my shoulders or my legs. The different parts of the body have different functions, and most important, they all need one another. As Paul says, "The head cannot say to the feet, 'I have no need of you.' " *Why then should we think we should mainly do spiritual formation all by ourselves in isolation from the rest of the body of Christ?* The idea of spiritual formation as a lonely pursuit of nirvana all by one's self, with a how-to manual in hand, is a distortion of what the Bible and the Wesleyan tradition teach. Consider the early church, the church in its infancy as depicted in Acts 2 and 4.

They devoted themselves to the apostles' teaching and to fellowship, to the breaking of bread and to prayer. Everyone was filled with awe at the many wonders and signs performed by the apostles. All the believers were together and had everything in common. They sold property and possessions to give to anyone who had need. Every day they continued to meet together in the temple courts. They broke bread in their homes and ate together with glad and sincere hearts, praising God and enjoying the favor of all the people. And the Lord added to their number daily those who were being saved. (Acts 2:42-47)

All the believers were one in heart and mind. No one claimed that any of their possessions was their own, but they shared everything they had. With great power the apostles continued to testify to the resurrection of the Lord Jesus. And God's grace was so powerfully at work in them all that there were no needy persons among them. For from time to time those who owned land or houses sold them, brought the money from the sales and put it at the apostles' feet, and it was distributed to anyone who had need. (Acts 4:32-35)

These two rich paragraphs need to be unpacked. Notice that the earliest Christians were always *together*—together in their homes, together in the temple courts. Notice second that Christian formation took place through their sharing not only in the apostle's teaching and prayer, but also through the ordinary activities of eating together and equally sharing their property so that there were no early Christians in want of a meal or a coat or a roof over their heads. *Can you imagine what a witness it would be if there were no hungry, naked, homeless Christians in the world? Can you imagine how it would form you as a part of a body of Christ that took so seriously the whole gospel for whole persons in the whole world, ministering wholeheartedly? Don't you believe that the world would have to take notice?*

Third, notice that this shared worship and fellowship was done with glad and sincere hearts. We are not talking about dry and boring, mere going-through-the-motions ritual and calling *that* worship. No, indeed. The energy and enthusiasm of the early church was contagious. And this brings me back to this point: spiritual formation happens when you forget yourself and get caught up in acts of piety and charity—the spiritual *and* social dimensions of the gospel.

Perhaps it is worth saying what this unity of the original body of Christ did *not* involve: (1) Most of them did not quit their day jobs. Indeed their day jobs and inheritance provided them with the resources to support the gospel initiatives. (2) They did not all sell their homes and abandon their families and go on the road. Some made this extreme sacrifice, but it was not required of all to be true followers of Jesus. (3) They did not go off somewhere and create a commune or a spiritual cloister. They met in ordinary homes regularly *and* in the temple courts, not just one or the other. (4) From Acts 5, we read the story of Ananias and Sapphira and discover that the earliest Christians did not practice some ancient version of communism. What they practiced was *communalism,* meaning that they made sure no one in the community was in want or need. They did not sell *all* they had and put the money in some central storehouse of goods to be distributed equally to all. As Peter pointed out to Ananias, even after Ananias sold some goods, the resources were still his to either give to the apostles or not. Ananias's sin was not that he didn't give everything he had; his sin was lying to the Holy Spirit about how much he had given. But there can be no doubt that these early Christians were committed to self-sacrificial living to build up the body of Christ and support one another, and this free and generous giving to one another was tremendously freeing and spiritually formative. Let us look at some of the other marks of the earliest Christian community that formed them spiritually.

"They devoted themselves to the apostles' teaching."

Genuine Christian teaching and learning is *in itself* spiritually forming. I sometimes get a little irritated when someone asks me, "So what are you doing in your classes to spiritually form your students?" as if there needed to be something *beyond* merely teaching them to accomplish this goal. My response is simple: "I am teaching them the true meaning of the word of God with enthusiasm and helping them learn how to study it and apply it."

I also get a little impatient with those who ask me personally, "Do you have devotional time in God's word?" My response is, "I always have devotional time whenever I am studying God's word." I always study God's word wide open to God and his Spirit and to whatever God wants to convey to me. I am always in a doxological mode when I study God's word. I do not divide out the so-called academic study of God's word from something else that is supposed to be more "spiritual." In fact this makes no sense to me at all. If I am not in the Spirit when I am doing my scholarly New Testament work, then I am not myself. If I am not listening to God when I am reading the Greek New Testament, then I am not myself. I consume and am consumed by God's word, which he uses to form me, over and over and over again. But the same is also true for you when you study and learn from God's word.

"They devoted themselves to fellowship."

Actually, I am not really happy with the translation of the Greek word ***koinonia*** as "fellowship" in the Bible (see a later chapter on this), though I do like Tom Skinner's old definition of fellowship: a bunch of fellows in the same ship rowing in the same direction. The word ***koinonia*** has an active sense. It means the sharing in common or participation in common with others in something. The result of such participating in common can be fellowship, but **koinonia** is the process, not the product; the activity, not the outcome.

Also, "devoted themselves" can be translated "they attached themselves to." We are indeed here talking about a conscious activity. The verb is reflexive, referring to what a person or group of persons does to themselves. And it is right to hear in this verb the sense that this was wholeheartedly undertaken. There was nothing casual or accidental about this. They devoted themselves to the apostles' teaching and to sharing things in common, breaking bread together, and praying. The spiritual bonding and forming came in the group, during the group activities they shared in common.

But the question to be asked of all of us is: have we *wholeheartedly* devoted ourselves when we gather together as the body of Christ? Or do we come to worship tired, distracted, twittering and tweeting and texting, but not really spiritually bonding with others and with God? Do we look at our communal gatherings as some sort of spiritual respite from having to do anything or think anything or commit to anything? Do we just sit in the pews and casually listen and let our minds wander, zoning in and out on what is happening? If any of this is even usually true, then we are not worshiping, and we are not being spiritually formed.

"They devoted themselves to the breaking of bread."

In too many Protestant services there is no eating. There is no taking of the Eucharist—Communion. There is no fellowship meal before, during, or after; there is nothing physical consumed during the service. And sadly, sometimes not even the word of God is taken in. What is so important about eating together? Put another way, why was it in the breaking of bread that the disciples at Emmaus reckoned it was Jesus who was the host of the meal? To understand all of this, we need to understand something about ancient hospitality.

First, the word we normally translate from the Greek as "hospitality" is ***xenophilia,*** which literally rendered means "the love of strangers." In the ancient biblical world, when you welcomed people into your tent or into your home, even if they were strangers or enemies, the guests became, at least for that period of time, a part of the family. They were greeted with the kiss of greeting at the door; their cloaks were taken; their heads were anointed; their feet were washed, cleaning the dirt from the road off them; and then at last, they broke bread and shared in a meal together. The earliest Christians made sharing in a family meal a regular part of what they did because they believed they genuinely were family. They believed they really were brothers and sisters in Christ, and what could be more natural for brothers and sisters to do than eat together? What we often forget is that, in the ancient world, often the strongest bonds were between siblings, not between parents and children. The language of brother and sister in this context connoted the *strongest* possible family bonds, now made possible through sharing in Christ together. Let me illustrate what this sort of experience can, and what it should never, mean.

In the late 1980s, I was invited to preach at an old Church of the Brethren congregation in Ashland, Ohio. These folks are called the Dunkers. Their distinctive practices included a three-fold immersion at baptism, in the name of each member of the Trinity, and foot-washing along with the Eucharist—*and* the Eucharist was served always in the context of a meal. After what I will call the main part of the worship service in this old church, we became a moveable feast and all went downstairs into the fellowship hall where there was a full meal for all of us to share, and in the context of that meal, we also took the Eucharist, and there was foot-washing. As a good Methodist, I had never taken my shoes off in church. Indeed, it would not have been "an odor pleasing unto the Lord." But all of a sudden an elderly saint of this church, who had been calmly sitting next to me, got up from his chair, knelt beside me, and started taking off my shoes and socks, with a towel and basin nearby. Do you know that my immediate reaction was identical to Peter's or even John the Baptizer's? I wanted to cry out, "No way are you going to wash my feet. If that's going to happen I am going to respect my elders and do it for you." But I didn't say anything and it was a tremendously humbling, holy thing to have my feet washed by someone who had "devoted himself to the apostolic practice."

Let us contrast that holy moment with just the opposite—what I can only call "the trivializing of the sacred." In a large megachurch in the Midwest, there was a seeker service; and on this particular day, the ministry team decided to "do Communion" a little differently, using cheese crackers and fruit punch. I kid you not. After the service, a woman came up to the head minister and said, "You know what I really liked about that service?" "No," replied the minister. The woman then said, "I liked that you stopped in the middle of the service and had snacks." At that juncture, an unacceptable image came into the mind of the minister, *This is my snack, given for you.*

Scholars of Luke's Gospel are divided on whether the phrase "the breaking of the bread" is Luke's way of talking about the Lord's Supper. This may well be the case, since he does not mention the practice in other terms. But why would the phrase "the breaking of the bread" connote the full Eucharist, which involves so much more? It is because when Jesus introduced these new elements into the Passover meal, he broke bread and said, "Take, eat, this is my body broken for you. . . . Do this in remembrance of me." The act of breaking bread symbolized the breaking of Jesus' body on the cross, not in the sense that his limbs were literally broken, but in the sense that he gave up his life, poured out the vial of his life force, put his body upon the cross, for us.

So it seems likely that the phrase "they devoted themselves to the breaking of bread" means not merely that they resolved to eat together regularly. It probably meant that they resolved to share in the Lord's Supper whenever they met together, and if we look at 1 Corinthians 11, where we hear the earliest form of the "words of institution," we hear two things: (1) the ritual begins, "For I received from the Lord what I also passed on to you: The Lord Jesus, on the night he was betrayed, took bread, and when he had given thanks, he broke it" (vv. 23-24); and (2) Paul says that this sharing in the Lord's Supper should and did take place "when you come together [in one place]"(see vv. 18 and 33).[3] No wonder John Wesley counseled constant communion. He saw it as a means of grace for Christians; and indeed, he came to see the Lord's Supper as such a powerful means of grace that it could be a converting as well as a confirming sacrament.

It is interesting that when the earliest Methodists got together, the first thing they asked one another was not, "How is your favorite sports team doing?" or "How is the job coming along?" No, the first question Methodists asked one another was, "How is it with your soul?" In other words, the very context of their meetings, the very essence of what they were about when they came together, was always spiritual formation in the collective context of the body of Christ. And this brings me to the last of the clauses in this portion of Acts 2.

"They devoted themselves to prayer."

This is not a reference to private prayer. No, Luke is talking about corporate and public prayer, prayer shared together when the body of Christ meets. There is, of course, a long tradition of prayer in the Bible. There are plenty of prayers in the Old Testament, and there are the psalms, which could be called sung prayers in many cases—not merely spiritual singing, nor merely praying, but sung prayers. We are not told what sorts of prayers were included in those early Christian days in Jerusalem, but it is likely they included prayers of praise, of thanksgiving, of petition, of intercession, and of penitence or repentance—the same kinds of prayers we pray today. The point is, that all such prayers were appropriate as part of corporate worship, and the earliest Christians devoted themselves to them.

John Wesley also encouraged not just reciting the Lord's Prayer in worship, but also what he called "extempore" prayer, or what we would call "spontaneous acts of praying," in various ways and for various things. According to Wesley, although prayer should be a deeply personal act, it is not meant to be a mere private act. To the contrary, praying together apparently has cumulative force—"If two or more agree together about anything..." says the scripture. In fact, Wesley had a theology of prayer.

John Wesley was certainly not a Calvinist like George Whitefield, his friend and fellow evangelist. Wesley actually believed that prayer was a change agent. By this I mean he believed that God, while he could have done it directly, has condescended to use our prayers to accomplish his purposes. We are partners with God in the bringing of the Kingdom on earth. Prayer is not merely our conforming our own wishes and ideas to the things God has preordained and predetermined from before the foundation of the universe. No, prayer in the Wesleyan tradition can and is used by God to accomplish God's ends. When Jesus tells his disciples that only prayer and fasting can exorcise some demons, he does not mean that God has already determined long before the prayer and fasting whether the demon is coming or going. He means that the praying and fasting are essential to the accomplishing of the exorcism. It is not a predetermined matter. As Paul says in 1 Corinthians, we are God's coworkers, and prayer is one of our weapons in the fight against the powers of darkness. Indeed, prayer in the Wesleyan tradition is *dangerous.*

Be careful what you are prayerful about. Here is a poem called "Prayer (I)" by George Herbert for reflection on this very matter.

Prayer, the church's banquet, angels' age,
  God's breath in man returning to his birth,
  The soul in paraphrase, heart in pilgrimage,
The Christian plummet sounding heaven and earth;

Engine against th' Almighty, sinner's tower,
  Reversèd thunder, Christ-side-piercing spear,
  The six-days' world transposing in an hour,
A kind of tune, which all things hear and fear;

Softness, and peace, and joy, and love, and bliss,
  Exalted manna, gladness of the best,
  Heaven in ordinary, man well dressed,
The Milky Way, the bird of Paradise,

Church bells beyond the stars heard, the soul's blood,
  The land of spices; something understood.

Prayer does not turn God into our cosmic bellhop, jumping whenever we ring, at our beck and call. Indeed, God often has to answer some prayers with an emphatic "NO!" God will not do anything that is contrary to his will. It is worth remembering that when we sign Jesus' name to a prayer, we ought to have first reviewed the prayer and asked, "Is this in character with what Jesus would pray?" Too often we fire up prayers as if they were a child's requests for Christmas presents, hardly thinking about whether the prayer is even appropriate or the sort of thing God might say yes to.

I do love the audacity in Herbert's poem about prayer, calling it an "engine against th' Almighty." What he means is not merely that God listens and nods approvingly, but that God responds. Our relationship with God is not a one-way street; and prayer is not a one-way street either—it's interactive, done in the context of an ongoing relationship with him. And this brings me to one last thing.

Spiritual formation is and should be undertaken in the context of one's ongoing relationship not only with God but also with God's people. It is not about one's personal and private quest for transcendence. As one's relationship with God in Christ and with the body of Christ grows and develops, one's sanctification level improves and one is spiritually formed—increasingly so.

CONCLUSION

In this chapter, I have focused on corporate worship and fellowship as the primary contexts in which spiritual formation happens and should happen. In the coming chapters I want to address another important matter: the relationship between character formation in the body of Christ and spiritual formation, the relationship between working out our salvation together and spiritual formation, the relationship between piety and purity, between ethos and ethics. First, however, we have to talk about the beginning of spiritual life at all—namely conversion or the new birth. We have only just begun our journey into a new way of looking at spiritual formation, a new and more biblical and Wesleyan way, which not accidentally or incidentally involves the imitation of Christ.

Questions for Reflection

1. Do you regularly take time for worship? Do you have Christian friends and fellowship?
2. What do you think about your own spiritual formation? Where are you in your spiritual journey?
3. Share a time when you felt close to God. Share a time when God was close but you may not have known it at the time.
4. How is the congregational singing in your church? How could it be better?
5. Share what the Lord's Supper means to you. How do you "break the bread" at your church?
6. What could your church do to help people worship? How could your church help people devote themselves more fully to prayer? How could your church fellowship help people grow closer to Christ?

CHAPTER TWO

THE ROOT OF SPIRITUAL FORMATION: CONVERSION

As a pastor, I've seen people slip through the cracks, ripped violently through the eye of the needle, caught in a great dragnet, cut down and gathered for harvest, pursued all the way into the wilderness, drawn unto him, invited. It is, for me, living proof that God was in Christ and reconciling the whole wide world. —Will Willimon[1]

When we talk about spiritual formation, what we usually discuss is how the spiritual life of those who are already Christians can be improved; how they can draw closer to God; how they can be better, more Christian persons. There is nothing wrong with such conversations, but too often they have a sort of fuzzy or generic or indefinite character, as if one size fits all; and more important, they often reflect a profoundly private and individualistic view of salvation. In this chapter we want to go back to the root of the issue—the whole way conversion is viewed in large sections of the Protestant Church. Let me explain what I mean.

I grew up not only in the shadow of Billy Graham's home in Charlotte, North Carolina, but also in the era when Billy Graham was the world's most famous evangelist and seemed to be constantly on TV. I even remember one day when my family was watching him on TV and when the call was made to come down front to where Dr. Graham was—a call made at the end of his sermon—my little sister said, "Let's get up close to the TV." Conversion was viewed as a matter of making a personal commitment to Christ, after which one should join a church, and there were ushers at the crusade standing around to help with part B. You might even have been asked to fill out a commitment card saying now that Jesus was your personal savior you were ready to make a commitment to the church. And indeed, the essence of the way evangelism was done in that whole era of the 1950s, 1960s, and 1970s—and is still done today in many circles—was that you asked an individual, "Do you have a *personal* relationship with Jesus/the Lord/Christ?" with emphasis on the word *personal.*

There is something odd about this whole question because the New Testament says absolutely nothing about individuals having a "personal" relationship with Jesus, in that precise sort of language, especially if by "personal" one means private or individualistic apart from anyone else's relationship with Christ. This way of viewing Jesus has even been satirized in a song by a rock group called Depeche Mode. The song is called "Personal Jesus," and in fact in the course of the band's thirty or so years, it is by far their biggest hit. What is being satirized is the notion that Jesus is at our beck and call and that when I "ask Jesus into my life" (yet another phrase nowhere to be found in the New Testament) I have access to all sorts of power and emotional highs. Jesus becomes my personal bellhop to meet my never-ending demands and needs. What is wrong with this picture?

What is wrong with it is that *while it is true that God in Christ becomes central and thus a vital part of a Christian's life after conversion, what primarily happens at conversion is not Christ becoming a part of "you" or being absorbed by "you" but quite the reverse—you become a part of Christ's body; you become "in Christ." The dominant language in Paul's letters about this matter refers to persons who are "in Christ." In fact the phrase "in*

Christ" is the Pauline equivalent for "Christian"—he does not use the term "Christian" to refer to converted individuals!

It is indeed a striking fact that the term "Christian" is missing in action in Paul's letters. He doesn't refer to individual converts that way; he refers to them as being "in Christ." Yes, there are occasionally, rarely actually, phrases like "Christ in you, the hope of glory," but this is not where the emphasis is placed in Paul or in the New Testament. The emphasis is placed on our being incorporated into Christ and his body in some way, rather than his becoming a part of who we are as individuals. What does it mean then to be "in Christ," and what does spiritual formation look like when we take that seriously? To answer that question we need to go back to square one and look at the New Testament and Wesleyan language about conversion, about being a new creature in Christ, about the new birth or being born again. Once we get our heads screwed on straight about all of that, we will be in a position to ask and answer what spiritual formation is, when it begins, and what its relationship is to initial salvation and initial justification by grace through faith.

It is obvious that when we first come to Christ, it is entirely likely that we do not really know all it entails and means. I remember vividly being at an InterVarsity Christian Fellowship meeting at the University of North Carolina in the early 1970s, and a young lady who was a new Christian stood up and gave her testimony. What she said was, "The way I see it, it all works out very well. I like committing sins and God likes forgiving sins. Salvation is by faith, not works, so my deeds don't much matter to God." Clearly, she had not gotten the memo about the Ten Commandments and other ethical exhortations in the Bible.

NEW CREATURES IN CHRIST

Paul puts the matter directly in 2 Corinthians 5:17-18: "So if anyone is in Christ, there is a new creation: everything old has passed away; see, everything has become new! All this is from God, who reconciled us to himself through Christ." Notice two things about that first clause. We have the ubiquitous phrase "in

Christ" to describe the state of being saved, and it is said that this "anyone" is now part of something called "a new creation," with everything old having already passed away. Then finally it is said that "all this is from God" and "through Christ." In other words, the initiative for salvation comes from God, the "hound of heaven," not from us. Before we even had an inkling of it, God was reconciling the world to himself through Christ. The initiative lies entirely with God. In fact notice when Paul particularizes the matter even more he says, "God reconciled *us*"—not merely *me* but *us*—to himself through Christ. God is not interested in having a bunch of isolated individual converts with no connection to one another. He is interested in having a people, a body of Christ, a Church.

This passage preserves the balance between the individual and the group, the one and the many, the personal effect of salvation and its being shared with a group properly. It isn't about each one of us having a "personal Jesus" or even a private relationship with Jesus. It is about us becoming part of something bigger, better, and more comprehensive than our individual lives. Indeed it is about us becoming part of the living body of Christ on earth, the most dynamic, important, eternal group of human beings in all of human history!

One more thing: 2 Corinthians 5:17-18 also makes clear that conversion is much more than just a spiritual tune-up, much more than just a self-help program. It is a radical reorientation of one's life. Once "anyone" becomes a new creature, he or she is "in Christ" and his or her old identity; old rugged individualism; old self-centered, self-seeking, self-improving character must pass away. *Whatever spiritual formation is, it can't be anything that denies the radical nature of conversion in and to Christ. It can't be anything that ignores the primary emphasis in the New Testament that we have become part of a whole new humanity, a new people of God, Jew and Gentile united in Christ.*

Another text that absolutely helps us get a clearer picture of the real nature of things, spiritually speaking, is 1 Corinthians 12:12-13: "For just as the body is one and has many members, and all the members of the body, though many, are one body, so it is with Christ. For in the one Spirit we were all baptized into one body—Jews or Greeks, slaves or free—and we were all made to drink of one Spirit." Frequently commentators who are dealing with this passage try to suggest that Paul is simply using an analogy. Life in the church is like the way the human body works and so we should all work together in the church for the common good. We've all heard that sermon before. But in fact, Paul is saying something much more radical than that. Notice that he does not say, "Just as a body has many members, so by analogy it is with the body of Christ." No, Paul says, "Just as the body is one and has many members...so it is with Christ." That is, Paul believes he is speaking about a spiritual reality, a spiritual union between Christ and his people such that we are directly connected to Christ the head, through the body. The hand is not directly connected to the head, nor is the foot, nor is the leg, but they are all connected to Christ through the body of Christ.

What Paul is struggling against in Corinth is precisely the disease the modern Protestant Church has: factionalism, party spirit, disunity, radical individuality. This is exactly why Paul describes conversion in collective terms and as follows: "For in the one Spirit we were all baptized into one body...and we were all made to drink of one Spirit."

There are many important points to be made about this verse, but we must be content with just a few:

(1) The Spirit is the one who actually joins us spiritually to the body of Christ, a spiritual reality. The language used here is that of baptism. Notice that Paul says "we" were all baptized into the one body. It's a shared experience, one we all must have to be saved, and the point at which we join the body of Christ is at conversion, when the Spirit links us not just to Christ, the head of the body, but to the body of believers that already exists. Conversion is into Christ and into his body, and these things happen simultaneously. It's not about us first making a commitment to Christ and then later, if at all, joining a church. We have been

plunged into Christ and his people by conversion, and the baptizer is the Holy Spirit himself!

(2) If Paul had been asked, he would have stressed that spiritual formation is chiefly the work of the Holy Spirit from new birth to the new body when we are raised by the Spirit when Christ returns. The Spirit is the change agent, and the Spirit is the one who continually convicts, convinces, changes, fills, renews, restores, reminds, gifts, bears fruit, stirs up songs, and sanctifies us. You can't understand spiritual formation without understanding the vital, dynamic relationship any real Christian has and must have on an ongoing basis with the Holy Spirit. Spiritual formation in the first instance has to do with the work of God in the spirits of human beings who have been joined to the body of Christ and so are "in Christ."

(3) Paul would also tell us, and does tell us in 2 Corinthians 5 and 1 Corinthians 12, that conversion means the death of the old self; as 2 Corinthians 5:17 indicates, "Everything old has [already] passed away." Spiritual formation in Christ is not about trying to put a stake in the heart of the old sinful self we once were so that we can get on with being new creatures in Christ. A converted person can say with Paul, "The old *has already passed away; behold the new creation is here.*"

Yes, there is a tension in the Christian life, but it is not between old self and new self; rather it is between flesh (sinful inclinations) and Spirit, as defined in Galatians 5. Paul also says it is an outer/inner tension—while outwardly our bodies are wasting away, inwardly the Spirit is working so that we are renewed day by day. We will talk more about the tensions in the Christian life in the next chapter. Finally, if we want to talk about baptism in or of the Spirit, Paul would insist this happens at conversion, not subsequently. Indeed, the only place he uses the language of baptism in conjunction with the Holy Spirit is precisely when he says, "For in the one Spirit we were all baptized into one body" (1 Cor 12:13). Here he is speaking about conversion into Christ, being joined to the body of Christ. Since the Spirit is said to be the baptizer in 1 Corinthians 12, Paul is not likely talking about the ritual of water baptism, which may take place before, during, or after the Spirit baptism.

Saying that "Spirit baptism" happens at conversion is not to say that we cannot have many dynamic or even crisis experiences in the Spirit subsequent to conversion. Of course that is true. Not only is sanctification progressive, it can have moments of dramatic improvement as well, thanks be to God. But no event *subsequent* to conversion should be called the baptism in or of the Holy Spirit. That's unbiblical because we have no instances of this phrase being used for a subsequent-to-conversion experience in the New Testament.

It is also wrong because we do not get the Holy Spirit on the installment plan—some now, more later. Why not? Because the Holy Spirit is a *person—the third person of the Trinity*. The Holy Spirit is not merely a power or force, as in "May the force be with you." The Holy Spirit is a person, and when the Holy Spirit joins an individual to the body of Christ, and comes and dwells within the believer, who is spiritually united to the body of Christ, the believer has the whole Spirit in her or his life. You can no more have a little bit of the Spirit in your life than a woman can be a little bit pregnant! Either the person of the Spirit dwells within you, like a new baby dwells within a new mother, or the Spirit is not in you at all. However, it is true that over time the Spirit gets hold of more and more dimensions of you as the Spirit progressively renovates your mind and your will, heals your emotions, and so on. But once the person of the Spirit is in your life, you can't get a further installment. He has already given his entire self to you just like the whole Christ is in you being the hope of glory. You don't get Christ on the installment plan; nor do you get the Spirit that way either. But what does Mr. Wesley have to say about conversion, the new birth, being a new creature in Christ?

MR. WESLEY ON THE NEW BIRTH

I used to have a colleague at Asbury who said that when he was a teenager he came to the altar in repentance so many times, and was born again so many times, that he had stretch marks on his soul!

Whatever else you say about the new birth, if it is genuinely the new birth it only happens once to a person, at the beginning of his or her Christian life. It does not happen again and again and again. You can no more be "a little bit born again" than you can be "a little bit born" in the first place. In fact talking about being "a little bit born again" is as much of an oxymoron as a person talking about being "a little bit pregnant." Nope. You either are or you aren't, and similarly you either are or you are not born of God.

Near the beginning of his sermon "The Marks of the New Birth," John Wesley makes unequivocally clear that conversion is a work of God. Quoting John 1:12-13, he says, **"We must become the sons of God,...believe on his name; [becoming sons] which were born, when they believed, not of blood, nor of the will of the flesh, not by natural generation, nor of the will of man, like those children adopted by men, in whom no inward change is thereby wrought, but of God."** Wesley thus stresses that the inward change that happens to persons, making them believers, happens through the work of God, not through human will. *God is the agent of initial spiritual formation, which we call conversion or the new birth, and we are not. God in the person of the Holy Spirit is also the primary ongoing agent of spiritual formation, and we are not.* It's a matter of our co-operating with what God is already doing in the body of Christ and in us as individuals as well. In fact, as much as anything, it has to do with *our getting out of the way of the Holy Spirit,* ceasing to quench or grieve the Spirit in our lives but rather opening ourselves up to the Spirit's renovating, gifting, character-forming powers.

When Wesley talks about our getting out of the way of the work of God in our lives, he even calls it "a renouncing of self." Too many times modern spiritual formation literature, with its indebtedness to psychology, presents spiritual formation as a series of things we can do to improve our sense of self-worth as Christians, or it presupposes the importance of having a healthy sense of self and self-importance in order to grow in Christ. Although I would not say that this is 100 percent wrong, I would say that it is mostly wrong. Here is how Wesley describes things:

The true, living, Christian faith (which whoever has it is born of God), is not only an assent, an act of the understanding; but a disposition, which God has wrought in his heart; "a sure trust and confidence in God, that, through the merits of Christ, his sins are forgiven, and he reconciled to the favor of God." This implies, that a man first renounce himself; that, in order to be "found in Christ," to be accepted through him, he totally rejects all "confidence in the flesh;" that, "having nothing to pay," having no trust in his own works or righteousness of any kind, he comes to God as a lost, miserable, self-destroyed, self-condemned, undone, helpless sinner; as one whose mouth is utterly stopped, and who is altogether "guilty before God." Such a sense of sin, (commonly called despair, by those who speak evil of the things they know not,) together with a full conviction, such as no words can express, that of Christ only comes our salvation, and an earnest desire of that salvation, must precede a living faith, a trust in Him, who "for us paid our ransom by his death, and fulfilled the law of his life." This faith then, whereby we are born of God, is "not only a belief of all the articles of our faith, but also a true confidence of the mercy of God, through our Lord Jesus Christ."

As usual, Wesley does not mince words. *"Spiritual formation exercises without repentance of sin avails us not,"* says our spiritual forebear. That deep trust in God that a true believer has is something wrought in the inner life of the believer by God himself in the person of his Spirit. In order to be "found in Christ" we have to first "renounce ourselves." Notice that Wesley does not say we must renounce or give up *some things,* like giving up chocolate for Lent! No, it is *ourselves* that we must renounce. Jesus of course says the same thing, "If anyone would come after me they must deny themselves [not merely deny themselves *something*], take up their own crosses, and follow me."

The beginning of spiritual maturity comes with a clear sense of our own sin and guilt before God. Too little spiritual formation literature even talks about sin and the way it gets in the way of being conformed to the image of Christ, but think about it for a moment. Christ was the sinless one. Wouldn't spiritual formation that has the aim of Christlikeness have as one of its major tasks dealing with sin in the life of the believer? We have come to such a sorry place in American culture that we think we can be spiritual without being repentant of our sins, reconciled to God, and on the path of conformity to the image of Christ. Indeed, bumper stickers are popping up everywhere that say things like, "I'm spiritual, not religious."

WHATEVER BECAME OF SIN?

Of course part of the problem in America these days is that we have ceased to be an honor-and-shame culture. Even the church has, in too many cases, become part of the "feel good" self-actualizing culture. I never will forget sitting on the platform next to Dr. Robert Schuller in the Crystal Cathedral, with the choir singing that great Isaac Watts tune "When I Survey the Wondrous Cross," when to my shock and dismay Schuller handed me his bulletin where he had underlined the hymn phrase "and pour contempt on all my pride," and next to the word *pride* he had written "NO!" And beside that he had written, "Pride in self is a good thing." Mr. Wesley thought otherwise. When a culture loses its sense of sin and shame, it loses its understanding of true honor and salvation. No amount of spiritual disciplines will help if there is no repentance of sin.

In *Amazing Grace,* that wonderful movie about William Wilberforce and his mentor John Newton, there is a very po werful scene where these two men are meeting and discussing vital things. Newton says, "These two things I know: that I am a great sinner and that Christ is a great savior." Here was a man who knew the need for repentance, full wholehearted repentance, for he had once been a captain of a slave ship and had been party to the enslaving of hundreds and hundreds of Africans. When Christ invaded his life, he not only became a minister of Christ; he also spent much of the rest of his life repenting of his many sins. Those who do not have a strong sense of sin and guilt hardly understand the need for the mercy of God, hardly grasp that salvation is not a self-help or spiritual tune-up program. It is a radical rescue that must involve our denying ourselves, or as Wesley puts it, "renouncing ourselves."

FRUITS OF SPIRITUAL CHANGE

What happens to the new convert when the spiritual formation of conversion invades his or her life? What is the first spiritual fruit of the Spirit changing us? Wesley has no doubt about what it is:

An immediate and constant fruit of this faith whereby we are born of God, a fruit which can in no wise be separated from it, no, not for an hour, is power over sin;—power over outward sin of every kind; over every evil word and work; for wherever the blood of Christ is thus applied, it "purges the conscience from dead works;"—and over inward sin; for it purifies the heart from every unholy desire and temper. This fruit of faith St. Paul has largely described, in the sixth chapter of his Epistle to the Romans. "How shall we," he asks, "who" by faith "are dead to sin, live any longer therein?" "Our old man is crucified with Christ, that the body of sin might be destroyed, that henceforth we should not serve sin."—"Likewise, reckon yourselves to be dead unto sin, but alive unto God, through Jesus Christ our Lord. Let not sin therefore reign" even "in your mortal body," "but yield yourselves unto God, as those that are alive from the dead." "For sin shall not have dominion over you.—God be thanked, that ye were the servants of sin,—but being made free,"—the plain meaning is, God be thanked that though you were, in time past, the servants of sin, yet now—"being free from sin, you are become the servants of righteousness."

The first great effect of spiritually being changed is power over sin—both inward and outward sin. The old self has been crucified and is buried with Christ in baptism (Rom 6); behold the new has come to pass. One of the real differences between spiritual formation discussions in the Wesleyan Way and some other Protestant discussions of spiritual formation is that *Wesleyans do not believe Christians are still in the bondage to sin.* They believe that the Spirit has set us free from the principle of sin and death (Rom 8:1-2). For freedom Christ has set us free, so we need no longer dwell in the past.

John Wesley was quite convinced that we must take 1 John 3:9 in complete earnestness: "Those who have been born of God do not sin." He cautions in this self-same sermon on the new birth that that text should not be amended by adding the term *habitually* as if it read, "Those who have been born of God don't sin with regularity." Wesley, however, defines sin more narrowly than in some places in Scripture. He means conscious willful sin whether inward or outward sin. He does not mean sins of omission or accidental sins and the like. His point is that we have power over conscious willful sin and can avoid it by the power of the Spirit.

Wesley believes that what begins to happen at conversion is that the peace, hope, and love of God begin to fill the human heart. Not only does one gain confidence that one is a child of God, but in addition to that settled confidence comes a sense that one is at peace with God. So one has hope for the future, and one is able to love God and one's neighbor, and one has the joy of the Spirit. The spiritual formation of the fruit of the Spirit is what we must turn to in a subsequent chapter. But here there is still more to mine from this sermon. Wesley notes in that great chapter in Romans, chapter 8, which is filled with the discussion of the Spirit, that one thing that happens *when the Spirit enters the believer's life is it enables and empowers his or her prayer life; and of course prayer is one of the main disciplines discussed in modern spiritual formation literature.*

"You have received the Spirit of Adoption, whereby we cry, Abba, Father!" Yes, as many as are the sons of God, have, in virtue of your sonship, received that selfsame Spirit of

Adoption, whereby we cry, Abba, Father: We, the Apostles, Prophets, Teachers, (for so the word may not improperly be understood,) we, through whom you have believed, the "ministers of Christ, and stewards of the mysteries of God." As we and you have one Lord, so we have one Spirit: As we have one faith, so we have one hope also. We and you are sealed with one "Spirit of promise," the earnest of your and of our inheritance: The same Spirit bearing witness with your and with our spirit, "that we are the children of God." (Rom 8:14-16)

So close is the connection between the activity of the Spirit in the believer and the activity and response of the believer to God that Paul says here that it is the Spirit by which "we cry, Abba, Father." That is, we can't even say the Lord's Prayer and mean it without the prompting and empowering internal work of the Spirit. We are dependent on the Spirit not just for our character formation, but also for the unction to function as those who boldly address God as "Abba."

What we have seen in this chapter is that the root of spiritual formation, the beginning of that process, comes at conversion, and that the Spirit provides us with all that is necessary not just to begin that process, but also to continue it, even when it comes to overcoming sinful inclinations and even when it comes to prayer. This chapter stressed as strongly as possible that salvation is incorporation into a body of believers; that once we are born again, the Spirit baptizes us into the body of Christ. Spiritual formation in the primary sense happens in that way and in that context. The chapter also stressed that conversion is not mainly about Jesus being incorporated into our lives as "our personal Jesus," but rather it is about our being incorporated into Christ; becoming "in Christ"; becoming a part of a living organism, not an organization. And that organism is called the body of Christ. We will explore more about how the Spirit shapes our spiritual character in a later chapter. But here let us leave this discussion with a word of encouragement.

The normal Christian life is a busy life—busy with family, work, children, rest, and even play. It involves all sorts of activities, all of which should be done to the glory of God and for our edification. If that is our orientation, then all that we do and refrain from doing can be part of our spiritual formation. But more than that, we cannot do our spiritual formation *alone*. For one thing, God is already at work in us to will and to do. For another thing, God's Spirit has joined us to a body of believers and we are all on the same pilgrimage. Spiritual formation is chiefly part of body life, part of things we do together. We should not be putting ourselves on a guilt trip if we don't have time to spend hours and days on a weekly basis doing certain kinds of supererogatory spiritual formation practices like fasting or praying all night or endlessly journaling. The good news is that the Spirit never sleeps and is at work in us all the time. And the Spirit is the primary agent of our spiritual formation; *we are not*. In any case, what we do together with our fellow Christians is already *the fundamental* means of our spiritual formation. Everything else should be seen as a supplement to, not as supplanting, our life in the body of Christ.

Questions for Reflection

1. Share how you came to Christ.
2. How does being part of a church make you a better person? How could it?
3. How connected are you to a congregation?
4. Where do get your spiritual nourishment? What refreshes your spirit?
5. Describe a time when you or someone you know was tempted. What helps when facing temptation?
6. What fruits of the Spirit (see Gal 5) are most evident in your life? in the life of your small group? in the life of your church?
7. How is it with your soul? Are you comfortable sharing this with people you know?

CHAPTER THREE

THE IMITATION OF CHRIST—NO, REALLY!

The gift of holiness is not something given primarily for the benefit of the individual or the few but for the sake of the community so that no one will settle for a halfhearted pattern of Christian discipleship but will aspire to conformity with Christ. The perfect do not constitute a self-enclosed holy club; they are leaven; they are signs for the church and lights for the world. —Edgardo A. Colón-Emeric[1]

I remember vividly my junior high Sunday school teacher saying over and over again, "Be like Jesus," long before there were any WWJD bracelets to be found. There was also a little voice in my head that said, "Yeah, right. How am I going to do that? Jesus is like a comic book superhero. He has a God button to push to get him out any tight scrapes. Me? Not so much." This reaction in fact is a pretty common one when we hear the exhortation "Be imitators of Christ." Some people just roll their eyes; others laugh; some flatly say, "I can't do it." Others stand there in stunned silence. The exhortation to imitate Christ may not fall on deaf ears, but, as one student said to me, on complacent lives, and so it is ignored. This was not John Wesley's reaction to the exhortation. Indeed one of his favorite spiritual classics to read, which he recommended enthusiastically to his Methodists, was the Thomas à Kempis classic *The Imitation of Christ.*

But in what sense are we called to imitate Christ, and what has that to do with practicing our faith? Here is where I say that *Christian* ***character*** *formation is at the root of spiritual formation.* And character formation is not something done in isolation for the most part, because it involves following good models, such as Christ, and it also involves the internal work of the Holy Spirit.

HAVING A CHRISTLIKE MENTAL OUTLOOK

Our starting point must be a powerful text found in Philippians 2:5-11 where theology is used in service of ethics and character formation, with the end result that actual self-sacrificial behavior is called for—behavior like Christ's. It is quite amazing but many New Testament commentators on Philippians 2:5-11 have done everything they can to deny the straightforward meaning of what Paul says ("Have this mind in you, which was also in Christ Jesus.") as if this were merely a call to a new attitude and not also a call to action, Christlike action, imitating the behavior of the Son of God. But in fact the theology of this beautiful Christ hymn is used in service of the ethical enjoinders before and after it.

Most New Testament scholars agree that we do have a christological hymn here, in a V pattern, speaking successively about the preexistence, earthly existence, and exalted existence in "heaven of the Son of God. One of the most striking things about the hymn is that the first half of it involves active verbs, telling us what the Son of God did: he did not consider being equal something to be taken advantage of; instead he emptied himself; he humbled himself; he became obedient even unto death. By contrast, the second half of the hymn involves passive verbs telling us what God did on behalf of the Son of God: he exalted him and he gave him the most exalted name. We need to examine this in some detail.

First, the hymn tells us that the Son of God has equality with God, or more literally, "In being, he is equal to God." Nevertheless, though he had this equality, the Son of God decided not to take advantage of this. Instead, he stripped or emptied himself. Emptied himself of what? Since Paul elsewhere is perfectly clear that the one called Jesus was born and remained the Son of God during his earthly life, what can Paul be talking about here? The answer is that this is Paul's way of saying that the Son humbled himself and accepted human limitations in order to become fully human—limitations of time, space, knowledge, power, and mortality. The great paradox of the Incarnation is that while the Son remained fully divine, he also became fully human, and the way this worked is that the Son had to limit himself, strip himself of his divine prerogatives. Notice, however, that Paul is equally clear that the Son does not come in sinful flesh but only in the *likeness* of sinful flesh. He appeared to be and was fully human, except he did not accept or bear the mar and mark of sin. He didn't have a fallen human nature. What we should deduce from this is that sin is not a natural property or quality of being human. It is a result of human misbehavior. Jesus was like us in all regards save without sin. But what does this truly mean?

For one thing, it means Jesus' life was not a charade. When he says in Mark 13:32 that no one, not even the angels, not even the Son, knows the timing of the Second Coming—no one, that is, but the Father—he is not joking. He has accepted the limitations of knowledge that all humans have, and he reflects them. Or, for example, when he asks in a crowd, "Who touched me?" he doesn't mean, "I really know who touched me but I am just pretending not to know so she or he will come forward and self-identify." No, he is genuinely seeking knowledge in that story. Notice as well that Luke 2:52 tells us that Jesus' consciousness was progressive, by which I mean he grew, he learned over time, he gained wisdom, and so on. This is an inherent part of being fully human. Jesus also endured the frustration of not being able to be everywhere at once and at the same time. When he was across the Jordan he was not in Bethany, and Lazarus died. It was a perfectly natural thing for Martha to say to Jesus when he finally showed up: "If you had been here Lord, my brother would not have died." But he wasn't there. He was elsewhere. There were limitations of power as well. In Mark 6, in the story about Jesus preaching in his hometown, we are told that he could not do many miracles there because of the lack of faith. We could cite many more examples, but these must suffice. What we must explore next may come as a shock—the great temptation of Jesus during his earthly life was to push the God button, to cease to be fully human and so obliterate his humanity. Let me explain.

If you explore the temptation scenes in Jesus' life, at the beginning and the end of his ministry, in the wilderness (Matt 4 and Luke 4) and in the garden of Gethsemane, what are depicted there are not ordinary human struggles with sin. Yes, it is true that Hebrews says he was tempted like us in all respects, save without sin (Heb 4:15), but mundane temptations are not the subject of Jesus' testing in the wilderness and in the garden of Gethsemane.

Consider it from this angle: have you ever met a sane person who was tempted to turn stones into bread? While I have known some people who could turn bread into stones by overcooking it, I have never met a sane person who faced the temptation to turn stones into bread. We are not talking about a normal human temptation here. We are talking about a temptation only a person who was both divine and human could have. Notice that in the threefold temptation in Matthew 4:1-11 each time Satan begins the temptation with, "If you are the Son of God. . . ." No one else on earth had ever faced a temptation like that before, and Satan certainly *does* assume Jesus is and has access to the power to do the things he is suggesting. But herein lies the point: the Son must resist the temptation to draw on his divine power to do things no mere mortal can do. He must resist the temptation to push the God button because no other humans have a God button, *and Jesus came to provide the perfect exemplar of how we should behave, including how we should behave under temptation.*

Or consider the second temptation—to throw oneself off the pinnacle of the temple. If I did that, all I would be likely to experience is a heavy bit of gravity. The Son of God, however, has ten thousand angels he can summon to catch him if need be.

Jesus must resist the temptation to use divine power in a way that invalidates his true humanity, to use it purely for selfish, self-preserving purposes. That's not why he came to earth, as the Christ hymn in Philippians 2:5-11 makes evident. "[He] came not to be served but to serve, and to give his life a ransom for many" (Mark 10:45). Or consider how in the garden of Gethsemane he faced no ordinary temptation. He faced the temptation not to be the Savior of the world by dying on the cross and exhausting God's just demands regarding our sin. He resisted the temptation to not drink the cup of God's judgment on sin. These were no ordinary temptations. They were temptations only the Son of God would or could face, for only he had the capacity to do what he was being tempted to do or, in the case of the garden temptation, to avoid.

Here is another collateral point that usually comes up at this juncture. "What about Jesus' miracles? Aren't they proofs of his divinity?" The answer actually is no. Jesus promised, and the disciples enacted, the very same miracles after his ascension. Look at the miracles Peter and Paul and others performed in Acts. Those miracles certainly do not prove the disciples' divinity, and they were no less great miracles than Jesus'—the disciples even raised the dead. In fact, what the Gospels tell us is that Jesus resisted the devil and performed his miracles drawing on the two resources we also have—the word of God and the spirit of God. Jesus himself announces, "If I by the Spirit cast out demons, then the Kingdom has broken into your midst" (Matt 12:28). Notice he says he is doing it by the power of the Spirit, the same Spirit that dwells within the people of God. And notice that the way he resists temptation in the wilderness is by quoting Scripture, the same resource available to us.

The point of stressing all this is that *the Incarnation is real, and so is Jesus' humanity. He is not 90 percent divine and 10 percent human. He is 100 percent both!* Jesus really did accept the limitations we face of time and space and knowledge and power and mortality. He lived his life drawing on the resources of the word and the Spirit to live a perfect life, and his temptations were very real. He resisted the temptation to draw on his divine nature and prerogatives when dealing with life. Why, you may be asking, are we dealing with all these intricacies of theology in this context? *Because it explains how Jesus can be and is our pattern, our exemplar, for our behavior. It explains why Paul can exhort, "Have this mind in you, which is also in Christ Jesus."* We have the same resources Jesus had to live our Christians lives—the word of God and the Spirit of God. Indeed, we have the benefit of hindsight and a much bigger canon of the word of God; we have the whole New Testament, which Jesus did not have.[2] But there is much more to say.

Notice the three clauses "[He took on] the form of a slave"; "He humbled himself"; "[He] became obedient to the point of death." Perhaps you have never thought about this, but isn't this exactly what Jesus told his disciples to do and be? "Be a servant"; "Take up your cross and follow me"; "Be obedient and faithful even unto death." We talk all the time about servant leadership or taking up our crosses or being faithful or obedient until death claims us, but too seldom is this connected to our following the life pattern of Christ himself and being like Jesus. The more we study the New Testament, the more we realize the writers in the New Testament were not holding up some utopian ideal; they were absolutely serious about our following the example of Christ in our behavior, and they believed this was possible by the power of the Spirit and the enlightenment of the word. Christians are called to live a Christlike life; a life without excuses; a holy life, in thought, word, and deed.

This brings us to an interesting point. Here is a literal translation of Philippians 2:4: "Let each of you look not to your own interests, but rather to the interests of others," which is then followed by, "Have this mind in yourself. . . ." If you have a translation that reads, "Let each of you look not *only* to your own interests but *also* to the interests of others," throw it away. In no manuscript of the Greek New Testament is the word *only* found in this sentence. Paul is not calling us to be *sort* of self-sacrificial. He is calling us to be *completely* self-sacrificial like

Christ himself was. We are to be self-forgetful, not both self-concerned and other-concerned. We are to truly follow the example of Christ, who lived a slave's life and died the death of a rebellious slave—crucifixion.

The verb *tapeinoo,* which is translated here as a reflexive verb ("humbled himself"), did not have a positive meaning in Philippi or elsewhere in the Greco-Roman world. Indeed, it would usually be rendered, "Be base-minded, have a slavelike or slavish mind." That was no compliment and was not seen as a virtue for any nonslave in the Greco-Roman world. In fact, humility was not seen as a virtue in the Greco-Roman world. Rather, boasting, self-promotion on honorific columns, and personal pride were seen as normal parts of being a good Roman citizen. The slogan "Humility is a virtue" would have been seen as an oxymoron, unless you were talking about the virtues slaves should model. Only in the Judeo-Christian context was humility seen as some kind of a virtue for all persons, and *only in Christianity was it said to be a virtue modeled by the Messiah of the Jews and Savior of the world—Jesus.*

Sometimes Christians make a mistake and assume humility chiefly has to do with an attitude about oneself. In fact, in this Christ hymn, *humility* is an action word. It has nothing to do with feelings of low self-worth; it has nothing to do with what my grandmother used to call "poor-mouthing," self-pity, self-loathing, or a lack of self-confidence. If there was one person who walked the earth who was self-confident, it was Jesus. If there was one person on earth who knew exactly who he was and knew his great worth, it was Jesus. *Humility in this text is the posture of a strong person stepping down and serving others, even to the point of death on the cross.* It has nothing to do with low self-image or the like. If Christ is the model of humility, it can't possibly have anything to do with negative self-appraisals.

The Christ hymn in Philippians 2 has as its second half what the Father did for the Son as result of the sacrifices the Son made. The fulcrum or nadir of the V pattern has the word "therefore." We could also translate it "because" or even "as a result."

Because of what Jesus did, God highly exalted him to his right hand and gave him the divine name of "risen Lord." (Note well: he already had the human name of "Jesus." The name "Jesus" is not the name above all names, which he gained at the Resurrection; rather it is the Old Testament name of "Lord" that he is given from that point on).

Now to a preening, prideful, self-congratulatory culture like the Greco-Roman world, Paul is offering countercultural virtues and behavior patterns. He is saying, "Leave the glorifying in God's hands, as Jesus did. Leave the honoring in God's hands, as Jesus did. Leave the kudos and praise in God's hands, as Jesus did." Even in these matters, we are to follow the example of Jesus. There is of course much more we could say on the basis of this rich christological hymn in its original context, but this must suffice, for now we must consider some things John Wesley stressed about the imitation of Christ. Like Paul, John Wesley did not see the imitation of Christ as "mission impossible." He saw it as realizable by the power of the word and the Spirit in our lives. *Although we cannot imitate the divinity of Christ, we are called to model ourselves, our character, and our behavior on the true and full humanity of Christ.*

JOHN WESLEY ON À KEMPIS'S *IMITATION OF CHRIST*

Perhaps more than any other devotional book of its time, John Wesley pointed his Methodists to a book he came to call *The Pattern of Christ* by Thomas à Kempis. A book originally written in Latin for the Brethren of the Common Life in about 1411, Wesley saw such merit in this book that he translated excerpts of it into English, calling the work *The Christian's Pattern*. We know it today as *The Imitation of Christ*. Typical of Wesley, he not merely told his audience to read the book; he told them *how* to read it, as he wanted them to absorb it and then change the way they practiced their Christian lives. For example, Wesley says:

I. As it is impossible for anyone to know the usefulness of this treatise, till he has read it in such a manner as it deserves: instead of heaping up commendations of it, which those who have so read it, do not want, and those who have not, will not believe, I have transcribed a few plain directions on how to read this (or indeed any other religious book) with improvement.

II. Assign some stated time every day for this pious employment. If any indispensable business unexpectedly robs you of your hour of retirement, take the next hour for it. When such large portions of each day are so willingly bestowed on bodily refreshments, can you scruple allotting some little time daily for the improvement of your immortal soul?

III. Prepare yourself for reading by purity of intention, whereby you singly aim at your soul's benefit; and then, in "a short prayer," beg God's grace to enlighten your understanding, and dispose your heart for receiving what you read: and that you may both know what he requires of you, and seriously resolve to execute his will when known.

IV. Be sure to read not cursorily . . . but leisurely, seriously, and with great attention; with proper intervals and pauses, that you may allow time for the enlightenment of divine reason. Stop frequently to recollect what you have read, and consider how to reduce it to practice. Furthermore, let your reading be continued and regular, not rambling and desultory. It shows a vitiated palate, to taste of many dishes, without fixing upon, or being satisfied with any; not but that it will be of great service to read over and over those passages, which more nearly concern yourself, and more closely affect your own practice or inclinations; especially if you add a particular examination upon each.

V. Labor for a temper that corresponds to what you read; otherwise it will prove empty and unprofitable, while it only enlightens your understanding without influencing your will, or inflaming your affections. Therefore intersperse here and there pious aspirations to God, and petitions for his grace. Select also any remarkable sayings or advices, treasure them up in your

memory to ruminate and consider; which you may either in time of need draw forth as arrows from a quiver against temptations, against this or that vice which you are more particularly addicted to; or make use of as incitements to humility, patience, the love of God, or any other virtue.

VI. Conclude all with a short prayer to God, that he would preserve and prosper this good seed sown in your heart, that it may bring forth its fruit in due season.—And think not this will take up too much of your time, for you can never bestow it to so good advantage.

If we carefully read through Wesley's excerpts from the classic by à Kempis, whereas we might think that this is yet just another how-to manual for our private devotions, this would in fact be a mistake. What Wesley is trying to do, and what à Kempis was originally trying to do, is inculcate an attitude of humility toward all of life, not just one's devotional life. In this respect it corresponds quite closely to what we find in Paul's Christ hymn in Philippians 2:5-11 in its original context. In some ways, what we find in Wesley's presentation of this classic is very similar to the work of Søren Kierkegaard, who spoke about purity of heart coming from willing the one good thing. Wesley is trying to deal with the root cause and motivator of all our actions, sometimes called "purity of intention," a cause that we have absolute control over, unlike the lack of control of the outcome and consequences of all our actions. Wesley is not merely trying to inculcate a certain kind of private devotional practice, though that is one manifestation of following à Kempis's advice. Indeed, Wesley is not merely concerned with spiritual practices; he is concerned w*ith all Christian behavior*. Thus, for example, he quotes à Kempis in the very first chapter of his extract as saying that we are indeed called to imitate the praxis of Christ. The goal is to live a virtuous life, not merely to be a more spiritual person. Thus we read:

We are admonished, that we ought to imitate his [Christ's] life and manners, if we would be truly enlightened and delivered

from all blindness of heart. Let therefore our chief endeavor be to meditate upon the life of Jesus Christ.

What will it avail you to dispute sublimely of the Trinity, if you are void of humility, and are thereby displeasing to the Trinity? Truly, sublime words do not make a man . . . a virtuous life makes him dear to God. I had rather feel compunction, than know the definition thereof.

If you did know the whole Bible, and the sayings of all the philosophers by heart, what would all that profit you without the love of God?

Vanity of vanities! All is vanity, but to love God and serve him only. It is therefore vanity to seek after perishing riches. It is also vanity to seek honors.

It is vanity to follow the desires of the flesh, and to labor for that for which you must afterwards suffer grievous punishment.

It is vanity to wish to live long, and to be careless to live well.

It is vanity to mind this present life, and not those things which are to come.

It is vanity to set your love on that which speedily passes away, and not to hasten to where everlasting joys remain.

Notice that this is primarily about not striving after riches and honor but instead living humbly before one's God. Wesley was perfectly happy to exhort people on how to spend their money and what to strive for in life. Indeed, late in his ministry, the second most frequently preached sermon of all of Wesley's sermons was "On the Use of Money."[3] The net effect of reading à Kempis is that one is called to live a simple Christian life, a message John Wesley's Puritan-born parents ingrained into him from childhood. The book is not just about humility and prayer and private spiritual disciplines. It is about living out humility by self-sacrificial service of others; by choosing a simple, not a self-indulgent, lifestyle; by walking what we talk as we follow the actual behavioral example of Christ. *The problem with many modern readings of Wesley's treatment of à Kempis is that it is read through the lens of modern individualistic Christianity, which tends to spiritualize and privatize even social and public praxis and behaviors.*

We must bear in mind that à Kempis's advice was given to a group of Christians, the Brethren of the Common Life, to practice *together*. He did not expect individual Christians to manage this all alone as a private devotional practice. Consider the example of Jesus' first disciples. He called them as a group to be his disciples and come and follow the pattern of his life. Usually they were called in pairs, and they were always sent out in pairs to do mission. He did not expect any of them to be a singular superman or superwoman for Christ. They were called to be part of the fellowship of followers, supporting one another, encouraging one another, lifting up one another, and helping one another on the bumpy road to the Kingdom. Read what à Kempis says in the second chapter of the extracts:

He that knows himself is vile in his own eyes, and is not pleased with the praises of mortals.

If I understood all things in the world, and had not charity, what would that help me in the sight of God, who will judge me according to my deeds.

Cease from an inordinate desire of knowing, for therein lies much distraction and deceit.

This is interesting from several points of view. à Kempis calls us away from an inordinate desire to know things instead of simply practicing our religion and following the pattern of Christ. Spiritual formation in this mold chiefly has to do with *action* more than contemplation or reflection. By "charity" in the quotation above is of course meant *caritas*—that is, love; and love here refers not to a feeling but a wholehearted devotion that prompts and impels deeds of piety and charity (in the modern sense of the term). Doing and being are intertwined and à Kempis is suspicious of an inordinate focus on learning and contemplation as a part of spiritual formation.

In the third chapter of à Kempis we read this:

All perfection in this life has some imperfection mixed with it: and no knowledge of ours is without some darkness. A humble knowledge of yourself, is a surer way to God than a...search after science. Yet knowledge is not to be blamed, it being good in itself and ordained by God; but a good conscience and a virtuous life is always to be preferred before it.

O if mortals bestowed as much labor in the rooting out of vices, as they do in the probing of questions, there would not be so great wickedness, nor so much hurt done in the world. Surely at the day of judgment we shall not be examined about what we have read, but about what we have done: not how well we have spoken, but how religiously we have lived.

The thing to notice about this section is not merely that à Kempis is reacting to medieval scholasticism and its bookish tendencies, which he is, but that he is stressing that the best way to model one's life on Christ is by a virtuous life and by rooting out vices, though he is not anti-intellectual in this exhortation. He says knowledge is a good thing and comes from God, if it is true knowledge. However, he reminds us that the accountability we will all face at the judgment seat of Jesus (2 Cor 5:10) is for the deeds we have done in the body, not for which books we have read.

At the very heart of spiritual formation is a "conscience void of offense," as Wesley would put it, regarding what one has said and done. à Kempis's strong urging in the following chapter of his work is that we rely not on our own insight and reflections if we want to be like Christ. Rather, he says, **"Consult with a wise**

and conscientious man, and seek to be instructed by one better than yourself, rather than to follow your own inventions." One must look *outside* one's self, and one's private reflections about one's spiritual life, and take wise counsel. Remember, à Kempis was saying this to monks called out of the world. Even they were not to practice too individualistic a model of spiritual formation.

There is much more along these lines that we could reflect on, but I believe we have captured the essence of what Paul was getting at and what Wesley wanted us to discern from reading à Kempis. We, together as a band of disciples, are all called to follow Christ—to follow his example, to behave as he behaved, and to model our character on his character. We are to pursue the virtues of self-sacrifice and avoid vices and temptations, for our deeds will indeed come up for review when Christ returns. Spiritual formation should have one eye on the horizon, on that eschatological accountability we all have, which provides a double reason to model ourselves on Christ: (1) he is the best example of virtue ever, and (2) he will be the final judge of our behavior as well.

When I was a small child, I really admired my grandfather. He was a stalwart Southern Baptist, a real straight arrow, and also a great public servant, being the fire chief of the fire department in Wilmington, North Carolina. While I was still a young man I remember asking him one day, "Pop, why are you such a straight arrow?" His answer was clear and direct: "Heaven is too sweet and hell too hot, to mess around in this life." He clearly had his eye on the afterlife, on the horizon. Spiritual formation, as modeling ourselves on Christ, has to do not only with purity of intent, not only with having the right attitude about ourselves (neither thinking too highly or too lowly of ourselves); it also has everything to do with modeling the character of Christ through our words and deeds. This indeed is a chief means of spiritual formation for us all. We become what we admire, and as Paul says, "Those who look with unveiled faces on the face of Jesus are being transformed from one degree of glory into another" (2 Cor 3:18).

We are, by the internal work of the Spirit and the external modeling of ourselves, of Christ, being conformed to the image of Christ, a process that only concludes when "we shall be fully made like him" at the resurrection of believers. It is a consummation devoutly to be wished for. The good news is that it's not mere pie in the sky by and by. It's a reality that we are already living into and that God means to see is brought to a successful conclusion in and for us. Are you so deeply in love with Christ, and all that he was and said and did, that you long to be like him? Hear the good news: God is working to will and to do in your life, to make that happen, now and when Christ returns.

Questions for Reflection

1. Share a difficult decision that you made. Did you pray before you made the decision?
2. When you hear, "Be an imitator of Christ," how do you respond?
3. Share an example where someone put his or her own interests aside for you. Think of a time when someone sacrificed something for you.
4. Who are you willing to sacrifice for? What do you expect, if anything, in return?
5. What is the difference between healthy pride and unhealthy pride? How does a prideful person act?

CHAPTER FOUR

SALVATION AND SPIRITUAL FORMATION

[Jesus'] life implies that we are fully human, not in our solitude or loneliness, but only through a web of relationships and connections with others, including God.... God in Jesus Christ is encountered not through solitary walks in the woods, or even by reading a book, but rather at a mundane dinner table... sharing food and drink with friends. —*Will Willimon*[1]

The term *spiritual formation* is, of course, not in the Bible and can be subject to a variety of interpretations and explanations. I remember a very interesting debate at Duke Divinity School some years ago about whether the study of spiritual formation was actually an academic discipline. At the time, the majority opinion seemed to have been that it was not, and so they would not tenure someone whose discipline was spiritual formation. Perhaps part of the problem is terminological. In any case, most people deeply concerned about the spiritual lives of Christians are more interested in the pastoral side of this issue rather than the academic debates about a discipline called spiritual formation. But it also must be admitted that the term was not part of the Methodist revival in the eighteenth century. It is modern terminology.

Perhaps some of the debates about spiritual formation can be obviated or avoided if we realize or accept that what we are talking about is part of the process of the sanctification of Christians. That is, spiritual formation, properly speaking, is about things that one does to grow in Christ and draw closer to God, and there are a myriad of activities that fit this description. Spiritual formation falls under the heading of sanctification and so, in the Wesleyan schema of things, under the heading of salvation.

Salvation? Yes, salvation. "But wait," a Christian might say, "I am already saved. I've been justified by grace through faith. I have experienced the new birth. And John Wesley preached over and over again that justification was by grace and through faith." This is true. He also preached, however, that there are three tenses to salvation: I have been saved; I am being saved; and I shall be saved to the uttermost.

The new birth, in the Wesleyan schema of things, is only the beginning of one's salvation, and it does not make the rest of the process inevitable. Wesley did not believe that once a person was justified by faith, final salvation was inevitable and unavoidable, and this was because he believed in the possibility, however remote, of apostasy, of Christians rebelling against God, abandoning their faith, and walking away from the kingdom of God. This is precisely what Wesley talks about in his famous sermon "On the Wilderness State," which should be compared to the companion sermon "On Wandering Thoughts."

John Wesley associated the "dark night of the soul" with the process of jettisoning one's faith in Christ, and so he did not accept the view of Saint John of the Cross—that such a condition was good for your soul. On the contrary, he thought it should be avoided like the plague. External trials and temptations were one thing. Every Christian faced them, and if responded to positively, they could strengthen one's Christian character. Apostasy and the dark night of the soul were a whole different ball game. They were the opposite of spiritual formation; they were spiritual deformation and deterioration. It becomes evident, then, that we need to reflect on some of the biblical texts that were crucial to Wesley's ways of thinking about this matter, as it will help provide an orientation so that we may better understand the relationship between spiritual formation and salvation.

WORK OUT YOUR SALVATION

When you talk to some Christians, if you use the word *work* and the word *salvation* in the same sentence, they assume you are making a serious theological blunder. Salvation has nothing to do with works; nothing to do with human striving; nothing, in fact, to do with human behavior. Salvation is *sola gratia,* purely a matter of God's grace zapping persons and keeping them saved to the end. It comes as something of a shock, then, when you tell them, "That was not Paul's view of salvation," because for Protestants, their understanding of salvation, in the wake of the Reformation, is largely formed by a certain kind of reading of Paul, or as I would say, a misreading of Paul. Let's take an example from Philippians again—this time Philippians 2:12-16. This text will require some examining. First, here is a somewhat literal translation of this text.

So then my beloved, just as you have always obeyed, not only in my presence but now much more in my absence, with fear and trembling, do your best to work out your salvation. For God is the one working in your midst both to will and to act for the sake of goodwill/purpose. Do it all without grumbling and arguments in order to become blameless and guiltless children of God, unblemished in the midst of a crooked and perverse generation in which you shine as the stars in the cosmos, holding fast to the word of life for my boasting at the Day of Christ, so that I am not running a pointless [empty] race nor laboring pointlessly.

As a simple preliminary observation to be kept in mind as you read the next few paragraphs, notice in the very first clause of verse 12 the connection between obedience and working out one's salvation. Obeying God is directly correlated with working out one's salvation. Paul begins in verse 12 to work his way to the conclusion of his first main argument, his first appeal for following good examples—in this case, the example of Christ. The transition from the example to the exhortation is easy to see: as Christ was obedient even until death (2:8), so the Philippians are called to keep on obeying, following the example of Christ (2:12). Thus Paul moves quite easily from commending to commanding. What we have here are three Greek sentences (vv. 12-13; 14-16; 17-18) building toward an outburst of joy—joy over sacrifices made by Paul and his converts—climaxing the pathos of this section. It will be seen that along the way Paul emphasizes negative examples (the allusion to the grumbling Israelites) and positive examples (himself and his audience).

Thus, one of the first things one notes when turning to verse 12 is that Paul has returned to the imperatival mode of speaking, which we see in 2:1-4 and in the transition verse, verse 5. The need to live out the gospel (1:27; 2:12), the assurance that their salvation is from God (1:28; 2:13), the call to unity (1:27; 2:14), and the suffering for the gospel both by Paul and the audience, a fact that binds them together (1:29-30; 2:17), show that Paul is examining what it means to live a life worthy of the gospel.

Verse 12 may be taken as an allusion to Paul's possible coming to visit the Philippians again once he is released, however in view of the contrast in the verse between ***parousia*** and ***apousia*** (noting the aural and rhetorical effect of this combination), we should probably translate these words as "presence" and "absence." Paul refers to, and by implication calls for, the continuation of the Philippians' obedience to their apostle, even in his absence. He gives them a pat on the back saying they have always obeyed in the past (see 2:8) and should just continue to do so. The issues in Philippi are not such that Paul needs to offer a stern corrective and a demand for a dramatic change of course. Rather he can build on the positive foundation that exists and strengthen the unity they need to maintain. Paul is not calling them from disobedience to obedience, but rather to continue to live out their obedience to the gospel.

And what does obedience look like? Paul exhorts them, "Work

out your own salvation with fear and trembling," and then goes on in the next verse to add, "For God is working among you to will and to act for the sake of goodwill/purpose." The grammar clearly indicates that this is the first major exhortation based on the hymn—"Christ has done all the listed deeds and has been exalted *so that* you might work out," goes the logic.

The term ***soteria*** or "salvation" is of course much debated in this verse because some would see a certain reading of this verse as contradicting the Pauline doctrine of salvation by faith alone, thought to be obvious from other Pauline texts. Thus some have argued for the translation "well-being" with the idea that the word could have a social sense of bringing about harmony and well-being and spiritual health within the community. But there are no *other* examples of that being the meaning of this word in the Pauline corpus. Paul is indeed talking about personal salvation, in this case sanctification and final salvation, and he is saying that both the believer and God, and indeed the community collectively, have a role to play in this matter. But it is "your own" salvation, not some abstract concept but something deeply personal affecting and transforming each individual.

One key to making a decision about this matter is that we must note that the "yous" in these verses *are plurals*; however, the phrase ***en hymin***, "within or among you," here probably has the same sense as it does in 2 Corinthians 4:12, namely "within each one of you." Paul is not here exhorting each individual to work out his or her private or individual salvation all by himself or herself. That much is clear. But he is talking about the community helping one another work out their personal salvation. It is true, but not sufficient, to say that this is an ethical text telling the Philippians how saved people live out their salvation, namely in obedience to God and his gospel. This is correct, but not the whole story.

What Paul says has implications for: (1) the cooperative nature of progressive sanctification, and (2) the importance of that cooperation when it comes to the matter of final salvation. Paul does indeed believe that the behavior of Christians subsequent to conversion affects both the current process of sanctification (and so spiritual formation) and, if something drastic like apostasy happens, their final salvation as well.

It seems to me that in light of Philippians 1:28 Paul does have eschatological salvation in view here, not merely well-being or even social harmony. *But, salvation has a corporate dimension as well as social implications.* This conclusion is almost required if one sees 2:12 as a further development of 1:28. Paul is not talking about initial salvation or justification by grace through faith. What then would it mean for the Philippian community to work out their shared common salvation as God keeps working in them to will and do to bring about that final salvation? One thing seems clear: it means that they must make strenuous efforts to be united and harmonious, standing together as the body of Christ against external pressures. They are to work together with a sense of awe and even trembling not only because God is in their midst energizing and enabling them to will and to do, but also because God will hold them accountable for their behavior and their social relationships. According to 3:12-14, that behavior affects obtaining the goal.

Notice Paul does not say, "work *for* your salvation," as if it could be obtained by mere human effort and as if they have as yet no salvation to claim. Rather he says, "work *out*" what God is working into your midst, and that is a different matter. The "thrust of this passage is not on how individuals get saved. It is rather on how the Philippians' shared gift of salvation is presently 'worked out' in the context of the Christian community and the pagan world."[2] In other words, sanctification (which involves both the actions of God and the saved) leading toward final salvation is in view here. The grammar indicates that working out their common salvation is part of their continued obedience to both their apostle and their God. It is hard to miss the emphasis here that the Philippians' working out of their salvation requires their full cooperation and effort. It does not happen automatically.

The phrase "fear and trembling" is in the emphatic position in the Greek and so Paul is placing strong emphasis on this attitude.

This phrase occurs in texts like Exodus 15:16; Isaiah 9:16; 1 Corinthians 2:3; 2 Corinthians 7:15; and Ephesians 6:5; and here it most likely refers to the Philippians' reaction to God's presence, not to emotions caused by intrahuman relationships or behavior. These words suggest that God is present with them and observing their behavior and so they should act like God is in their midst and behave! Of course Paul wants to be proud of his converts on Judgment Day, the Day of Christ (see 1:6, 10; 2:26), when Christians will be held accountable for their behavior (see 2 Cor 5:10). Salvation is an already *and* not yet matter in Paul's thought, and it is not completed until the return of the Savior (Phil 3:20) and the final conforming of the believer to his image by means of resurrection. Notice that Paul says in Philippians 3 that even he has not yet obtained that final salvation condition and goal. We should see the discussion here in light of the discussion in 1:9-11 where sanctification leading to glorification is in view.

The grammar here in verse 13 indicates that the exhortation to work out their salvation is not mere idealism but rather is viable "*because* God is working in their midst to will and to do." Were God and his grace not constantly working in the believing community in a powerful way, believers would not be able to obey this command of Paul's. In fact the word *God* is in the emphatic position in this clause to emphasize *who* it is that is enabling compliance with this imperative. Salvation is worked out in community and with the empowering of God. To attempt to work it out on one's own and/or under one's own power is a mission doomed to failure. At the same time, Chrysostom is absolutely right that God's willing does not replace or supplant our voluntary willing; it rather enables and increases our willing and our power and our freedom to do what God requires (Homily 8 on Phil 2:12-16). But we must work out what God has worked into the midst of the community. The Philippians should be exhibiting a healthy body of Christ that manifests the saving activity of God in their midst.

Paul also indicates in verse 13 that they can and should do this manifesting of their salvation in their ways of relating to one another, "willing and doing for the sake of goodwill." But whose goodwill? In Romans 10:1 the term is used to refer to human goodwill, indeed Paul's own heartfelt desire. In our own discourse of Philippians 1:15, Paul uses it to refer to a human disposition. It is, however, possible that Paul is referring here to God's good purpose or favor. But both the immediate context, which is focusing on human willing and doing, and Philippians 1:15 favor the conclusion that Paul is talking about human beings behaving and being well disposed and benevolent toward one another. Paul's views on the issue of divine sovereignty and human free will seem not to be far from those of R. Akiba, who famously said, "Everything is foreseen [by God], yet freedom of choice is given; and the world is judged by grace, yet all is according to the amount of the work" (m. 'Abot 3.19). Only that last phrase would Paul likely disagree with, though he certainly believed in rewards for work well done in Christ for the sake of the gospel (see 1 Cor 3). Indeed, he believed we were redeemed in part to do good works (Eph 1).

In verse 14 we likely have an allusion to the grumbling of the Israelites when they were wandering in the wilderness, for Deuteronomy 32:5 (LXX, the Septuagint) is probably partially quoted or alluded to in the immediately following verse. As in 1 Corinthians 10 (see especially 10:10), Paul seems to be using the behavior of the Israelites to tell his converts how *not* to behave. They are not to be like that wandering, deceitful, sinful generation. Notice the comprehensive nature of the exhortation "Do *everything* without grumbling and disputing." ***Panta*** or "everything" is in the emphatic position. But grumbling against whom? Arguing with whom? If there is a concrete reference here and one presses the allusion with the Israelites, this suggests a grumbling in regard to local leadership and an arguing that involves those leaders, which would point us to the discussions about Euodia and Syntyche in Philippians 4:2-3.

Rather, verse 15 says they must be blameless and pure and indeed faultless, shining like stars in the Philippian night sky. This is a clear allusion to Deuteronomy 32:5. It is possible, though far from certain, that Paul may be preparing for the critique we will find in Philippians 3 where he will discuss the enemies of the cross. This conclusion is supported by the fact that the allusion here to Deuteronomy is to the grumbling and complaining *among* the people of God. The phrase "crooked and perverse generation" in its original context referred to Jews, and whereas we might expect here for it to refer to Gentiles, the reference to circumcision and "dogs" in Philippians 3 suggests Paul is reversing the polarity of the term "dog" usually used of Gentiles. If this is correct, Paul is already warning about Judaizers[3] and their effect on the Christian community, namely as agents of division, which this discourse is combating. Murmuring and disputing or arguing are not the sorts of behavior that promote community unity. Avoiding such behavior is one of the ways persons become blameless and pure and faultless children of God (which is family language, not friendship language), and thus they will stand out as starkly in the midst of their agonistic culture as stars in a night sky. An allusion to Daniel 12:3 is possible here.

What have we learned from this cursory walk through Philippians 2:12-15? First, Paul believes that salvation is a community matter as well as an individual matter, and in this text he is urging us individually and collectively to work out our shared salvation. One of the clearest implications of this surely is that we must together work out and on our spiritual formation as part of that process of sanctification of the body of Christ and of the individual. Second, *spiritual formation as part of a process of sanctification is not something entirely separate from obedience or good works, or how we treat our fellow Christians, or how we act when life throws us a curveball.*

Paul is not interested in cultivating a spirituality unconnected with the obedience of faith. Indeed, it ought to be obvious that ethical integrity is one of the things that most affects our spiritual condition and our sanctification. Paul in fact believes that all of us will have to give accountability to God for our behavior when Christ returns (2 Cor 5:10) and that our behavior affects not merely our spiritual condition but also our final salvation if we persist in sinning and commit either moral or intellectual apostasy. Paul isn't kidding in Galatians 5 when he says to Christians—in this case to those persons who not merely make occasional mistakes but whose regular patterns of behavior could be characterized by terms like "fornication," "licentiousness," "idolatry," "enmity," "jealousy," "drunkenness," or "orgies"—"I am warning you, as I warned you before: those who do such things will not inherit the kingdom of God" (Gal 5:20). Although good behavior and good works cannot earn you final salvation and a place in God's kingdom, for no one is worthy of being saved, bad behavior can certainly ruin your Christian character and keep you out of the final Kingdom. *The close connection between sanctification and spiritual formation is very important in the Wesleyan tradition, or put another way, holiness is an essential part of spiritual formation in the image of Christ.* The command "Be holy, as I am holy" in some ways is the beginning of wisdom about Christian spiritual formation in the Wesleyan way.

WESLEY ON THE WILDERNESS STATE

At the outset of his sermon "The Wilderness State" in typical fashion Wesley does not mince words:

What is the nature of this disease, into which so many fall after they have believed? Wherein does it properly consist; and what are the genuine symptoms of it? It properly consists in the loss of that faith which God once wrought in their heart. They that are *in the wilderness,* have not now that divine "evidence," that satisfactory conviction "of things not seen," which they once enjoyed. They have not now that inward demonstration of the Spirit, which before enabled each of them to say, "The life I live, I live by faith in the Son of God, who loved me, and gave himself for me." The light of heaven does not now "shine in their hearts," neither do they "see him that is invisible;" but darkness is again on the face of their souls, and blindness on the eyes of their understanding. The Spirit no longer "witnesses with their spirits, that they are the children of God;" neither does he con-

tinue as the Spirit of adoption, "crying" in their hearts, "Abba, Father." They have not now a sure trust in his love, and a liberty of approaching him with holy boldness. "Though he slay me, yet will I trust in him," is no more the language of their heart; but they are shorn of their strength, and become weak and feeble-minded, even as other men.

Lest we might be prone to blame God for this dilemma, Wesley quickly adds:

What are the causes of the wilderness state? These indeed are various. But I dare not rank among these the bare, arbitrary, sovereign will of God. He "rejoices in the prosperity of his servants: He delights not to afflict or grieve the children of men." His invariable will is our sanctification, attended with "peace and joy in the Holy Ghost." These are his own free gifts; and we are assured "the gifts of God are," on his part, "without repentance." He never repents of what he hath given, or desires to withdraw them from us. Therefore he never *deserts* us, as some speak; it is we only that desert him.

The most usual cause of inward darkness is *sin*, of one kind or another. This it is which generally occasions what is often a complication of sin and misery. And, first, sin of commission. This may frequently be observed to darken the soul in a moment; especially if it be a known, a willful, or presumptuous sin. If, for instance, a person, who is now walking in the clear light of God's countenance, should be any way prevailed on to commit a single act of drunkenness, or uncleanness, it would be no wonder, if, in that very hour, he fell into utter darkness. It is true, there have been some very rare cases, wherein God has prevented this, by an extraordinary display of his pardoning mercy, almost in the very instant. But in general, such an abuse of the goodness of God, so gross an insult on his love, occasions an immediate estrangement from God, and a "darkness that may be felt."

I would differ a bit from Wesley's dramatic language at this juncture, as he did himself differ elsewhere in his writing. A serious sin, a sin of commission and premeditation, definitely grieves the Spirit within the believer. But as Wesley elsewhere says about the inward witness, the Spirit will not willingly leave the believer; rather, the Spirit will seek to convict the believer, to prick his or her conscience into repentance. It is a chain or pattern of sins, repeatedly committed knowingly and willfully, which becomes a habit, that leads to "the wilderness state" or apostasy. His analogy of pouring water on a fire or withdrawing fuel from a fire is a good one. Sin pours water on the fiery Spirit within us, and if in the course of sinning we are led to neglect the worship and fellowship of God, and to neglect the spiritual disciplines, that withdraws positive fuel from the fire. Wesley puts it this way:

Perhaps no sin of omission more frequently occasions this than the neglect of private prayer; the want whereof cannot be supplied by any other ordinance whatever. Nothing can be more plain, than that the life of God in the soul does not continue, much less increase, unless we use all opportunities of communing with God, and pouring out our hearts before him. If therefore we are negligent of this, if we suffer business, company, or any avocation whatever, to prevent these secret exercises of the soul, (or, which comes to the same thing, to make us hurry them over in a slight and careless manner,) that life will surely decay. And if we long or frequently intermit them, it will gradually die away.

In the first half of this book I stress the corporate and collective dimensions of spiritual formation, but I must quickly add that the more private and individual dimensions of spiritual formation are also vital to spiritual health. Above all Wesley stresses private prayer. It can be added as well that when your personal prayer life dries up, there is something amiss in your spiritual life. It is a telltale sign that something has gone wrong, whether through outward or inward sin, whether through sins of commission or omission. It is important to mention, however, that Wesley talks about private prayer as part of a larger prayer practice that also involves prayer in the congregation as well as family prayer.

As if Wesley were speaking directly to our biblically illiterate culture, and sadly our almost as biblically illiterate church, he stresses that *pure ignorance is a major cause of spiritual degeneration and apostasy*. Here is how he puts it:

Another general cause of this darkness is *ignorance*; which is likewise of various kinds. If mortals know not the Scriptures, if they imagine there are passages either in the Old or New Testament which assert, that all believers without exception, *must* sometimes be in darkness; this ignorance will naturally bring upon them the darkness which they expect. And how common a case has this been among us! How few are there that do not expect it! And no wonder, seeing they are taught to expect it; seeing their guides lead them into this way. Not only the mystic writers of the Roman Church, but many of the most spiritual and experimental in our own, (very few of the last century excepted,) lay it down with all assurance as a plain, unquestionable Scripture doctrine, and cite many texts to prove it.... "But is not darkness much more profitable for the soul than light? Is not the work of God in the heart most swiftly and effectually carried on during a state of inward suffering? Is not a believer more swiftly and thoroughly purified by sorrow, than by joy?—by anguish, and pain, and distress, and spiritual martyrdoms, than by continual peace?" So the Mystics teach; so it is written in their books; but not in the oracles of God. The Scripture nowhere says that the absence of God best perfects his work in the heart! Rather, his presence, and a clear communion with the Father and the Son: A strong consciousness of this will do more in an hour, than his absence in an age. Joy in the Holy Ghost will far more effectually purify the soul than the want of that joy; and the peace of God is the best means of refining the soul from the dross of earthly affections. Away then with the idle conceit, that the kingdom of

God is divided against itself; that the peace of God, and joy in the Holy Ghost, are obstructive of righteousness; and that we are saved, not by faith, but by unbelief; not by hope, but by despair!

What Wesley is talking about here is precisely the teaching of Saint John of the Cross and his disciples that suggests that the dark night of the soul is not merely normal; it could be good for your spiritual formation! Not so, says Mr. Wesley. This is an unbiblical notion. What would Wesley as a pastor have us do if we saw someone in the process of committing moral apostasy or intellectual apostasy? What would he have us do if a person was stubborn about her or his sins and refused to repent or give them up? Listen carefully to what he says about preachers who preach peace and mercy and compassion that are without any accountability or repentance for sin:

Accordingly, they know and use but one medicine, whatever be the cause of the distemper. They begin immediately to apply the promises; to *preach the gospel,* as they call it. To give comfort is the single point at which they aim; in order to which they say many soft and tender things, concerning the love of God to poor helpless sinners, and the efficacy of the blood of Christ. Now this is *quackery* indeed, and that of the worse sort, as it tends, if not to kill men's bodies, yet without the peculiar mercy of God, "to destroy both their bodies and souls in hell." It is hard to speak of these "masons with untempered mortar," these promise-mongers, as they deserve. They well deserve the title, which has been ignorantly given to others: They are *spiritual mountebanks.* They do, in effect, make "the blood of the covenant an unholy thing." They vilely prostitute the promises of God by thus applying them to all without distinction. Whereas, indeed, the cure of spiritual, as of bodily diseases, must be as various as are the causes of them. The first thing, therefore, is to find out the cause; and this will naturally point out the cure.

As a good doctor of souls, Wesley says that one must be a good spiritual diagnostician. If a person merely is depressed, perhaps from losing a loved one, then there is occasion to preach peace and offer comfort. But if his or her subdued or diminished spiritual state has a root in sin or ignorance or even idleness, then that is another matter. The cures of "the wilderness state" are as numerous as its causes: outward or inward sin; deliberate or accidental sin; ignorance or sloth. On the latter, following his Puritan forebears, Wesley stresses:

Perhaps it is this very thing, the want of striving, spiritual sloth, which keeps your soul in darkness. You dwell at ease in the land; there is no war in your coasts; and so you are quiet and unconcerned. You go on in the same even track of outward duties, and are content there to abide. And do you wonder, meantime, that your soul is dead? O stir yourself up before the Lord! Arise, and shake yourself from the dust; wrestle with God for the mighty blessing; pour out your soul unto God in prayer, and continue therein with all perseverance! Watch! Awake out of sleep; and keep awake! Otherwise there is nothing to be expected, but that you will be alienated more and more from the light and life of God.

From this quotation you can see clearly how much Wesley believed in an active approach to spiritual formation but how at the same time he wanted a wholehearted, not a halfhearted, approach to the matter. A going through the motions of outward rituals without heart religion would not do. But at the same time, a purely private, inward, and mystical approach to spiritual formation was also not a Wesleyan or biblical approach.

Wesley knew that at times a Christian could suffer from heaviness on account of many trials and temptations. The lamplight of joy is burning low in such a situation, and to such a person a word of reassurance that no temptation has overcome a believer that is not common and can be prevailed over (1 Cor 10) is the appropriate medicine. The causes of darkness must be diagnosed before the cures can be administered. Perhaps most important of all, Wesley had an absolute abhorrence of those who, like Job's comforters, would want to ascribe every trial in life to God himself, including even the dark night of the soul.

No, says Mr. Wesley, God does not willingly withdraw from anyone, and darkness is not something that strengthens one's spiritual character. On the contrary, it weakens it. Love, joy, peace, patience, and kindness—in other words, the fruit of the Spirit—are what forms us spiritually from the inside out. Whereas trials and temptations may *test* our character, the inward work of the Spirit and the outer partaking of the grace and knowledge of God through the word and the sacraments are the normal means of spiritual formation, the means of *strengthening* our spiritual character, which certainly has as much do with what we do together as Christians as it does with what we do when we are alone with our God.

No wonder Paul said in good Southern fashion, "Y'all work out y'all's salvation with fear and trembling, for it is God who works within all y'all to will and to do." Notice these last two verbs. God empowers the willing and doing of his good works and purposes on earth. God doesn't just inspire good intentions; he enables willing and doing. He enables the obedience of faith, without which spiritual formation cannot properly or fully transpire. For what God intends by spiritually forming us, is to make us his holy and loving people; joined together in harmony as one body of Christ; at peace with one another; experiencing wholeness and wellness in our life together as the church.

Questions for Reflection

1. How is your faith working out for you? Have you ever had to stand up for your faith? Have you experienced discrimination because of your faith?

2. In what ways can a small group of Christians help you grow in your faith?

3. Does it help you to set goals for your spiritual growth or make yourself accountable to others?
4. For some people speaking up in a group is difficult. How could you help others feel more comfortable in order to share more deeply?
5. When do you pray? Do you have a special prayer place or time? How has prayer helped you on your spiritual journey?

CHAPTER FIVE

THE FRUIT OF SPIRITUAL FORMATION

Membership in the Kingdom is not limited to those with enough leisure and resources to sit around thinking spiritual thoughts; it's accessible for all, particularly those whom many of the presumed righteous exclude by their rules and rituals. Jesus simply announced that God is present, that God is already establishing God's rule.... Jesus' challenge was not, "How can I have a more purposeful life?" but rather, "How can I get my life aligned with God's purposes for creation?"... When we forgive our enemies, when we bless those who persecute us, Jesus is not calling us to be pious doormats for the hobnail boots of the world. Rather we are living out, and living out of the Kingdom that has already begun to come, which has begun to revolutionize the world and the way we look at the world.
—Will Willimon[1]

We've all met persons who are enormously talented and yet profoundly immature. We've even met people who have not just natural talents but gifts from the Holy Spirit, and yet the way they exercise those gifts is hardly mature. As a musician, I am afraid I have run into more than my share of such people in church choirs. I once had a choir director in one of my churches who asked me if she had to give up being the choir director just because she was having an extramarital affair. Apparently, the connection between exercising one's spiritual gifts and basic

Christian ethics and bearing spiritual fruit was not clear to her!

John Wesley, in his discussions of the Holy Spirit, on more than one occasion stressed that the gifts of the Spirit should be exercised or guided by the fruit of the Spirit. That is, mature Christian character should guide how one exercises one's gifts. And spiritual formation is about character formation in the first instance. It is about becoming a more Christlike, and therefore a more ethical, person. We need to spend some time examining several texts that have to do with the fruit of the Spirit and Christian virtues formed in us by the Spirit, but there is one more point that should be made at the outset of this chapter.

Somehow, some way, spirituality in the modern era has been disconnected from ethical integrity. I keep running into tremendously "spiritual" persons, even "spiritual" Christians, who nevertheless have no problems with ethically problematic things ranging from abortions of convenience to conspicuous consumption and shopping until they drop to the occasional venturing into sexual sin, called euphemistically "a fling." *But when we study spiritual formation and its fruit, it is all about character formation and becoming a better, more virtuous, more Christlike person.* In fact, it's all about becoming a more obedient person—obedient to God and his word—which such "spiritual" persons too often caricature as some sort of "legalism" from which their spirituality has set them free.

If your spirituality has set you free from "a long obedience in the same direction," I can promise you it did not come from the Holy Spirit. The Holy Spirit is not called the Holy Spirit for nothing. The spirit of God sanctifies the imagination, life, heart, actions, and patterns of behavior of Christ so that they are increasingly conformed to the image of Christ. And frankly, the spirituality of Jesus entailed a high degree of ethical rigor, as even a glance at the Sermon on the Mount will show. Jesus didn't come to abolish the Law and the Prophets but to fulfill them, and indeed in some cases even to intensify their demands (e.g., no adultery committed even in one's thoughts).

Here I must also make an important distinction on behalf of John Wesley's views. John Wesley, and Jonathan Edwards as well, talked a good deal about "religious affections." This should never be confused with mere human emotions. Unfortunately, in our "affective" age, Wesley has too often been interpreted as an advocate of what he would call "pure enthusiasm," emotions and emotional experiences being thought to be the essence of true religion. This is not what Wesley meant by "affections," nor did he mean that affections made a person affectionate. My colleague Ken Collins, a leading Wesley scholar, puts things this way:

Emotions are fleeting, ephemeral. Dispositions or tempers are habituated; they are long-lived and enduring. The Holy Spirit, through the means of grace, transforms the dispositions of the heart, orienting them to their proper end, which is God. This transformation of the tempers of the heart, which make up the will, is what sanctification is all about.[2]

By religious affections I mean what Collins means by dispositions or tempers. We are talking about the internal work of the Spirit in the human mind or heart that disposes a person toward all that is good and true and noble, and of course above all, toward God. According to Wesley, the heart then has settled dispositions and convictions created by the work of the Spirit. Bearing these general considerations in mind, let us consider the fruit of the Spirit.

THE FRUIT OF THE SPIRIT: *CARPE* THE *KARPOS*!

Let's start with the first and most obvious thing. Paul in Galatians 5 does not speak about the fruits (plural) of the Spirit, even though we probably have heard sermons where the plural was used in reference to this text. No, the word *fruit* (***karpos*** in the Greek) is definitely in the singular. All the qualities, temperaments, attributes, and virtues listed under that heading are collectively called "fruit." This makes clear that it will never be sufficient for a mature Christian person to say, "I have self-control and my wife has patience and my friend Teddy has joy, so it takes all of us to make up the fruit of the Spirit." No, Paul is not calling *us* fruits, nor is he suggesting different strokes for different folks with different personalities. He is calling all of us *to manifest all the fruit of the Spirit.* And note that he is talking about something the Spirit produces in the believer and in the Christian community. He is not talking about natural tendencies in this or that believer, and he is certainly not talking about mere emotions.

If we look at the larger context of Galatians 5:19-23, we can see that Paul is holding up three mirrors to the audience: the mirror of their pagan past (the desires and behaviors of the "flesh"); the mirror of the present and possible future if divisions and factions continue to persist and grow under the malign influence of the Judaizers; and finally the mirror of the true Christian community, which is what the fruit of the Spirit is meant to depict. Paul is especially concerned to contrast the social sins that are now beginning to plague the Galatians' churches with the fruit of the Spirit, as follows:

WORKS OF THE FLESH		FRUIT OF THE SPIRIT
Acts of hatred	vs.	Love and joy
Discord	vs.	Peace
Anger (quick temper)	vs.	Patience
Fits of rage	vs.	Acts of kindness
Acts of selfish ambition	vs.	Acts of generosity
Dissensions leading to factions	vs.	Faithfulness to others
Acts of envy	vs.	Acts of considerateness[3]

The first column, "Works of the Flesh," depicts people who are selfish, mean-spirited, and generally out of control. The second column describes persons or groups that are other-directed, community-spirited, and have self-control. In fact Paul ends the fruit list with one of the classic virtues of the ancient Greco-Roman world, self-control. The point is that when a Christian community is being its best self, it not only models the virtues at the heart of the Mosaic code (love of neighbor) but also the highest and best virtues of the Greco-Roman world. The Spirit produces such character and such behavioral traits in the Christian community and such dispositions in the converted heart.

Here is where we note, then, that Paul is contrasting the works (plural) of the sinful inclination (called the "flesh" here) and the fruit (singular) of the Spirit. Sin is always divisive—it always splits up families and communities; whereas the fruit of Spirit produces unity without uniformity—harmony—which involves different persons singing different notes, in the body of Christ. These qualities, dispositions, and behaviors are something the Spirit who dwells within the Christian community, as well as within the individual believer, produces. They are not something believers acquire, develop, or achieve *on their own*. But it is a mistake to emphasize pure passivity when talking about the fruit of the Spirit, as if it were only about character traits and dispositions and not also about behaviors and virtues.

Here again, we have a case of the *community* working out what the Spirit is working in *it*. The community is to manifest these traits or qualities in godly behavior. Look again at the chart above and you will see how many times the fruit implies action, not mere attitude. The normal Christian life and the normal Christian community should manifest all these traits, and manifest them all in appropriate interpersonal behaviors. We must be patient with one another or self-controlled in relationship to one another or love one another, to give but three examples. Nevertheless, it is right to say, as one of the New Testament scholars I first learned from said, "Fruit is not produced by act of parliament or exhortations; it is produced organically from a tree that is properly planted, watered, fertilized, and grown." Similarly, the fruit of the Spirit does not show up in a Christian's life merely because someone exhorted him or her to be more patient. It happens because of the ongoing internal working of the Spirit in a believer's and in a community's life.

In this list, as in an encomium like 1 Corinthians 13, love comes up for first mention. *Love* is an action word involving decisions of the will and attempts to do things, not merely a feeling or attitude in the Bible. This is why love can be—and is—commanded of the believer. But this is love that comes from the Spirit into our lives and community. Romans 5:5 talks about God pouring his love into our hearts. As Augustine put it, God gives what he commands and then commands what he wills.

Although we may take the term *love* as almost a cliché, it is striking that the noun ***agape*** (a Greek word meaning selfless, sacrificial, unconditional love—the kind of love with which God loves us) is basically not found in classical Greek literature or in the writings of Paul's Jewish contemporary Josephus. It is basically not found in Greco-Roman virtue lists either, and yet it dominates the discussion in the New Testament—not only the discussion about our relationship with God, but also the discussion about our relationship with one another. Love, as Paul says in 1 Corinthians 13, is the manner in which a Christian should do all things. Hence in Galatians 5:6 he talks about faith working through love, or speaking the truth in love, and in Galatians 5:13, serving one another through love, and so on. Love is the *sine qua non* of the Christian spiritual life and character and should be the guide of all its behavior. *At the heart of spiritual formation is loving God with your whole heart and loving neighbors—even strangers and enemies—as one's self. And this of course is not natural; it is supernatural. It is a product of the Spirit's prompting, equipping, and internal transforming of our lives. Loving God with whole heart and neighbor as self is also, not incidentally, the essence of what Wesley meant by perfection or entire sanctification.*

Joy is another signature quality of the Christian life and community. Notice that for Paul this is not a quality produced by circumstances or ephemeral pleasures, but rather something generated by the internal work of the Spirit in the believer and in the Christian community. Again, it is not produced by emotions, nor is it simply an emotion; it is a disposition of the heart that is inclined toward God. It is precisely that living presence of God within us that gets us excited and gives us joy and assurance and hope. If God is for us and dwells in our midst, who can be against us?

There is a famous legend told about when Nero was having various Christians set alight in the Roman Circus Maximus (the Colosseum did not exist in the A.D. 60s). The story goes that as they were being tied up on crosses and set alight, they began singing beautiful hymns of praise. This maddened Nero, and he reportedly asked, "Why are they singing? How can they be joyful as they are being killed?" The answer lay within—greater is he who is within us than anything the world can do to us. Joy in the Spirit can often and is often manifested in spite of our external circumstances. Eschatological joy involves a forward-looking attitude that is hopeful (Rom 5:2, 11; 14:17; 15:11).

Please note that Paul is describing social or interpersonal traits, not primarily inner qualities of individuals or their individual souls. This especially has to be stressed in dealing with the word *peace*, which is grounded in the Hebrew concept of *shalom* rather than in the Greek concept of "serenity." The Greek concept has to do with a quiet mind, the absence of activity, or especially the absence of pain and other disturbances. The Jewish concept, by contrast, has to do with personal wholeness, with healthy relationships, rather than with the absence of pain or trouble. This is why it is sometimes called "the peace that passes understanding." This peace comes from the living, healing presence of God in the person and in the Christian community when they are in right relationship with God and with one another. God is a God of peace and not of chaos and destruction, and this should affect the way Christians relate to outsiders (Rom 14:19). To wish other people *shalom* is to wish them the presence of God in their lives and what comes with that—peace with God and possibly good health, but in any case, a strong sense of well-being.

One more term in this list of traits needs a bit of examining: ***makrothumia***. Literally this term means "having a long temper," or as we would say, a long fuse—patience. Usually in the New Testament it refers to having patient endurance of some wrong or suffering without responding in anger or taking revenge (cf. 2 Cor 6:6; Eph 4:2; Col 1:11; 3:12).

Some of these traits, which lead to behaviors, would have been seen as countercultural, and some would have been seen as the highest virtues of the culture whether Jewish or Greco-Roman. This is one of the interesting aspects about how the issue of character traits and virtues are treated in the New Testament. Spiritual formation is indeed about character formation, which of course is a work in progress.

At the Billy Graham Museum in Charlotte, North Carolina, there is a little garden with the tombstone of Ruth Bell Graham. The stone reads: "End of Construction—Thank you for your patience." To a real extent, we do need to see ourselves as Christians under construction, not persons who are fully formed and always mature in Christ. But the more we are "in Christ" and "in his community" and around mature Christians and communities that manifest the fruit of the Spirit, the more we ourselves are likely to mature and to know what is expected of us and what Christ-likeness really looks like. As Wesley said, the fruit of the Spirit should guide the exercise of the gifts of the Spirit, however ecstatic or dramatic. Love builds up the community; hubris puffs up the individual. You will know the tree by the fruit it bears.

THE ALMOST AND THE ALTOGETHER CHRISTIAN

One of the more crucial of John Wesley's early sermons, preached at Oxford University at the beginning of the Methodist Revival in England, was entitled "The Almost and the Altogether Christian." John Wesley was apt to say that you can be as orthodox as the devil (for the devil knows the truth about Jesus and God but that truth has not transformed him) and still not be saved. For Wesley the heart of religion was the religion of the heart, by which was meant real internal conversion of the human mind and spirit by means of the spirit of God, and then the reforming of the basic dispositions of the heart in a Godward direction. Wesley described the result of such a genuine conversion as follows:

Do good designs and good desires make a Christian? By no means, unless they are brought to good effect. "Hell is paved," says one, "with good intentions." The great question of all, then, still remains. Is the love of God shed abroad in your heart? Can you cry out, "My God, and my All"? Do you desire nothing but him? Are you happy in God? Is he your glory, your delight, your crown of rejoicing? And is this commandment written in your heart, "That he who loves God love his brother also"? Do you then love your neighbor as yourself? Do you love every man, even your enemies, even the enemies of God, as your own soul? As Christ loved you? Do you believe that Christ loved you, and gave himself for you? Have you faith in his blood? Do you believe the Lamb of God has taken away thy sins, and cast them as a stone into the depth of the sea? That he has blotted out the handwriting that was against you, taking it out of the way, nailing it to his cross? Have you indeed redemption through his blood, even the remission of thy sins? And does his Spirit bear witness with your spirit, that you are a child of God?

Wesley placed a lot of emphasis on the internal witness or testimony of the Holy Spirit, telling a person he or she is a child of God, and he placed a lot of emphasis on the character transformation that accompanied the witness, namely one is filled with a heart full of love for God and others and begins to manifest that in one's life. But lest we think that Wesley is just talking about an inner experience that an individual has and should have if he or she is a saved person, it becomes clear the more one reads, that Wesley sees the experience as the means of character transformation, which in turn should and can lead to the transformation not merely of ones "tempers" (attitudes, feelings, inclinations) but also to the transformation of one's behavior.

In his "Notes on the New Testament," Wesley adds a few telling comments about the fruit of the Spirit. He says:

Verse 22

***Love*—The root of all the rest.**

***Gentleness*—Toward all men; ignorant and wicked men in particular.**

***Goodness*—The Greek word means all that is benign, soft, winning, tender, either in temper or behavior.**

Verse 23

[23] Meekness, temperance: against such there is no law.

***Meekness*—Holding all the affections and passions in even balance.**

Notice that Wesley does not just think the fruit is and should be manifested between Christians. No, he particularly thinks gentleness must be exercised toward nonbelievers, which, it must be said, is not the normal approach of censorious preachers of his day or ours. What is especially interesting is the final comment on meekness, which Wesley equates with keeping all the affections and passions in even balance. This understanding of the term seems almost stoic and does not really fully comport with the way the term is used elsewhere in the New Testament, even when speaking of Christ himself. Meekness, to be sure, is not weakness, but it does mean a sort of mild-mannered approach to relating to others—a humble approach rather than a rude and arrogant one. It also refers to a person who is self-controlled, proactive in the way he or she relates to others rather than reactive.

In an interesting letter, written near the close of his life, Wesley stresses, "When the witness and the fruit of the Spirit meet together, there can be no stronger proof that we are of God" (John Wesley, Letter, 31 March 1787). *It was not just the inner sense of assurance of salvation, or even just changed dispositions, that indicated a person was of God; it was also the evidence of changed character and behavior.*

In his reflections called "Faith and the Assurance of Faith," Wesley provides a chain of logic to help us understand the relationship between holiness and love and the internal testimony of the Spirit that we are children of God. He says:

We must be holy of heart and life before we can be conscious that we are so. But we must love God before we can be holy at all, this being the root of all holiness. Now, we cannot love God until we know he loves us—"We love him because he first loved us" and we cannot know his love to us until his Spirit first witnesses it to our spirit. Until then, we cannot believe it.

What is striking about this is not merely the clear connection made between knowing God loves us and loving God in return, which is said to be the root of all holiness. Even more striking is the notion that *we can be holy of heart and mind and that we can know we are.* We could equally well say that the root of spiritual formation is being loved by God and loving God in return, which reforms and transforms our character into a more holy character. There is no spiritual formation practice more important than the active loving of God with whole heart and loving neighbor and others as self. And the interesting by-product of such loving is that we become holy people; we become set apart for God; we become like God, who is both holy and love. God is not holiness without love (thank goodness); nor is God love without holiness (praise God). God's love is always a holy, sanctifying, sin-conquering, sin-exterminating love.

Sometimes what happens in discussions about Christian maturity and spiritual formation is that instead of being encour-

aged, people get discouraged, because they think that they are being exhorted to become super-Christians, to strive for a sort of spiritual life that frankly they don't see themselves ever achieving. They are not working on sainthood; they are working on just being good Christian people, and it's all they have time for. For those who feel that way, hear the good news: spiritual formation is not an achievement; it is what goes on invisibly every day in the life of the true believer, even when that believer is unaware of it. God in the person of the Spirit is at work in us every single day, transforming us. Paul puts it this way, "So we do not lose heart. Even though our outer nature is wasting away, our inner nature is being renewed day by day" (2 Cor 4:16). It will be seen that we have reached the point where it's time to talk about spiritual formation as it has to do with what the individual Christian does on his or her own, and sometimes by himself or herself. We will begin that discussion in the next chapter.

Questions for Reflection

1. How is the fruit of the Spirit evident in your life? family? church? small group?
2. How do you show love to those around you?
3. God is transforming us every day into the image of Christ. How has your faith "ripened" in the last year?
4. Where do you turn for renewal, strength, courage, or faith?
5. *Shalom* means "wholeness" and it is a word often used for peace. What are the characteristics of people who have their wholeness in Christ?
6. Some people leave a particular church because they are hurt or angry. How can your church be more loving?
7. What is the reputation of your church in your community? in your denomination? What is your reputation? Can a person tell by your actions that you are seeking to live like Christ?

PART TWO

The Individual Context: The Believer as a Member of the Body

CHAPTER SIX

THE BELIEVER AND THE MEANS OF GRACE

The modern world has many ways of turning us in on ourselves, eventually to worship the dear little god within. Christianity, the religion evoked by Jesus, is a decidedly fierce means of wrenching us outward. We are not left alone peacefully to console ourselves with our sweet bromides, or to snuggle with allegedly beautiful Mother Nature, or even to close our eyes and hug humanity in general. A God whom we couldn't have thought up on our own has turned to us, reached to us, revealed to be someone quite other than the God we would have if God were merely a figment of our imagination—God is a Jew from Nazareth who lived briefly, died violently, and rose unexpectedly. This God scared us to death but also thrilled us to life. —Will Willimon[1]

It was, without question, a shock to my system. My wife and I moved to England for my doctoral work in 1977. I came as a person on the way to full ordination in The United Methodist Church in America. The two churches I had been part of since birth, Wesley Memorial United Methodist Church in High Point, North Carolina, and Myers Park United Methodist Church in Charlotte, North Carolina, were both large churches with very traditional liturgy. I had been raised a high-church Methodist who regularly partook of the creeds, the responsive readings, the Gloria Patri, the Doxology, the reading of several Scriptures,

Holy Communion, the sermons, the prayers of the people, the offering, and of course the singing, including both congregation hymn-singing and choir anthems. I was used to robed ministers and liturgically rich services. When I got to Durham, England, I was nearly immediately put on the Durham and Darlington circuits as a preacher, but what I found in these various churches was a shock. Their worship services consisted of the "hymn sandwich," as they put it: a hymn, a prayer, a hymn, a scripture, a hymn, a sermon, a hymn, an offering, and a hymn. Did I mention hymns? And we sang a lot of verses of a lot of hymns (often to tunes I had never heard before and some of which I never wish to hear again). I love and loved music, having been a musician all my life, but this was like going to a songfest and hoping a worship service broke out.

I asked my senior pastor at Elvet Methodist Church in Durham, "How come it's like this?" He explained in some detail that Methodists in England had to define their ethos and identity over against the dominant Church of England as well as the highly liturgical Catholic Church. The result was very low-church Protestantism. I was even told, "Don't ask them to recite a creed. They will think you are a closet Anglican or Catholic." Wow. In America, by contrast, where there were no high-church denominations dominating the religious landscape, Methodists didn't feel they needed to denude the service of liturgy. They could just be themselves, as Mr. Wesley had encouraged. Indeed, he had even encouraged them to go to both Methodist and Anglican services.

To ask what spiritual formation looks like for Methodist individuals depends on where they are located and what sort of Methodism they have experienced. Methodism in Singapore doesn't look the same as Methodism in Zimbabwe, or in England, or in Estonia, or in America. I know because I've been to all those places and many more where there are Methodists. Because of these varieties of Methodist practices, we must concentrate in the second half of this book on things both the Bible and Mr. Wesley suggested that *all* good Methodists should do to improve and grow their spiritual lives. The right place to start is with what Wesley says about the "means of grace." What are the means of grace for ordinary, normal Methodists?

WESLEY ON THE MEANS OF GRACE

One of the questions John Wesley regularly had to answer during the Methodist Revival in the eighteenth century was: "Since salvation comes through preaching the gospel, do we have any need of and are there any 'ordinances' we must follow?" This question meant: are there any means of grace ordained by God that Christians are obliged to use and practice in order to grow in Christ, or do Christians just need to keep listening to the preacher, since preaching and hearing is how grace and the new birth came to people in the first place?

Before we answer that question, it is important to note that Wesley believed that preaching the word of God is indeed a means of grace. He would want to do nothing to minimize that. To those worshiping at Bedside Baptist, Posturepedic Presbyterian, or Saint Mattress Methodist, which is to say, staying at home in bed on Sunday, Wesley exhorts such lazy Christians that although they can come in contact with general revelation in all of creation, the one place they can most assuredly come in contact with the special revelation of the gospel is in church or in revival meetings, and they dare not neglect the preaching. But what of other means of grace?

At the beginning of his famous sermon "The Means of Grace," Wesley rightly cautions about the danger of mistaking "the means" for "the ends." He warns:

Some began to mistake the *means* for the *end,* and to place religion rather in doing those outward works, than in a heart renewed after the image of God. They forgot that "the end of" every "commandment is love, out of a pure heart," with "faith unfeigned;" the loving the Lord their God with all their heart, and their neighbor as themselves; and the being purified from

pride, anger, and evil desire, by a "faith in the operation of God." Others seemed to imagine, that though religion did not principally consist in these outward means, yet there was something in them wherewith God was well pleased: something that would still make them acceptable in his sight, though they were not exact in the weightier matters of the law, in justice, mercy, and the love of God.

What Wesley is warning against in this paragraph is mere formalism, a sort of faith that thinks, If I just participate in the ordinances, if I just go to church, if I just take the sacraments, I am a good Christian and will be saved. That would be mistaking the means for the ends, which is of course the grace and salvation of God. John Wesley did not believe that even the sacrament of baptism automatically conveyed grace to the recipient regardless of his or her spiritual state, but he did firmly believe sacraments did so for those who were open to receiving the grace of God. Wesley warns not merely against formalism, but also against those who think we need no forms or liturgy at all to worship God. Wesley's view is that the abuse of the means of grace does not rule out their proper use.

But what exactly does Wesley mean by, and include in, the means of grace? This may come as something of a surprise, even to some Methodists today. First, the definition Wesley insists on is this: **"By 'means of grace' I understand outward signs, words, or actions, ordained of God, and appointed for this end, to be the ordinary channels whereby he might convey to men, prevenient, justifying, or sanctifying grace."** He does not deny there are other, extraordinary channels of grace; but here he is referring to the ordinary ones, the very ones that normal Christians have a chance to encounter normally, even on a day-by-day basis.

If you are expecting Wesley to suddenly break forth into a long harangue about baptism and the Lord's Supper, you will be surprised to learn that the first words out of his mouth are:

The chief of these means are prayer, whether in secret or with the great congregation; searching the Scriptures (which implies reading, hearing, and meditating thereon); and receiving the Lord's Supper, eating bread and drinking wine in remembrance of Him: And these we believe to be ordained of God, as the ordinary channels of conveying his grace to the souls of men.

In fact, Wesley is not going to talk about baptism at all in this context! Why not? Because it is a one time—and one time only—ordinance per person, and almost every single person Wesley addressed in England, whether churched or not, had at least been christened as an infant and listed in a church registry. If you have already been baptized, this cannot be a means of grace for you going forward or thereafter.

Indeed, the Anglicans considered the whole country their parish and you were on their contact lists even if you were an ardent Baptist. I never will forget how my wife and I regularly got the Anglican parish letters and announcements in the mail, quite unsolicited and mailed to the caretakers house at Elvet Methodist Church! They were claiming us as part of their parish flock, even if we only went to the Methodist church. That's the way it is when you have an official state church in various European countries. Wesley, then, is going to discuss the means of grace from the perspective of an audience for whom baptism could not or could no longer be a means of grace in the future.

Notice the three means of grace he expects his audience to participate in regularly: (1) prayer, both individual and collective; (2) searching the Scriptures, or, as we might call it, Bible study and devotional reading of the Bible; and finally, (3) "constant" Communion. Dealing with the three means of grace that Wesley mentions in this sermon is going to take us some time, so we will be treating these three in an introductory way and examining prayer in some detail in this chapter, and then in subsequent chapters we will deal in more detail with searching the Scriptures and Communion.

Lest someone take a magical view of any of these three means, Wesley stresses once more:

> **Whoever, therefore, imagines there is any intrinsic power in any means whatever, does greatly err, not knowing the Scriptures, nor the power of God. We know that there is no inherent power in the words that are spoken in prayer, in the letter of Scripture read, the sound thereof heard, or the bread and wine received in the Lord's Supper; but that it is God alone who is the Giver of every good gift, the Author of all grace; that the whole power is of him, whereby, through any of these, there is any blessing conveyed to our soul. We know, likewise, that he is able to give the same grace, though there were no means on the face of the earth.**

Here of course Wesley is arguing against Catholic theology in particular when it comes to the Lord's Supper. The grace and power lie in God, not in the elements or the activities *themselves*. Thus a magical view of what the means can accomplish apart from a receptive heart, a heart of faith, is avoided.

Furthermore, Wesley wants to stress that partaking in these means is not meritorious. It does not earn one brownie points in heaven, much less earn one salvation. Wesley adds this:

> **The use of all means whatever will never atone for one sin; that it is the blood of Christ alone, whereby any sinner can be reconciled to God; there being no other propitiation for our sins, no other fountain for sin and uncleanness. Every believer in Christ is deeply convinced that there is no merit but in Him; that there is no merit in any of his own works; not in uttering the prayer, or searching the Scripture, or hearing the word of God, or eating of that bread and drinking of that cup. So that if no more be intended by the expression some have used, "Christ is the only means of grace," than this,—that He is the only meritorious cause of it, it cannot be disputed by any who know the grace of God.**

This is a salutary warning even for us today, for the temptation is to believe that "if I just engage in these spiritual practices and this much prayer and this much church attendance, God will have to reward me for this and bless me for this." A modern example of this sort of misguided thinking is how some have used the prayer of Jabez, whereby if one simply follows that prayer, God is somehow forced or compelled to "enlarge one's territory," make one prosperous, and so on. Wesley is avoiding this sort of magical view, even of prayer. You can pray with all sincerity until you are blue in the face, but if it is not God's will to do X, Y, or Z that you are pleading for, it isn't going to happen just because you recited some biblical prayer with all your heart. That approach is what my old pastor called "rabbit's foot religion," and it is not the religion Wesley urges his Methodists to practice to improve their Christian life.

Wesley is also writing against those truly low-church Protestants who kept saying, "All you have to do is believe to be saved, so skip all this stuff about practicing the means of grace." Wesley's answer is: **"If you say, 'Believe, and you shall be saved!' He answers, 'True; but how shall I believe?' You reply, 'Wait upon God.' Well; but how am I to wait? In the means of grace, or out of them? Am I to wait for the grace of God which brings salvation, by using these means, or by laying them aside?"**

The phrase "wait actively" is a key phrase for understanding Wesley's view about how Methodists should practice their religion and grow in grace. His basic view is that we should participate in the normal means of grace as often as we have time to do so. Wesley first provides several telling examples from the teachings of Jesus to make clear that we should always pray and never give up praying.

"Ask, and it shall be given you; seek, and ye shall find; knock, and it shall be opened unto you: For everyone that asks receives; and he that seeks finds; and to him that knocks it shall be opened." (Matt 7:7, 8) Here we are in the plainest manner

directed to ask, in order to, or as a means of, receiving; to seek, in order to find, the grace of God, the pearl of great price; and to knock, to continue asking and seeking, if we would enter into his kingdom.

WHAT'S THE POINT OF PRAYING?

Here it will be wise to pause for a moment and meditate on why we pray, both according to the Bible and according to Wesley. First, we do not pray to inform God of something he does not know. Anyone who knows his or her Bible knows that God is all-seeing and all-knowing. Prayer then cannot be a matter of reminding a deity, who is so old he has senior moments, of forgetting something he should have known, or browbeating a truculent and reluctant deity to do something he was otherwise not planning on doing. These sorts of views of prayer did characterize some ancient pagans, but not God's people at their wisest and best.

Why do we pray then, besides the obvious fact that God has commanded it? The answer is that God uses prayer to work out his will in the world, and through prayer it is **WE** who become informed about what we do not know or see, and we become God's agents of redemption, healing, and hope in the world. But this is not all, for what I have just been talking about is prayer of intercession or petition. Of course there are other sorts of prayers as well that God uses to shape our own spiritual lives: prayers of praise and thanksgiving and prayers of repentance and lamentation. And of course *it is also true that a function of prayer is not merely to better inform us about God's will, but also to actually draw us closer to God himself.* People who love one another wholeheartedly are always talking to one another. They are in ongoing living relationship and conversation with one another, and so it should be between God and us. The question is: Are we listening to God when we pray, rather than just talking all the time?

Wesley stresses that God responds to both corporate and private prayer. In regard to the latter, Wesley urges:

A direction, equally full and express, to wait for the blessings of God in private prayer, together with a positive promise, that, by this means, we shall obtain the request of our lips, he hath given us in those well-known words: "Enter into your closet, and, when you have shut the door, pray to your Father which is in secret; and your Father, who sees in secret, shall reward you openly." (Matt 6:6)

One of the most interesting things Wesley goes on to point out is that Jesus is not talking merely about the prayers of born-again Christians. Indeed, there were *none* when Jesus said this! He is simply talking about people asking in sincere trust for God's help, and Jesus says clearly that God hears and responds to such prayers. Were this not the case, there would be no point for unbelievers to ever pray a sincere prayer!

Sometime ago, a not very wise but very public TV minister was asked if God hears the prayers of non-Christians—of say agnostics, Muslims, Jews, Hindus, Buddhists, and so on—and his curt answer was an emphatic "NO!" The problem with this is that Jesus himself says otherwise, *so long as the prayer is directed to the right deity, the God of the Bible.*

Wesley makes mincemeat of such a bad theology of prayer, citing James 1:5 and 4:2, saying:

The gross, blasphemous absurdity of supposing *faith,* in this place, to be taken in the full Christian meaning, appears hence: It is supposing the Holy Ghost to direct a man who knows he has no faith (which is here termed *wisdom*), to ask it of God, with a positive promise that "it shall be given him;" and then immediately to subjoin, that it shall not be given him, unless he has it before he asks for it! But who can bear such a supposition?

ON SEARCHING THE SCRIPTURES

Though he spends considerably less time on it in this particular sermon, Wesley goes on to stress that searching the Scriptures is absolutely a means of grace for those who do it. He aptly compares John 5:39, Jesus' exhortation to the Jews to search the Scriptures and discover they speak about him, to the story in Acts 17:11-12 about how the Bereans searched the Scriptures and by so doing became believers, finding that the grace of God saved them through that act.

Bible study is not, however, just a means of grace for those seeking God. Indeed, it is also a means of grace and Christian growth for those who are already in Christ. Wesley puts it this way:

> **This is a means whereby God not only gives, but also confirms and increases, true wisdom, we learn from the words of St. Paul to Timothy: "From a child thou hast known the Holy Scriptures, which are able to make thee wise unto salvation through faith which is in Christ Jesus." (2 Tim 3:15) The same truth (namely, that this is the great means God has ordained for conveying his manifold grace to man) is delivered, in the fullest manner that can be conceived, in the words which immediately follow: "All Scripture is given by inspiration of God;" consequently, all Scripture is infallibly true; "and is profitable for doctrine, for reproof, for correction, for instruction in righteousness;" to the end "that the man of God may be perfect, thoroughly furnished unto all good works." (2 Tim 3:16, 17)**

John Wesley, like so many of his forebears, believed that the Bible is the living word of God and that it changes lives. What would he say to a church today that is largely biblically illiterate but yet cannot understand why it is not growing in grace and in the knowledge of God? Wesley would rightly say, "It's because these things inherently go together." You want to know God better but you don't want to study the Scriptures? What's wrong with this picture? Studying the Scriptures is one of the most obvious and normal means to know God better and to grow in grace. Ignorance is not bliss when it comes to Christian spiritual formation. To the contrary, ignorance leads to darkness and a lack of spiritual growth.

Some people today of course say, "Let's just practice relationship Christianity. We shouldn't have to study to be real Christians; we can just associate with and listen to others who are real Christians, such as our pastors or Sunday school teachers, and that should be enough." Or others say, "Well, I am not much of a reader, and anyway I got out of school a long time ago. I don't need to study the Bible, as I already have Jesus in my heart." But think about these attitudes for a minute. In the former case, there is the problem that unlike the Scriptures, which are the inspired words of God in the words of human beings, your friends and pastors are fallible Christian people. They don't always get it right; and the way you know this, is by knowing the Scriptures. It's not enough to be "hearsay" Christians who do not themselves search the Scriptures.

Second, those who think study is too tedious, and unnecessary since they are already born again, are forgetting that birth is only the beginning of the process of the Christian life. Infants may well not be able to read, but they are supposed to grow up and learn and be able to read and write and so on. *Too many Christians are arrested in a state of spiritual infancy and mistake pablum for real food.* But the point of the spiritual life, like the point of life itself, is to grow in wisdom and stature and in favor with God and human beings. Even Jesus needed to do that; and you will notice in Luke's story that Jesus is busy discussing and discoursing about the Scriptures in the Temple (Luke 2:41-52).

The third means of grace Wesley stresses in this sermon is the regular, indeed the constant, partaking of the Lord's Supper, as much as is possible. He argues cogently that this is precisely what Christ commanded us to do. It's not an optional extra; it's obligatory. Wesley puts it this way:

All who desire an increase of the grace of God are to wait for it in partaking of the Lord's Supper: For this also is a direction

Christ has given. "The same night in which he was betrayed, he took bread, and brake it, and said, Take, eat; this is my body;" that is, the sacred sign of my body: "This do in remembrance of me." Likewise, "he took the cup, saying, This cup is the new testament," or covenant, "in my blood;" the sacred sign of that covenant; "this do in remembrance of me." "For as often as you eat this bread, and drink this cup, you do show forth the Lord's death till he come." (1 Cor 11:23, &c.) You openly exhibit the same by, these visible signs, before God, and angels, and men; you manifest your solemn remembrance of his death, till he cometh in the clouds of heaven.

Only "let a man" first "examine himself," whether he understand the nature and design of this holy institution, and whether he really desires to be himself made conformable to the death of Christ; and so, nothing doubting, "let him eat of that bread, and drink of that cup." (1 Cor 11:28)

Here, then, the direction first given by our Lord is expressly repeated by the Apostle: "Let him eat; let him drink;" . . . both in the imperative mood; words not implying a bare permission only, but a clear, explicit command; a command to all those either who already are filled with peace and joy in believing, or who can truly say, "The remembrance of our sins is grievous unto us, the burden of them is intolerable."

It is hard to exaggerate how important John Wesley saw taking Communion regularly was to the normal Christian life and to growth in grace. In fact, so important was it to him that he wrote an entire sermon entitled "On Constant Communion" in which he argued that regular Communion was not enough!

In Wesley's view, spiritual formation, indeed Christian growth, needed to focus on prayer, probing the Scriptures, and taking the Lord's Supper—not on having a personal spiritual director; not on going on spiritual retreats; not on protracted periods of fasting; not on reading a lot of books on how to improve one's Christian life or discern God's will for one's life. However much there might be other things that can improve a person's spiritual formation, it is precisely and especially these three things that Wesley said "we Methodists" should concentrate on.

And notice this: although Wesley is exhorting us as individual Christians to do these things, all three of these things can involve something we do with other Christians; and in the case of taking Communion, we are talking about a practice that is not normally *supposed* to happen apart from when Christians come together. Let's spend some time seeing what the Scriptures themselves suggest about these things we ought to prioritize. Since this will take considerable examining, what we are going to do is spend the rest of this chapter on prayer, and then in the next chapter deal with searching the Scriptures as spiritual formation and a means of grace, and then have a chapter on Communion.

PRAYER IN THE NEW TESTAMENT

The place we must necessarily start the discussion of prayer in the New Testament is with the prayer that Jesus taught his disciples. This, of course, is the most widely prayed prayer in human history; and still today it unites the body of Christ worldwide. On any given Sunday, millions of Christians around the world pray this prayer. But what exactly are we praying? Are we just mindlessly reciting a familiar formula like when we daydream driving down an all-too-familiar road? Or is there something crucial about this prayer, which came as a response to a request that Jesus teach his followers how to pray?

The first thing to note about this prayer is that in one sense it can be called the Lord's Prayer, since he originated it, but in another sense it might better be called the Disciples' Prayer, for it was given for us to use. It is interesting, however, that it appears Jesus himself prayed in this fashion. For one thing, Jesus certainly prayed to God as *Abba*, the Aramaic word meaning "Father dearest." It is a term of intimacy, and interestingly a term that children used of their fathers; but it is also a term the disciples used of their Jewish teachers. It is not, however, slang or colloquial speech, so the translation "Daddy" is not appropriate, being too familiar and informal. Disciples never called their master teachers "Dad" or "Daddy," much less addressed their deity in this fashion.

Notice in Mark 14:36 Jesus is depicted as calling God "Abba," which Mark renders in Greek with the more formal "Father," not with "Daddy." Nevertheless, those who know about the prayer language of early Judaism, know that Jews would in fact use roundabout ways of talking to and about God to avoid mispronouncing the names for God. (For example, they would say, "Blessed be He," rather than, "Blessed be Yahweh," or they would talk about the kingdom of heaven instead of the kingdom of God, so sacred was the name of God and its right pronunciation.) So Jesus is initiating his disciples into a new level of intimacy in the way they address and relate to God, when he teaches them to pray saying "Abba." It is interesting that in Luke's form of the Lord's Prayer we simply have "Abba"/"Father" as the first clause, but in Matthew we have "our Father" because the prayer is being adopted for communal use, for use as a prayer we all pray together (cf. Luke 11:2 to Matt 6:9). This prayer was meant to be prayed both in an individual form and as part of the body of believers, and over the course of Church history it was the wisdom of the Church to emphasize the collective form of this paradigmatic prayer found in Matthew, *rather than the individual form of the prayer.* In fact, most Christians don't even realize there is any form of this prayer other than the collective form found in Matthew 6.

The beginning of this prayer is much like other early Jewish prayers, which talk about God's name being hallowed and his rule being present on earth or being invoked to come on earth as it is in heaven. In this respect, Jesus is simply modifying some preexisting Jewish prayer patterns, adopting and adapting them to his own disciples. There is some debate as to whether the second clause should be read as a statement ("Your name is hallowed") or as a directive ("Your name should be hallowed"). In light of the way early Jews used such a clause, it is probably a statement of recognition, not a statement of instruction. God's name is holy, and indeed is hallowed by believers everywhere. Unlike in our culture, where names are mere labels or ciphers, in Jesus' world a name connoted something about the nature of someone. What does it tell us about our God that he could be named "Father dearest"—and not just anybody's father but quite specifically both Jesus' Father and the believer's Father, hence "our Father"?

When I was growing up in the South, we actually used to pray the Lord's Prayer in public grade school at the beginning of the day. But the Lord's Prayer is not intended to be prayed by anyone and everyone. We must first become Jesus' disciples. The privilege of addressing God as "our Father" comes after we have been adopted as God's sons and daughters through a personal relationship with Jesus. As the hymn says, we must "come to the Father through Jesus the Son and give him the glory, great things he has done." This is why I suggested earlier that we should call this the Disciples' Prayer.

Since I have written another book on what is meant by the term Kingdom in the New Testament,[2] I will not repeat here all that I said there. Here it is appropriate to note that sometimes the Greek word ***basileia,*** and indeed the Aramaic word behind it, ***malkuta,*** has a more verbal sense and sometimes more the sense of a noun. That is, sometimes it refers to an activity and sometimes to the result of such activity. So in some places it refers to God's divine and eschatological saving activity and sometimes it refers to God's reign in someone's life, or somewhere, as a result of that divine saving activity.

This is why I suggest that the English word *dominion,* which can be either a verb or a noun, is a better equivalent for the Greek and Aramaic terms. A dominion can certainly be a place—the king's dominion—but a king can also have dominion over someone or somewhere. The problem with the English term *kingdom* is that it always has the sense of a place, such as the United Kingdom. More important, what Jesus is referring to here is the inbreaking of God's final saving activity on earth, which one day will result in God directly ruling everywhere on earth.

So when the disciple prays, "Thy kingdom come, thy will be done, on earth as it is in heaven," that disciple implies two things: (1) as of yet that is only partially true on earth, and we are praying for God to finish the job. But that also means we are praying for the end of human history as we know it. We are praying for God to finish what he has already begun, because he has already begun to rule here in the lives of his followers. (2) This implies clearly that there are various ways in which, and places in which, God's will is not being done on earth as it is in heaven. There are things still badly wrong on earth, and it would be untrue to say that whatever happens on earth is God's will, whether it is good, bad, or indifferent. Early Jews and early Christians were not fatalists. They did not believe that whatever turns out to happen must be God's will for this or that person or this or that group of persons. No, sin and evil are still rampant on the earth, which is precisely why the believer must earnestly pray, "Thy kingdom come, thy will be done, on earth as it is in heaven." It is simply bad theology to sing the old song "Que Sera, Sera (Whatever Will Be, Will Be)." The Christian knows that it is not true that all things have been predetermined on earth. This is precisely why we pray for things to change when we pray for the divine saving reign of God to come in fullness on earth as in heaven.

The next petition in the Lord's Prayer can be read one of two ways: "Give us today, the bread for tomorrow" or "Give us this day, this day's bread." It probably means the latter, and it reflects what Jesus says elsewhere in the Sermon on the Mount—that we should live day to day in dependence on God, not worrying about what we will eat, what we will drink, and what we will wear. If we think for a moment about the story in Exodus about manna from heaven, it will be remembered that this bread was given new each morning and it was not to be stockpiled. Why? Because the lesson was to teach God's people to remain in daily focus on, and dependence on, God. This means being aware every day that we need God, even for just the basics of life. Jesus does not encourage us to pray for luxuries or to pray to become conspicuous consumers or to pray for prosperity, which in our day is just a euphemism for praying to be rich. Indeed, Jesus warns about the spiritually deadening force of riches on the human heart.[3]

The next petition has to do with either debts or sins—or both—as a form of debt to God. In Matthew's form of the prayer we hear, "Forgive us our debts"—quite the appropriate prayer for a debtor nation like America these days. Luke's form, however, has "Forgive us our trespasses." However we view this petition, what is being asked for is debt forgiveness. This part of the prayer is penitential in character. We recognize not merely our indebtedness to God and others, but also our transgressions against God and others.

Notice the deliberate connection between being forgiven and offering forgiveness to others who owe us something or who have harmed us in some way. Jesus believes there is an inherent connection between receiving forgiveness from God and forgiving others—or at least there should be. We should forgive as we are forgiven. But there is probably something more implied. If we commit the sin of unforgiveness against others, we have put an impediment in our own hearts to receiving forgiveness from God. The connection between our relationship with God and our relationship with others and how the latter effects the former is especially clear here.

We do not have a private relationship with God, nor do we simply receive a private forgiveness from God, if by private we mean that what we receive from God is in no way affected by the way we behave toward others. It is not true that forgiveness is just between "me and the Lord." That is ignoring that our sin is not just between God and us. Indeed, as often as not, our sin is against our neighbor as well as against God, and forgiveness needs to characterize both our relationship with God and our interpersonal relationships. I am stressing once more that our relationship with God, and thus our spiritual formation, is indeed a deeply personal matter but not a private matter. Indeed, James, the brother of Jesus, exhorts us in James 5 to "confess our sins to one another" and not merely to God, presumably for the sake of accountability. The divine-human relationships are intertwined with the human-human relationships.

John Ed Mathison, a United Methodist minister in the United States, tells the story of a woman whose husband of some thirty years had betrayed her. He had run off with another woman and then divorced his wife. This devastated her; but instead of time healing her wounds and her becoming better, she just became bitter. John Ed could see that unforgiveness was shriveling up her soul and that she was becoming a cynical and cold person, still dealing with her anger about being betrayed.

John Ed called her in for a chat and they began to talk about the aftermath of the disaster that had happened to her. He told her, "We are going to try an experiment to see if we can improve at least your frame of mind and attitude toward life. I want you to verbalize that you forgive your former husband. I want you to say out loud, 'Frank, I forgive you.' The reason you must do this is because unforgiveness in your heart is eating up your spiritual life. You are in fact blocking receiving God's grace in your life by this attitude." The woman looked defiant but said, "I forgive you, Frank!" with venom and vehemence. It was almost a shout. "OK," said John Ed, "that's a start. Now let's try it again, only this time pretend you mean it and make it sound like you do." The woman lowered her voice and said quietly, "Frank, I forgive you."

"Now this time," said John Ed, "I want you to close your eyes and visualize Frank in front of you, and then imagine that Jesus is sitting beside you, holding your hand and giving you courage." The tears started rolling down her cheeks, and in a voice as quiet as a church mouse, but with sincerity, she said, "Frank, I honestly can't forgive you without Jesus' help, but he is helping; so since he forgives you, so do I." John Ed smiled and then said, "It's time to let it go so you can be healed inside." And so it was that forgiveness came into the life of a brokenhearted woman and gave her the power to forgive someone who had hurt her deeply. But of course forgiveness offered and forgiveness received are two different things; but forgiveness offered is as important for the giver and her or his spiritual life as it is for the receiver.

The next petition in the Lord's Prayer is confusing on two grounds. First, as James 1 says, God cannot be tempted and *"God tempts no one!"* Why in the world then are we praying to God, "Lead us not into temptation," if God never does that anyway? The second source of confusion comes from the second clause. Should it be rendered in an abstract way, "but deliver us from evil," or more personally, "but deliver us from the Evil One"? There is a difference. Jesus certainly believed in the reality of Satan; indeed Jesus had had notable encounters with Satan in the wilderness at the beginning of his ministry (Matt 4; Luke 4). If someone had asked him if he believed in Satan, he could have responded, "Believe in Satan? I've seen him in action!"

To further complicate things, we have here the word ***peirasmos*** and its cognates, which in fact can be translated either "tempt" or "'test." It is an old theological distinction, but a useful one, that whereas God will test us (see the book of Job), Satan will tempt us. What is the difference, especially if, as in the case of Job, what God intended as a test, Satan intended as a temptation? The difference in fact is enormous. A test is intended to strengthen our Christian character, development, or spiritual formation, whereas a temptation is intended to destroy that Christian character. On the whole, it seems best to translate these two clauses of the prayer, since we are praying to God and not to Satan (God forbid!), "Put us not to the test, but deliver us from the Evil One."

Though it is probably not a part of the original inspired text of Matthew, a few manuscripts add a sort of doxological conclusion to the prayer: "For thine is the Kingdom and the power and the glory forever, Amen." These words are an appropriate addendum and conclusion but are not in our earliest manuscripts, which is why they are left out in modern translations. What should we deduce from this paradigmatic prayer about what Jesus would have us pray and how he would have us pray?

First of all, this prayer is given in a context in which Jesus has also said, "When you are praying, do not heap up empty phrases as the Gentiles do; for they think that they will be heard because of their many words. Do not be like them, for your Father knows what you need before you ask him" (Matt 6:7-8). What this suggests to me is that Jesus is urging three things: (1) Less is more. God is not deaf, nor is he a reluctant hearer of our prayers, nor does he have senior moments and need to be reminded of things. It is not necessary to belabor your point. I take this to mean that it is unnecessary to drone on and on, especially since God already knows what we need before we ask. (2) The prayer should be sincere and heartfelt, not "full of sound and fury, signifying nothing." Prayer, even prayer for the body of Christ in a public setting, is not to be done for the purpose of impressing the audience; and in any case, God is unimpressed by pomposity. If there is a good reason to pray at length, for example, making petitions for a lot of different persons, that is fine. But bearing in mind that you cannot browbeat God, it is unnecessary to pray the same thing, the same prayer, over and over and over, ad infinitum, ad nauseam, pleading and pleading and pleading. God already knows how much you need or want something. You don't have to go overboard to prove it. (3) Avoid making a display of your piety when you pray in church. That would be only about ego and ego fulfillment. *A prayer should not draw attention to you in the congregation; it should draw attention to God and to the needs being mentioned.*

When we survey this paradigmatic prayer from the point of view of kinds of prayer, something else interesting comes to light. This prayer is a combination prayer. It begins with an address to the one and only God, continues with praise for that God (hallowing his name), and then petitions God that his dominion and will be fully manifest on earth. It then petitions for daily bread and forgiveness (it is interesting that we are to see ourselves as just as dependent on God for daily bread as for forgiveness); then there is the petition for protection and deliverance; and finally, in a later addition, there is a doxology directed to the Father. There are a variety of different kinds of prayers—prayers of praise; of thanksgiving; of petition for self; of intercession for others; of repentance; and in a sense we have all of these wrapped up into one prayer. Only a direct prayer of thanksgiving or a prayer of lamentation is not found in the Lord's Prayer. We should also note that the prayers of intercession and prayers for self coalesce here since it is "we" who together, in concert, are praying for daily bread, for forgiveness, and so on. There isn't really a petition here for others that we are not also praying for ourselves and vice versa.

PAULINE PRAYER

It was the practice of Paul, even when he was writing to converts who were giving him "Maalox moments," to pray a prayer of thanksgiving for the audience before instructing them. This was a part of Paul's doxological life pattern, and it tells us a lot about his own spiritual formation. He had learned to give thanks even for those who caused him trouble and to pray for their welfare. In fact, he had learned to thank God even for the very things about his converts on which he was having to correct them—in the case of the Corinthians, it was their spiritual gifts. Listen to Paul's opening prayer in 1 Corinthians 1:

I always thank my God for you because of his grace given you in Christ Jesus. For in him you have been enriched in every way—with all kinds of speech and with all knowledge—God thus confirming our testimony about Christ among you. Therefore you do not lack any spiritual gift as you eagerly wait for our Lord Jesus Christ to be revealed. He will also keep you firm to the end, so that you will be blameless on the day of our Lord Jesus Christ. God is faithful, who has called you into fellowship with his Son, Jesus Christ our Lord. (vv. 4-9)

Strictly speaking, this is not a prayer but Paul's *report* of what he had been praying. These are the things Paul had been thanking God for, in regard to these converts. Yet in 1 Corinthians 11–14, as a part of their ongoing spiritual formation and growth, Paul at length corrects how the Corinthians are using their gifts. And this brings up a good point. The reason you need both spiritual gifts and spiritual growth is so that you will use the gifts in ways that glorify God and edify the saints, ways that build up the church rather than puff up the individual.

Spiritual formation of yourself is a by-product of properly edifying others. This is why we must be wary of too much concentration on ourselves and our spiritual formation lest instead of making us more other-directed and Christlike it turns us into spiritual navel-gazers—self-seeking, self-focused, and self-absorbed. In some ways the best way to allow yourself to be spiritually formed is to forget about yourself and focus on God and others. And a big part of prayer and spiritual formation is understanding that *whereas God always responds to his people's prayers, sometimes the response is an emphatic "No!" But "no" is indeed an answer to prayer. We should not mistake the answer "no" for God being silent.* Let us consider the episode in Paul's prayer life where God said no. Here is 2 Corinthians 12:1-10:

I must go on boasting. Although there is nothing to be gained, I will go on to visions and revelations from the Lord. I know a man in Christ who fourteen years ago was caught up to the third heaven. Whether it was in the body or out of the body I do not know—God knows. And I know that this man—whether in the body or apart from the body I do not know, but God knows—was caught up to paradise and heard inexpressible things, things that no one is permitted to tell. I will boast about a man like that, but I will not boast about myself, except about my weaknesses. Even if I should choose to boast, I would not be a fool, because I would be speaking the truth. But I refrain, so no one will think more of me than is warranted by what I do or say, or because of these surpassingly great revelations. Therefore, in order to keep me from becoming conceited, I was given a thorn in my flesh, a messenger of Satan, to torment me. Three times I pleaded with the Lord to take it away from me. But he said to me, "My grace is sufficient for you, for my power is made perfect in weakness." Therefore I will boast all the more gladly about my weaknesses,

so that Christ's power may rest on me. That is why, for Christ's sake, I delight in weaknesses, in insults, in hardships, in persecutions, in difficulties. For when I am weak, then I am strong.

One of the things one has to keep steadily in mind in this passage is that Paul is engaging in a rhetorical technique called "inoffensive self-praise," and one also needs to know that he is doing it in a tongue-in-cheek way *in order to shame his audience into humility and shame his opponents for the wrong sorts of boasting.* Paul then is going to boast about things that for the most part no one in antiquity would ever boast about—trials, temptations, shipwrecks, beatings, and so on. These are the very things that in an honor-and-shame culture one never spoke publicly about, things one hid from the public gaze. Not so Paul.

It is a huge mistake to assume that boasting in Paul's world is simply identical to modern boasting in our contexts. It is not. Paul is using inverted boasting to silence the wrong sort of boasting in the audience. And there is a heavy dose of irony deliberately ladled into this whole passage. So, for instance, at the beginning of this passage, Paul, probably much like his opponents, the pseudo-apostles, recounts a vision he had many years earlier, but with a difference. Notice that he speaks about himself in the third person, says the man had a vision, and then says only that he *heard, not saw, some things in heaven.* Then he says that he can't tell them about the content of what he heard! This is a deliberate deflation device critiquing those who go on and on about "what the Lord said to them" and "what they saw in their mind's eye." Paul in effect says he had the experience but then does not relate the content of the experience! Paul says that when you have an experience like that, God forbids you to go around bragging about it lest it simply be a tool for self-aggrandizement. (Note well: to superspiritual persons who tend to brag, are you listening?)

But then something else remarkable happens in this passage. Paul begins to brag about his weaknesses; but he also talks about how God used a deflation device in his life to prevent him from getting too elated, too puffed up, too stuck on himself. He says God gave him a stake, or a thorn, in the flesh, some kind of ongoing physical condition that bothered him. He calls this stake in the flesh "a messenger of Satan"—that is, a reminder of his mortality, frailty, and temptability. Notice the answer God gave Paul when Paul prayed earnestly three times to have the stake extracted from his flesh. God answered, "NO!" Instead of taking away the physical problem, God increased his grace to Paul so that Paul would continue to rely on God and his grace and not on his own insight or physical health or the like. *God's power is made perfect in our weakness.* Now we are into deep spiritual waters. Let us see if we can see to the bottom of them.

First, God does indeed answer some prayers of sincere Christians with a resounding "no" from time to time. And "no" is indeed an answer to prayer, for we do not always know how to pray properly. Frankly, we should be thankful that God is not a cosmic bellhop, at our beck and call, jumping whenever we plead and doing everything he can to always please us. God is not a people pleaser, unlike many ministers, unless of course what pleases us is in accord with God's will and what pleases God in the first place. *The beginning of wisdom about spiritual formation is that prayer is not about getting God to do our will; it's about us being conformed and used as instruments of God's will.* There is *no* inherent power in prayer. There *is* inherent power in the God who answers prayer. And it is a huge mistake to use prayer as if it were some sort of magical wand that forces God to do our bidding. We can be as sincere as Paul was in pleading with God to have or remove something, and God is still free to say no, because God alone knows what is best for us, what will most help our spiritual formation.

Second, Paul was told that God would give him the grace to bear up under the stake he experienced. One of the things people who are often praying for healing don't understand is that God does not always heal people. There is a mystery to this, as prayer can be an instrument of healing according to God's will in a particular case. But there are plenty of folk who pray earnestly and don't get healing, and in many cases it has nothing to do with whether they have faith or with the quantity of faith they have. Let me tell you what it does have to do with.

We have mortal bodies, and there is no point for them to be propped up endlessly when death is inevitable. Sometimes God heals these bodies because he still has more for us to do in these bodies and in this life. But when we believe and know that there is resurrection life coming, we realize that this life is not all there is. As Christians we should not live by the beer commercial motto "You only go around once in this life, so you have to grab for all the gusto you can get." When we know that life is not too short because it's eternal, when we know we are going to go around twice in life, we understand why propping up these bodies as long as medicine can do it or through miraculous healing is not always God's will for us.

We have roamed far and wide in this chapter to begin to get a handle on what the normal Christian life looks like when it comes to individual efforts at spiritual formation. Mr. Wesley said prayer, searching the Scriptures, and constant Communion were the ways to go about that as an individual Christian. The good news is we don't all have to become monks, or fast for forty days and nights, or go on an infinite number of retreats in order to improve our spiritual state. There are simple things even the average busy Christian can do, indeed can do every day in many cases, to grow in grace. In the next chapter we will look at the second means of grace Wesley stressed: searching the Scriptures.

Questions for Reflection

1. All churches have a different culture, whether high church, low church, or in between. How would you describe your church? How does your church compare with other churches you know? In what kind of church are you most comfortable?

2. How do you understand the meaning of the means of grace?

3. Share a time when you or someone you know experienced the grace of God through worship, prayer, baptism, Communion, or searching the Scriptures.

4. How often do you commune with God? How often do you participate in Communion? in prayer? in other Christian practices like service?

5. Have you grown spiritually through edifying others? Share a time when someone edified you. How did you feel about him or her?

6. Describe how the Lord's Prayer edifies and teaches you about God as the beloved Father.

7. Some people have a difficult time understanding God as a loving Father because of their own personal history. How do you address God in your praying?

8. Can you think of a time when God said no to you and it was a good thing? Has God ever answered your prayer? Share that experience with some of your Christian friends.

CHAPTER SEVEN

SPIRITUAL FORMATION AND SEARCHING THE SCRIPTURE

Jesus is not here to get what you want out of God; Jesus is God's means of getting what he wants out of you. —*Will Willimon*[1]

The devotional use and reading of the Bible has gone on for as long as there has been a Bible, but when John Wesley refers to "searching the Scriptures" he is not referring to a particular kind of use of the Bible or a particular sort of way of reading it for spiritual benefit. *What Wesley means is that the Bible itself, however one may read it, is a book inspired by God, a spiritual book if you will, and as such it has spiritual effects on those who read it with eyes wide open and heart's door cracked and the Spirit resident inside the believer.*

The Bible is both inspired and inspiring. It is not merely a human record of God's word; it is the living word of God that transforms human beings and continually spiritually forms those who are open to its effect, as in the story of those two disciples at the inn at Emmaus who felt their hearts burn when Jesus spoke to them and broke bread with them. So, too, the Bible is the living word of God, the bread of life that if consumed provides not merely nourishment but indeed soul formation and enlightenment.

This conviction about the character of the Bible was of course profoundly important to Wesley. In his introduction to his *Standard Sermons* he says this:

To candid, reasonable men, I am not afraid to lay open what have been the inmost thoughts of my heart. I have thought, I am a creature of a day, passing through life as an arrow through the air. I am a spirit come from God, and returning to God: just hovering over the great gulf; till, a few moments hence, I am no more seen; I drop into an unchangeable eternity! I want to know one thing the way to heaven; how to land safe on that happy shore. God Himself has condescended to teach the way; for this very end He came from heaven. He has written it down in a book. O give me that book! At any price, give me the book of God! I have it: here is knowledge enough for me. Let me be "homo unius libri ['a man of one book']."

Here then I am, far from the busy ways of men. I sit down alone: only God is here. In His presence I open, I read His book; for this end, to find the way to heaven. Is there a doubt concerning the meaning of what I read? Does anything appear dark or intricate? I lift up my heart to the Father of Lights: "Lord, is it not your word, 'If any man lack wisdom, let him ask of God'? You 'give liberally, and do not scold.' You have said, 'If any be willing to do my will, he shall know.' I am willing to do, let me know, your will." I then search after and consider parallel passages of Scripture, "comparing spiritual things with spiritual." I meditate thereon with all the attention and earnestness of which my mind is capable. If any doubt still remains, I consult those who are experienced in the things of God; and then the writings which, being dead, they yet speak. And what I thus learn, that I teach.

Concerning the Scriptures in general, it may be observed, the word of the living God, which directed the first patriarchs also, was, in the time of Moses, committed to writing. To this were added, in several succeeding generations, the inspired writings of the other prophets. Afterward, what the Son of God preached,

and the Holy Ghost spoke by the apostles, the apostles and evangelists wrote. This is what we now style the "Holy Scripture:" this is that "word of God which remains forever:" of which, though "heaven and earth pass away, one jot or tittle shall not pass away." The Scripture therefore of the "Old and New Testament," is a most solid and precious system of divine truth. Every part thereof is worthy of God; and all together are one entire body, wherein is no defect, no excess. It is the fountain of heavenly wisdom, which they who are able to taste, prefer to all writings of men, however wise, or learned, or holy.

In his advice on how to read the Bible, Wesley in his preface to his *Notes on the Old Testament* stresses:

If you desire to read the scripture in such a manner as may most effectually answer this end, would it not be advisable,

1. To set apart a little time, if you can, every morning and evening for that purpose?

2. At each time if you have leisure, to read a chapter out of the Old, and one out of the New Testament: if you cannot do this, to take a single chapter, or a part of one?

3. To read this with a single eye, to know the whole will of God, and a fixed resolution to do it? In order to know his will, you should,

4. Have a constant eye to the analogy of faith; the connection and harmony there is between those grand, fundamental doctrines, Original Sin, Justification by Faith, the New Birth, Inward and Outward Holiness.

5. Serious and earnest prayer should be constantly used, before we consult the oracles of God, seeing "scripture can only be understood through the same Spirit whereby it was given." Our reading should likewise be closed with prayer, that what we read may be written on our hearts.

6. It might also be of use, if while we read, we were frequently to pause, and examine ourselves by what we read, both with regard to our hearts, and lives. This would furnish us with matter of praise, where we found God had enabled us to conform to his blessed will, and matter of humiliation and prayer, where we were conscious of having fallen short.

And whatever light you then receive, should be used to the uttermost, and that immediately. Let there be no delay. Whatever you resolve, begin to execute the first moment you can. So shall you find this word to be indeed the power of God unto present and eternal salvation.

And in his preface to his *Notes on the New Testament,* Wesley adds:

I advise every one, before he reads the Scripture, to use this or the like prayer: "Blessed Lord, who has caused all holy Scriptures to be written for our learning, grant that we may in such manner hear them, read, mark, learn, and inwardly digest them, that by patience and comfort of thy holy Word, we may embrace, and ever hold fast the blessed hope of everlasting life, which you have given us in our Savior Jesus Christ."

What we should deduce from all this is not merely that Wesley was in favor of devotional reading of the Bible or that Wesley believed the Bible was true or that Wesley saw such reading as important for spiritual formation. No, *he saw the reading and study of the Scriptures as essential if one wanted to be a Christian at all, because the Bible, coupled with the internal illumination of the Spirit, is what spiritually forms us and transforms us. It does not merely inform us.*

What did Wesley mean then about searching the Scriptures as a means of grace? Here several things come to light not only from the quotations above, but also from his sermon "The Means of Grace." First, searching the Scriptures means a wholehearted studying of God's word, giving it one's full attention. There is nothing casual about searching the Scriptures. It is planned, intentional, and often undertaken at certain times of the day, decided in advance.

Second, when Wesley talks about searching the Scriptures he is of course not talking about doing something like a Google search. There is nothing random about what Wesley refers to. He is talking about deliberately and carefully comparing one Scripture with another, especially in regard to what the Bible says about soteriology, the doctrine of salvation by grace through faith in Jesus Christ.

Third, Wesley is talking about truth seeking, not merely reference seeking or mere research. The Scripture he cites is the story of the Bereans searching the Old Testament to see if what Paul was preaching were true: "They examined the Scriptures every day to see whether these things [Paul had preached] were true" (Acts 17:11). This text is not merely about Christians reading the Bible; it is, in this case, about non-Christians reading it. And they are not reading it for their spiritual improvement; they are reading it to see if Paul's interpretation of the Bible was true! And this brings up an important point. Wesley did not distinguish between the honest open reading of the Bible by non-Christians and the same sort of reading of the Bible by Christians. Why not?

Two reasons. First, Wesley believed in prevenient grace, namely that the Spirit works on non-Christians to help them see the truth of God's word, and second, he believed in the inherently inspired word-of-God character of the Bible—it could change a heart of stone into a heart for the Lord, if received. *He would not distinguish between a truth-seeking way of reading the Bible and how a Christian reads it for his or her continued edification.* The issue was the work of the Spirit and the character of the Bible, not primarily a particular *way of reading* the Bible spiritually. In short, the Bible is inherently a spiritual book. Searching the Scriptures, then, is for everyone, whether a Christian or not, because in

Wesley's view, everyone needs to be saved; everyone can be saved; and Scripture is the tool for—or road map to—salvation, indeed it is the road map to heaven.

Modern distinctions between an academic study of the Bible and a devotional one are not really applicable because Wesley thought that the most spiritual benefit could be had from reading the Bible in its original languages! He thought that people should apply their whole selves and commit themselves to lifelong study of the Bible whether or not they were scholars. Wesley encouraged even lay people who were capable to read the Bible in Hebrew and Greek. This is because he believed that the Bible itself is inherently inspired, and a translation of the Bible, however good, is one step removed from the source. The more spiritual benefit one wants to get out of the original word of God, the better one ought to know its original voice in the original languages. This is not because he thought an English translation was inadequate for salvation or Christian growth. It is a matter of good and better.

My point is that "*spiritually* better" is defined by Wesley as what we today might call the highly academic learning of Greek and Hebrew in order to read the real Bible, not merely a translation of it. Of course Wesley would, however, distinguish between merely reading the Bible for information and reading it as a truth seeker, with eyes and heart open. It is the latter sort of reading he is commending whether by Christians or others. At this juncture it would be good if we went to the Bible itself, in this case the New Testament, and see what we can learn about how the biblical writers viewed both the oral word of God and the written text of Scriptures. There are some surprises that come to light when we do this sort of study.

WHAT IS THE WORD OF GOD AND HOW SHOULD THE BIBLE BE VIEWED?

When spiritual formation is the issue, the most important question to ask is, Is the Bible really God-breathed? Is it the powerful word, living and active, of a powerful God, or is it just another human book talking about God? The sort of spiritual formation Wesley predicates of the Bible presupposes a high view of Scripture itself; but what happens when we do indeed "search the Scriptures" looking for truth, not merely about the gospel of Jesus Christ, but about the Bible itself? What do we find? Here are some of the answers—answers, as you will see, that have convinced me that we are fully justified in believing the Bible is God's truth, a truth that can transform us and nourish us spiritually. But let me tell a story first.

His name was Ralph Cain and he was mentally challenged. He was a sweet Christian man, and when I knew him he was in his forties. About the only book he read regularly was the King James Bible. One day I was visiting with Ralph and he was puzzled. He said, "Dr. Ben, I don't understand the Bible here in the Twenty-third Psalm. I've been trying to memorize it, but the very first line confuses me. It says 'The LORD is my shepherd, I shall not want.' Why does it say, 'I shall not want?'"

I could see that this old English rendering troubled Ralph, so I explained, "Ralph, it means if the Lord is your shepherd, you shall lack nothing essential in life." Suddenly his face lit up and he responded, "That's good. I just knew it couldn't mean I shouldn't want him, because I do!" Even when you read the Bible with an open heart, seeking God, there are times when it can be very confusing. And we wrongly simply assume that because the Bible is inspired, its meaning should be immediately obvious to any sincere reader, without study or reflection. This assumption, however, is false, and it doesn't help that our culture is so different from that of biblical times.

Ours is a culture of texts.[2] The written word is king whether a persons texts, tweets, or reads. This is clear enough from the fact that we now have a whole line of lawyers called "intellectual property lawyers" who are prepared to go court in an instant if a client's words have been begged, borrowed, or stolen without permission. It is therefore difficult for those of us who are surrounded by texts to wrap our minds around the fact that the New Testament was written in and for a predominantly oral culture—a culture where the spoken word took precedence over the written word and the written word simply supported or at least served as a surrogate for the spoken word.

When I call the world of the New Testament an oral culture, I don't merely mean that most people couldn't read and write. That of course was true. The best we can tell, the literacy rate was never more than about 20 percent in the age when the New Testament was written. In many places it was less than that. Literacy was usually a sign of someone being of higher social standing, and therefore better educated, and of course was more likely to be exhibited by males in a male-dominated culture where often only men got a formal education. It is, then, a remarkable fact that a series of texts guided, goaded, and guarded the early Christian movement in its most crucial period of development—the second half of the first century A.D., when in fact every one of the New Testament books was written.

In the battles over whether and in what sense the Bible in general or the New Testament in particular can be called God's inspired word, very little ink has been spilt discussing the issue of the power and authority that texts had in an oral culture. In fact, especially in cultures that had and cherished certain sacred texts—texts that provided source material about one's religion—the text took on an almost magical quality. This is understandable especially in a Jewish context, for texts about biblical religion were normally kept in sacred spaces—in the Temple or in the synagogue. Scribes, who often were full-time employees of priests or Levites or the Temple hierarchy, carefully and lovingly copied them.

But it was not just in Judaism that texts were kept in sacred places. If one chooses to make the arduous climb up to Delphi, where the oracle was in southern Greece, you will discover many buildings called treasuries, just like the treasury in the Temple in Jerusalem. These treasuries were not just where money and valuables were kept. They were also places where important and crucial documents were kept, it was believed, under the watchful eye of one deity or another. Similarly, in Rome there were the

Vestal Virgins with whom one deposited for safekeeping wills, property deeds, treaties, and sacred documents. It is not a wonder then that many people in antiquity were convinced that texts themselves, especially religious texts, might well be invested with some of the divine qualities of the deity they were placed close to. They believed, for example, that curse tablets (tablets on which one wrote a curse formula against someone) themselves might engender a curse on someone, especially if the tablet was placed near or in the divine presence.

Many such examples could be given, but I want to offer one. The stories about the ark of the covenant are interesting for many reasons. Take a moment to read 1 Samuel 4-6 and then 2 Samuel 6. The ark of the covenant was constructed so that it contained the written covenant document in its lower part; but also on the top of the ark itself there were images of cherubim—angels—and between them it was believed the divine presence rested. The divine presence, the divine power, and the divine word were all right there together. So present was God with his word that when Uzzah reached out to prevent the ark from falling when an ox stumbled, and he actually touched the ark itself, he was immediately struck down and died on the spot (2 Sam 6:6-7). This of course scared David to death and it is said that thereafter he was afraid of the Lord.

It is not surprising that Israelites like David would associate God's word with power and inherent authority; nor indeed is it surprising that they would think that God's words were living things that had inherent power. After all, did they not have a creation story that told them that God created the world simply by speaking words? Hadn't they learned the tale of how God himself wrote down the essence of the Torah, the Law, on a tablet for Moses?

My point in mentioning all of this is simple. It shows so very clearly why ancients did not think words, and especially divine words, were mere ciphers or sounds. They believed words partook of the character and quality of the one who spoke them and that this was especially so when one was talking about God's words. And not surprisingly in an oral culture a premium was put on the oral word. The living voice was generally preferred, except of course when it came to holy words spoken to unholy people. Then there might well be a preference for a mediated conveying of God's word, a reading or proclaiming of his word by a spokesperson—a prophet or a priest; or a king, an apostle, a prophet, or an elder if we are talking about the Christian community. As the author of Hebrews says, the Israelites at Sinai heard "such a voice speaking words that those who heard it begged that no further word be spoken to them" (Heb 12:19). When a living voice proclaimed the living word, whether from God directly or through God's messenger or emissary, things were likely to happen. All of this helps us to begin to understand the use of the phrase "word of God" in the New Testament.

By general consensus among New Testament scholars (and that sort of nearly universal agreement is rare in the guild), 1 Thessalonians is one of the very first, if not the very first, of all the New Testament documents to be written. And from near the beginning of this discourse we hear about "the word of God." First Thessalonians 2:13 says, "When you received the word of God, which you heard from us, you accepted it not as the word of humans, but as it actually is, the word of God, which is at work in you believers." This verse deserves some examining. In the first place, Paul equates the message he proclaimed to the residents of Thessalonica with "the word of God." Clearly the phrase refers to an oral proclamation that was heard. If we ask what this message was that Paul proclaimed, whatever else it contained, it surely contained the good news about Jesus and perhaps in addition some quotations and interpreting of a few Old Testament texts.

Then Paul makes a remarkable statement. The Thessalonians received this proclamation as it actually was—not the words of human beings, cooked up or contrived by mere mortals, but a word from God, indeed "the word of God" to and for them! Clearly enough we see already in Paul's words here at least one expression of a theology of God's word. God's word, though spoken in human language, should never be confused with mere human speech or even mere human words about God, however accurate. Rather we are talking about divine speech that changes human lives. But then Paul adds another remarkable phrase: "which is [still] at work in you who believe." The word of God is seen as something living and active and having taken up residence in the lives of Paul's converts—and still is in the process of working on and in them!

The implications of these statements are enormous and they include the following: (1) Paul believes that he adequately and accurately speaks God's oral word and has the authority to do so. (2) From the context it becomes quite clear that this does not simply mean he is a good reader of Old Testament texts, though certainly he sees the OT as God's word written down. (3) What must be included here in the phrase "word of God" is what later came to be called the gospel or the good news of and about Jesus Christ. This of course was the heart and soul of Paul's message wherever he proclaimed it in the empire. (4) In and through these words that Paul proclaimed, God was speaking, and it should never be seen as merely the words of human beings. A profound theology of revelation and a clear conception of Paul being an inspired person who could truthfully convey God's message of salvation are presupposed. Ancients had little trouble in believing in the idea of divine revelation. It is we moderns who have trouble with the idea.

Another early Pauline text of relevance to this discussion is 1 Corinthians 14:36-37 where Paul asks his audience if the word of God originated with them or if they were the only ones it had reached. Of course, he is *not* talking about the Corinthians having received a shipment of Bibles from the Gideons! He is talking about their having heard and received the oral proclamation of God's word from Paul and others. But what Paul goes on to say in verse 37 is more than a little important. He adds: "If any think they are prophets or are spiritually gifted, let them acknowledge that *what I am writing is the Lord's command*." Here finally we have a reference to a text being "the Lord's command" and not just any text. In this case the reference is to Paul's own letter written to the Corinthians. Here we do indeed have the nodal idea of an inspired text being God's word, in this instance involving some imperatives.

But of course it is not only Paul who has this concept that the word of God is an oral proclamation that includes telling the story about Jesus and that it is a living and active thing. We see this in various places in the book of Acts. Several texts deserve brief mention. First we notice the reference in Acts 4:31 that speaks of the fact that the Holy Spirit of God filled all who were present (men and women) and that they all "spoke the word of God with boldness." In this text we begin to see the connection, which is already obvious in various Old Testament prophetic texts (cf. e.g., Isa 61:1—the spirit of God prompts the preaching of the good news), that it is the Holy Spirit, not merely the human spirit, that inspires the speaking of God's word. Here already the concept of prophetic inspiration and revelation is transferred to the followers of Jesus, apparently to all of them, and all on this occasion and in this place are prompted to speak God's word boldly. Again, we are not talking about preaching from a text or preaching a text. We are talking about an oral proclamation of a late word from God.

So much is the word of God (in this case the proclamation about Jesus) seen as a living thing in Acts that remarkably we have texts like Acts 6:7 where we hear how the word of God itself grew and spread. This is not merely a personification of an abstract idea. The author believes that God's word is alive and that when it is heard and received it changes human lives; it takes up residence in them. And so the very next sentence in this verse says, "The number of the disciples increased greatly in Jerusalem." Note also Acts 12:24 where it is said that God's word grew and spread.

We see this same sort of concept of the word of God in the book of Hebrews. Hebrews 4:12-13 is worth quoting in full: "For the word of God is living and active. Sharper than any double-edged sword, it penetrates even to dividing soul and spirit, joints and marrow; it judges the thoughts and attitudes of the heart. Nothing in all creation is hidden from God's sight." Here again the subject of the phrase "word of God" is an oral proclamation. The focus is not on the after-the-fact literary residue of that proclamation, which is perfectly clear because the author speaks of it sinking into the inner being of the listener. But even more remarkable is the fact that here the word of God inside the believer is said to be analogous to God's eyes—it penetrates the innermost being of a person and judges the thoughts of his or her heart or mind, laying everything bare. Our author, however, is not the originator of these ideas. We can fruitfully compare what is said here with Psalm 139, where the focus is on the work of God's presence or Spirit. What is said in Psalm 139 about the Spirit is said here about the living and active word. These two things are seen as going and working together. We have already seen the connection of word and Spirit in Acts 4 as discussed above.

Another text of relevance to this discussion is 1 Peter 1:23, which speaks of believers being born anew by "the living and enduring word of God." This can certainly refer to the oral proclamation; however the term *living* can also convey the sense of life-giving, as it does for example in the phrase "living bread" in John 6:51. We can compare this as well to 1 Peter 1:3, which speaks of a living hope, which surely means more than merely an extant hope, or we can consider 1 Peter 2:4-5, which speaks of believers as living stones of the new spiritual house of God. *When we hear the phrase "the living word of God" then, we are meant to think of something that is actually God's word and as such has life-giving potential. Normally the phrase also connotes an oral proclamation of God's word in some form.*

Notice that thus far we have said nothing about the other use of the phrase "word of God" in the New Testament—that is, as it is used to refer to Jesus himself (John 1)—or about the concept that the written Old Testament is the word of God as well. But we can now make some remarks about these other uses of the phrase. The Logos (the Greek word for *Word*) theology of the prologue to John's Gospel is often thought to be distinctive of this book, but we may well see it also in 1 John 1:1-2 where we hear of the Word of Life, which seems to be synonymous with both Jesus (who could be touched) and with the message about Jesus as God's incarnate Word. Similarly in Revelation 19:13 the name of God's Son is said to be "the Word of God." We have seen some hints already of the notion that texts could be the word of God as well, and now we must turn to more evidence of this by looking in detail at 2 Timothy 3:16.

Because of the enormous significance of 2 Timothy 3:16-17, we must necessarily go into a considerably more detailed explanation of these verses, since whole theories about the nature of God's word and the nature of inspiration have been derived from these verses. Here, clearly the subject matter is a written text, in this case what Christians now call the Old Testament. The Old Testament was in fact the Bible of the earliest Christians because of course the New Testament had not yet been written, collected, or canonized. Indeed, even the Old Testament canon, or list of included books, was not completely settled before the waning decades of the first century A.D. Here we must make an important distinction between "the Bible" as one form that God's word took—the written form—and the "word of God" that is, as we have already seen in this chapter, a much broader category that refers to inspired and powerful spoken words. The earliest Christians were neither without a Scripture (the Old Testament) nor without the living voice, the oral word of God, which in their view now included Christian proclamation, especially the good news about Jesus.

It is an interesting fact that the New Testament writers tend to say more about the inspiration of the Old Testament than the Old Testament writers themselves. For example, in Mark 12:36 Jesus tells his audience that David "by the Holy Spirit, declared..." and then a portion of a psalm is quoted. And in Acts 1:16 we hear that the Holy Spirit, through the mouth of David, predicted what would happen with Judas. Second Peter 1:21 can be compared at this point. We are thus not surprised to hear about the inspiration of Old Testament figures in the New Testament, but

2 Timothy 3:16-17 goes a step beyond that in talking about an inspired text itself.

Second Timothy 3:16 is surely the most famous of the verses of 2 Timothy, cited more than one hundred times in the patristic literature. There are, however, various ways it could be translated and each causes a variable in its meaning. It could read, for instance, "Every ***graphē*** (i.e., Scripture) is God-breathed and profitable/useful . . . so that/with the result that the person of God is ready, equipped for good works." Usually when ***pas*** (all/every) is used with a noun without the definite article it means "every" rather than "all." Thus the meaning seems likely to be "every Scripture" or perhaps "every passage of Scripture." Paul does use ***graphē*** in the singular to refer to the whole of Scripture in Romans 11:2, but there we have the definite article (cf. also Gal 3:22). Of course this means that "all Scripture" is included, but the emphasis would be on each one being God-breathed. Paul does not envision any Scripture that is not God-breathed.[3] It would also be possible to read the verse to mean "every inspired Scripture is useful," but against this view is that it is more natural to take the two qualifying adjectives as relating to the noun in the same way as in 1 Timothy 4:4.

A further issue is what to make of the adjective ***theopneustos***. Its literal meaning is "God-breathed." Greek words with the ***–tos*** ending tend to be passive rather than active, so we should not take this to mean "every Scripture is inspiring," but rather "every Scripture is inspired." What is meant is that God speaks through these words. God breathed life and meaning and truth into them all (see similarly Num 24:2; Hos 9:7; 2 Pet 1:21).

Note that we are not given an explanation of how that works. This text by itself does not give us a theory of inspiration or its nature. Does the Spirit lift the mind of the writer to see, understand, and write, or is it a matter of mechanical dictation? These questions are not answered here. What is suggested is that whatever the process, the product is God's word, telling God's truth.

The emphasis here is actually on what it is good or profitable for—as a source of teaching about God and human beings and their ways, as a means of refuting false arguments or errors and offering positive "proofs" and rebuking sin, and as a means of offering constructive wisdom and teaching on how to live a life pleasing to God. It will be seen then that the Old Testament is largely viewed here as a source for ethical instruction and exhortation, which is not surprising given the emphasis in this letter. There is no emphasis here on it being a sourcebook for Christian theology, which would come more from the Christian *kerygma* and Christian tradition. We may also want to consult other places where Paul speaks about the nature of the Old Testament Scriptures such as in Romans 15:3-4 or 1 Corinthians 10:11, which confirm that Paul thinks that what we call the Old Testament is very suitable for Christian instruction, especially for training in righteousness and other ethical matters.

There is debate about verse 17 as to whether we should see it as a purpose or result clause. Is it the purpose of Scripture to fit a person of God for ready service, or is it the result and effect of Scripture that that happens? Probably this is a result clause. The result of learning Scripture is that one is equipped. It seems likely as well that since this is directed specifically to Timothy here, "person/man of God" refers to a minister of some sort. Paul then would be talking about equipping the minister by means of studying the Scriptures. *In other words, the Bible itself spiritually forms us as we hear, heed, and learn it.*

Paul brings the list of what Scripture is useful for to a climax and conclusion with the phrase "training in righteousness." Here righteousness surely has an ethical rather than a forensic sense, in keeping with the ethical focus of the rest of what Scripture is said to be useful for. Chrysostom puts it this way: "This is why the exhortation of the Scripture is given: that the man of God may be rendered complete by it. Without this he cannot grow to maturity" (Homily 9 on 2 Timothy). Clearly, with this text, we are well on the way to a full-blown theology of inspired written texts being God's word, being God-breathed. What is interesting is that neither Paul nor the author of Hebrews view the Old Testament as an example of what God *once* said, relegating the revelation and speaking to the past. No, it still has the life and power and truth of God in it, and it still speaks in and to the present. More important for our purposes, as Chrysostom says, *the Bible is essential to our growing up in Christ, to our ongoing spiritual formation.*

One more text is of direct relevance to this sort of discussion, particularly in regard to the issue of inspiration and revelation. Second Peter 1:20-21 says, "Above all, you must understand that no prophecy of Scripture came about by the prophet's own interpretation of things. For prophecy never had its origin in the human will, but prophets, though human, spoke from God as they were carried along by the Holy Spirit." It is indeed normally about prophets and prophecy that we hear about the notion of inspiration, and this text seems to add a bit more to the discussion than 2 Timothy 3:16.

First of all, there is here a contrast between prophecy that made it into Scripture and other prophecies. The author says that whatever may be the case about other prophecies, in regard to Old Testament prophecy it cannot be a matter of purely private or individual interpretation or explanation. That is, the author thinks there is a meaning in the prophecy itself that makes a claim on the listener and that it is not for the listener to "determine the meaning" of the text but rather to discover it. Indeed he even means it wasn't up to the prophet to interpret it or add his own interpretation to it. He was constrained by the source of the information to speak another's words and meaning—namely God's. This is made clearer in what follows in verse 21. This latter verse speaks about the origins of true prophecy and insists that it does not originate as a matter of human will or ingenuity. To the contrary, it is the Holy Spirit who inspires the prophet. In fact, the text literally says the prophet is carried along or forcefully moved by the Spirit to say what he does. The prophet is so led by the Spirit that his words can be said to be God's words, originating from a divine source.

Much more could be said along these lines, but this will need to suffice as we draw this chapter to a close. The living word of

God is seen as an oral message, an incarnate person, and finally as a text, in particular the text of the Old Testament. Its life, power, and truth are a derived life, power, and truth, if we are talking about the oral or written word. The source is God, who inspires, speaks, and empowers the words with qualities that reflect the divine character. It is right to say that Paul thinks that what he says, God is saying. It is right to say that both Paul and the author of Hebrews think that what the Old Testament says, God says. It is right to say that these same writers think that what Jesus says, God says. Indeed, the author of Hebrews is audacious enough to suggest that the preexistent Christ actually spoke some of the Old Testament texts into existence! It is also right to say that for early Christians the emphatic center and focus of the proclamation of "the word of God" was Jesus and the Christ event in general. It is also right to say that some New Testament writers even reached the point of being able to talk about Jesus being the Word of God incarnate, come in the flesh; *thus, when Jesus spoke on earth, he not merely spoke for God, he spoke as God, and indeed spoke about himself*. The message and the messenger are one in this case.

Let us return to a crucial question about the Bible, as it has a direct bearing on the issue of spiritual formation. What did 2 Timothy 3:16 tell us the Bible was written for in the first place? The Bible is useful for teaching, correction, rebuking, and training in righteousness. Here is where we learn that spiritual formation in the biblical sense is subsumed under the heading of "training in righteousness." *That is, the spiritual use and content of the Bible must not be separated from its moral use because the point of spiritual formation is to make us more like Christ, and that includes making us more moral people. There is no dividing of spiritual and moral formation or for that matter spiritual and theological formation.*

Equally important, we have found in the text of the New Testament itself justification for looking at the Bible the very way that Wesley and many others did—as a living word of God that is spiritually formative in and of itself if one will but hear and heed it, receive and believe it. In other words, the book itself is not merely spiritually nourishing; it is inherently divine or sacred in character, takes on a life of its own, and has life-giving potential. We don't have to read it in some specifically "spiritual" or devotional way; we just have to read it with eyes and heart wide open.

The modern attempt to separate spirituality from morality or even from theology dies a quick death in the Bible when we actually look at the statements in it that talk about the spiritual character of the Bible *and what it was originally intended for*. The other side of this coin is that the Bible was also never intended to be studied as a purely secular or human document. Any sort of study like that is bound to come up short of fully understanding or using the Bible in the way it was intended to be used. Although the Bible can be taught without one believing it is telling the truth about God and a host of other subjects, the biblical writers were convinced that it *ought not* to be taught that way. It ought to be taught as God's truth; and it ought to be taught in a way that transforms lives and trains people in righteousness. *A spirituality that is not about seeking truth and not about pursuing a life of righteousness is not a biblical spirituality.*

Last, it's also not about reading the Bible in a theological or ethical way any more than it's about reading it in a spiritual way. The Bible is inherently, irreducibly, theological and ethical and spiritual in character. There is no escaping that fact, and any reading of the Bible that tries to denude it of its theological and ethical character is inherently reductionistic and inadequate. It is like the famous story of the five blind men, each feeling a different part of the elephant and trying to explain what it is they all are touching. Alas, not one of them can get a glimpse of the whole, even though they do indeed get a hold of a part of the creature, and precisely because they cannot get a glimpse of the whole, they can't tell what it is or what it is for.

The sort of spiritual formation the Bible calls us to is being saved persons, for it is salvation that opens the eyes of the blind, and salvation is what the Bible was written for in the first place. This is why Wesley said, "At all costs give me this book, and let me be a man of one book." The Bible itself is the most spiritually formative document that has or could ever be written, for it is the tool God uses to save the world. Even the ordinary, normal Christian can read the Bible and have his or her soul nourished. Even the non-Christian can search the Scriptures and learn that they are true. Spiritual formation is just another way of talking about salvation and sanctification.

Let me conclude this chapter with a brief story. In August of 1979, my wife Ann was expecting our first child. We had gone to the Lamaze natural child-birthing classes in Durham, England, and were good to go, when the doctor threw us a curveball. Ann's blood pressure was too high and she was placed in the hospital for observation. The blood pressure got bad enough that the doctor told us on August 13 that he was going to induce Ann with drugs the next day. Ann, wanting to have this baby *au naturel,* was distraught. She knew far too much about what drugs do to infants in the womb. That night in the hospital, I was reading to Ann from Ezekiel. We had been reading straight through the book and fortunately—or unfortunately—we had arrived at the doom-and-gloom chapters. This was not helping until I read the words, "And I will keep you safe...and I will multiply your kindred...and you will come home soon," in the middle of a lot of other negative stuff. A little light came on in my brain and I said to Ann, "Honey, I think it will be all right. The baby is going to come on her own."

I knew perfectly well that Ezekiel was speaking to Jews in exile in Iraq in the seventh century B.C. I was not so egocentric as to think that these words were written specifically and in the first place for Ann and me on Aug. 13, 1979. The point was that we were reading the Bible wide open to how God would speak to us *using* those God-whispered words of old. We were listening with our hearts as well as with our minds, believing God was alive and well and could help us. The meaning of the words was not different, but those words were now being applied in a different way. I should add that there was nothing particularly *spiritual,* in the narrow sense of that word, or metaphorical about God using these words to reassure us. For us, it was a mundane physical promise to keep Ann safe and multiply our kindred and that all would come home soon.

Sure enough, Ann's water broke at about four in the morning, and when my neighbor showed up with his car to take me to the hospital (we had neither car nor phone) he was stunned to find me wide awake, dressed, and pacing the floor. When he asked how I knew, I just smiled and said, "We had advanced divine warning." Our daughter Christy was born alive and well only hours later, without the aid of drugs. God is like that, and God uses his living word to address one generation after another of those who listen closely, intently, and with an open mind. God's word spiritually forms, informs, and transforms us whether we are seeking spiritual formation or not. The Bible is just that kind of book.

Questions for Reflection

1. How does the Bible help you seek the truth?
2. What is your favorite Bible story? Why?
3. What favorite Bible passages do you call to mind when you need help?
4. How has the Bible opened your eyes and deepened your relationship with God?
5. Share a time when God spoke to you through your study of the Bible.
6. How does it feel to be inspired? Share a time when you had an inspiration.
7. Has your understanding of the Bible changed over time? Have certain passages of the Bible spoken to you differently at different times?
8. God's truth is not meant to be used in an offensive manner or as a weapon for attacking others. How can you offer's God's truth to others so that they will hear?
9. Select a Bible verse that "speaks" to you now and memorize it.

CHAPTER EIGHT

THE LORD'S SUPPER AS SPIRITUAL FORMATION

Why Jesus? Because for humans like us, love has to be embodied to be fully grasped, both literally and mentally and emotionally. God didn't just send us abstract truths, he sent an incarnate truth—his Son. What convinced the crushed disciples that Jesus was alive was not an empty tomb, subject to many explanations. No, it was that the risen, embodied touchable Jesus appeared to them and dined with them once more. —Ben Witherington III

As we have seen earlier in this study, John Wesley not only saw the Lord's Supper as a sacrament, a means of grace; he also urged his Methodists to take Communion constantly, in part on the theory "the more grace, the more growth." But in fact, many of Wesley's newly minted Methodists had not come from a life in the Anglican Church, had not regularly taken the Eucharist in the past, and did not much like being told that now that they had become Methodists they should also go to their nearby Anglican churches and take Communion. Because so few Methodist leaders were ordained, most of them couldn't serve the Eucharist to them. But what was the rationale of Wesley to urge all his Methodists, whether it was easy to accomplish or not, to take Communion "constantly"? We must explore this question.

In his sermon "The Duty of Constant Communion" the first

rationale Wesley provides for why this is a Christian duty is that Christ commanded us, "Do this in remembrance of me." In other words, his first point is that Communion is not a supplement to or an optional part of the Christian life; it is a command of the Lord that must be obeyed. Indeed, it is said to be a command for us as the body of Christ to do this "until he returns."

A further reason for taking Communion constantly is because of our constant need of forgiveness, since we keep sinning. Wesley puts it this way:

A second reason why every Christian should do this as often as he can, is, because the benefits of doing it are so great to all that do it in obedience to him; viz., the forgiveness of our past sins and the present strengthening and refreshing of our souls. In this world we are never free from temptations. Whatever way of life we are in, whatever our condition is, whether we are sick or well, in trouble or at ease, the enemies of our souls are watching to lead us into sin. And too often they prevail over us. Now, when we are convinced of having sinned against God, what surer way have we of procuring pardon from him, than the "showing forth the Lord's death;" and beseeching him, for the sake of his Son's sufferings, to blot out all our sins?

In other words, Communion is not only a way to receive forgiveness for the sins of the past; it is also a way to strengthen or shore one's self up to face temptation in the present and future. Communion strengthens us to love and obey God, and Wesley would add that it "leads us on to perfection." Think of it this way: would you not want to draw closer and closer to the person you love, and if a means were provided by which you could do this, would you not regularly avail yourself of it? Such is the case with Communion and the Lord. We draw closer to him as we take the tokens of his body and blood into ourselves. For Wesley, Communion is the ultimate means of spiritual formation.

The next rationale that Wesley provides for constant Communion is that the early church followed this practice. Here is what he says: we should follow the example of

> **the first Christians, with whom the Christian sacrifice was a constant part of the Lord's day service. And for several centuries they received it almost every day: Four times a week always, and every saint's day beside. Accordingly, those that joined in the prayers of the faithful never failed to partake of the blessed sacrament. What opinion they had of any who turned his back upon it, we may learn from that ancient canon: "If any believer joins in the prayers of the faithful, and goes away without receiving the Lord's Supper, let him be excommunicated, as bringing confusion into the church of God."**

Wesley seems to take the summaries in Acts 2 and 4, which speak of breaking bread together, as references that include the Lord's Supper (and he may be right about that), but in addition he is citing the Apostolic Constitutions, which do not go back to the apostles themselves. What they describe is the early medieval practice in some parts of the church.

So vital was taking Communion for spiritual strengthening that Wesley was prepared to say that even if you don't have time to do the preliminary prayers and self-examination, you should still take Communion.

> **It is highly expedient for those who purpose to receive this, whenever their time will permit, to prepare themselves for this solemn ordinance by self-examination and prayer. But this is not absolutely necessary. And when we have no time for it, we should see that we have the habitual preparation which is absolutely necessary, and can never be dispensed with on any account or any occasion whatever. This is, First, a full *purpose* of heart to keep all the commandments of God; and, Secondly, a sincere *desire* to receive all his promises.**

In order of importance, Communion was more important for one's soul than the penitential prayers and self-examination that usually preceded the rite. This quotation makes very clear just how much of a sacramentarian Wesley was. Whereas prayer is a means of grace without question, Wesley puts even more emphasis on Communion.

One of the regular issues that arose in early Methodism, and indeed in church history in general, was that the warnings of Paul in 1 Corinthians 11 were taken to mean that unworthy people should *not* take Communion. We will say more on this shortly, but by way of correction here, what Paul is talking about is taking the Lord's Supper *in an unworthy manner*. He is not talking about our *being worthy* in order to take it at all. On that criteria no one should take Communion for no one is worthy of Christ's sacrifice on the cross. It's not about our meriting taking Communion. Wesley urges:

God offers you one of the greatest mercies on this side heaven, and commands you to accept it. Why do not you accept this mercy, in obedience to his command? You say, "I am unworthy to receive it." And what then? You are unworthy to receive any mercy from God. But is that a reason for refusing all mercy? God offers you a pardon for all your sins. You are unworthy of it, it is sure, and he knows it; but since he is pleased to offer it nevertheless, will not you accept of it? He offers to deliver your soul from death: You are unworthy to live; but will you therefore refuse life? He offers to imbue your soul with new strength; because you are unworthy of it, will you refuse to take it? What can God himself do for us further, if we refuse his mercy because we are unworthy of it?

What sort of view of the sacrament does Wesley actually have, since he is clear that he doesn't believe in an inherent dose of grace in the sacrament regardless of the condition of the recipient, nor in the notion of the sacrament actually being the physical body and blood of Jesus? Sometimes it has been suggested that Wesley took the Zwinglian view that the "real spiritual presence of Christ bestowing blessing" is what we encounter in the Eucharist. This I think is basically Wesley's view. He doesn't think the Lord's Supper is merely symbolic; to the contrary, he believes it can really convey or mediate grace and blessing, if partaken of in a worthy manner. But who are the proper recipients of this means of grace? To answer that and other questions we must turn to the New Testament itself.

THE LORD'S SUPPER IN THE NEW TESTAMENT

The word ***koinonia*** gets bandied about a great deal in Christian circles. We talk about having ***koinonia,*** and some churches have ***koinonia*** rooms and ***koinonia*** meals and so on, without really realizing the significance of the term, which is unfortunately all too often translated as "fellowship." This, however, is *not* the real sense of the term. As I have mentioned before, Tom Skinner once defined fellowship as a bunch of fellows in the same ship, but ***koinonia*** does not refer to simply being locked into the same experience with someone else. It is not a passive term at all. It is in fact the same root as the term ***koine,*** as in *koine* Greek, usually taken to mean common Greek.

When we actually look at the use of the term ***koinonia*** in the larger Greek literature it refers to business deals that two or more parties actively engage in together! Perhaps a much better translation would be "sharing or participating in common" with someone. In other words, you can't have ***koinonia*** by accident, and you can't have it all by yourself. It involves an active partnership. For example, in Philippians 1:7 Paul speaks of how he and his converts in Philippi are joint participants in the grace of God, and at Philippians 4:4 he speaks of them being joint sufferers with one another in the cause of Christ. This most crucial means of grace for an individual is nonetheless something we should only participate in together with others.

This brings us to 1 Corinthians 10:14-17. "Is not the cup of thanksgiving which we drink a joint participation in the blood of

Christ, and is not the bread that we break a joint participation in the body of Christ," asks Paul rhetorically. Of course Paul's answer to these questions is yes and yes. He then makes an assertion: "Because there is only one loaf, we who are many are one body, because we all participate in the one loaf." Notice again the emphasis on active participation. We need to examine these ideas carefully.

The first thing to notice is that one of the implications of 1 Corinthians 10:17 is that if we don't actively participate in partaking of the body of Christ *WE ARE NOT ONE BODY*. What follows from this is that in some undefined way the failure to share in the Lord's Supper prevents believers from having unity with one another and with Christ. This may well explain one reason in low-church Protestantism we have so much fragmentation of denominations and splitting of groups, not to mention of hairs. We do not take seriously enough the spiritual transaction that is happening in the Lord's Supper. We also too seldom actually partake of the Lord's Supper together and as a result we do not get the unifying benefits of doing so.

One of the keys to understanding Paul's argument in 1 Corinthians 10 is his use of the term *spiritual* (***pneumatikon***). In what sense were the rock, the food, and the drink spiritual (10:3-4)? Paul is not talking about figurative food and drink but rather real food and drink; neither is he talking about the character or quality of that real food and drink. The term *spiritual* here has the very same significance that it does in 1 Corinthians 15:44. There the contrast is between a natural body and a spiritual body. The contrast has to do with the *source* of the body. God's Spirit provided the food and drink in the wilderness, and God's Spirit will provide the resurrection body as well. The food, like the body, is a real and material substance, but its origins are different from ordinary food or bodies. A spiritual body, then, means a body given by, and perhaps entirely empowered by, the Spirit. It does not refer to a nonmaterial body. Similarly, spiritual food and drink here refer to real food and drink, but spiritually or miraculously provided. There is then nothing here to suggest that

Paul saw the Lord's Supper elements as something magical or "spiritual" in themselves. To the contrary, he is trying to *counter* magical views of religious rituals and ceremonies in Corinth.

A further clear application of 1 Corinthians 10, and also 1 Corinthians 11 for that matter, is that sharing in the Lord's Supper is meant to be an act of the body of Christ. There should be no such thing as private Communion or individual Communion. That would be a violation of the very meaning of the word ***koinonia***: a sharing in common with another in something; an active participating or partnering with another in something. The Lord's Supper is part of body life in Christ. This is applicable to serving a married couple Communion while everyone else only watches. If one is going to do Communion, one had better invite the whole body present to participate. Otherwise the Lord's Supper goes from being what it is intended to be, to being a subset of a marriage ceremony, which it was never intended to be. The Lord's Supper was meant to unite us all together, not set apart a newly married couple's union from the union the rest of those present can share. But there is more.

The Lord's Supper is an active sacrament. You must take and eat; you must take and drink; and Paul says we should do this "as often as we come together as the body." This is not something meant to be fast-food grace or an afterthought tacked on to the end of the worship service. Furthermore, as Paul says so clearly in 1 Corinthians 11, no one should partake of this sacrament "without discerning the body." Now scholars have debated this endlessly. Does this mean without discerning Christ's spiritual body in the bread, or does it mean without discerning that this is an act of the body of Christ—the church—that we are supposed to share in common? It is probably the latter since we know in 1 Corinthians Paul is trying to unify that many-splintered thing called the Corinthian Church.

This brings us to what is for some Protestants the biggest surprise about this text in 1 Corinthians 10:14-17. Paul says that what we are sharing in common or participating in common in when we do Communion is not just body life of the church, but also *the very blood and body of Christ himself*. The reference to sharing in the blood makes clear he is not just talking about our having fellowship at the table, for blood, unlike body, is never a metaphor for the church. Paul is deeply concerned not only about the Corinthians trivializing the Lord's Supper and turning it into a mere part of the larger banquet; he is actually concerned about *sacrilege*.

He warns in 1 Corinthians 11 that the reason some have gotten sick and died is because they have not partaken of the Lord's Supper while recognizing the "body of Christ" being present. Now we are getting down to the heart of the mystery, and mystery it is for sure. When we drink of the cup of thanksgiving, we are jointly, actively sharing in common the blood of Christ. And when we partake of the loaf, we are not loafing around; we are jointly, actively sharing in common in the body of Christ. Christ himself, in other words, is present in and with the sacrament, and we partake of him, not just of the elements, in some undefined way.

That is, there is a vertical as well as a horizontal dimension to this meal—we do not just share with and share in one another as body when we eat and drink; we share with and share in Christ himself and the benefits of his death when we do so, and if we do not discern that this is what is happening, Paul says we eat and drink judgment upon ourselves! What this clearly implies is that we should not be practicing infant Communion, as infants cannot discern much of anything theological or spiritual about what is happening. Baptism, by contrast, is a passive sacrament, something done for the person in question as a rite of passage, and if indeed baptism can be a sign of God's prevenient grace, of what God does for us even before we respond, then there isn't a problem with infant baptism. In fact, there may be more of a problem with baptizing adults long after they have become Christians because the point of that ritual is that it is a rite symbolizing the passing from outside to inside the body of believers.[1]

The sense of the sacredness of the act, the holiness of the act, the grace and yet gravity of the Lord's Supper act, is so potent and clear in 1 Corinthians 10–11 that we dare not trivialize these great mysteries. In Paul's view the Lord's Supper is not a mere manipulation of symbols; it is a sharing in a sacrament with either gracious or grave potential outcomes. To be sure, I doubt Paul would have endorsed later theologies of transubstantiation or consubstantiation, as he is not talking about a magical change of the elements or a physical imbibing of Christ's actual body or blood. Nor would he have endorsed a merely symbolic trivialization of the rite. Something somewhere in between these extremes is the truth, and at a minimum it means that the real presence of Christ is spiritually present and blessing in and with the sacrament. And there are endless testimonies that can be given about how the Lord's Supper properly received and shared in can produce dramatic results of reconciliation and healing, among other things. I will tell one true story.

On the Sunday after Ulysses S. Grant and Robert E. Lee signed the treaty at Appomattox, there was a worship service in the Episcopal church in Richmond. As with almost every Episcopal Sunday service, the Eucharist was to be offered on that day, and up until that Sunday the practice had been that the slaves sat in the upstairs wraparound balcony, the white folk sat downstairs, and there were two calls to Communion, first for those downstairs and then afterward for the slaves upstairs. But on this Sunday when the first call to Communion came, a former slave slipped downstairs and began down the aisle. There was a gasp in the congregation downstairs; that is, until an older white-haired, bearded gentleman stepped up beside the slave and went arm in arm with him to the Communion rail. That bearded gentleman was Robert E. Lee, who had told Abraham Lincoln at the beginning of the war that he could not accept command of the Union forces. He added that he did not favor slavery but he could not oppose his beloved Virginia. On that first Sunday after the Civil War ended, reconciliation began to come between former slaves and former masters at the Communion rail in Richmond.

We now need to examine some of the deeper spiritual significance of Paul's recitation of the Lord's Supper ritual found in

1 Corinthians 11:17-34. One of the things that becomes clear as one works through 1 Corinthians 11:17-34 is that Paul expects the meal Christians share to be far more egalitarian in nature than a normal Greco-Roman meal. He is trying to construct a social practice that will go against the flow of the culture's norms in several respects, not the least of which is that he wants all, from the lowest to the highest status, to wait for one another and partake together. Paul's strategy is to make a distinction between private meals in one's own home and a meal shared in and by the "assembly of God," the ***ekklēsia*** as Paul calls it. Here is another telltale piece of evidence that it is a clear mistake to assume that Paul simply applied the patriarchal and stratified structure of the household and its conventions to the community of faith.

Even though the community meets in the household of one of the more socially well-off Christians, Paul insists that they carry on in a way that comports with the equality that exists in the body of Christ, without regard to social distinctions and social status. The meeting does not involve a matter of sacred space or sacred buildings but rather sacred times, occasions, and events. Paul does not talk about holy buildings but rather holy persons and holy actions of worship and fellowship. These occasions are to be regulated by sacred traditions; in this case the narrative of the Last Supper provides certain norms. The Lord's Supper is seen as a sacrament or ceremony of Communion, both vertical and horizontal in character. It is clearly not seen as a rite of incorporation. Meals in antiquity were occasions for either gaining or displaying one's social status, as they were microcosms of the competitive nature and values of the culture as a whole. Paul's attempt to deconstruct some of this socially stratifying and individualistic behavior as it was happening at the Lord's meal goes directly against what many would have seen as the real function of such meals—an attempt to show off, to strut one's stuff.

First Corinthians 11:20 mentions coming together in one place. Apparently there were enough Corinthian Christians that they did not always do this. But what is crucial for our purposes is that Paul implies that the reason for the bigger meeting is *the partaking of the Lord's meal.* This was something the whole body was to do together. Here we may think back to Acts 2:43-47, which suggests that *they all met together in one place,* were of one accord, and all partook of the Christian meal together. Paul knows of that paradigm and the Corinthians were far from emulating the model. Clearly, in Corinth the Lord's Supper was a part of a larger meal and meeting, something Acts 2 also suggests. Since Paul says some are drunk at the Lord's meal, we must imagine that the Lord's Supper was taking place after the normal meal, perhaps even after the drinking party as well, though the text is not clear on this point. It would appear that the Lord's Supper was not viewed as, or had not at this juncture been transformed into, a ritualistic act that was part of a worship act distinguishable from a fellowship meal. On the contrary, meals, the Lord's Supper, and worship were all part of one ongoing event.

First Corinthians 11:21 suggests that the wealthy are being served first and getting the better portions while the poor are in the atrium getting the leftovers. The end result is that one is gorged and drunk and another goes hungry. This hardly amounts to a shared common meal. The problems that Paul deals with in 1 Corinthians primarily have to do with things that work against the unity of the group. The goal of Paul's rhetoric here is to remove obstacles to that unity.

In one sense, knowing even a little about human nature, we can easily understand how this problem arose. The host was reasonably well-to-do, and so quite naturally he invited his friends to dine with him in the dining room, while the socially less elite were left to fend for themselves in the atrium or garden. The result was further stratification of an already divided group of people.

First Corinthians 11:22a makes very plain that the problem is the well-to-do people who have houses grand enough in which to have their own dinner parties. Notice that Paul does not rule out such sumptuous feasts. His point is that pagan rules of dining protocols absolutely have no place in a Christian meal situation, much less in a Christian meeting and dinner that also involves the Lord's Supper. The better-off Christians are showing no respect for the have-nots; but even worse, they are not showing the proper respect for the Lord and his meal. The meal itself is being violated, not just general fellowship or even the ***ekklesia*** in general.

It is not surprising, then, that Paul's way of correcting the problem is to remind the Corinthians of the traditions he and they share about the Lord's Supper. In 1 Corinthians 11:23 he uses the semitechnical language of Judaism for the passing on of sacred traditions. This text suggests there was a deliberate passing on of this story in a rather set form, and now it has made its way to Corinth. But Paul is not mentioning this for the first time here. This is a tradition Paul had already passed along to the Christians in Corinth. Indeed, it seems to have been one of the first things he handed on to them, presumably in order to set up the practice of the Lord's Supper meal from the outset of the community.

This is a tradition Paul received, and we must take this to mean from the Jerusalem community itself, perhaps even from someone like Peter, who was present at the Last Supper (see Gal 1–2). Paul presumably does not mean literally that it was Jesus who handed him this tradition but that it goes back to Jesus himself ultimately. That this was a tradition other Christians mediated to Paul is shown by the closeness of the Pauline form of the tradition of the words and story to the Lukan form as well as by its differences from the Markan and Matthean forms of the story and words. I would prefer to say that the Lukan form reflects the Pauline form, rather than the converse, since Luke wrote at a later time and after being Paul's sometime companion over the years. The important point is this: Paul's record is chronologically the earliest we have of this crucial material. Unfortunately, he only selectively quotes his source, as he is busy correcting abuses and problems, not making a positive exposition of things.

First Corinthians 11:23 makes clear that the Lord's Supper was a tradition involving a historical memory of an actual event. It is thus set off from pagan memorial meals of various sorts.

One of the regular features of the latter sorts of meals was that the person about to die would leave in his will a stipend and stipulation that there be a memorial feast in his honor. Diogenes Laertius, for example, records that Epicurus left provision for an annual celebration "in memory of us" (10.16-22). The Corinthians may well have seen the Lord's Supper as a funerary memorial meal. One of the main differences, of course, would be that in the Lord's Supper one does not merely celebrate the life of the deceased Jesus; one *communes* with the living Christ and, by having his meal and by other means, one also proclaims his death until he comes again. The pagan funerary meals were often eaten on the graves of the deceased because it was believed that although they were in the underworld, they were still alive and could partake of the meal with the living in some sense. Archaeologists have in fact found pouring spouts going down into the graves so that wine could be poured into them! The Lord's Supper stands out from Passover as well in that the Lord's Supper celebrates a historical person and his deeds, whereas Passover celebrates the divine actions of Yahweh in the Exodus-Sinai events. There were salient differences between these three sorts of memorial meals.

The reference to Jesus' betrayal or being handed over (***paredideto*** can mean either in 1 Cor 11:23) marks off the Lord's Supper from all pagan celebrations that focused on myths. There is poignancy to this beginning of the ceremony as it reminds us that one of Jesus' own disciples betrayed him and did this in the context of a meal meant at least to bind the disciples closer to Jesus and to indicate the forgiveness they had from him! If we look carefully at this text, the following points come to light: (1) There is no association here of the breaking of the bread with the breaking of Jesus' body, despite the later textual variants that tried to slant the tradition in this direction. Nothing at all is suggested about reenacting the Passion in this ceremony. The breaking of the bread would not be a reenactment anyway, since no bone of Jesus' body was broken. (2) Notice the double reference to "for my memory/memorial" or "in remembrance of me" after both the bread and the cup words. This may be Paul's own emphasis here, since only Luke and Paul have the memory clauses.

(3) Only Paul says they are to celebrate the Lord's Supper as often as they drink of the wine cup. Not all meals involved wine. For the poor especially, this would be for special occasions. (4) In the Last Supper meal the language was clearly figurative, following the lead of the symbolic use of language in the Passover. This had to be the case, since Jesus was not yet dead; indeed he was physically present with them at the Last Supper. Jesus seems to have been modifying elements in the Passover meal and referring them to himself. This must count against any sort of overly literal interpretation of the "words of institution." (5) The phrase ***hyper humōn*** ("that is for you") is found only in the Pauline/ Lukan form of the tradition (1 Cor 11:24; Luke 22:19-20). It probably alludes to Isaiah 53:12, indicating that Christ gave his body on the believers' behalf and/or in the believers' place. The breaking of the bread is associated with and reminds us of that act of self-giving of his body and life. (6) What Jesus did at the Last Supper should not be seen as a funerary rite. This is not Jesus' last will and testimony, for the word *new* here, referring to a new covenant or testament, is fatal to such a view. The term ***diatheke,*** or "covenant," should be seen as a reference to the founding of a new covenant relationship through the shedding of Jesus' blood. Thus the remembering here is not merely a matter of a yearly memorial service for Jesus, like the pagan funerary meals. Indeed, the mention of having this meal whenever all the Corinthians come together suggests a frequent occasion, a regular ceremony involving something more positive than just a funerary remembrance rite. The ceremony of the Lord's Supper is a visible word proclaiming the dead but risen Jesus until he comes, as well as what he has done for them in his death and resurrection. (7) Jesus is said to have broken the bread only after giving thanks. This does not prove he was celebrating a Passover meal, since the giving of thanks was part of any Jewish meal. Nevertheless, the other features of this historical memory certainly suggest he was celebrating a Passover meal. (8) The reference to the wine cup coupled with the reference to some getting drunk makes perfectly clear that the early celebration of the Lord's Supper did involve wine with some alcoholic content; it was not mere grape

juice. (9) Notice that Paul does not specifically link the cup to Jesus' blood. It is rather called "the cup of the new covenant," which is "in my blood" (i.e., instituted by the death of Jesus). It is certainly beyond either Jesus' or Paul's meaning to suggest that the audience was being asked to drink Jesus' blood, something Jews would react to in horror, as would pagans. Paul says nothing about the wine being or representing Christ's blood. That is found in the Markan tradition. (10) Paul stresses that the meal involves both eating and drinking, but it also includes the words said—proclaiming Christ's death until he returns. Thus the meal has a past, present, and future orientation. It does not just focus on the past. One may suspect that the Aramaic cry ***maran atha*** (cf. 1 Cor 16:22), "Come, O Lord," was an integral part of the earliest Jewish Christians' original celebration of the Lord's Supper. The Lord's Supper, then, is an essential witness to the crucified, risen, and returning Lord. The Lord's coming mentioned here prepares for the discussion about coming judgment in the following verses.

The reference in 1 Corinthians 11:27 is to Christ's actual body, which was crucified, as the reference to blood makes evident. ***Anaziōs*** has been translated "in an unworthy manner" and sometimes has been thought—incorrectly—to modify not the *way* of partaking but the character of the persons partaking. *But Paul refers to those who are partaking in an unworthy manner, not those who in themselves are unworthy,* which presumably Paul would see as including any and all believers. No one is worthy of partaking of the Lord's Supper; it's not a matter of personal worth. Rather, Paul is concerned with the abuse in the actions of the participants, or at least some of them. Paul says that those who partake in an unworthy manner, abusing the privilege, are liable or guilty in some sense of the body and blood of Jesus. They are, in addition, partaking without discerning or distinguishing "the body."

Perhaps Paul means such abusers are guilty of standing on the side of those who abused and even killed Christ—an atrocious sacrilege. Perhaps, like the author of Hebrews (see Heb 6), he is indirectly accusing them of crucifying Christ afresh. The concept of sacrilege was widespread in Paul's era. For example, Dionysius of Halicarnassus says, "Those who tried to abolish a custom were regarded as having done a thing deserving both the indignation of human beings and the vengeance of the gods... a justifiable retribution by which the perpetrators were reduced from the greatest height of glory they once enjoyed to the lowest depths" (*Rom. Ant.* 8.80.2). Paul is saying something similar to this about those who have become sick and died. Those Corinthians had partaken of the Lord's Supper in an unworthy manner and God had judged them for doing so. Paul uses this as a solemn warning against continuing to abuse the Christian meal.

Paul believes that the Corinthians are bringing judgment on themselves both temporally, in the form of weaknesses and illnesses, and possibly even permanently, in eternal condemnation. Paul even says that because of this very failure "some have died" (11:30), a shocking conclusion. Paul must have believed he had some prophetic insight into the situation, which we at so great a remove do not have. It is presumably not the food that made them ill, but rather the judgment that came upon them for partaking in an unworthy manner. Such disasters can be avoided, says Paul, if the Corinthians will simply examine themselves and their behavior and before they partake remember their fellow believers who are their equals in Christ (11:31). Perhaps Paul sees the judgment of illness as a temporal judgment meant to prevent the worse disaster of being condemned with the world of nonbelievers at the last judgment when Christ returns. If this is correct, Paul may view the illness as corrective or remedial rather than some sort of final judgment on a person.

First Corinthians 11:33 then provides a final word of remedial advice. The verb ***ekdesesthe,*** while it may mean "wait for one another," is perhaps more likely in this context to mean welcome one another, show gracious hospitality to one another, partake together with one another without distinctions in rank and food. The point of the Lord's meal is something other than satisfying hunger, or at least this is not the main point. Thus the meal must not be treated as just another banquet. These reminders should also remind us that *if we treat the Lord's Supper as simply a means of improving our own individual spiritual formation without awareness that this is an act necessarily involving sharing in common with our fellow Christians, we are hardly being less individualistic than the converts in Corinth who Paul criticized.*

It appears clear, after a somewhat detailed examination, that Wesley's orientation to the Lord's Supper, both as a sacrament and also as something that should be a regular part of Christian worship and every Christian's spiritual life week to week, is a natural extension of the emphases of Paul in 1 Corinthians 10–11. Instead of a means of grace it had become a means of disgrace for the Corinthians because of how they participated in the sacrament; indeed it had become a means of judgment on their spiritual lives. If there is one thing that becomes clear from examining both Wesley and Paul on the Lord's Supper it is that in order to do spiritual formation right, one needs to have an adequate ecclesiology, an adequate understanding of sharing in common in the body of Christ. *We are all in this journey of spiritual formation or salvation or sanctification together, and it has been mandated that we not see that journey as some sort of individual or individualistic spiritual quest for transcendence or self-improvement. Improvement—growth, salvation, grace—comes from the Lord, and it comes in the context of body life.*

This means, among other things, that we have to overcome our shyness or even antipathy toward persons we don't exactly enjoy communing with in our church settings and realize that the people kneeling at the Communion rails with us are our forever family, our brothers and sisters in Christ, and that Communion is meant to break down those barriers and impediments that prevent real ***koinonia*** with them and with Christ. We may as well get used to being with all sorts of folk who might make us uncomfortable now, because we will be sharing eternity and Christ with them forever. *Christian spiritual formation is not just about improving our relationship with Jesus. It's also about learning how to live as and with the body of Christ, our fellow believers.*

Let's conclude these reflections with a brief story. Our daughter Christy loved liturgy. When she was growing up we lived in a small town in Ohio, and the Methodist church there was liturgy impoverished most of the time. So we compromised and went to the early service at a good local Lutheran church before attending Sunday school and the later service at the Methodist church. But when the time came for Christy to go through Confirmation she chose to the do the two-year catechism class at the Lutheran church, which climaxed with Christy and others taking their first official Communion at the altar. Everyone was dressed up and the sense of a special occasion was in the air. The teenagers were excited. They were both joining the church and, as their first official act as members, taking Communion as adults. They had studied the meaning of the ritual and this would be no mere *pro forma* march to the altar rail. A special photographer came and took a picture of the whole group smiling and looking nice in their special dresses and suits. I suspect that Paul would have approved of partaking of the Lord's Supper in this worthy manner, making it something very special, very sacred, a time for joy and celebration.

In our next chapter we must consider what Wesley called "works of charity" as a means of spiritual formation. We will discover that when a person gets lost in serving others, spiritual formation happens to us as a by-product.

Questions for Reflection

1. Describe how Communion is served at your church. How often is it served? Do you take Communion individually, all together, or some other way?
2. Share a meaningful Communion experience. Have you ever had the opportunity to help serve Communion? If so, what was it like for you?
3. How might Communion strengthen you?
4. Through Communion we say that Christ poured out his life for us. How do you pour out your life for others?

5. Communion represents the new covenant with God. Discuss what it means to live in covenant with God and with one another. How faithful are you in keeping your covenant? How faithful is your church in keeping its covenant with God? How can we be more faithful?

6. In Communion we remember what Christ did for us, but we also celebrate Christ's life, death, and resurrection. How can you remember and celebrate at other times, in other ways?

7. Reread the Communion rituals in the hymnal. What parts are meaningful for you? Do you need to learn more to more fully understand what Communion is? If so, who can help? What resources do you need?

CHAPTER NINE

WORKS OF CHARITY AS SPIRITUAL FORMATION

> *There is a world of difference separating] the manner of building up souls in Christ taught by St. Paul, from that taught by the Mystics!... For the religion these authors would edify us in, is solitary religion.... Directly opposed to this is the gospel of Christ. Solitary religion is not to be found there. "Holy solitaries" is a phrase no more consistent with the gospel than holy adulterers. The gospel of Christ knows of no religion, but social; no holiness, but social holiness. —John Wesley,* Hymns and Sacred Poems, *Preface*

Like most young Methodists, I was involved in service projects as a member of the Methodist Youth Fellowship (MYF). On one occasion the project involved giving up my Easter holiday and going to work in Appalachia, near Burnsville, North Carolina. My job was to work with the children of some of the coal miners, organizing a Christmas party. There was one particular family who lived well back in the mountain woods. They had a five-year-old son named Carl who had never seen any other children apart from his numerous siblings. After some long conversation on Good Friday, I managed to convince Carl's mother that it would be good for Carl to go to the party I was organizing for Saturday, which included, among other things, an Easter egg hunt.

Bright and early Saturday morning I drove the truck back up into the Carolina hills to collect Carl. Now you need to understand that he and his family were dirt poor. They had next to nothing and lived in a rundown shack. When I came up to the house, there was Carl, sitting on the clapboard porch with his cheeks all rosy from his momma scrubbing them vigorously. He had on his only decent clothes and shoes, and as I got out of the truck I could see he was holding something. Carl had exactly one prized possession—his goose. When he came over to me smiling he handed me a big goose egg and said, "Here. This is for the children who don't have any Easter eggs." I looked into that little face and I saw the face of Jesus. I heard the voice of Jesus say, "Just as you did it to one of the least of these... you did it to me." Those sorts of experiences you never forget. When a poor boy gives up a prized goose egg for others, grace is in the air. And the thing was, I had gone there to serve, not to be spiritually formed or informed. But without question a by-product of being a MYF volunteer in the mountains of North Carolina on that day was my own spiritual formation. Carl had been more help to me than I ever was to him, though I have to admit he had a pretty great time meeting a lot of other children his age on that Easter Saturday.

WESLEY ON WORKS OF MERCY or CHARITY

There is really very little debate that Wesley believed devoutly that there is no spiritual holiness without social holiness and vice versa. He also believed that spiritual formation entailed social engagement in works of mercy or charity. He calls the latter another means of grace and he defines such acts as including, but not being limited to, visiting the sick and the prisoners; feeding the hungry and clothing the naked; opposing heinous social sins such as slavery; charitable giving; and doing good in whatever way one can in general. Wesley was so ambitious that he wanted his Methodists to preach and practice the whole gospel in the whole world.

In the context of discoursing on the Sermon on the Mount,

which he saw as a credo for Christian living, he says this about works of mercy:

> **"Take heed," says he, "that you do not your alms before men, to be seen of them: Otherwise you have no reward of your Father which is in heaven." "That you do not your alms:"—Although this only is named, yet is every work of charity included, everything which we give, or speak, or do, whereby our neighbor may be profited; whereby another man may receive any advantage, either in his body or soul. The feeding the hungry, the clothing the naked, the entertaining or assisting the stranger, the visiting those that are sick or in prison, the comforting the afflicted, the instructing the ignorant, the reproving the wicked, the exhorting and encouraging the well-doer; and if there be any other work of mercy, it is equally included in this direction. ("Upon Our Lord's Sermon on the Mount")**

To the end of being generous to others, Wesley believed that his Methodists should live a simple lifestyle—eat simply; dress simply (or "plainly," as he called it—so that they could free up their resources to be charitable toward others. In his famous sermon "On the Use of Money" (the second most preached of all his sermons after "Justification by Faith") Wesley stressed that Christians should "make all they can by honest means, save all they can, in order that they might give all they can." Mincing no words, Wesley added that if you do the first two of these things without the third, you may be a living person but you are a dead Christian. Wesley himself was responsible for building orphanages, setting up soup kitchens for the poor, providing housing for abused women, helping alcoholics get rehabilitated (and saved), and many more such things. He set it as a professed goal to get to the point where upon his death he had given everything away. He did not quite succeed, since the revenues from his many books and tracts kept coming in. One can only imagine the forensic polemic that would have come out of John Wesley had he ever encountered the "prosperity gospel," a phrase that is an oxymoron if there ever was one. *The point about all this in terms of spiritual formation is that if your "social" life does not include "social holiness" this impedes or even corrodes your spiritual formation in ever so many ways.*

It should be added at this point that Wesley also believed eating right, staying in good health, and fasting were also means of grace for Christians, not least because these practices kept them in a condition in which they could continue to serve God actively, and as a by-product such practices helped spiritually form the persons doing them. In other words, such practices were not ends in themselves, as if people were trying to save themselves or spiritually improve themselves simply by fasting or eating right. No, this was only a means to being of more service to the Lord, and in that service the Lord, for whom they were "spending and being spent," spiritually molded them.

To the end of getting his Methodists to be ethically serious about their service to God, Wesley also saw once-a-year covenant renewal services as a good thing. Such services were seen not only as a means for grace, but also as a way of getting Methodists to commit themselves to works of charity as well as piety. Here is the famous introductory prayer from the covenanting service:

Commit yourselves to Christ as his servants. Give yourselves to him, that you may belong to him. Christ has many services to be done. Some are more easy and honorable, others are more difficult and disgraceful. Some are suitable to our inclinations and interests, others are contrary to both. In some we may please Christ and please ourselves. But then there are other works where we cannot please Christ except by denying ourselves. It is necessary, therefore, that we consider what it means to be a servant of Christ. Let us, therefore, go to Christ, and pray:

"Let me be your servant, under your command. I will no longer be my own. I will give up myself to your will in all things. Lord, make me what you will. I put myself fully into your hands:

put me to doing, put me to suffering, let me be employed for you, or laid aside for you, let me be full, let me be empty, let me have all things, let me have nothing. I freely and with a willing heart give it all to your pleasure and disposal. I do here covenant with you, O Christ, to take my lot with you as it may fall. Through your grace I promise that neither life nor death shall part me from you. I make this covenant with you, O God, without guile or reservation. If any falsehood should be in it, guide me and help me to set it aright. Mighty God, let this covenant I have made on earth be ratified in heaven. In the name of the Father, Son, and Holy Spirit. Amen."

Wesley was perfectly clear that spiritual formation could come through suffering, through persecution, and through becoming poor, as Jesus did. He took quite seriously the words of Paul when he told us, "For you know the generous act of our Lord Jesus Christ, that though he was rich, yet for your sakes he became poor, so that by his poverty you might become rich" (2 Cor 8:9). What Wesley rightly took this to mean is that we have here an allusion to the Christ hymn in Philippians 2:5-11 (see above). Whereas the last use of the term rich in 2 Corinthians 8:9 has a metaphorical or perhaps spiritual sense, Paul is quite clear that Jesus deliberately stripped himself of all his heavenly benefits and became a slave among human beings in order to save the world. Wesley believed we should imitate Christ in living a plain life as well, and he believed it would do us spiritual good too.

For Wesley, deeds of mercy included teaching, feeding, and clothing poor children; furnishing gainful employment to the jobless; giving loans to struggling entrepreneurs; visiting the sick and the prisoners; and providing food, money, clothing shelter, books, medicine, and other essentials to the needy. Wesley did not ask his Methodists to do things he himself never did, and it was unusual for a person of his social station to do such things for the poor. Wesley established free medical clinics in London, Newcastle, and Bristol. Wesley's Foundry Clinic was apparently one of the first free public medical clinics in London.

Wesley believed education to be pertinent not only to train children, but also to help uneducated adults. So it was that Wesley founded schools in many places, including Bristol, Newcastle, and at the Foundry. Most famously he founded the Kingswood School in 1748. Wesley also established a publishing system on behalf of the adults to provide cheap books or pamphlets to educate the poor on the knowledge of the world and the Christian faith. Unlike many preachers of his age and since, Wesley didn't just talk about doing works of charity, doing good works; he put his hand to the plow and did them, even if it involved huge burdens financial and otherwise.[1] Wesley believed that if we would but weary ourselves in well doing, the result would be our spiritual improvement in two ways: (1) we would do good, and (2) we wouldn't have time for sinning and mischief.

Near the end of his famous tract "On the Character of a Methodist" Wesley stresses:

> **As he has time, he "does good unto all men;" unto neighbors and strangers, friends and enemies: And that in every possible kind; not only to their bodies, by "feeding the hungry, clothing the naked, visiting those that are sick or in prison;" but much more does he labor to do good to their souls, as of the ability which God gives; to awaken those that sleep in death; to bring those who are awakened to the atoning blood, that, "being justified by faith, they may have peace with God;" and to provoke those who have peace with God to abound more in love and in good works. And he is willing to "spend and be spent herein," even "to be offered up on the sacrifice and service of their faith," so they may "all come unto the measure of the stature of the fullness of Christ."**

This is an expansion on Paul's statement that Christians should do good to all persons, and especially to the household of faith. Wesley believed not only that doing such things was helpful to others, and a good Christian witness to them, he also believed it affected one's own sanctification positively. Wesley would in no case be surprised to hear that the Catholic Church would consider a person like Mother Teresa for sainthood. The tree can be known by its fruit, and if the fruit is good, the tree must be as well.

CREATED IN CHRIST FOR GOOD WORKS: RETHINKING SPIRITUAL FORMATION

Paul in his encomium called "Ephesians" makes an interesting contrast between how initial salvation or justification is something we have "by grace through faith and not as a result of our works, lest anyone boast." *But if* we ask *not* how we were initially saved, but rather what we were saved for, Paul adds, "For we are what he has made us, created in Christ Jesus *for good works, which God prepared beforehand to be our way of life*" (Eph 2:8-10). A more literal translation would be: "For you have been saved by grace through faith, and this not from you, [but rather] the gift of God, not from works, lest anyone might have boasted. For you are his handiwork, created in Christ Jesus for good works, which God prepared beforehand in order that we might have lived in them." Let's break these verses down a bit.

Verse 8 picks up the parenthetical remark of verse 5b, which said we are saved by grace through faith. The question then becomes, what does the ***touto*** ("this") in verse 8b refer to—faith, or the whole salvation event? Probably the latter, but it is worth stressing that Paul is referring to salvation in the present tense; more specifically he is referring to initial salvation. The work of initial salvation, including the gift of faith, is all the work and gift of God to the believer; it is not our own doing or striving, though certainly believers must exercise that gift of faith and appropriate its benefits. God will not and does not have faith or exercise faith for us.

In verse 9 "works" refers to human efforts, not works of the Law. Paul will deal with the latter later in the discourse. Thus there is no reason for the believer to boast, as if he or she accomplished his or her own salvation. Rather, saved people are God's handiwork. And they have been saved to serve, created in Christ

Jesus for a specific purpose—to do good works. These works are done not to earn God's praise or favor but out of a grateful heart and obedient spirit, responding to the gift of salvation. Believers were not saved simply to revel in the benefits of the salvation experience. Rather God renovates a people so that they will do his will. God prepared this sort of result of salvation beforehand so that there was a way believers should live once they were saved, if they intended to do what God had in mind when he saved them.

One of the things that comes to light from this passage is that since initial salvation is a gift from God, we are called to stop worrying about our own spiritual condition, stop focusing on ourselves, and get on with the purpose for which God created us—doing good works for the benefit of others.

This notion that we were created for others, created for serving others, and created for doing good works on behalf of others is not a new theme here in Ephesians. Indeed, the creation story itself tells us that Eve was created for Adam, for it was not good for man to be alone. Human beings were created for relationship, which means they were not created to be self-conscious and self-centered. What the story of the Fall tells us is that Adam and Eve only became self-conscious, self-protective, and self-centered as a result of their sin. In fact, the very definition of sin is "the heart turned in upon itself" (*coeur in curvatus in se*).

It cannot be an accident that the heart of God's commandments to his people, the Great Commandment, urges us to love God with our whole heart and our neighbor likewise. *In other words, the Great Commandment tells us not to be self-focused but rather to focus on the Other and the others.* Spiritual formation, then, needs to be in accord with this fundamental mandate of God to humankind, a mandate that Christ himself reiterated. And so it is absolutely no surprise that when salvation is spoken of, we are told that it's time to get back to the basics of the great commandment—namely, loving others. Salvation has the specific purpose of making us Other and other-focused once again! We were saved to serve; saved to get over ourselves and love others; saved to do good works.

But what does it mean that God has prepared such things beforehand in order that we might live into and live in them? Once the habits or tempers or dispositions of the heart become other-focused, then there is to be an other-focused pattern of life for us to follow. I suspect that Paul has in mind not only the Great Commandment but also the various works of mercy that have been stressed in both the Old Testament and in the teaching of Jesus, which are regularly labeled "good deeds." God has not merely prepared for us golden opportunities to help others; he has already given us golden rules regarding what these works should look like. The phrase "that we might live in them" indicates not merely sporadic forays into good deeds, but rather living and breathing good works, making it a way of life. And we can say once more that one of the serendipitous side effects of living this way is one's own spiritual growth and sanctification.

It will be worthwhile to look at a different take on this same thing, offered by Jesus' own brother. What did James mean after all by "Faith without works is dead"? We will take the time to look in depth at the whole of James 2. First though, an initial quotation from someone who reflected long and hard on both James and Paul is in order, namely John Chrysostom, who has much to say about one of Wesley's favorite subjects and a means of grace—works of mercy.

Mercy is the highest art and the shield of those who practice it. It is the friend of God, standing always next to him and freely blessing whatever he wishes. It must not be despised by us. For in its purity it grants great liberty to those who respond to it in kind. It must be shown to those who have quarreled with us, as well as to those who have sinned against us, so great is its power. It breaks chains, dispels darkness, extinguishes fire, kills the worm and takes away the gnashing of teeth. By it the gates of heaven open with the greatest of ease. In short, mercy is a queen which makes humans like God. (Catena 13)

Sometimes the heritage of the Reformation is more of a burden than a blessing, especially when it comes to Martin Luther's defective opinions about the homily called "James." What we are dealing with in James 2:1–3:12 are supporting arguments for the theses already alluded to or enunciated in James 1. In these chapters James advises his audience that partiality is inconsistent with faith (2:1-13), that faith without works does not profit (2:14-26), and that not many should become teachers (3:1-12). James is concerned that partiality, dead orthodoxy, and too many attempts at authoritative teaching without first listening to the word may and probably do exist in some of the Jewish Christian congregations he is addressing, and he aims to nip the problems in the bud with various sorts of patterns of persuasion and dissuasion. Let's consider a fresh translation of James 2.

My brothers, don't keep the faith of our glorious Lord Jesus Christ in partiality. For if a man with a gold ring and luxurious clothes enters the meeting, but also a poor man in filthy rags [comes in], but you look at the luxurious clothes he is wearing and you say [to the former], "Be seated here in a good place," and to the poor man you say, "You stand here or sit at my feet," do you not make a distinction amongst yourselves and are judges [using] false standards of judgment?

Listen, my beloved brothers, has not God chosen the poor in the eyes of this world to be rich in faith and inheritors of the Kingdom which he promised those who love him? But you slight [dishonor] the poor. Is it not the rich who oppress you and with their own hand drag you into court? Are they blaspheming the good name, the name called over [given to] you? If, however [or indeed], you observe the supreme [or sovereign] law according to scripture "love your neighbor as yourself" you do well.

But if you show partiality you commit sin, being convicted by the law as a transgressor. For whoever keeps the whole law, but stumbles at one point, is answerable for [the breaking] of all of it. For he who said, "Do not commit adultery" also said, "Do

not murder." But if you do not commit adultery, but murder, you have become a transgressor of the law. So speak and so act as those who will be judged by the law of freedom. For judgment without mercy will be shown to those not having mercy. Mercy overrides [triumphs over] judgment!

Of what use is it, my brothers, if someone says they have faith, but cannot have works? Is that [sort of] faith able to save him? If a brother or sister exists with little [or no] clothes and lacking food for the day, but one of you says, "Go in peace [i.e., Good-bye] warm and feed yourself," and does not give them the bodily necessities, of what use is it? So even faith, if it has not works, is totally useless [dead] by itself. But if someone says, "You have faith and I have works." Show me your faith without works, and I will show you faith by my works. You believe God is one? You do well [Good for you]. Even the demons believe [that] and shudder. But you wish to know [for certain], O empty headed person, that faith without works is useless? Abraham, our Father, was he not vindicated by works, offering Isaac his son upon the altar? You see that faith cooperates with his works, and by his works faith was perfected, and the Scripture was fulfilled saying, "But Abraham believed and it was reckoned to him as righteousness, and he was called God's friend." You see then that a person's vindication is from works and not from faith alone. Similarly, even Rahab the whore, was she not justified by works, entertaining the messengers and sending them out another way? For as the body without [the] Spirit is dead, so also faith without works is dead.

The first section of the two major sections of chapter 2 (2:1-13 and 14-26) deals with the matter of showing partiality, especially vis-à-vis the rich and the poor. In the background of course is the idea that God is no respecter of persons, with the implication that neither should his people be. Our author is picking up earlier discussions in Jewish Wisdom literature that are against favoritism and that stress God's impartiality (see Sir 7:6-7 on the former and Sir 35:10-18 on the latter). James addresses his audience as "my brothers" once more, so we can be sure he considered them Christians. However, from James's point of view, they are Christians under construction and require instruction.

The issue is showing favoritism or partiality, and what he intends to prove is that partiality and faith in the glorious Lord Jesus are incompatible. That some Christians would exhibit both together is unacceptable and reprehensible for it amounts to a violation of the love commandment. An important point about this crucial thesis statement of this part of the argument is that the key phrase reads literally "keep/hold the faith of the Lord." Though this is regularly rendered "faith in the Lord," this is not exactly what James says, and if that was what he meant he could have used the prepositional phrase beginning with ***en***. This in turn may well suggest that Jesus is seen here as the exemplar of impartiality and that believers are to keep the "faith of the Lord" (i.e., his trustworthy and faithful ways) by modeling themselves on his behavior. In a stratified world of showing or giving face to one person or another who was thought to be of higher status or more honorable, James and Jesus both deconstructed this practice of "sucking up" to the well heeled.

It is significant that the phrase we find here, ***en prosopolempsias,*** which can be translated "with your acts of favoritism," involves a term that literally means "to receive face" and that is found at Leviticus 19:15 LXX, which says: "You shall not render an unjust judgment; you shall *not* [receive/give face] to the poor or defer to the great: with justice you shall judge your neighbor." This suggests of course that one must be impartial to all and not show any favoritism to the poor or the rich. The phrase suggests those who make judgments on the basis of "face"—that is, the outward appearance of someone—just as we might talk about the "face value" of something.

But is James suggesting, contra the text in Leviticus, that one *should* show partiality to or a preferential option for the poor? No, actually he is not. He is saying that one should not show favoritism to the rich, which is then unfair to the poor; nor should one slight the poor and so dishonor them. All persons should be treated fairly regardless of their socioeconomic status. Of course one can argue that since there is imbalance in a fallen world full of self-centered acquisitive persons that God is concerned about balancing the scales, about justice for all, and in a fallen world this may appear to be partiality for the poor. Divine and human advocacy for the poor is necessary just to overcome the inequities the poor experience. This I think is what James has in mind and is in accord with what Leviticus says about impartiality.

Verse 2 is more difficult and moves into a hypothetical or possible example of showing partiality. We know it is likely a hypothetical example because it is a conditional clause using ***ean*** plus the subjunctive and thus the author sees it as a "more probable future condition." A definite possibility, to be avoided, is in mind, but not something already plaguing the audience. Verses 2-4 provide us with the reason or causal basis for the exhortation that will establish its truth. Here we have a proof from example, with the punch line coming in verse 4, that proves the point—partiality and faith in Christ or faithfulness to the example of Christ are inconsistent because they make a person a partial judge of other persons, indeed of other Christians.

James here is likely speaking of a Christian worship assembly. If it was like Jewish worship in a small building or home, some might have had to stand and others sit. It is evident from later sources that visitors were allowed in and ushered to a spot, a duty deacons later had. It was Jewish custom to have special and honored places in the synagogue for distinguished people and benefactors (cf. Matt 23:6; Mark 12:30; Luke 11:43, 20, 46). It would not be at all surprising if Jewish Christians carried this custom over into their life in the church. Both the poor and the wealthy examples here are likely viewed as visitors since both are directed as to where to sit. Nothing is said in the telling of this tale about why the rich man and the poor man came into the assembly, and the partiality issue is raised not in regard to their behavior but rather in regard to the behavior of the one seating them, which implies a judgment on the Christian usher's part.

James, however, finds this behavior unacceptable. The contrast between the rich man and the poor man may be played up a bit, but the wearing of gold rings and fine clothes was, of course, widely practiced among the well-to-do Jews and Gentiles in first-century culture, and the description of the poor man as both in bad clothes and as being dirty may suggest he is a beggar. It is possible that the reference to a man with a gold ring is a reference to a person of equestrian rank—the rank signaled by the wearing of a gold ring—and thus a potential benefactor to the congregation. Verse 3 makes quite clear that the believer who is seating these visitors is judging them purely by appearances—which often leads to partiality. "The rich person is invited to sit rather than to stand, to proximity rather than to distance, to comfort or prestige rather than to discomfort and dishonor."[2] The verb here (***epiblepsete***) can have the sense of "look upon with favor" as is clearly the case in Luke 1:48 and 9:38, the other two uses of the term in the New Testament (cf. Pss 12:4; 24:16; 32:13; 68:17, all in the LXX). Notice as well that the verb is in the plural, suggesting this sort of favoritism involved more than one Christian usher or leader.

The problem is that these Christians who are welcoming the visitors are showing partiality, which is unacceptable regardless of what status these visitors have as far as believing or honor is concerned. When the visitors are with the believers they are considered part of the worshiping group. The partiality is happening in Christian worship, which is the last place it should happen since worship is supposed to be where God is perfectly glorified and people are treated as God treats them. Judging by appearances (vs. 3a) is judging by a false and all-too-human standard of judgment (vs. 4). It is probably right to hear echoes of the teaching of Jesus here in parables like those found in Luke 14:7-14 or Luke 16:19-31 where we have the dynamics of the dramatic contrast of rich and poor and how they are treated in this life. In the former parable we hear about places of honor at a gathering as well. *The point to be made for our purposes is that spiritual formation has as much to do with how we treat others in the small things of life as it has to do with specific spiritual exercises or disciplines.*

Verse 5 begins another thought and we have here a statement about the poor followed by two about the rich. Partiality to the rich is bad for the poor and makes no sense because the rich are oppressors of Christians. The three questions serve as a way of amplifying the point that partiality is inconsistent with Christian faith, with the most disturbing question left for last as a climax. The idea of God showing special concern for the poor is, of course, well known from the Old Testament (cf. Deut 16:3; 26:7). Jesus, too, in Luke 6:20 picks up the idea of the election of the poor, and we have similar thoughts from Paul (1 Cor 1:27-29—God chose the lowly things of this earth). Verse 5 speaks of the poor, who are poor from the world's point of view but rich in what really matters—faith. It also speaks of what comes through faith—the status of being inheritors of the Kingdom.

It does not follow from this, either, that James "romanticizes" poverty, and even more to the point, by "poor" James really means economically poor, not merely "poor in spirit." In fact he will suggest that spiritually these folk are far from poor—indeed they are rich. ***Plousious*** ("riches") refers to their being rich in the realm of faith. It is not implied that they had more or more abundant faith in comparison to others—no comparison is made. It is quite clear that the Kingdom mentioned here is viewed as being in the future; it is what God has promised to those who love him, a promise not yet fulfilled. The poverty spoken of is both physical and spiritual, as is the wealth, but no one person in the contrasting example embodies both kinds of wealth or poverty. The poor in question are believers; they may be rich in faith, but this does not give permission for other Christians to treat their physical poverty as if it did not matter.

Alfred Plummer rightly urges:

He does not say or imply that the poor man is promised salvation on account of his poverty, or that his poverty is in any way meritorious. . . . He is spared the peril of trusting in riches, which is so terrible a snare to the wealthy. He has greater opportunities

of the virtues which make man Christ-like, and fewer occasions of falling into those sins which separate him most fatally from Christ. *But opportunities are not virtues, and poverty is not salvation.*[3]

Notice as well that the poor as described here are said to be heirs of the Kingdom.

In verse 6, ***etimasate*** means "dishonor," to show disrespect, to those whom God has especially showered favor upon. As we have seen, Paul shares a similar view about shaming those who have nothing, and the social context that presupposes disunity and favoritism in the assembly is also similar (see 1 Cor 11:22). This is a very unwise course of action and verse 12 indicates the perpetrators are accountable for such actions on Judgment Day. The standard of judgment is the "law of liberty"—that is, the new law of Christ that combines something old and something new. Playing up to the rich doesn't make sense on another score either. Generally speaking, it's the rich who are oppressing believers and having them hauled off to court. James may have some particular incident in mind, but the remarks seem to be generalizations here.

Thus, we have irony here: the Church is oppressing that one poor fellow who came in, while the rich oppress "you"—that is, the Church as a collective whole. What sense then does that behavior make considering God's word and standards? asks James. In verse 7, the rich are labeled "blasphemers"—blaspheming Jesus' good name—perhaps because they profess to be pious but their deeds are impious. And if we didn't get the point already from verse 1 that James believes Jesus embodies the glorious presence and nature of God, this verse makes it clear.

The drift of the argument here is that even if you keep all the (other) commandments of the Law but by showing partiality to the rich neglect the one commandment to love your neighbor (the poor brother), then you are in fact guilty under the whole Law. Thus, if we take into consideration this continuation of the argument, it would appear that the commandment of Leviticus 19:18 is regarded as one among many that the faithful Christian is to keep.

I would suggest that a more careful scrutiny of what Paul (see Gal 5:14) and James say about the Law as it applies to Christians shows that they in fact have similar views on this subject. Verse 8 makes evident that perhaps the most serious problem with showing favoritism is that it is a blatant violation of the great love commandment to love neighbor as self.

Verse 9 comes out and makes the point in as drastic a fashion as possible—playing favorites is not only unacceptable to James; it is a sin against God, one for which one will be convicted under the Law as a transgressor. To show partiality is to fail to love the poor neighbor, and to fail to do this is to violate the whole Law. You don't have to violate all the commandments to be a lawbreaker. But the conceptual idea here is this: the Law is "one" because God, who is One, gave it to believers. It is his word. James here is offering a short form of a syllogism, an enthymeme that requires that one supply the missing premise, in this case the minor premise. In full form it would look something like the following:

Major premise—Whoever keeps the whole Law but fails in one point

Minor premise—Showing partiality is a failure to keep a part of the Law.

Conclusion (vs. 9)—If you show partiality you are a transgressor of the whole law.

Verse 11 provides us with a second enthymeme, which makes the same point a slightly different way, as follows:

Major premise—God, who said, "Don't commit adultery," also said, "Don't kill."

Minor Premise—If you break any individual command you break the Law, since they are all from one source.

Conclusion—If you don't commit adultery but do kill, you have still become a transgressor of the whole Law.

Notice that verse 11 has the phrase "he who said," which indicates that the author saw the Law as God's very words—God spoke it. There is no higher endorsement for the Law. Paul also expresses the unity of the Law in Galatians 5:3, as does Jesus in Matthew 5:18-19 and 23:23. Being under the Law obligates one to obey the whole Law (Rom 2:13). To draw an analogy, it is like one who drops a single drop of food coloring in a glass of water—all the water is affected. One sin taints the whole character, and one sin means *the* Law, not just *a* law, has been broken. The remedy is not stated here but it is obviously not to ignore the Law. Was there perhaps a common Christian ethical code grounded in the Old Testament, the teaching of Jesus, and some Christian instructions from the apostles that both James and Paul knew and were adhering to? For sure, this code, if it existed, did not just involve the Mosaic Law as reinterpreted by Jesus, not least because Jesus added his own imperatives, some of which were at variance with what the Mosaic covenant demanded.

Verses 12-13 draw this first elaboration of an argument to a conclusion in the form of an epicheireme, which is a completely stated argument where the audience need not supply the minor premise.

Major Premise—For judgment without mercy is shown to one who has no mercy.

Minor Premise—Yet mercy triumphs over judgment.

Conclusion—Therefore speak and act as though you will be judged under the law of liberty.

Verse 13 may draw on the teaching of Jesus in the Sermon on the Mount again, in particular Matthew 5:7, "Blessed are the merciful, for they will receive mercy," and Matthew 6:12,

"Forgive us our debts as we forgive ..." James, however, turns the beatitude into its converse to make his point. The theme of mercy is common in Wisdom literature (see Sir 27:30–28:7).

The life the believer lives after conversion indeed affects his or her status before God at the Last Judgment. Paul, too, knows of the idea of salvation by faith, coupled with a judgment of the believer's deeds (cf. 2 Cor 5:10). There also apparently comes a point where the disjunction of profession and practice is such that one's salvation is in jeopardy—the good tree will produce good fruit, and if it does not, it may be judged to be not a good tree after all, no matter what label is put on it. Judgment without mercy means severe, unrestrained judgment—the full wrath of God. Verse 13b may involve the quoting of a proverb meant to give hope: "Mercy triumphs over, or overrides, judgment." God, of course, looks on human hearts as well as on human lives. In fact, we could render this maxim: "Mercy boasts over judgment," or as we might say, "Mercy has the bragging rights over judgment" in God's way of viewing things. God expects complete loyalty and obedience. Obviously there are times when humans are unable to do what they intend to do, whether because something internal or external prevents it in a fallen world or because we are dealing with fallen people. Those who do strive to do God's will and still fall short have both repentance and the mercy of God to fall back on; otherwise no one will stand on the Judgment Day (see 1 Cor 3:13-14). But more than this, James would have us know that if believers are merciful instead of judgmental they are mirroring the character of God and fulfilling an essential requirement of the royal Law. We must now turn to James 2:14-26.

James 2:14-26 can be called the storm center of this sermon, or certainly the portion that has drawn the most attention and most fire, and not just from Luther. That it has been troublesome in Protestant circles more than in Catholic is of course because of the vital aspect of justification by faith alone, in Protestant thinking.

We must not see James 2:14-26 as a direct response to what

we find in Galatians (or Romans, for that matter). Both Abraham and Rahab were favorite topics of discussion when it came to the matter of faith and works in early Judaism. The discussions in Wisdom of Solomon 10:5, Sirach 44:20, and 1 Maccabees 2:52 should all be consulted, and we might mention Hebrews 11:17 and Matthew 1:5 from the Christian writings as well. James's discussion of Abraham is closer to the earlier Jewish one than to the later Pauline one for the good reason that not only does James focus on the binding of Isaac story; he also stresses that Abraham is an example of faith that manifests itself in action, in obedience to God. James is pursuing the same line of discourse that we find in Matthew 12:37—a person is vindicated, or even "justified" or accounted righteous, as a result of what he or she has done or said. This is a different matter than the discussion of the basis of initial justification or salvation. Clearly, James is more likely drawing on the earlier Jewish discussion of these figures of faith than on the later Pauline one. And once and for all we must stress that when Paul speaks of works of the Mosaic Law, in fulfillment of the Mosaic covenant, he is talking about something very different from James's discussion of works that come forth from and express Christian faith. James and Paul do not mean the same thing when they speak of "works."

All of this, however, does not rule out the possibility that James is dealing with some issues that Jewish Christians raised from what they heard, and perhaps misunderstood, about the teaching of Paul in its early stages in the early 50s. At that time there were in fact Judaizers from Jerusalem going behind Paul in Antioch, Galatia, and perhaps elsewhere trying to add observance of the Mosaic covenant to the Pauline gospel, even for Gentile Christians.

It may also be said that both James and Paul were concerned about what later came to be called "dead orthodoxy"—faith without its living expression in good works. Whereas it may be true that "'faith without works' spares individuals the embarrassment of radical disruptions in their lives and relationships,"[4] the truth is that both Paul and James were all about radical disruptions in the lifestyles people had previously been accustomed to. James here is busy deconstructing various prevailing social customs and habits and offering up in sacrifice various sacred cows, but Paul did the same thing in his own way. We may assume Paul and James knew something of each other's "gospel" both from personal conversation and hearsay but not from reading each other's letters.

It is important for us to note that we do indeed have connections between the first and second half of James 2. Both verses 1-13 and verses 14-26 use the diatribe style, choosing some polemical examples to punctuate the points being made, and the underlying problem of mistreatment of the poor believers surfaces in both parts of the chapter as well. In both sections faith and works are seen as inevitably and intimately connected, and in both sections impartiality is seen as a hallmark of real faith. *The implications of this for our spiritual formation is that spiritual formation, if it is to be genuinely Christian, must involve both faith and good works, works of piety and charity.*

Here we have the diatribe form—including debate with a straw man, **tis** ("someone"), that James sets up and refutes—but in the form of a deliberative Jewish homily with careful parallelism in two stanzas, each with two parts:

Part 1—verses 14-17, 18-20

Part 2—verses 21-24, 25-26

James thinks that at least some of his Jewish Christian audience know well these Old Testament stories and their context, if not also the way they were interpreted in Jewish circles. It would be hard to overestimate how strongly the issue of faith and works and salvation is stressed here. Some nine of the twenty uses of the term ***pistis*** ("faith") in James occur in this passage, as do twelve of the fifteen uses of the term ***ergos*** ("work") and one of the five uses of the verb ***sōdzō*** ("save"). In other words, twenty-two of the words in this brief passage (217 total Greek words) are these three words, or some 12 percent of the passage.

James begins in verse 14 by asking his Christian audience whether a faith without works is useful or useless. The nature of the conditional sentence here shows that he thinks this question might well arise. The second remark is also a question: "Is your faith able to save you?" This is a rhetorical question to which the answer implied is no—if by faith is meant the type of faith that James is attacking. James has here broadened the previous discussion to the more expansive topic of faith and works. Crucial to understanding this verse is recognizing the use of the anaphoric definite article before the word *faith* here. The question should be translated, "Can that [sort of] faith save him?"

James is following the rhetorical advice that suggests one should stick with, and reiterate, one's strongest point the longest (see *Herr.* 4.45.58) precisely because all of the rest of the argument rests on this crucial point about the necessary connection between living faith and good works. Notice that the discussion here has moved on from talking about visitors to the assembly of faith, to "brothers and sisters." Christian treatment of fellow Christians is at issue here.

There follows a little parable in verses 15-16, also begun by ***ean,*** indicating a condition that is future but probable. Certainly there were plenty of destitute Christians in the first century needing aid from the community. We see a scantily clad and hungry brother or sister. ***Gymnoi*** need not imply naked, but rather underclothed or poorly clothed as opposed to unclothed. This person is so indigent he does not even have enough food for today. The response in verse 16 is meant to seem shaky and shallow. It sounds pleasant enough, even concerned in a superficial way—"Hope you are well fed and clothed." But in fact this is an anti-Christian and unloving response that is unacceptable. Beneath the surface is the idea that deeds of mercy are not an option but an obligation for those who profess and have real faith.

"Go in peace" is what the person says to the indigent man. In fact this was a stereotyped parting formula and often meant no more than "good-bye," though it could have the fuller sense of "blessings" (cf. Gen 15:15; Exod 4:18; Judg 16:6; 1 Sam 20:42;

Mark 5:34; Luke 7:50). This seems more likely here. It appears also that we should translate ***thermainesthe kai chortazesthe*** in verse 16 as middles, not passives; in which case it means "warm yourself" and "feed yourself," not "be warmed" and "be filled," as a sort of wish. If this is right then the person in question is being very callous indeed. He is juxtaposing warm words with cold deeds. He, like so many others since, is saying in effect, "Pull yourself up by your bootstraps," or, "Do it yourself." Quite clearly, what was being asked for was not some luxury item but rather the necessities of the body—clothing and daily bread; but even so, the person in question did not even give these. As Luke Timothy Johnson says, "It is not the form of the statement [depart in peace], but its functioning as a religious cover for the failure to act."[5] *Perhaps the worst thing that can happen, if we are talking about spiritual formation, is the overspiritualizing of the commands of the Lord in order to avoid acting on their obvious social sense. Christ is not just interested in the poor in spirit; he is interested in our serving and helping the physically poor, and that is part of our spiritual formation.*

To this behavior James rejoins: "If you say you have faith and fail to help, of what use is it? What good does it do you or anyone else?" Possibly, in verse 17, we should translate ***kai*** as "even" and read, "So [or in the same way] *even* faith, if it does not have works, is dead by itself." James has thus made two key points: (1) living faith necessarily entails good deeds, and (2) faith and works are so integrally related that faith by itself is useless or dead, unless coupled with works. Or as Peter Davids summarizes well:

For James, then, there is no such thing as a true and living faith which does not produce works, for the only true faith is a "faith working through love" (Gal. 5:6). Works are not an "added extra" any more than breath is an "added extra" to a living body. The so-called faith which fails to produce works (the works to be produced are charity, not the "works of the law" such as circumcision against which Paul inveighs) is simply not "saving faith."[6]

Throughout verses 18-20 the opponent starts the debate and the "you" is James or his ally. James has his imaginary opponent accuse him of being a "faith without works" person, whereas the speaker takes the supposedly higher ground of touting his works. The proper rhetorical order of protocol is that he or she who speaks first in such a debate should first state his or her own proofs and only then rebut the arguments of the opponent (see Aristotle, *Rhet.* 3.17.1418b.14). This is what happens here, and rebuttal only comes after the opponent has stated his view in verse 18a. But in fact the opponent is taking a reactionary and defensive posture here—"I have works, while you have faith"—thereby apparently placing himself in the positive category as a person of Jewish orthopraxy (correct action), while James has only orthodoxy (mere faith) on his side. But James's position is that the two things cannot and must not be divorced, while the opponent suggests they can be. Thus, he accuses James of mere faith, and so of hypocrisy in effect. The examples James will cite prove the point that *real faith works,* the two go together. Paul thought the same and this is the gist of his phrase "the obedience of faith"—that is, the obedience that necessarily flows forth from real faith (Rom 1).

Perhaps here James envisions two believers hypothetically debating with each other. And then he interjects a rebuttal at verse 18b. The problem here is very clear. This "person" is still separating faith and works, as if they could be separate gifts of different Christians. The argument would be, "Works are all right, but that's not my gift" (or vice versa). To this sort of dichotomizing James responds, "Show me a person with faith but without works, and I'll show you my faith by my works." The point here for our discussion of spiritual formation is that it necessarily involves social holiness—deeds of charity and mercy, as Wesley would say. You cannot be a spiritually whole or well person in the New Testament sense and not care about and do something about the lot of your fellow human beings.

To the believer who prides himself on right belief (and clearly in verses 18 and 19 faith means something else than what it usually means for James—not trust in or active dependence on God, but rather mere belief that God exists), James says, "So you say you believe God is one. Good for you; however, so do demons and they are shuddering in their belief—fearing the wrath of God to come. A lot of good that faith did them." The sarcasm in verse 19 is hard to miss. The demons are the ultimate example of faith divorced from praxis, or right confession from right living. Wesley often preached on this very text, using it to illustrate the difference between the almost and altogether Christian.

Here James is stressing essential matters and probably he is implying, "You believe in the unity of God; you ought also to believe and practice the unity of faith and works." The reference to the demons existing and believing is also characteristic of what we find in the Gospels (cf. Mark 1:24; 5:7). The demons were perfectly orthodox and perfectly lost.

In verse 20 James becomes even more sarcastic: "So you want evidence, O empty headed one (cf. Rom 2:1; 9:20), that faith without works is useless/without profit (***argos***); let's turn to the Scriptures." Another way of translating ***argos*** here would be "workless"—faith without works is workless, or as I would prefer to put it, *faith without works won't work! Wesley would have said deeds of piety without deeds of charity are not adequate for spiritual formation*. The two examples from Scripture that James cites were very standard examples of true faith among the Jews. He is choosing the most stellar example, Abraham, and in some ways the most scandalous example, Rahab the harlot.

James knows how much Abraham was idolized in the Jewish tradition. For example, Jubilees 23:10 says, "Abraham was perfect in all his deeds with the LORD, and well-pleasing in righteousness all the days of his life." Sirach 44:19 says, "No one has been found like him in glory." More important of course is 1 Maccabees 2:51-52, which says Abraham was reckoned righteous not on the basis of his faith but as result of passing the test and remaining faithful and obedient when he was asked to sacrifice his son. Clearly James does not push his use of the exemplary Abraham to these extremes, but he stands in the tradition of seeing Abraham as the *exemplum par excellence*. It is of more than passing interest that the use made of Genesis 22 here is closely similar to the use made in Hebrews 11:17-19, which says that it was by faith that Abraham, when tested, brought forth his son Isaac and offered him. This may suggest that there were some standard interpretations of the key Old Testament figures that circulated in Jewish Christian circles.

James refers to two separate texts in Genesis—the promise in 15:6 and the story about the offering of Isaac in 22:12-16. As is frequent in midrashic exegesis, the two texts are combined. James is stressing that it was on the basis of Abraham's obedient offering of Isaac—that is, his deed of obedience—that he was ***edikaiōthē***, justified or vindicated. Principally, he is thinking of Genesis 22:16 where God promises his blessing as a result of Abraham having done what he did. This may be compared to the word of blessing in Genesis 15:6. In verse 22 the verb ***synergei*** ("working with") should be seen as an iterative imperfect, which implies that faith was working along with works at the same time side by side, or put another way it implies these two things coexisted in Abraham's life over a period of time. So James can go on to say, "You see that faith cooperates with his works, and by works his faith was perfected. The two go together hand in hand, works perfecting faith, which is by implication imperfect without it." The concept of righteousness here at least in verse 21 seems to be Jewish: not counted righteous or considered righteous but declared to *be* righteous—that is, "*is* righteous by means of deeds." Abraham's belief was belief in action.

The point of James's argument, then, has nothing to do with a forensic declaration of justification at someone's conversion; the argument is simply that Abraham did have faith, which here, unlike other places in James, means monotheistic belief. For this, Abraham was famous in Jewish tradition; but he also had deeds flowing from that faith. Thus, James is not dealing with works of the Law as a means to become saved or as an entrance requirement. Notice he never speaks of "works of the Law." He is dealing with the conduct of those who already believe. He is talking about the perfection of faith in its working out through good works. "Work out your salvation with fear and trembling" was how Paul put it. Or better, in Galatians 5:6 Paul speaks of faith working itself out through love, whereas James speaks of faith coming to mature expression or its perfect end or goal in works. These two ideas are closely similar.

This still leaves us with the difficulty of verse 24, a statement Paul would never have made. However, if, as we should, we take the vindication in verse 24 as referring to that final verdict of God on one's deeds and life work, then even Paul can be said to have agreed. Even he speaks of a final justification or vindication that is dependent on what believers do in the interim (cf. Gal 5:5 and what follows it). It is this final vindication or acquittal in view here. Paul would agree that one cannot be righteous on that last day without there having been some good deeds between the new birth and that last day in the spiritual pilgrimage. Thus verse 24b only apparently contradicts Paul, not least because not even Paul thought faith alone kept one in the Kingdom, though it did get one into it.

As a secondary and more daring example, which is intended to illustrate the same ideas (***homoios***—"similarly"—makes this clear), Rahab entertained the Hebrew spies and chucked them out (hence ***ekbalousa***—literally "cast out") the back window when the enemy approached. The point here is, if everyone from Abraham to Rahab received final vindication because of faith *and* works, so shall the followers of Jesus. Rahab's faith is not mentioned, but it was widely held to by Jews. We may also think that the rhetorical strategy here involves forestalling the objection "But I am not a towering figure of faith like Abraham," to which the proper reply is, "At least you could follow the example set by Rahab!" The last example then removes all excuses for doing nothing and shames the audience into action. Finally, one can also suggest that since both Abraham and Rahab are examples of those who exercised faith and hospitality, which contrasts nicely with the first example in this section where no hospitality is shown to the poor, this may in part explain why these two historical examples are cited here. *Wesley insisted that hospitality was an important part of spiritual formation.*

James is not dealing at all with the question, On what basis do Gentiles get to enter the community of faith? But rather, What is the nature of the faith, of true Christianity? Does it necessarily entail deeds of mercy? It is of course possible that James got wind of some sort of perverted or garbled Pauline summary that his audience had heard, but even this is not a necessary assumption. Jews were fascinated with Genesis 22 and the story of Abraham, and both James and Paul drawing on the useful examples of faith when joined with works explains much of the common terminology; but alone, faith is just dead, totally useless. *Dead orthodoxy has absolutely no power to save and may in fact even hinder the person from coming to living faith, a faith enlivened by works of charity (i.e., deeds of love). Neither can spiritual formation without works of charity and mercy be seen as valid and valuable, or comprehensive spiritual formation. We must beware of overspiritualizing spiritual formation*!

We have labored for a while in the vineyard of James to understand better the relationship of faith and works because it has enormous implications for the discussion of spiritual formation, some of which we must now enumerate. Just as faith without works is dead, so spiritual formation that consists purely in works of piety without any works of mercy is also in grave danger of being dead, or at least is an orientation too narrowly focused on an individual's private attempts at spiritual improvement. James is absolutely devastating in his critique of hypocritical piety that ignores the needs of the poor and does nothing to help them.

Let's close this section with a story. It was pouring cats, dogs, and frogs in Charlotte, North Carolina, and I was at a gas station filling up our car. I happened to glance up to the corner of the two busy intersections where this gas station stood. There, standing on the corner, absolutely soaked to the bone, was a hooded man with one of those signs. You know the kind I mean. It said, "Homeless. Please Help. God Bless." I quickly looked in my wallet and found what cash I had. While the gas was autofilling my tank I ran through the rain to this poor soul and gave him what I had. He looked up and a smile cracked his wrinkled face. He said, "Oh thank you so much Sir, and may God bless you." The fact is, God had just blessed me in that very moment. I saw the face of Jesus, and he smiled at me in the rain. Nothing I did the rest of the day mattered as much as that moment.

IN SUM

Spiritual formation in the biblical and Wesleyan tradition has and wants nothing to do with the divorcing of faith from good works or spirituality from ethics or spiritual formation from sanctification. Indeed, spiritual formation in the biblical and Wesleyan tradition suggests that focus on the Other and the others has as its by-product growth in grace and progress toward spiritual maturity. Spiritual formation in the biblical and Wesleyan tradition is outwardly not inwardly focused, and it certainly does not believe that the dark night of the soul is a necessary or good part of proper Christian spiritual formation.[7]

Spiritual formation in the biblical and Wesleyan tradition believes that as we imitate Christ and obey his teachings we are conformed to his image, and that is spiritual formation. Spiritual formation is what happens to us when we become self-forgetful and concentrate of getting on with what we were created in Christ Jesus for—good works. Spiritual formation in the biblical and Wesleyan tradition certainly values spiritual disciplines like fasting or practicing the lectio divina, but it is not in the main a reiteration of medieval monastic piety. It is much more Jewish and deed-centered than that.

For one thing, the primary emphasis must be on formation in the collective context of the body of Christ—the individual is formed in and with the group. For another thing, even when prayer as a spiritually formative practice is the subject, corporate prayer, congregation prayer, and shared prayer as well as private and extemporaneous prayer are emphasized. It is never just about going into one's prayer closet and praying. It is never just about one's private devotional time, though both of those things are good and necessary for spiritual formation. Nowhere is this clearer than in Wesley's sermon "The Means of Grace" where he emphasizes not merely the importance of prayer and searching the Scriptures, but also taking Communion constantly with the body of Christ.

Spiritual formation in the biblical and Wesleyan tradition in fact starts with a different view of God and salvation than in the Reformed tradition. In both the Bible and in the Wesleyan tradition, life is not viewed as essentially predetermined by God, and prayer is not simply about getting in touch with what God has already decided about things from before the foundation of the universe. To the contrary, prayer is a means of grace God uses to bless others, and we have the privilege of participating in the enacting of God's will on earth, both freely and without predetermination. Prayer looks different when prayer matters to someone else's salvation or healing or the like. Doubtless, God could have predetermined everything in advance, but instead he chose to use his people as his coworkers in saving and healing the world.

The biblical and Wesleyan tradition also stresses that spiritual formation is a part of sanctification, a part of working out our salvation, and what we do after conversion affects that process of maturation and moving on toward perfection, by which is meant mirroring the full image of Christ, having a heart completely filled with love for God and neighbor. Spiritual formation, then, also has to do not only with theology but ethics as well.[8] It cannot endorse false gospels like the health-and-wealth gospel, which distorts the truth about what God wants for us. He blesses us to be a blessing to others, not to revel in conspicuous consumption and self-centered materialism.

It is my hope that this little study will at least help those in the Methodist orbit and tradition do a rethink about how we have been thinking about and doing spiritual formation. The Bible and our tradition urge us to do so. May God help us see things more clearly, practice our faith more accurately, obey God more completely, use all the means of grace more frequently, and so go on to perfection, as the Bible and Mr. Wesley urged us to do.

Questions for Reflection

1. How do you and your church minister to the poor? What ministries do you have in place? Are more needed?
2. Most people do not tithe (give 10 percent), but give only about 2.3 percent of their income for works of charity and mercy. What percentage do you give?
3. Make a list of places that your church supports through its giving. These might include schools, missionaries, hospitals, food pantries, shelters, job creation programs, natural disaster-relief, and so forth. These might be local, national, and/or international. What works of mercy and charity does your denomination support?
4. Wesley was perfectly clear that spiritual formation could come through suffering, through persecution, and through becoming poor, as Jesus was. In what ways have your sufferings and hardships shaped you spiritually?
5. Share a time when you generously gave of your time, gifts, and talent.
6. Why does what a person does speak louder than what that person says?
7. Faith and works strengthen each other and cannot be separated in a person's life. How might doing more acts of mercy and charity make you a stronger Christian? How might these acts strengthen your church?
8. Have you experienced "warm words with cold deeds"? Or has anyone ever expected you to "pull yourself up by your bootstraps" or "do it yourself"? Share what happened. What is the line between encouraging people to do it themselves and helping them do it. Give some examples.

AFTER WORDS: WHAT DOES A NORMAL CHRISTIAN LIFE ENTAIL?

In saying we believe God will raise our dead bodies to new bodies, we are saying that we believe in the resurrection of persons with recognizable personalities. . . . The Jesus movement was a corporate social movement; not a conglomeration of religiously inclined individuals. —Will Willimon[1]

Christians today, including Wesleyan ones, are busy people. Especially considering the way the world economy has been going, Christians are finding they have to work more and more just to survive and put food on the table, clothing on their children, and a roof over their heads. The temptation, and the danger, is to neglect everything else other than work and rest in such a situation. This is certainly a mistake, but an understandable one. How is it even possible that there are enough hours in a day to also be concerned about one's spiritual growth, one's spiritual formation?

The good news is as follows: much of the essential spiritual formation every Christian needs can be obtained simply through being faithful attenders of church, where indeed God's people pray together, search the Scriptures together, and share Communion together. This is the primary context for our spiritual formation according to the Bible and to Wesley as well. To this should be added private prayer and time in the word as well as family prayer and time in the word, as time and opportunity present themselves. Reading good Christian books as time allows is also good, of course. And once in a while going on a retreat is an excellent idea.

Unless a person is in some sort of spiritual crisis, it's not necessary to have a spiritual advisor or to practice a sort of extreme asceticism that vitiates one's ability to function in one's life work and so on. Spiritual formation in the biblical and Wesleyan mode does not envision us becoming so heavenly minded that we are no earthly good. It does not require that we all become some sort of spiritual athletes constantly focusing on our own spirituality. Remember biblical spirituality is Other and other-directed, not self-centered. It is not a human self-help program. It is grace that transforms and heals us and helps us grow in Christ. Works of piety and charity as discussed previously are more than enough for us to focus on in order to become what we admire—Jesus Christ himself. And in fact one of the best ways to do that is get lost in serving and loving others as an expression of our love for God.

Wholeheartedly loving God and neighbor is not merely enough of a spiritual and ethical orientation for a normal Christian life; it's also what Wesley meant when he talked about going on to perfection and imitating Christ. It's not a vision of life for monks alone. It's a vision all Christians great and small can practice without giving up their day jobs or abandoning their families or seeking out a spiritual guru or too regularly retreating into some cloister to get away from the world. After all, Christians are called to be in the world, while not being of it. As Paul promised, if Christ and his Spirit are in our lives, and their presence is in the body of Christ, then the saying is true—while outwardly we are wasting away, inwardly we are being renewed every single day. Greater is he who is in our midst than any of those things in the world that drag us down. The future is as bright as the promises of God, and that includes the future of our spiritual growth.

May God help us move away from spiritual formation models that divorce spirituality from theology, ethics, and social holiness.

May God help us leave behind self-centered, overly self-focused models of spiritual formation. May God help us understand that spiritual formation primarily takes place in the context and in the life of the body of Christ. It's not about our going on a lonely spiritual quest to become spiritual supermen or superwomen. Spiritual formation is of course a deeply personal matter; but it is never a private matter, for our God is a public God who lives in the community of the Trinity, and if we would mirror the divine life, we must live in the community of his body, not isolate ourselves from it.

If these reflections on spiritual formation in the biblical and Wesleyan way have stirred up minds into active thought, so that we may begin to consciously take stock of whether we are being spiritually formed in good and godly ways, and then we act on what we learn after the personal inventory, then I am content. Bear in mind what it takes to hear from Jesus at the end of days: "Well done good and faithful servant" or "Inherit the Kingdom" (Matt 25:31-46). It requires a living faith that works, doing works of piety and charity. This is what not only John Wesley said; it is what Jesus and James and Paul said as well. And the testimony of those four witnesses is true, for there is no higher commandment than loving God with all that we are and all that we have, and likewise loving our neighbors in ways that help and heal and save. This is not merely spiritual formation; it is sanctification. And it is not merely sanctification; it is the way we may all "go on to perfection" being conformed to the image of our Savior, Jesus Christ.

Questions for Reflection

1. What kind of witness are you for Jesus in your daily living?
2. Where are you in your spiritual journey? What are you doing well? Where do you need help?
3. What are the ways that your church can help its members live more like Jesus?
4. Who do you know that lives a spiritually fulfilling life?

5. Can Jesus say to you and to your church, "Well done good and faithful servant"?
6. Make a plan and commit to following Jesus more closely and to loving him and all God's people more fully, especially those closest to you.

Notes

1. Loving and Worshiping God Wholeheartedly

1. All quotations from the works of John Wesley are from the Jackson edition, which is in the public domain and readily available in various places online. What I have done is simply contemporized the speech a bit and Americanized it (e.g., dropping the "u" from "labour").

2. *The United Methodist Hymnal* (Nashville: The United Methodist Publishing House, 1989), vii.

3. For more on this topic see my book *Making a Meal of It: Rethinking the Theology of the Last Supper* (Waco, TX: Baylor University Press, 2007).

2. The Root of Spiritual Formation: Conversion

1. William H. Willimon, *Why Jesus?* (Nashville: Abingdon Press, 2010), 83.

3. The Imitation of Christ—No, Really!

1. Edgardo A. Colón-Emeric, *Wesley, Aquinas, and Christian Perfection: An Ecumenical Dialogue* (Waco, TX: Baylor University Press, 2009), 57.

2. Sometimes at this juncture someone will ask, "But what about Jesus knowing what was in the hearts of other human beings? Surely, that is Jesus' divine mind, a mind we don't have." Actually, if you look closer at such texts, you discover that Jesus gained this insight through being perfectly in tune with the Spirit. It is the Spirit that revealed

these things to him, just as is depicted of Paul and others in Acts and elsewhere.

3. See the appendix to my *Jesus and Money: A Guide for Times of Financial Crisis* (Grand Rapids: Brazos Press, 2010), where the text of that sermon is quoted in full and discussed.

4. Salvation and Spiritual Formation

1. William H. Willimon, *Why Jesus?* (Nashville: Abingdon Press, 2010), 39–40.

2. Dean Flemming, *Philippians: A Commentary in the Wesleyan Tradition* (Kansas City, MO: Beacon Hill Press, 2009), 130.

3. Judaizers were Jewish Christians who insisted that Gentile converts to Christianity be circumcised and obey the laws of Moses—that is, to become a Christian, a Gentile had to first convert to Judaism. Paul and Simon Peter opposed this.

5. The Fruit of Spiritual Formation

1. William H. Willimon, *Why Jesus?* (Nashville: Abingdon Press, 2010), 92–95, excerpts.

2. Private correspondence, June 29, 2011.

3. For a detailed discussion of this passage see my *Grace in Galatia* (Grand Rapids: Eerdmans, 1998), 402–5.

6. The Believer and the Means of Grace

1. William H. Willimon, *Why Jesus?* (Nashville: Abingdon Press, 2010), 6.

2. *Imminent Domain: The Story of the Kingdom of God and Its Celebration* (Grand Rapids: Eerdmans, 2009).

3. See my *Jesus and Money: A Guide for Times of Financial Crisis* (Grand Rapids: Brazos Press, 2010).

7. Spiritual Formation and Searching the Scripture

1. William H. Willimon, *Why Jesus?* (Nashville: Abingdon Press, 2010), 116.

2. For a much fuller form of this discussion see my *The Living Word of God: Rethinking the Theology of the Bible* (Waco, TX: Baylor University Press, 2007).

3. Nor is it likely that the word *writings* in the previous verse refers to both the OT and the Gospel message, which at this stage was not yet a written Gospel in all likelihood. "Sacred Writings" is simply a collective noun for the works we call the Old Testament.

8. The Lord's Supper as Spiritual Formation

1. One can read a good deal more on both these subjects in my *Making a Meal of It: Rethinking the Theology of the Lord's Supper (*Waco, TX: Baylor University Press, 2007), and my *Troubled Waters: Rethinking the Theology of Baptism* (Waco, TX: Baylor University Press, 2007).

9. Works of Charity as Spiritual Formation

1. There is a fine article by Ryan Snider at http://www.lagrange.edu/resources/pdf/citations08/WorksofMercy.pdf where he shows at some length not only what constituted Wesley's works of charity, but also the way Wesley viewed their relationship with sanctification. Snider concludes, "This change of attitude toward works of mercy and the realization of its vital role in sanctification might be a missing element that leads people to social apathy, but it might also be a missing link in the state of one's own spiritual life. Works of mercy cannot be overlooked as a means to experience God and to receive God's graces, ultimately playing a part in defeating sin and becoming restored to the image of God." This is certainly something Wesley would have affirmed.

2. Luke Timothy Johnson, *The Letter of James* (New Haven: Yale University Press, 2005), 222–23.

3. Alfred Plummer, *The General Epistles of St. James and St. Jude* (London: Hodder & Stoughton, 1891), 125.

4. Pheme Perkins, *First and Second Peter, James, and Jude* (Louisville: Westminster John Knox Press, 1995), 13.

5. Johnson, *Letter of James,* 239.

6. Peter H. Davids, *The Epistle of James: A Commentary on the Greek Text* (Grand Rapids: Eerdmans, 1982), 122.

7. It is important and wise to compare Wesleyan spiritual formation with other sorts, not least because Wesley drew on all sorts of sources from the church fathers in his teachings on this subject. There are even some surprises in the sources he used, such as Ephrem of Syria. A very helpful reader in Christian spirituality in general is the volume edited by Ken Collins, *Exploring Christian Spirituality: An Ecumenical Reader* (Grand Rapids: Baker Books, 2000). What one learns from working through this reader is that Wesleyan spiritual formation has more of a social edge than some other forms of Protestant and Catholic spirituality, but it is by no means unprecedented to find spiritual and social holiness combined in a single vision of spiritual formation before Wesley. A good example of this would be someone like John Chrysostom.

8. See my *The Indelible Image: The Theological and Ethical Thought World of the New Testament,* volumes 1 and 2 (Downers Grove, IL: IVP Academic, 2009, 2010).

After Words: What Does a Normal Christian Life Entail?

1. William H. Willimon, *Why Jesus?* (Nashville: Abingdon Press, 2010), 124–25.